Beyond the Plough

Born and brought up in Parkstone in Dorset, Janet Woods now lives in Perth, Western Australia, although she returns to her English roots on a regular basis to visit family and friends. Janet is the author of several historical romances, the most recent of which, *Daughter of Darkness*, won the 2002 Romantic Novel of the Year Award in Australia.

Beyond the Plough

Janet Woods

POCKET BOOKS

LONDON • SYDNEY • NEW YORK • TORONTO

First published in Great Britain by Simon & Schuster, 2004
A Viacom Company

Copyright © Janet Woods, 2004

3 5 7 9 10 8 6 4

Simon & Schuster UK Ltd
Africa House
64–78 Kingsway
London WC2B 6AH

www.simonsays.co.uk

Simon & Schuster Australia
Sydney

A CIP catalogue record for this book is available from
the British Library

ISBN 0 7434 6800 7

Typeset by SX Composing DTP, Rayleigh, Essex
Printed and bound in Great Britain by
Cox & Wyman

This book is dedicated to my friends and fellow authors,
Anna Jacobs and Sharon Milburn,
with whom I have shared a decade of critiquing.
Thanks, ladies

*

The author is happy to receive feedback from readers.
She can be contacted via her website
http://members.iinet.net.au/~woods
or by mail
PO Box 2099
Kardinya 6163
Western Australia

1

Dorset 1837

The hallway of Cheverton Manor was decorated with ivy and prickly holly boughs bright with blood-red berries. A huge log blazed in the hearth. Pine cones and needles had been added for the fragrance they provided, causing sparks to explode up the chimney as the resin heated.

Siana Forbes paused on the stairway on this, her second New Year's day without her husband. She was young to be a widow, barely twenty-two. Of medium height, her figure crackled with pent-up energy. It seemed long ago that she'd flown in the face of convention and discarded the black of mourning. Her burgundy-coloured riding habit followed the curves of her waist and breasts. Beneath her skirt she wore white silk pantalettes, but not for warmth. Her late husband had introduced her to such undergarments on her wedding day, now they were part of her daily apparel.

Edward Forbes gazed down at her from his portrait. Silver-haired and elegant, he appeared to be the essence of propriety, but in fact he'd been downright wicked in his ways. However her grief had been genuine when he'd died before he'd had a chance to see his son and heir.

The young baronet was upstairs in the nursery. Christened Ashley Edward Joshua, the little squire was a strong child who resembled his father in his features. His hair was a glossy sable, his eyes a dark, mysterious green, the colour of pines. The colouring had come through her, supposedly passed down through the blood of the Welsh marcher lords, the ancestors her mother had claimed as their own.

Siana loved Ashley with all the intensity a mother feels towards her first child. He was unaware yet that Cheverton Manor and the estate surrounding it would be his life work. It was a lot of responsibility for such a small boy to shoulder.

It was early as she made her way to the door, stopping only to greet the servant who came to tend the fire. Her own maid was still abed. No doubt Rosie would scold her for going out with her hair hanging in a loose braid down her back. Not that anybody would be abroad at this early hour on New Year's day to see her.

Outside, the morning was raw. The night mist still lingered, floating in shifting layers to writhe around the stark winter tree shapes and hide the sky. The air was sharpened by woodsmoke, which rose from the manor's chimneys to be trapped within the damp blanket of vapour.

Siana slipped the bridle over her mount's head and led Keara from her stall. Her horse stamped impatiently on the stable floor with her hoof and snickered softly when Siana struggled to lift the saddle to her back. A pretty bay, with a dark tail and mane, her soft brown eyes were ringed with dark lashes.

'Stand still, Keara,' Siana told the mare, as the saddle began to slip sideways.

She jumped when the steward took over the task, admonishing, 'You should have had the groom kicked out of bed, Lady Forbes.'

Siana eyed Jed Hawkins warily. He was a big man, bigger than her late husband, to whom he'd been devoted. Grey-bearded, and weathered, with eyes like dark honey, the enigmatic and taciturn steward was totally to be relied upon, but slightly intimidating on occasion. She hadn't heard him coming up behind her.

'It's the first day of the new year,' she said by way of an excuse.

'New year or not, the groom still has his duties to perform. One of them is to escort you. Surely you were not thinking of going out alone?'

'Sometimes I need to be alone, Jed. I have a strong urge to visit the place I grew up in. I've not been back there since my mother died.'

As he tightened the cinch around her mount's belly his eyes softened. Gruffly, he said, 'All right, lass. I'll follow on after you and you won't even know I'm there.'

'You're not my father, you know,' she dared to say.

He gave her a level look. 'No, but I would have made a better one than that preacher man, Gruffydd Evans, ever was.'

She cocked her head to one side, trying to fathom him out. 'Perhaps you should wed and produce children of your own instead of trying to be a father to me.'

3

Jed chuckled at that. 'Your husband asked me to watch out for you and I intend to, whether you want me to or not.'

'It's odd that your loyalty to him stretches beyond the grave. What were you to him?'

He lowered his eyes. 'Youthful companion, comrade-at-arms, friend.'

Before she knew it, Jed's large hands had circled her waist and he'd lifted her on to the saddle. She hooked her knee around the horn and gazed angrily at him. 'I could have managed by myself. Wherever you were going at the crack of dawn, you can continue on.'

'I was going nowhere. I've just come back.'

Her eyes flared with curiosity. 'From where?'

'You'd be surprised.' Jed grinned slightly to himself, a gesture which reminded Siana forcibly of her late husband when his mind had been absorbed by the ways and means of love.

Jed was unmarried, but no doubt he would be aware of how to obtain the certain intimacies necessary to men. She clicked her tongue and rode out before he could see the colour flood her cheeks, feeling sorry she'd embarrassed herself by asking, but, nevertheless, her curiosity about Jed now biting at her.

Half an hour later she stood under the winter-bare limbs of an oak tree. This was the spot where her mother, Megan, had died giving birth to a still-born infant. Her mother's blood had poured from her body to nourish this tree. A little way off stood the remains of a labourer's cottage. The walls were blackened by fire and grass grew amongst the tumbled bricks.

4

Her mother's bastard daughter, Siana had been brought up in the cottage. Although she'd survived the constant brutality of the Skinner family, her mother had not. The last of the Skinners still living were Siana's half-siblings, Josh and Daisy. They shared the blood of her own mother, and had become Siana's responsibility upon Megan's death.

She smiled as she thought of them. Despite his youth, at the tender age of sixteen, Josh was well on his way to becoming a man of substance. Five-year-old Daisy lived at the manor with Siana.

Melancholy crept over her. She'd sworn never to come back to this place of sorrow again. For a day or two, though, something had been drawing her back. She'd tried to ignore this uneasy fey sense of hers. It was inherited from the Welsh side of the family, who had cast her mother from their hearth and home – kin Siana had never met.

But the previous night she'd dreamed of her mother. The cottage had been undamaged, and Megan Skinner had beckoned to her from the doorway. When she woke, Siana realized she could ignore the call of the sight no longer.

Leaving her horse to graze, she strode across the grass and into the miserable remains of the cottage. A glance behind her showed Jed a little way off, motionless inside the drifting breath of the mist. Her heart gave a little tug. Jed was a good, honest man and she was sorry now that she'd snapped at him.

She closed her eyes, listening for the first sigh of wind over the hill. It usually came keening in from the sea at

5

this time, travelling five miles over the land to bring with it the sharp smell of brine and seaweed. It was too early, perhaps, for the wind remained mute and the silence pressed against her ears.

There was something here in these sad ruins, something alien to it. She listened for its voice, connected with a faint whisper. It was the sound of a breath, but not a breath expelled. It was held inside, trapped within heartbeats thundering with panic. Whatever it was, it was scared of her. A stray dog? She stretched out her hands and could feel its presence tingling warm against her palms.

She smiled. The sight she'd inherited from her great-grandmother Lewis had not visited her for some time. In the past it had sometimes brought her a warning. At other times the gift of healing. This time, she sensed something both needful of her and precious.

'You needn't be afraid,' she murmured and, opening her eyes, gazed around the gloomy interior of the place. It was not a place of happy childhood memories for her. Here, she'd known nothing but misery. That emotion still lingered within the burnt spaces, as if the heat of the fire had shrivelled it, but hadn't been fierce enough to kill it. She should have the ruins pulled down, scatter the stones far and wide.

The kitchen had caved in long ago, the bricks piling in one on top of the other. The sky showed through the remains of charred roof timbers, which supported nothing but mist. Over to her left, where the second-storey wall was still intact, a rough shelter had been built with the charred bricks. Inside, something moved a fraction.

It was not a dog, but a small child huddled against a bundle of dark rags. The girl whimpered with fear as Siana picked her way over the fallen bricks, ignoring the faint, sweet stink of corruption in the air.

Siana held out her arms to her. 'Don't cry, my sweet little angel. Come to me, I promise I won't hurt you.'

The waif came creeping into her arms, cold and quivering for comfort like a wretched runt of a kitten. The dark rags became the form of a woman in a donkey-brown gown.

Siana removed her jacket and cuddled the child within its warmth, moving her away from the sight and smell of death, so she could begin to forget. The thin little body pressed against hers, a pair of dark blue eyes regarded her intently for a moment, then closed. The child's honeyed hair clung in damp ringlets against her scalp.

'You have me now,' Siana whispered to her, her heart aching for the child's plight, for she'd almost been in the same situation herself once, though not of an age to be aware of it.

As she left the cottage with her burden the first breath of wind came over the hill to push at the mist. Then it blasted with some force against her body, flattening her thin shirt against her shift and chilling her to the bone. She moved into the shelter of the trunk of the oak tree, waving to Jed to come forward.

He towered over her, gazing down at the thin scrap of humanity in her arms. 'Not one of ours,' he said, dismounting. Removing Siana's jacket from the girl, he handed it back to her, then tucked the child cosily inside his topcoat. Siana used his bent knee as a mounting block to scramble into the saddle.

She gazed down at him. 'Her mother is in the cottage. She's dead.'

'I can smell it on the child. The poor soul must have been there for several days. As soon as we get back I'll send some men out with a cart to take the body to the undertaker.'

She couldn't help but tease him a little whilst he tenderly stroked the child's head. 'You're right, Jed. You would make a good father.'

'Aye,' he said comfortably and, giving a quiet chuckle, mounted one-handed and brought his great, black gelding under control. They started back towards Cheverton Manor side by side, the child asleep against his chest.

Francis Matheson was pleased to discover it wasn't Siana who was ill.

She greeted him with a spontaneous smile. 'I'm so happy to see you, Francis.'

Handing his topcoat and hat to a servant, he followed her up the stairs. There, on the landing, out of sight of the servants' prying eyes, he pulled her into his arms and kissed her.

Her nubile young body moulded into his, his own response forcing him to remember the years of abstinence following his wife's death. The heat he discovered in himself was hard to handle, and the ardent response from her soft lips displayed a new hunger. He dared to ask, 'Have you decided when you'll wed me?'

'Soon.' Her eyes lit up with mischief. 'Soon, I will give you an answer.'

'My sweet one,' he murmured. 'If I have to wait for you, I will.'

Her arm slid around his waist and her eyes were dancing now. Pushing open the door to the nearest guest chamber she pulled him inside. 'Make love to me now.'

Even as he experienced shock, his body reacted so positively he could hardly contain his urge to push her down on to the bed, toss her skirts over her head and take his fill of her.

But he wanted to feast on her, not indulge in quick satisfaction. So, although sorely tempted, Francis regretfully shook his head. 'Unfortunately, I'm on my way to the infirmary, and wasn't there someone in need of medical attention? Is it Ashley or Daisy?'

She shrugged slightly. 'It is neither. Tell me, Francis, will you be so cold with me after we are wed?'

He tried not to let his surprise show as he held her at arm's length to gaze at her flushed face. Had he been cold? If so, it was unintentional. But his refusal had embarrassed her, and his courting skills were sadly lacking. He kissed the end of her nose. 'I love you, Siana. But I've loved you for too long, and respect you too much to take our relationship lightly. That doesn't mean I'm cold.' He grinned at the thought. 'I'm trying to keep some distance between us, for without a wedding day in sight the consequences could be disastrous for you.'

She nodded, accepting his comment with a flirtatious toss of her head. 'You do not think too badly of me for being forward, then?'

9

'How could I?' Briefly, he kissed her again, not daring to do more than that if he was to keep his mind on his work all day. 'Now, who is this mysterious patient?'

'It's a girl I have found amongst the ruins of my childhood home. Her mother is dead and the men have gone to pick up the woman's body.'

'A cadaver to examine,' he grumbled. 'Did you have to pick today to go to the cottage?'

Compassion filled her eyes. 'If I hadn't, the child would have spent another cold night in the dark with only her dead mother for company. Would you rather have that happen, Francis? I think not.'

A few minutes later he was gazing down at the child, pleased that Siana had possessed the sense to isolate her in case she was infectious. 'What's the girl's name?'

'She is called Marigold.'

'A pretty name.'

'She's named for the colour of her hair, I think.'

'Was there anything on her mother's body to indicate who she is, or where she came from?'

'I didn't look, and the child hasn't spoken yet.'

'Then how the devil do you know her name?'

Siana shrugged and, avoiding his grey, probing eyes, fussed with a piece of lace at her cuff. 'Perhaps I was mistaken and she whispered it before she went to sleep.'

Francis knew evasiveness when he heard it, and was familiar with the strange way Siana had with her sometimes. 'And perhaps you just know, aye? I'll take her with me to the infirmary if she's fit to travel.'

'You can't. She's my child now.' Siana bit down on

her lip. 'Something drew me to her side; I was meant to find her.'

Francis sighed, because he already knew he was going to lose this battle. 'The girl is a foundling. You can't just keep her.'

'Why not? She has nobody else.'

'We don't know that and there are procedures.'

His reasoning was swept aside. 'If she had somebody, she and her mother wouldn't have been sheltering in the cottage ruins in the middle of winter. And since you're on the board which runs the infirmary, I see no difficulty with procedures. Besides, Marigold will be your child when we are wed, so nobody will dare object. I thought next summer might be a good time for the wedding. Does that suit you?'

Astounded by her blatant manipulation and bemused by the sudden lurch his heart gave, he nodded. 'That's only a few months away.'

'So it is.' Gently she kissed his cheek. Judging from the laughter evident in her voice she knew she'd just dealt herself the winning hand. 'I'll go and play with Ashley and Daisy whilst you examine Marigold, shall I?'

'Please stay. She might wake and feel scared by the sight of a strange man.'

'She'll grow to love you as much as I do.'

He almost purred at her flattery, then smiled at his susceptibility. He wrote in his notebook with a graphite pencil. *Female foundling of unknown origin – to be known as Marigold Forbes (Matheson?). Aged about four years. Suffering from malnutrition.*

He took a good look at the child. He'd visited just

about everyone in the district over the past few years, and this little girl was certainly not one of his patients. She had a delicate and dainty air to her, like a porcelain figurine. Her limbs were thin, but without too much muscle wastage, her stomach was slightly distended. She was dirty and dehydrated and smelled of death, but her heart beat strongly.

She opened her eyes and stared at him. They were the colour of cornflowers. Her hair was a mass of tangled gold curls, freckles danced sparsely across her nose. Her gaze was direct, without curiosity, yet slightly assessing. Francis was disconcerted by it.

'Can you tell us your name?' he said gently to her.

Her gaze moved on to Siana and she gave a tentative smile. Her voice was a piping little lisp, like that of a bird. 'Mariglows.'

He slid Siana a glance, absorbing her innocent expression, the gleam of triumph in her eyes. 'I shall call her Goldie,' she said.

'Do you have a second name?'

The child stared at him, uncomprehending.

Behind him, Siana expelled a sigh of a breath and reached out her hand to close the smaller one inside it. When Francis looked again, the child was asleep.

'It was meant to be,' she said calmly. But deep in her heart she felt uneasy, as if Goldie was hers only for a short time. She shook the feeling off, pessimism didn't sit easily on her these days.

'The girl is free of external parasites,' Francis informed her. 'We don't know what her mother died of yet, so have her bathed as soon as possible. Feed her on milk-sops, oatmeal and chicken broth for a day or two. Inspect her for worms when she functions.'

'Yes, Doctor.'

'Her appetite will be small to begin with.' When she kissed him on the corner of his mouth he grinned, forced to abandon his professional mantle.

'Thank you for not making a fuss about her, Francis.'

He gazed sternly at her. 'You do understand that you can't take in every child who is orphaned, don't you? As it is, we're going to start married life with five children to care for.'

A wide grin spread across her face. 'Don't look so horribly fierce about it. Be warned, as soon as possible I intend to present you with a son, then there will be six. He can grow up with Ashley for companionship and you can teach him to be a fine doctor, like yourself.'

He pulled her against his body, his hand splaying across her back. 'Now we have a wedding date, I'm almost tempted to get some practice in for this son of ours.'

Her breath chuckled against his ear, making him shiver. 'Make up your mind to this, Francis. Once I have you in my bed you will not escape too easily. Now, as you pointed out earlier, you are expected at the infirmary. So, be gone.'

'So I am.' They sprang apart, laughing as a knock came on the door and Siana told whoever it was to enter.

Rosie came in carrying a large bowl and a jug of water.

'Leave them on the table, I'll bathe her myself,' Siana said, seeing the doctor to the door. She was about to give

Francis a chaste peck on the cheek when he gave a chuckle and swept her into his arms. When he'd finished kissing her entirely to his satisfaction, he strode off, laughing inside as she stood there, hot-faced and flustered.

Rosie was grinning from ear to ear when Siana turned towards the child. Siana couldn't quite meet her knowing eyes. 'Indeed, I don't know what came over Dr Matheson,' she said to the maid, fanning her face with her hand.

'Looks like he might be a right lusty fella, the doctor, with the pair of you always kissing in corners where you think you can't be seen.'

Siana tried not to grin. 'You think so?'

'Stands to reason, don't it? Since his wife died he ain't had time for a woman, until he sets eyes on you.' She lowered her voice. 'Built like a stud bull, too, but I suppose you'm noticed that.'

'Rosie!' Siana exclaimed, half in protest, half in laughter. She wouldn't have taken this familiarity from any other servant, but Rosie had been her maid since her first marriage, and had become her confidante and ally in her transformation from peasant girl to lady. 'You should not say such things.'

''Tis only the truth. You'll be walking around with a smile on your face from the word go. Now, when's the wedding going to be?'

'August . . . and Dr Matheson doesn't mind Goldie becoming one of the family.'

'Have you told him you want him to move into the manor?'

Siana shrugged. 'I'm sure he won't mind.'

Rosie's look was measured. 'Best you talk to him soon, with the wedding not far off. The doctor has his pride, he'll want to provide for his wife and children himself.'

Siana promised herself she'd ask Francis as soon as possible. After all, what objections could he possibly have to moving into Cheverton Manor?

2

Although Goldie settled in quickly, a month later it became obvious that Daisy resented the presence of another female in the nursery.

Having lost her mother at too young an age to remember her, Daisy had automatically transferred her affections to her older sister. Daisy called her 'Mamma' now, and Siana didn't bother to correct her. After all, her sister had only just turned five; what harm could it do? Daisy couldn't remember her former impoverished existence in the mean estate cottage, either, for she'd lived a life of comfort ever since. When Daisy was old enough to understand, then Siana would explain the situation to her.

Daisy had welcomed the birth of Ashley almost two years before, but she seemed to regard the presence of Goldie with suspicion, as though the girl was competing for Siana's affection. And indeed, Goldie was a rival. The empathy between Siana and the orphaned child was unmistakable. Something inside Goldie tugged at something in Siana, as if they were twin souls.

Now, Siana dried Goldie's tears and scolded the

defiant Daisy who stood with her legs apart and hands on hips, glaring indignantly at the younger girl.

'Please don't smack her again, Daisy. She's smaller than you.'

Daisy's bottom lip stuck out in a fat pout. 'She took my doll from her house. I hate her.'

Goldie snuggled into Siana's side, a livid welt decorating her cheek, the small wax figure held in her hand. 'I was only looking at it,' she whispered.

'You should have asked Daisy first.' Giving a sigh, Siana drew Daisy's stiff little body against her other side. She stroked the golden curls at her temple. 'It wouldn't hurt you to share your toys, Daisy. Say sorry to Goldie.'

After a moment her sister relaxed a little. 'But I'm not sorry, Mamma. If I say I am it will be a lie, and you told me I mustn't tell lies.'

Siana stifled a grin. The wretch! Who could argue with such logic? 'Then promise me you won't hit Goldie again.'

For a moment, Daisy hesitated, then said, 'I promise I won't hit her if she promises not to steal my things.'

The time had come to lay down the law. 'You have too many toys to play with all at once. If you don't share them I'll take them away from you. And I'll turn you over my knee if you smack Goldie again. Do you understand?'

'You're not Goldie's mamma; she's buried in the cemetery,' Daisy said rebelliously. 'You found Goldie.'

'And now I'm her mamma, and I love her as much as her own mamma did.'

'You love her better than you love me.' Daisy's bottom lip began to tremble.

'That's not true, Daisy. I love you both, but I've loved you for longer, because I've known you since you were a baby.' Siana cuddled the girls against her sides and was eventually rewarded by a kiss on each cheek. 'Now, make friends. Dr Matheson is waiting for me and I have to ready myself. We're visiting the Reverend White to arrange for the marriage banns to be called, and if the pair of you don't behave yourselves I won't allow you to be there on the day.'

The pair exchanged a glance of such consternation that Siana nearly laughed.

'I'll be friends if you will,' Daisy said grudgingly.

Goldie hesitated for a moment, then in the quiet, trusting way she had, she nodded. Slipping from Siana's side, she delicately replaced the little wax figure on her chair in the doll's house.

When they skipped off towards the table, Siana heaved a sigh of relief and went through to the nursery, where Ashley was taking a rest. Her son was lying on his back sound asleep, his thumb sucked firmly into his mouth. Long lashes swept against his soft pink skin and his hair was a mass of dark silky curls. Love for her son overwhelmed her, making her unreasonably emotional, so her eyes moistened and she knew she'd be unable to speak coherently.

'My dearest Edward, thank you for leaving me with this sweet son of ours,' she choked out, 'for I love him so much.' Vulnerable under the influence of something so precious, she hugged the feeling to her, feasting on it.

Edward had honoured her by making her his wife. He'd caged her, but she'd loved him in her own way and missed the exciting intimacy of their life together. However, she tried not to think too much of her late husband, especially in the face of her forthcoming marriage to Francis, whom she loved completely and without reservation.

The nursery maid smiled when Siana stooped to kiss Ashley's cheek. 'He might be looking like an angel now, but he's been as lively as a flea on a dog this morning. Fair wore me out, I can tell thee.'

Siana chuckled as she left, wishing she had more time to share with the children. But most of her time was taken up by the affairs of Cheverton Estate. And now she had her wedding to arrange.

Changing into a gown of amber brocade, with a velvet shoulder cape for warmth, she allowed her maid to tie the lace-decorated strings of her bonnet under her chin. They made a becoming frill which set off her centre parting and allowed her ringlets to escape into fashionable disarray.

'Pretty as a picture,' Rosie said with satisfaction. 'Now don't you be forgetting your cloak. 'Tis cold outside and, although I told the groom to heat some bricks for your feet to rest on, you can't be too careful.'

Hot bricks, was it? Not long ago, her warmth came from her mother's old shawl and a pair of hand-me-down boots, and grateful she'd been for them, too. Still, it was nice to be cosseted.

Francis was waiting for her in the drawing room, his hands cupped around a steaming tankard of hot, spiced brandy. The remains of ham and cheese and a crusty loaf of bread rested on a plate. There was a special edge to his smile today. 'You won't mind if I come with you in the carriage?'

'I will mind if you don't. Finish your drink, Francis. The horses will wait.'

His mount came with them, tied behind the carriage, for Francis was the only doctor in the district, and never knew when he'd be called on to visit those suffering from disease or accident.

The coachman clicked his tongue and the Cheverton blacks set off, their heads nodding, their breath steaming and leathers creaking and clinking. The ground was hard. In the shadows the frost hadn't yet cleared. The iron-shod hooves of the carriage horses threw up stones, snapped twigs, and chopped up clods of decaying leaves.

How evocative the smell of winter was, Siana thought. The air was redolent of the woodsmoke curling from the chimneys of the labourers' cottages, seasoned with the cold and spiced by salt carried on the wind blowing off the sea. The pine trees retained their fragrance under a taut skin. The sap was no longer liquid, but a hard amber vein waiting for the rise of spring. The trees stood in a carpet of rust and fallen cones, their needles dark, bristling spikes.

The land belonged to Ashley, the son of her first marriage, who was the product of a liaison between an aristocrat and a peasant. The day after their marriage she and her aristocrat had made love in this carriage, on the way to the horse sales.

Her quiet chuckle turned Francis's eyes her way.

They contained an unspoken query. It was one she couldn't answer, for memories such as this one could not be shared with him. She leaned forward, took his hands in hers and gently tugged. 'Come and sit beside me, Francis.'

The winter grey of his eyes registered amusement as he resisted. 'So you can tease me?'

The laughter suddenly left her when she realized the depth of her hunger for him. 'Are you so easily teased by me, then?'

'You know I am.'

Softly, she said, 'Dearest Francis, you allow your background to show when you play the drawing-room aristocrat. Your manners and control don't impress me in the least, especially when I so long to be loved by you.'

His smile returned at that. 'I've forgotten how to play courtship games, Siana.'

'I know.' Taking his face between her hands she tenderly kissed him, whispering against his lips, 'Are you so frightened of loving me that you must keep me at arm's length?'

'Aye,' he said. 'For to have you in my bed before our wedding night would be disrespectful to you, and wrong for us.'

'Even though I'm a peasant by birth?'

His eyes became glacial. 'You make too much of your low birth. You have risen above it now. You move in different circles and must accept different standards of behaviour. I will not be the one to push you down again. It seems I must show restraint for both of us.'

Which struck her as being slightly hypocritical, for

she'd learned that what these people did in a public way and what they did privately often contradicted each other.

'"*Manners maketh the man*",' she said almost accusingly, dredging the words out from she knew not where.

He was cutting. '"*Manners maketh man*." If you are going to quote, quote correctly.'

Giving a tiny gasp she pulled away from him, colour rising to her face. 'You are displaying very few manners, Francis. Your words are wounding. You mock my lack of education, and speak as if you believe the peasants are little more than animals.'

The expression in his eyes softened. 'You know that's far from the truth. I've always been straightforward in my speech. You know I love you, Siana, but you must learn to be less spontaneous in demonstrating your affection . . . in public, at least.'

'Perhaps it should be you who learns to be more spontaneous.'

He shrugged. 'When we are wed, be assured, I will prove my mettle to you, for I'm not a man to hang back without reason.'

She turned to gaze at the countryside passing by, hurt beyond measure by his rebuke. Gradually, she came to realize that in being too forward she'd embarrassed him. Francis was more conventional than Edward had been, and she must adjust her behaviour accordingly. So when the church tower came into her view she turned apologetically to him. 'I'm sorry, Francis.'

He took her hand in his and kissed her knuckles. 'I must apologize for being so churlish. I find it hard to display affection in public, but if it's any consolation, you're constantly in my thoughts. I did not seek to mock you, for I'm proud of what you've achieved. I'm totally ashamed of myself.'

The Reverend Richard White's smile was wide when he saw her. When Siana had been younger and in need, the reverend had taught her to read and then employed her in his house. She could not forget the fact that the help had been withdrawn when she'd needed it most, but kept it in mind that he'd been manipulated by others, her late husband in particular. Although he was verging on portly, and past middle age, Siana found Richard to be likeable. But she no longer held as much respect for him as she had in the past.

Their interview was formal, as Richard sought to make sure they both understood the duties attached to the marriage vows. Sounding bored, Francis told him, 'Both of us have been wed before and are well aware of what is required.'

'Quite so.' Richard sighed. 'I have not seen you in church lately, Francis.'

Francis's mouth twisted wryly. 'Winter has brought its usual diseases to haunt the villagers. We have lung sickness, rheumatism and stomach ailments at the moment. There has been a case of lockjaw, and several deaths from malnutrition amongst children from the larger families. I must put my vocation above all else at times.'

Tears pricked at Siana's eyes. 'Is there anything I can do to help?'

'They wouldn't welcome your charity.' He slid her an apologetic look. 'I know you've done your best, Siana, but the improvements to the cottages have had little effect, since whitewash doesn't keep out the draughts or the rain, and most of them need rebuilding. What the villagers need is good, nourishing food.'

'Then I'll talk to Jed Hawkins and see if the estate can manage a rise in wages again.'

Richard nodded approvingly. 'Siana tells me you'll be moving into the manor once you're wed, Francis. You'll be in the position to do something about conditions, then.'

Siana opened her mouth, then shut it again when Francis gazed at her with a slight frown. 'The estate belongs to Edward's son, not to Siana. I'm not a trustee, so I'll not be in the position to administer any inheritance there may be. As for me moving in, this hasn't yet been discussed between us.'

Picking up the slight current of tension, Richard gently coughed. 'You'll stay for refreshments, won't you? Mrs Leeman has so looked forward to your visit, Siana.'

Francis rose to his feet as if he were about to refuse, then he seated himself again when she appealed to him, 'Have I time to visit my mother's grave?'

'Aye,' he said, his voice slightly gruff and ashamed. 'Do you want to be alone, or shall we take refreshment first, then stop off on the way home?'

'We'll take refreshment, for I expect Mrs Leeman has prepared it, and I'd like to pass some time with her if I may.'

The housekeeper had aged, but was delighted to see

her. The reverend invited Mrs Leeman to join them and she presided over the teapot, self-conscious and pink-cheeked. Siana made a mental note to invite her to the wedding.

'Have you heard anything from my father?' she asked Richard.

'The last I heard of Gruffydd Evans he was preaching in Hyde Park, in London, to a large crowd. But that was several months ago. He has a companion travelling with him. A theology student taking a sabbatical from his studies, I believe.'

After tea, they took their leave, pausing at the church-yard, where Siana's mother and stepfather were buried. She gazed at the tombstone her deceased husband had erected, murmuring, 'Mourned by Lady Forbes. I always resented Edward for trying to make me some-thing I wasn't.'

'And now you resent me.' Francis turned her round to face him. 'Take my word for it, Siana. There's nothing mysterious about people. Clad in silks or sacking, we're all the same naked, and become nothing but dust after we die.'

'Yet you go to church and pray on occasion.'

'And so do you. It's convention and fear of the unknown, my pagan princess.' He grinned. 'The com-bination is a damned nuisance.'

She chuckled. 'You've been as prickly as a hedgehog today.'

'I was up half the night, battling for a child who was near to death.' A smiled drifted across his face. 'He recovered.'

'Despite God.'

'Now, there was a battle.'

'My father would condemn you to suffer for your sin, one day.'

'If I do, it will be worth it for the life of that one child.' She gently caressed his cheek. 'I love you.'

Taking her in his arms, he held her close. 'Do you want to visit Edward's grave whilst you're here?'

'No, we've said goodbye.' She gazed at her mother's tombstone again. 'You're right, they're only dust.' She lifted her head and gazed into his eyes, a faint smile on her face. 'But I know my mother still lives, for sometimes she looks back at me from the mirror or through the eyes of Josh and Daisy.'

His arms tightened around her and they stood there for a moment, his chin resting on her head, his body sheltering her from the bitter wind that had sprung up, as if she were a delicate hot-house plant. 'I love you,' he murmured, 'never doubt it,' and he tipped up her chin and kissed her with so much tenderness she wanted to cry.

Then his horse stamped and whinnied and the spell was broken. She shivered. 'Take me home, Francis. My brother Josh is bringing Elizabeth over to stay for a few days. She's going to help me with the arrangements for the wedding.'

They strolled back to the carriage hand in hand.

'Your friendship with Elizabeth never ceases to amaze me. By rights, you should be enemies.'

'Because of Edward?' She laughed. 'Their relationship was over before I married him. Elizabeth is the most generous woman on earth. As you know, she suffered greatly when she was married to my step-brother, who was a bully. Elizabeth and I needed each other at the time; she became my mentor and my friend, and I love her dearly.'

'When did you intend to tell me of your plans to have me live at Cheverton Manor?' he teased, handing her into the carriage.

'Ah yes, I've been waiting for the right opportunity to ask you.' She could hardly meet his eyes. 'Would you mind very much if we lived there? There's plenty of room for the children, and if I move out, half the servants will be without work. Will the fact that I was married to the previous owner bother you?'

He placed a finger over her mouth, hushing her. 'Today, I realized that your love for Edward Forbes was more deeply rooted than I imagined. The thought made me feel jealous, and I reacted badly to that.'

'You mustn't ever be jealous. Yes, I loved Edward, for he was good to me when I desperately needed someone. I love you in a much deeper way, Francis. You complete me.'

He smiled at that. 'There's a notion that pleases me.'

'If you wish to live elsewhere, we shall.'

'Someone has to guide the young Sir Ashley in his gentlemanly occupation as squire of the district, I suppose. I was going to suggest it myself.'

'I couldn't think of anyone better. Are you sure it won't be too much of an imposition? I know how busy you are.'

Settling himself across from her he smiled with a certain amount of smugness. 'I've taken another doctor into the practice. His name is Noah Baines. If I move into the manor it will solve the problem of finding him decent accommodation.'

She grinned. 'That means you'll have more time to spare with your family, then.'

'How perceptive of you, my dear.' He held out his hands. 'Come over here so I can kiss you.'

'Certainly not, sir.' Her eyes gleamed with mischief. 'As you so rightly pointed out earlier, I would be acting like a strumpet, which would hardly be circumspect.' The words had hardly left her mouth when he grabbed her hands and jerked her forward. She landed on his lap, laughing.

He traced a finger over her mouth, reducing the laughter there to a smile, then to a sober, trembling response. His grey eyes held hers to his, brought her into his intensity. 'I want you to know how much I love you,' he whispered, and his mouth reached gently to capture hers, then deepened into a kiss of such passion she was powerless to stop it.

Every part of her became yearningly alive, and she speculated on what it would be like to be loved by this man. He took his time over the caress, exploring the depths of her mouth, his tongue encouraging hers to flirt and dance. He released her in his own time, a delightfully rueful look on his face as he stated, 'Sometimes a man can be his own worst enemy.'

'And a woman's.' Siana knew of several ways to ease his desire, but it wouldn't be wise to reveal all that she had learned about loving – not yet!

*

Josh Skinner whistled as he urged the horses on. Driving a coach and four, a vehicle that took passengers from one town to another, he was enjoying every moment. He'd had a full coach from Poole through to Wareham, and would pick another load up on the return journey.

At sixteen, Josh resembled the Skinner family with his mousy-coloured hair and blue eyes. He lacked the Skinner stockiness, though. His slim, wiry build and fine features were inherited from the Welsh side of the family, for the mother of Siana, Daisy and Josh was Megan Lewis. Not that they were acquainted with the Welsh side, for their mother had been cast out of her village for conceiving Siana out of wedlock, and had never seen her family again.

Recently, Josh had gone into partnership with one Giles Dennings, former head clerk at the bank where Josh kept his account. The pair had bought a coaching business from a company which was going bankrupt.

'I've had my eye on this un for some time. The owner is drinking the profits away and it's only a matter of time before he starts to go under,' Josh had told Giles. 'Everyone is frightened the railways will put 'em out of business, so the coach company can be picked up cheap. Things move slowly in these parts and I reckon the railways won't get here for years to come. By the time they do, at five pence a mile sitting inside the coach, and half price outside, we'll have made ourselves a bleddy fortune.'

Giles had watched Josh's bank account swell rapidly since he'd started his business with a mule and cart as a ragged twelve-year-old. The head clerk had surprised

Siana's brother when he'd thrown in his lot with him. It was as if Giles had known he would be incapable of juggling the various tolls, licences, government charges, horsing costs and other etceteras that were part of the coaching business. But like Giles had said, he saw no avenue to advance from his present situation, so might as well take a gamble on his own skills.

'We'll take it over lock, stock and barrel – drivers, outriders and all,' Josh had told him. 'You run the business and scheduling side and I'll handle the horses and the employees.'

Jasper would be right proud of him if he had known. Jasper was the old mule Josh had started out with. A framed likeness of him hung on the wall of his new office. It had been drawn by Josh's side-kick, the stunted deaf-mute boy he'd aptly named Sam Saynuthin. The mule stood between the shafts of a light cart, its ears pricked alertly forward. A figure bearing a remarkable resemblance to Josh was at the reins. *Josh Skinner, Cockles and Cartage,* it said on the side of the cart.

Now Josh handled his new acquisition with pride. Sam Saynuthin grinned, then gave a prolonged blast on the post horn before Josh turned through the gates of Cheverton Manor. His sister-in-law Elizabeth, and her pretty little daughter, Susannah, were tucked cosily inside the coach.

Josh saw his sister come running out on to the porch. She was a bonny sight. Then Jed Hawkins appeared, a tall, silent figure, who stepped forward when the coach came to a halt to hand Elizabeth and her daughter down.

Josh noticed the glance Jed and Elizabeth exchanged

and silently whistled. Jed Hawkins had visited Elizabeth on several occasions of late, even sleeping in the guest bedroom one night, when his horse had thrown a shoe. He wondered what Siana would say when she found out. Still, it weren't any of his business – or Siana's, come to that.

'Good day to you, Josh. That team is a bit of a step up from old Jasper.'

'A grand old mule, he was, Jed. Jasper did me proud, and he was much easier than driving this team. These buggers need to learn to keep in step. Old Jasper brought me in a shillin' or two from the knacker when he died.'

The steward nodded and, running an approving eye over the coach, grinned at him. 'That's a big rig.'

Josh grinned back, for the pair had put the past rancour aside now Edward Forbes was dead, and they were comfortable with each other. 'Carries fifteen passengers at once, it do.'

By crikey, he was going up in the world when a man like Jed Hawkins stopped to pass the time of day with him. Money talked, and no one would ever call the Skinners vermin again, Josh thought. At least . . . not to their faces.

Isabelle Collins was not a happy woman.

'That Skinner harlot has put in a bid for the Bainbridge Emporium,' she hissed at her husband, Ben. 'She's pushing the price up.'

'I don't know why you lets the woman get you so tempered up, Issy.'

She couldn't tell Ben that she hated Elizabeth Skinner for lots of reasons, but mainly because she was everything Isabelle wanted to be herself – a lady. Elizabeth Skinner's breeding shone through even though her conduct had been blatantly immodest over the years.

Isabelle chose to forget that her own modesty had been sadly lacking at one time – she chose to deny that the real bone of contention between them had been the old squire, to whom she'd been promised in marriage. Edward Forbes had jilted her for the peasant girl, Siana Lewis who, in her turn, was a good friend of Elizabeth Skinner.

Isabelle hated both of them. But she was wary of the peasant girl, for she'd already come off worst in a confrontation with her.

It was said that both women had shared Edward Forbes's bed at the same time. Both were beautiful to look at, amusing and popular. She'd always imagined the pair laughing at her awkwardness and her ugly body though, had she but known it, neither of the women gave her more than a passing thought.

Isabelle was unhappy, and when she was unhappy she became the coarse farm girl she'd once been – before her aunt, Caroline, had sent her to school to improve her manners, and before she'd inherited the fabric warehouse and shop.

'That strumpet sells all manner of scandalous things, most of them fit only for whores like herself to wear. No decent woman would wear silk garments and lace next to her body.'

'And you shouldn't be using bad words in front of

little Alexandra. You want her to grow up to be a nice little lady, don't yer?'

Her husband was prancing around on his hands and knees, looking for all the world like an overgrown infant himself. His son, George, and their daughter, Alexandra, both clung to his back. Shrieking with laughter, they fell sideways when he flattened on to his belly. He turned over and gazed up at her, grinning. 'Aren't you goin' to out-bid her, then?'

'I want that Emporium, but I ain't going to let her ruin me. The building itself needs expensive repairs and it's a fire trap. You've got to consider resale value. If she keeps pushing up the price it won't be worth buying it. It would be cheaper to build a new one.'

'Then burn it down, buy the site and build a new one on it.'

Ben didn't often say anything so sensible. Isabelle's eyes narrowed. This bore thinking about, but she must take no action that could be put down to her.

As Ben gazed at her his tongue came out to moisten his lips. 'You looks all pink and pretty in that gown. Why don't you come down here, give your Ben a nice juicy kiss and play horsies with him, too?'

Excitement raced through her. 'We can't conduct business in front of the children.'

'Of course we can't.' He nodded to them. 'You two go and visit Great-aunt Caroline in her sitting room for an hour. Tell her that your ma and I have got urgent business to discuss, and you can stay for tea with her. She'll like that.'

Isabelle blushed as the children raced away. She

locked the door after them. Even after three years of marriage, Ben Collins's desire for her was still hot and strong.

He grinned at her, murmuring. 'I reckon your arse would look right pretty in a pair of silk pantalettes.'

'Get on with you, Ben Collins,' she said, giggling when he pulled her down on the floor beside him and fumbled with the fastenings of her bodice.

Isabelle was a large woman. Her bosoms were as round as melons, her thighs and hips dimpled and cushiony. Ben smiled happily when she emerged from her bodice, and said with great reverence, 'They be a beauteous pair of titties, our Isabelle. Lord knows, I must be the happiest man alive.' As he bent to kiss each swollen button, he slid a hand up under her skirt. 'Your Ben's got a right need on him today, so where's his fat little puddin' hidin' then?'

Isabelle relaxed her thighs with a tiny shiver of anticipation. Ben's eyes gleamed when he gazed at what she revealed. He liked looking at her, and the fact that he'd been the only man who'd ever thought her attractive made her want him all the more.

She glanced at his stem, rearing thick and proud when he loosened the opening in his trousers. Lord, he was a lusty man! But she was more than a match for him. She reached out to tease him, wondering if they made silk pantalettes in her size.

She'd get back to the problem of Elizabeth Skinner and the emporium later.

Elizabeth and Siana had always been able to talk frankly

34

to one another. Now Josh had gone on his way and Susannah was happily installed in the nursery, the two women smiled across the tea tray at each other.

After the refreshment, they started work on the guest list. Francis had handed Siana a list of names from his sister-in-law, the countess. Prudence had placed herself and her husband, the Earl of Kylchester, top of the sheet of paper. Francis's other four older brothers were then listed, along with their wives and children of the two with families. Then came a plethora of aunts and uncles, cousins, friends and acquaintances too close to ignore, in order of precedence.

Siana gazed at the list in dismay. 'I had no idea Francis had so many relations.'

Elizabeth seemed amused. 'There's no need to invite William Matheson. The invitation wouldn't reach Van Diemen's Land until after the wedding. Out of courtesy, you must notify him of the event, however, for he may wish to send you a gift.'

'From a wild land on the other side of the world? What sort of gift could he send us? It would serve him better for us to send him one. A wife, perhaps.'

'I've heard that William Matheson has become quite wealthy as a farmer there.'

Siana choked out a laugh. 'What use is wealth when one has no family or children, and all around you is wilderness? Although I've heard of the place, because it's a prison colony, I cannot find it on the globe in the library. Francis told me it's an island at the bottom of a huge continent in the southern waters of the world called Australia. It must be a dreadful place in which to

35

live, for I've also heard the place is overrun with fierce and terrifying natives who throw spears at people.' She shrugged. 'Now, let's get on with this task. There's nobody from my side except you, Mrs Leeman, Josh, Daisy and Goldie.'

There was a momentary hesitation in Elizabeth, then she said, 'Daniel and his wife will be in the district at the time.'

Siana's mouth tightened as her eyes came up to meet Elizabeth's. Usually, they avoided mentioning Elizabeth's son, who had been fathered by Edward Forbes.

3

'Daniel is Ashley's brother,' Elizabeth said.

'Half-brother.'

Elizabeth conceded Siana's point with a nod. 'Daniel is leaving his legal practice in London and moving back to the district shortly. He has expressed a desire to see Ashley.'

Siana cleared her throat. 'Daniel and I argued when we met at the reading of Edward's will. He insulted me at a time when I was grieving.'

'He's ashamed of what he said.' Leaning forward, Elizabeth placed a hand over hers. 'My dear, surely you cannot hold that small incident of so many months ago against Daniel. He was grieving, too. You must remember that you loved each other once, and he felt betrayed when you wed his father. He was not to know then, that others had conspired to keep you apart, and he spoke without thinking.'

Their eyes met for a moment of challenge, then Siana said gently, for she didn't want to cause a rift between them, 'I wonder if Edward would approve.'

There was a pause – a pause fraught with tension,

then a reproachful glance came her way. 'Probably not, but Edward wouldn't have approved of your marriage to Francis, either, for he was a self-centred man who liked to keep control of his possessions – even when he had no further use for them.'

Which was the closest his former mistress had ever come to revealing how hurtful Siana's marriage to Edward had been for her. Siana could find nothing in Elizabeth's words to dispute, so she held her tongue as Elizabeth's hand was withdrawn and folded into the other in her lap.

Elizabeth rarely allowed her anger to penetrate her calm façade, so Siana waited, for it was obvious Elizabeth had more to say.

'Edward is dead. This estate now belongs to Ashley. Would your son want to grow up ignorant of the strong bond that exists between them? Edward accepted the concept of *noblesse oblige* towards lesser blood ties. Didn't he take his own half-brother in? They served in the army together and became almost inseparable.'

Gazing at her in astonishment, Siana stammered, 'Edward mentioned no brother.'

Elizabeth looked about to say more, then she shrugged and offered an apologetic smile. 'It was not a relationship either of them wished to acknowledge in a public manner. But there, I have been indiscreet, and we mustn't quarrel. Shall we drop the matter of the guest list for the moment, and pass on to other matters? Would the Countess of Kylchester lend you some of her servants, d'you think?'

The change of subject disconcerted Siana for a

moment. She knew she'd have been more kindly disposed towards Daniel if he'd apologized to her himself, for his words when they'd last met had been cutting. He'd accused her of marrying Edward for position and money. But as Elizabeth had said, the past should be left behind, and wasn't she being overly protective of Ashley?

Siana didn't often think of Daniel now, rarely remembering he was brother to her own son, fathered by the same man. Of course Edward would have approved of Ashley knowing his brother. He'd never hidden his own relationship to Daniel, just denied his elder son's legitimacy and the right to inherit – which, to her mind, was the very thing Daniel's heart most desired. It was a motive she could understand.

Picking up the pen and dipping the nib into the ink well, she smiled at Elizabeth as she carefully added Daniel and his wife to the guest list.

It wasn't until after Elizabeth had returned home that Siana remembered the matter of Edward's brother. It had to be Jed Hawkins, of course, because, now she knew, the resemblance was obvious. She was about to summon him to the drawing room, but her hand stilled on the bell pull. Edward had never mentioned the connection and Jed might be embarrassed if she asked him about it. He'd certainly been treated with less indifference than his other employees by her late husband, but not as familiarly as close kin. She decided to let it lie for the moment and might ask Francis's advice on the matter once they were wed.

She doubted whether, unlike Jed Hawkins, Daniel would keep his kinship with Ashley a secret, for he'd never been discreet about his aristocratic connection, which had exposed Elizabeth to public shame and scorn.

The wonder of it all was that Edward had fallen in love with herself, a destitute peasant girl, Siana mused, and he had followed it up with marriage. He'd changed her life and she'd always be grateful to him for that.

Spring arrived late; clouds saturated with soft rain showers came to water the crops. Green shoots sprang from the earth and speared towards the sky. Everything changed colour quickly. An abundance of golden daffodils in April were joined by a carpet of bluebells in May, white daisies lifted their heads in the grass to greet the arrival of blue forget-me-nots and fragrant wallflowers.

Summer's arrival had a suddenness to it, bringing soft balmy breezes to caress the land. Vibrant red poppies, bracts of pink and cream roses, purple honesty and toadflax rejoiced in the warmth. Losing its verdancy, the corn became an ocean of undulating gold.

Francis Matheson was taking tea with his daughters. Both of them were dressed in blue gowns. The bodice of the one Maryse wore was sprigged with hand-embroidered cornflowers. His elder daughter presided over the tea service, an ornate silver affair of swirled metal and roses. It had been a wedding gift for their mother from his brother, the Earl of Kylchester – a much too grand gift for a country doctor of modest means, and always a source of amusement to them, for it could never be lifted comfortably.

Maryse, handing him a slice of cake, gazed at him anxiously as he took a bite, for she'd made it herself under the tutelage of Mrs Tibbet, his housekeeper. He nodded and smiled at her, watching the anxiety flee from her eyes. His Maryse was a gentle soul, good at womanly pursuits. He expected her to make a good marriage, for she had grace as well as charm.

Pansy would rather employ her mind with mathematics and the sciences. She should have been a boy instead of a girl, he mused. There was a badly darned hole in her stocking he could see as she lounged in her chair with her feet crossed at the ankles. She turned her head to give him a swift, bright smile, her long brown hair swinging. His heart turned over at that smile.

Both were more woman than girl now, he thought with a sudden shock, noticing the line curving from shoulder to waist. They resembled their mother, their delicate facial bones and sweetly curving mouths the very image of hers. Their eyes were Matheson grey.

'Siana said she will buy Maryse and me our very own horses to ride,' Pansy told him, her eyes sparkling. 'But we have to ask your permission, and then we can accompany her with Jed Hawkins and the groom to the horse sales to help choose one.'

'You must not presume too much on Siana's generosity, Pansy.'

'Siana said the horses will be a special gift to welcome us to Cheverton Manor. She said she'll be glad to have some pleasant company to ride out with, for there are lots of places we can explore together – and she knows of some Roman ruins I can sketch.'

'You don't mind me marrying Siana, do you?' It was a statement rather than a question, for the answer was written on their faces, which pleased him mightily.

Maryse gazed up at him, her eyes almost glowing with adoration. 'Of course not. She's so pretty that you can't help but admire her. And she's clever, funny and interesting, despite her background. It will be fun having a stepmother who's still young. She has asked us to help her choose colours and decorations for the bedrooms we shall occupy.'

'I like her enormously, too.' Pansy broke in. 'Siana doesn't have any airs and graces. She's not frightened of spiders or mice and doesn't keep telling me to be ladylike, or to sit still. She told me that if you lie very still and gaze up at the sky, you can feel the world turning. So I tried it, and I did. Only I got the back of my dress dirty, and Aunt Prudence said she *despaired* of me.'

Francis chuckled. 'Your aunt means well.'

Pansy's eyes were round and indignant. 'Siana would never say anything like that. She said dirt can be washed off, and she likes me exactly as I am.'

'So do I,' Francis managed to get in, but Pansy's flow of words refused to be stilled.

'I can tell her secrets, and she doesn't make fun of me or tell anyone else – not even Aunt Prudence, who wants to know everything about us . . . even private things.'

Maryse kicked her sister's ankle and they both turned very pink. Pansy turned to gaze out of the window, biting her lip.

'More tea?' Maryse mumbled, her slender wrist barely supporting the weight of the teapot.

Francis nodded, thinking a little sadly. Thank goodness they had someone to talk to besides himself. His girls, so sweetly tender in their flowering, would never regard Siana as their mother, she was too young. But they had certainly found a friend they could relate to.

'We're invited to sleep at Cheverton Manor tomorrow. The stable puppies are nearly ready to leave their mother, and we are to choose one each. We're also having fittings for the gowns we will wear to your wedding.'

Francis frowned slightly. 'I have business in Poole and will be leaving whilst you're still in your beds.'

'Pansy and I can walk over,' Maryse said. 'It's not far, and Mrs Tibbet will come with us if I ask her. The stable boy can bring her home in the cart.'

But come morning, Mrs Tibbet was looking decidedly harassed as she bustled about. She was none too pleased with the interruption to her plans. Hands supporting her back, she gazed at the pair of them. ''Tis laundry day, and if I don't get started now it won't be dry by nightfall. I'm not as fleet of foot as you two young ladies. It would take me a good hour to walk over to that there manor. That's going to put me behind with my work – and me with a room to prepare for the new sawbones. Have you forgotten he's arriving tomorrow?'

Maryse and Pansy gazed at each other in consternation, then Pansy suggested, 'We're old enough to go by ourselves, Mrs Tibbet. It's a glorious day, and if we cut around the fields and through the woods, nobody will see us. We'll be there in no time at all.'

Mrs Tibbet gazed at them with doubt in her eyes. 'I don't know what your father would say to that.'

Maryse smiled at her. 'I'm sure he won't mind. I've already packed our night wear. We can carry the bag between us. Then we'll be out from underfoot.'

After a moment or two, Mrs Tibbet nodded. The two girls grinned at each other, pleased to be granted this unexpected freedom. They went off down the lane, their bonnets shading their faces from the sun, swinging a calico bag between them.

Pansy found a willow stick and swiped at the long grass.

The day was promising to be as glorious a day as August could produce. Flower perfume drifted in the air, so now and again their noses were assailed with delicious scents. The grasses had grown high and were beginning to seed. The air hummed with the industrious sound of the bees gathering pollen.

Pansy clambered over the stile with agile grace. Maryse handed the bag to her sister and followed more slowly, making sure her stockings didn't catch on the rough wooden crossbeams and the moss didn't stain her gown.

It had been a good summer. The hay was being dried and stacked upon stone staddles, which would allow the air to circulate. To lose the hay fodder to rot would be a disaster for the farmers, and mean starvation for the animals who wintered on it. When the corn had been successfully harvested and stacked, the ricks would be thatched to guard against winter storms. In the meantime, the sheep were set in pens woven from slender hazel-branches, to graze upon the fresh grass growing amongst the hay stubble. The pens would be moved from place to place, the flock's last function before being slaughtered, to fertilize the soil for next season's crop.

At this time of year the field labourers worked long hours, whilst the farmers prayed and kept an eye out for the weather. Itinerant labourers worked alongside the locals, young men for the most, who'd teamed up, slept rough and earned a wage the best way they could.

The field the two girls had entered was dotted with such people. Men worked abreast, using small sickles to cut the wheat. Their muscles bulged as they moved, their faces, toasted nut brown from the sun, were sheened with sweat. The field was a hive of activity, kept that way by the overseer. Rest breaks were rotated for the various teams of five, who also competed for a small keg of scrumpy cider, which would be awarded at the harvest supper.

It was a perfect day. The air was balmy and swifts flitted over the field to snatch up the insects disturbed by the workers. Above, in the infinite blue of a seamless sky, a small hawk hovered, seemingly motionless. Field mice sprang like squeaking acrobats from beneath the labourers' tread, to disappear back into the stubble again.

Maryse would have liked to linger and watch for a while, but they had to traverse half the length of the field to reach the woods. As they walked, the girls kept their eyes on the picturesque scene, so familiar to them both.

The Matheson girls presented a picture of innocence to the watching eyes of some of the labourers. Sweet in their bonnets and dainty gowns, they were unaware of the three young men lounging in their path under the shade of the hedge – of the avid eyes taking notice of their womanly curves. The sight of a trim ankle would set the blood running rampant in the veins of these young stallions.

The lads were conversant with country ways. They'd seen first-hand how nature worked, and were aware of their place in it. Between them, they'd initiated many a young wench, willing, or sometimes the reluctant, who they'd managed to convince.

Henry Ruddle, a strapping lad of eighteen with dark good looks, slate-coloured eyes and a pock-marked face, grinned. 'Here be coming a couple of innocents.'

'They be gentry by the looks of them,' Patrick Pethan warned.

Silas Barton gave a high-pitched snigger. 'I ain't never had a gentry maid, nor likely to be offered one. Does he reckon they be different under their skirts from the peasant wenches?'

'Sweeter, I reckon. The gentry keeps their daughters under lock and key.'

'Then what's this pair doing, cavortin' about the countryside by themselves?'

'Lookin' for adventure, I reckon.' Henry cupped his crotch in his hand. 'This here would be right honoured to oblige them, too.'

'Leave them be, Henry. There be plenty of country

rump on offer in these parts, and those two are hardly out of the schoolroom.'

'I'll just have a bit of fun with them, that's all.'

'Make sure it is just fun. I don't want to get messself hanged. Nor do I want to be gelded by some beefy farmer with a rusty sickle in his hand, or have my balls nailed to his barn door.'

Maryse came to a sudden halt, uttering a soft 'Oh,' when she spied the booted legs stretched out in front of her. Pansy clutched her arm and tried to pull her around the leg, but they were stopped by the sight of another labourer. When they took a step back, their retreat was blocked.

The man who'd been seated rose to his feet and gave a sweeping bow. 'Who have we here, then?'

'Stand aside,' Maryse said, trying to disguise the wavering in her voice. 'How dare you detain us?'

He chuckled. 'We ain't detaining you, missy. We be trying to be friendly and make your acquaintance. I be Henry, that there is Silas and the one behind you be Pat. What be you two beauties called?'

'That's none of your business. Stand aside.'

Henry lost his smile. 'That don't be very friendly, like. Where be you off to this fine mornin'?'

'To the manor. We're expected . . . and if we don't get there soon the steward will come looking for us.'

The one called Henry scratched his dark, greasy thatch. 'Doubt that. We see'd Jed Hawkins headin' off into town a little while ago, didn't we, boys?'

The other two nodded their heads. 'I heard he's got a

woman there. I bet a sweet little thing like you has got a sweetheart, too?' He reached out to touch her ringlet.

Maryse jerked her head away. 'No, I haven't. I'm not old enough.'

'You be old enough fer me, and a right pretty piece. How 'bout you give Henry a kiss.'

Beginning to panic, Maryse tried to push past him, her heart pounding as his arm blocked her. 'Out of our way, please.'

'We can't let you go through the woods by yerself. You never know who might be lurking in there. Some of those thievin' tinkers be camping up on the common, and they be out gatherin' scroff for the camp fires or trappin' rabbits, most like. If they get a hold of you two, there'll be no knowin' where you'll end up. You'll be taken away and sold as slaves in some foreign parts, I reckon.'

Maryse's eyes widened with horror as her sister crowded against her.

The man's hand gripped her arm above the elbow. 'Come on, my lovely, there's a gap in the hedge. I'll show you something you might like better.'

'Leave her alone, you bully,' Pansy screeched and, lashing out with the willow stick, striped Henry's face with a welt. Her second swipe caught him across the eyes, making them stream with tears.

His hands went to his face and he cursed horribly. The one called Silas swung back his fist, catching her a numbing blow on the upper arm.

Partially raised with her boisterous cousins and, finding she had courage a-plenty when needed, Maryse kicked him hard, then, swinging the bag around, knocked him flat on his back. Patrick had made no move towards them. Now he jerked his head towards the stile, indicating they make their escape.

They fled when someone gave a loud roar. It was the overseer, a stout, ruddy-faced man with a neck as thick as that of a bull. 'Stop messing about with them wenches and get back to work, you three, unless you want your wages docked.'

The sisters made it safely to the stile, scrambled over it into the woods and didn't stop running until they were out of breath. For a few moments they doubled over, gasping in air. Still breathing heavily, they stared at each other.

Pansy gave a nervous giggle. 'Papa will fume for a month when he finds out.'

'Then we mustn't tell him.' Straightening her bonnet, Maryse took her sister's hand and gazed nervously around them. She'd been made uneasy by the encounter and felt threatened as well as soiled. 'What if there *are* tinkers in the woods? It's rumoured that they steal babies and eat them.'

Pansy picked up a stout stick, stating with bloodthirsty relish, 'Well, we're not babies, and I'll knock those thieving tinkers on the head if they try and sell us into slavery. Pick up that stick with the knob on the end, Maryse. If I miss their heads, you can bang them on the nose. Remember how cousin Ned's nose bled when I accidentally punched him? It dripped all over his jacket. He swore at me, and got a good thrashing for his trouble.'

'And you got a lecture about unladylike behaviour from Aunt Prudence.'

Pansy giggled. 'I know all her lectures by heart.'

It was quiet in the woods, which smelled pleasantly of mushrooms, moss, pine needles and boggy grass. Buoyed up by Pansy's false courage, they proceeded cautiously along the track, careful not to trip over the gnarled and twisted tree roots, and jumping at every snap of a twig or rustle of a leaf.

Finally, they left the tree line, coming into the grounds of Cheverton Manor at the back of the house. The house was of comfortable proportions, built solidly of Portland stone. Ivy rambled over the walls and the morning sun gleamed warmly on the windows.

They heaved a great sigh of relief when they saw people about, a maid shaking the dust from a rug and a gardener digging in the kitchen garden.

Pansy threw her stick aside and gazed at her sister. 'Should we tell Siana about those field labourers bullying us?'

'No, we'd better not. Siana might feel she had to tell Papa. She'd certainly dismiss them, then she'd be short-handed. We must be careful not to go into the fields again, that's all. Those men will leave the district after the harvest is in, then we'll be safe.'

It was a decision Maryse would later come to regret.

Siana was in the nursery. She put Ashley down, giving both girls a hug when they appeared at the door. 'Goodness, you two look flushed.'

'It's warm outside,' Maryse mumbled, reddening even more with the guilt of her evasiveness.

'I hope it remains that way whilst the corn harvest is underway. We're short-handed as it is, without the weather turning against us.' The smile she gave them was as warm as summer. 'Where's your papa? Did he come with you?'

Pansy slid a grin towards Maryse. 'He had an early appointment in Poole, but he sent his love.' Siana felt her smile grow wider.

Her attention captured by Daisy and Goldie, who had abandoned their milk and biscuits to compete for her notice, Pansy turned to them. 'Hello, you two. How are the lessons, then?'

Daisy and Goldie gazed at each other and grimaced, united in the things they were finding hard to master – reading, writing and learning their sums. Miss Edgar, their governess, was nice, though. She didn't treat them like babies, and played singing games with them, as well as allowing them to draw pictures.

Miss Edgar came bustling in now, her face wreathed in smiles. 'Good morning, Miss Matheson, Miss Pansy. A lovely day, isn't it? Finish your refreshment, please, Daisy and Marigold. It's nearly time to come through to the schoolroom for your reading lesson.'

Daisy gazed pleadingly at Siana. 'Do we have to, Mamma?'

'Most certainly. You don't want to grow up to be ignorant, do you?'

Goldie solemnly shook her head and picked up her milk.

'You don't even know what higgerant means,' Daisy accused her.

'Yes I do.' Head slanted to one side, a milky moustache decorating her upper lip, Goldie aimed a cool, blue gaze towards Daisy. 'Higgerant means you're stupid.'

Miss Edgar gazed at Goldie in astonishment. 'Good gracious!'

Daisy swallowed her milk and made a face. 'I'm not higgerant. I knew what it meant all the time.'

Siana exchanged an amused glance with the governess, who took the girls' hands and began to lead them away, saying, 'What clever pupils I have today. That's good, because we have a spelling test later on.'

Ashley had wandered off to become exuberantly involved with kicking a rag ball around the room. Siana snatched him up as he ran past, to give him a parting hug.

His skin was like satin against her lips. He giggled when she blew against the fragrant folds of his neck, pummelling her with his podgy fists to be set free. Love for him filled her, like warm milk running into a jug, when she put him down. Indeed, the jug overflowed as she watched him scamper off, his dark curls bobbing. What a sturdy, handsome boy her little squire was becoming. Had Edward lived, he would have been so proud of him.

Her arms slid around the waists of the two girls, almost as tall as herself and well on their way to becoming beautiful young women. They went down the wide staircase like that, side by side. How lucky she was,

Siana thought. Soon, she would be stepmother to these two girls – and their father would be her husband. Before too long she hoped to bring another child into the family, one who would span the two families and unite them even more. Then nothing would be able to spoil her happiness.

But, just as the thought was released, a shiver of unease trickled coldly up her spine to set the hairs at the nape of her neck on end. Despite the warmth of the day, Siana felt a slight chill. It had been a long time since the strange, fey sense, which she'd inherited from her Welsh ancestors, had shown itself so strongly.

She shook off the flicker of dread it brought with it and, pushing the feeling to the back of her mind, turned to the girls. 'We must go and choose your puppies later, before Jed gets it into his head to dispose of them.'

The bitch was a descendant of one of Edward's two spotted coach dogs, which had died of old age within weeks of each other the previous spring. It was small, vaguely terrier by appearance and more so by nature. It didn't have a name. Siana supposed it was her dog and thought that one day she might ask Jed about it.

When Maryse and Pansy gazed at each other and grinned from ear to ear, she grinned too. It was such a pleasure to have the girls for company. 'We'll go and see them now.'

It didn't take long to choose. Maryse picked the only black one, a bitch with white ears and socks. After much deliberation, she named it Victoria, after the new queen. Pansy's pup was white and wore a black mask. He had a single black spot above his tail, after which he was promptly named.

'How will Jed dispose of the others?' Maryse said and, cuddling the squirming Victoria against her cheek, cast anxious eyes over the rest of the litter.

'They'll be sold at market, I expect. Good ratters can always find a home.'

A relieved smile touched the girl's mouth. She was soft-hearted, Siana thought, and too sensitive for her own good. When Maryse wed, she hoped her husband would be kind to her.

At the authoritative yelp of the puppies' mother, the chosen two were placed back on the teat with their less fortunate siblings, and nudged back into line.

At least the bitch would not lose all her babies, Siana thought.

Jed Hawkins came riding in just as they were leaving the stable. He dismounted and handed the reins to the stable boy, instructing, 'Leave him saddled. I'll be going out again soon to help with the harvest.' He sent her an enquiring glance. 'Unless you ladies need escorting somewhere, of course.'

'We're going to have a picnic in the manor gardens this afternoon, Jed, so the maids will be with us.'

'Keep away from the fields, if you would. There are strangers about, and tinkers. That could result in trouble.'

Maryse and Pansy exchanged a glance.

'I've just come back from a meeting with Squire Frampton and the local farmers. Since the Tolpuddle men were pardoned there has been trouble again. The

London Dorchester Committee is planning to welcome George Lovelace back home from Van Diemen's Land.'

Jed was referring to the leader of the other five Tolpuddle men who'd been sentenced to transportation to New South Wales for administering an illegal oath. It was common knowledge that the charge had been a trumped-up one; a punishment for trying to form a union to better the condition of the rural workers. Having been brought up in one of the estate cottages herself, albeit one of the better dwellings, Siana had experienced at first hand the degradation, sickness and hunger brought about by inadequate wages and shelter – so she held a sneaking sympathy for the lot of the labourers. She dared not say so to Jed, though.

'Well, I suppose they've learned their lesson,' she said blandly.

To this Jed muttered darkly, 'I doubt very much if they've learned anything, for they have too many supporters to quietly settle back in their former life. News of their pardon has incited more lawlessness, which will unsettle the district again. No doubt it will worsen when the men return home, for the ploughman, George Lovelace, is an eloquent lay preacher by all accounts. The landowners have decided to stand firm on keeping wages under control.'

'If the Tolpuddle men were pardoned, doesn't it indicate that their cause was just?'

She squirmed when Jed's honey eyes rested on her for a moment. 'Have the labourers worked more willingly for the weekly shilling you gave them?'

She didn't want to argue with him over estate wages. Wasn't it enough to know that the women always came off worst in the home? For they fed their menfolk and children first, and were forced to exist on the leftovers. It was the women who suffered most, who aged quickly from constant childbirth or lack of nutrition. Yet they were expected to work side by side with their menfolk and for a lesser wage, as well as run the household and look after the children.

Any attempts on her part to better the lot of her own workers was met by resistance from the trustees of the estate, as well as Jed. It was something in which she had no say, because she was a woman. The trustees were unanimous in their thinking. If conditions at Cheverton Estate were improved, then other estates in the district would be expected to follow suit. That would cost the landowners money – money they would rather keep in their own purses.

Giving a sigh, Siana nodded. 'You know I haven't got an answer to that, Jed. I'll be careful. We'll stay within sight of the house if that will put your mind at ease. There's a pleasant spot under the oaks.'

His smile reflected the relief he felt, for her compliance would mean less for him to worry about. 'That it will. They need me in the fields. The more hands there are out there, the quicker the harvest will be brought in. This good weather can't last for ever.'

'The girls have chosen a puppy apiece for themselves,' she informed him when he began to walk away. 'They're the black one with white ears and legs, and the one with the mask and dark spot above the tail.'

'Good choices,' Jed said, turning to smile at the two girls.

The sun touched his features. For a moment it was as if Edward was standing there. Siana gave a tiny gasp, reminded of the relationship Elizabeth had seen fit to inform her of.

'Is something wrong?' he said.

'No, nothing, it's just . . .' Perhaps it was time it was brought out into the open; if so, it would be up to her to initiate it, for Jed never would. But not in front of the girls. 'I'd like to discuss something with you, later, in private.'

'I'll be working until after sun-down, for there's book work to attend to.'

'I know, but what I have to say won't take a moment.'

'I know that look. Are you about to pry into my private life, missus?' he asked with soft menace.

'Could be.'

The paraphrasing of his laconic speech pattern made him raise a disbelieving eyebrow and shake his head. A grin cracked his face. 'Can you hold your curiosity until morning?'

'Join me for breakfast, then.'

When he nodded and walked away, Siana knew it would be all right.

4

Jed Hawkins didn't come right away to Siana's summons. He left her waiting for half an hour.

'Why didn't you come sooner?' she said crossly.

He stood perfectly still, balanced on legs slightly apart, gazing down upon her. His eyes were dark and expressionless, making her feel at a disadvantage. 'I've been working in the the fields since dawn. I'm going into Poole after breakfast and needed to wash and tidy myself.'

How hard he worked for his wage, and how useless he made her feel. In fact, his whole stance seemed to challenge her. It crossed her mind that he might have resented her taking over the estate. She dismissed the thought, Jed had never been less than kind or protective of her, and he'd always been taciturn. 'Why didn't you tell me you were Edward's brother?'

'Ah, so that's what's so damned important to you.' His expression didn't change as he considered her question, then slowly, he said, 'I didn't think it was any of your business.'

'Oh . . . I see.' She recovered rapidly from the set-down. 'You look older than Edward.'

He hummed slightly in his throat. 'That could be a fact, it could indeed. 'Tis in the eye of the beholder, though, for I be five years younger.'

'You're infuriating, Jed Hawkins.'

The corners of his mouth twitched. 'Only because you allow yourself to be infuriated. Is there anything else, or can I help myself to breakfast now? There's nothing like a bit of hard labour to put an edge on a man's appetite.'

'Don't stand on ceremony on my account.' Head slanted to one side, she scrutinized his face. 'You look like him, you know. Why didn't I notice it before?'

He chuckled. 'Could be you were plain dazzled when Edward was alive. He had that effect on people.'

'Tell me about your relationship with him.'

'Don't see any point, since it was private between us. Besides, some things are best left undisturbed.'

Jed was clad in the suit he wore to church on Sundays. He had recently shaved and his hair had been trimmed. A tiny suspicion lodged in her mind.

'You look as if you're off a-courting.'

His cheeks hollowed as he sucked in a breath, his eyes slid her a narrowed glance. His skin adopted a slight rosiness. 'There might be some truth in that. Then again, there might not.'

She sighed. 'You're not going to tell me, are you?'

Amusement filled his eyes. 'You always did allow your curiosity to get the better of you.'

Frustrated by his answer, she spat out, 'Damn you, then, Jed Hawkins!'

'And you, Lady Forbes.'

'You only call me that when you try to put me in my place.'

'Which is anywhere where you can't meddle in a man's business.' He heaped a plate with eggs, ham and several slices of bread, then seated himself at the table.

Taking a plate of lesser proportions, she slid into the seat opposite him. 'I'll find out, you know.'

'I daresay. Mind your nose don't get stuck where it don't rightly belong though.'

'*Ooh, men!*' she fumed.

He chuckled.

Then she realized Jed was uncle to her son. The management of the estate couldn't be in better hands. She grinned widely. 'Enjoy your breakfast, Uncle Jed.'

His eyes came up to hers and he began to laugh. 'I'll be glad when you're wed, that I will. The good doctor might be able to stop you from making mischief for others.'

Siana's wedding day arrived, sparkling with sunshine. For the second time, Josh escorted his sister to the square-towered Cheverton church where she was to exchange her vows with Francis. This time he was much more self-assured.

Siana had gowned herself in yellow to marry Francis – not a colour as bright as the daffodils that danced in spring amongst spiked leaves over every piece of open ground, but a softly glowing shimmer of pastel satin. Her wide-brimmed hat was a confection of peachy silk roses.

Daisy and Goldie were dressed in the merest blush of

peach to match the roses. In the charge of Francis's two daughters, who were clad in a tint of green, the effect was a celebration of summer. All four girls tried not to let their inner excitement show as they proceeded down the aisle under the scrutiny of the guests, dividing to sit in the pews either side.

When Francis caught Siana's glance his heart leaped. How deep and glowing her eyes were today. His mother had possessed a rare and highly prized gemstone called an Alexandrite which, depending on the light source, changed colour. Today, Siana's eyes were the same green as the gem exposed to natural light. He almost disintegrated under the loving look she gave him. She was seductive, this woman of his with the pagan heart.

He remembered his heart breaking into a thousand shards when she'd married Edward Forbes in this very same church just a few years before. Now a miracle had occurred and she was about to become his.

Then she was standing next to him. Francis couldn't help himself. He took her face in his hands and gently kissed the lush ripeness of her mouth. A ripple of amusement went through the guests. He grinned self-consciously, just as astonished that he'd made a public declaration of his affection for her.

She was laughing at his display, her mouth a delicious and wanton curve, her eyes full of mischief as they flirted with his, until the solemnity of the vows they exchanged sobered them both.

Then the ceremony was over. There was a dash to the carriage and they were being conveyed back to

Cheverton Manor, there to greet their guests as they arrived for the feasting.

'I love you, Mrs Matheson,' Francis told her as the carriage wheels measured the short distance to the manor.

When he leaned forward to steal a kiss she slid her arms around his neck and, afterwards, hugged him tight. 'I'm so happy, Francis.'

He freed himself from her grip. 'You'll crush your gown, and we have yet to greet our guests.'

'Were I to appear crushed, your brothers would applaud you and the women would envy me.'

'Then, crush you I shall.' He pulled her across the carriage on to his lap and proceeded to kiss the sense from her.

'Hah!' she said, revelling in this playfulness and laughing down at him as they turned in through the manor gates. 'You'd better compose yourself, husband, for we haven't the time to finish what we started satisfactorily.'

'Exactly what I feared when we started. If you must torture me, Siana, chose a more appropriate place, in future.' He chuckled when she made a face at him.

Soon, they were standing together inside the hall, her fingertips caressing the palm of his hand as they greeted their guests.

Daniel appeared, to bow over her hand. The fleshy contours of his face had matured into manhood. Although he resembled his father enough to still jolt her, he lacked Edward's charisma, for his mouth had a slightly sullen tilt to it and, when he smiled, his eyes no longer lit up. She couldn't imagine how she'd once thought herself in love with him.

Daniel's wife, Esmé, appeared older than Siana had imagined she would be, for she remembered reading a letter Daniel had sent to his father, describing her as girlish. She was thin featured and her mouth drooped at the corners a little, as if she didn't laugh much. She had pretty blue eyes and was pleasant enough, however.

Elizabeth had been given permission to take Daniel to the nursery to visit Susannah and Ashley before dinner was served. Although Susannah was Elizabeth's daughter, she was a guest until she left in the morning and Siana didn't like the routine of the nursery maids, or that of her children, disrupted unnecessarily.

Daniel caught her eye. He nodded, smiling his thanks when they came back down.

With the help of the borrowed chef and an army of footmen, the manor servants had produced a feast fit for a king. Enjoying a merry evening on this, the second occasion of marriage, Siana was better able to cope with the company she found herself in.

Throughout the evening Francis frequently engaged her glance, smiling in an altogether intimate manner which made her blush. He was teasing her for the incident in the carriage, and his brothers roared with laughter and slapped him on the back.

There were five of them present. In order of age, Ryder the Earl of Kylchester, with his countess, Prudence, dressed becomingly in pale blue. They were accompanied by their litter of sons. Siana was glad to meet the Matheson cousins at last, after hearing Pansy and Maryse prattle about their manly virtues. And a dashing lot they were.

Augustus was next, resplendent in his admiral's uniform. He considered himself lucky to be in port at the time of the wedding. 'Very lucky, for otherwise I would have missed meeting this exquisite creature.' His eyes twinkling, he elbowed Francis out of the way and looked into Siana's eyes. Then he swept her hand to his lips and placed a kiss in the palm. 'You should have wed me. I'm in need of a wife.'

'As long as it's another man's wife,' Francis said with a laugh.

Then came Beckwith, the tallest of the brothers, who was long faced and solemn and made his living practising the law. He scrutinized her intently, then nodded his approval at Francis. His wife was round, jolly and had a fussy manner.

Raoul came next. He was a widower with a sardonic manner, who was – Prudence had told her – involved in all manner of schemes.

'I'm an opportunist, I buy and sell items for profit,' he explained when she asked him. 'When Francis told me the colour of your eyes I had this Alexandrine set in gold for you.' Taking a ring from his pocket he slid it upon her finger.

'Thank you, it's a most beautiful ring, Raoul. I don't deserve it.'

His lips hardly moved, but they became a smile. 'If Francis loves you as much as he appears to, I'm quite sure you do.'

'Is that the stone that belonged to our mother?'

Francis asked, coming up behind them and thinking it an odd coincidence that he'd remembered the stone earlier in the church.

'She gave it to Bethany on our wedding day. Perhaps you and Siana will have a daughter to pass it on to one day.'

As Elizabeth had guessed, William, the former army officer, now resident in Van Diemen's Land, was absent.

Siana had never seen Francis looking so happy, or dressed so handsomely. His slim-fitting trousers, topped by an embroidered waistcoat and a dark grey cutaway jacket with winged collar, were of good cut and quality. Her heart melted every time their eyes met.

Maryse and Pansy were allowed to stay up late and dance with their cousins. At eleven they were packed off to the adjoining bedrooms Siana had had prepared for them. She blew them a kiss as they left. She was fond of the two girls, and hoped she'd prove to be a good stepmother to them.

In the past, that role had been taken by their aunt, Prudence, who was loath to relinquish it and let everyone know of her input into her nieces' upbringing. She insisted they must have a season in London in a year or two, to launch them into society. This was an endeavour to find them suitable husbands.

'It will not do them any good to marry beneath them,' Prudence brayed after they left the room, completely forgetting that their father had done just that.

As if by some unspoken agreement, the festivities finally came to an end. The guests departed in a flurry of good wishes, their carriages rolling off down the drive in convoy, their lamps gleaming in the darkness, their coachmen and outriders fully armed, in case of trouble.

Siana and Francis stood in the doorway, watching them go. Above them, ragged clouds sailed across the moon. The breeze raised goosebumps along her arms. Francis put his arm around her when she shivered, pulling her close.

There was a moment of awkwardness, dispelled when Francis smiled at her. Hefting her up into his arms, he headed up the curving staircase, whispering against her ear, 'Where do we sleep, Mrs Matheson?'

If she had her way there would be precious little sleep – and she *would* have her way. She grinned at the thought. 'Take a left turn at the top of the stairs and go to the end of the corridor.'

Francis nodded to Rosie, who hovered on the landing outside their two adjoining rooms. 'I doubt if your services will be required, Rosie. Off to bed with you.'

Siana chuckled when Rosie scuttled off, grinning to herself. 'I hope you're good at unlacing me, then.'

'I'm a physician. I've unlaced every garment you can name.'

'Yours is the room next door,' she said, when he shoved the door ajar with his foot.

He gazed down at her, eyes amused as he heeled the door shut behind them. 'Not tonight.' Setting her gently on the bed he plucked the pins and ornaments from her hair and watched it tumble down her back in a ripple of perfumed darkness. 'I've always wanted to do that.'

She smiled at this small secret yearning he'd revealed. 'Disrobe me, Francis.'

He hesitated for just a moment, then bunched her frothy petticoats in his hands, carefully sliding them up to her knees. Up and up his hands went, his thumb brushing against her dark core and sliding over silk and lace. He hesitated when he encountered her lacy demi-corset, sucking in a deep, shuddering breath.

'I was wrong. I've never unlaced garments such as these.'

Taking his face between her hands, she kissed him, her mouth a soft caress against his as she said. 'I hope the way I dress pleases you. Start with my bodice and skirt. Imagine I'm a gift you've just been given.'

She stood, presenting him with easy access to fastenings and strings. There was pleasure in his eyes as he gradually unwrapped her, until the only garments between him and her naked body were a tease of filmy chemise and a lacy demi-corset. When she moved slightly, the chemise slid over one shoulder, revealing the rise of one breast without exposing the nipple.

He gave a faintly bemused smile. 'The last time I examined you a maid uncovered a portion at a time.'

Her eyes widened. 'You remember that?'

'For a moment I forgot I was a doctor.'

'Tonight you'll forget it completely, I promise,' she purred, 'for it's my turn now.' Carefully she unwound his stock, then removed jacket, waistcoat and shirt. His chest was broad and muscular, lightly furred. She kissed the spot beating above his heart and felt its pace increase beneath her mouth. When her fingers went to the fastenings of his trousers, his hands covered hers, stilling them.

He kissed her mouth, her shoulders and the hollow of her throat whilst his fingers wrestled with the intricacies of her lacing. She gave a low gurgle of laughter when he cursed. He grinned when he won the fight, tossing the garment aside. The silk chemise followed it.

He gazed at her, standing in nothing but her stockings, and growled deep in his throat. Hopping from one leg to the other he kicked off his shoes, peeled off his trousers then reached out for her.

'Oh,' she whispered against his ear when their flesh came warmly together, deliberately provocative, 'can that all be you, my love?'

'You know you've made a stallion out of me.'

Her arms came up around his neck and his hands slid one under each of her buttocks as he lifted her and bore her down on to the bed. There had been no foreplay. Francis just slid deeply into her. Her disappointment at this was short-lived, though. He stayed there for a few moments, feeding her moistness with his presence, growing thick and hard to fill her, so she adjusted to the accommodation of him. Then, very slowly, he withdrew from his warm nest.

She whimpered when he touched his mouth against one of her breasts, gave a little cry of encouragement when it swelled against his tongue in joyous union. Too soon, everything came together in a sensuous feast of loving, until her wanting built to a fever pitch of hot, writhing flesh. She trapped him above her, her legs circled around his waist, her pelvis tilting towards him.

'Now, Francis. Now!'

His restraint crumbled and he drove into her with a

hard, bruising urgency. She'd not expected such strength and clung to him, helpless under the thrusting power of his passionate attack. Between them grew a concentration so intense, she felt his heat drive up into her, felt her muscles contract to grip and close around him.

Her gasp of delight coincided with his own triumphant grunt as he lost control, and plunged into his final possession of her. He drove the breath from her splayed body with each swift thrust, she pulling him back each time he retreated, so he could probe the very reaches of her, to finally explode in a rush of molten lust together.

Breathing harshly, he collapsed against her, she taking his weight and gentling his hair with her fingers. After a moment or two he said softly, 'I'll be damned. I thought I'd forgotten how.' He propped himself up on one elbow, to gaze down at her and delight in her dishevelment. His smile came, wonderingly at first, then he laughed in a most self-satisfied way.

'Stop looking so smug,' she said, not bothering to hide her laughter.

One of his fingers delicately traced around the contours of her face. 'I feel smug, especially since that was a delicious taste of what's to come.'

Everything in her tingled with expectation. 'There's more?'

'Of course there's more. I've waited too long for you to set you aside so soon.' His finger left her face to follow a shivering path down her neck and over her shoulders, to explore each swollen breast. Then he kissed her mouth, plundering it until it was soft and receptive to the ever-demanding advances of his tongue.

Inside of her, she felt a stealthy movement. Her eyes narrowed. Feeling like a great, lazy cat, she stretched seductively beneath him.

Although Francis remained conventional on the outside, it became evident to Siana that inside the bedroom, he was exactly the opposite.

Unlike Edward, he was possessed of great vigour and stamina, and was not averse to a little experimentation of his own, a trait she intended to encourage. Kept satisfied by his attention, Siana felt secure in his love – her only regret was that she didn't become pregnant during those first few weeks.

Despite having a new partner in the medical practice, Francis was called out to urgent cases often, or made himself available for consultation in the patient rooms opened at his premises.

With the children being tutored Siana had time on her hands. Due to the simple fact that she'd been born a female, Jed Hawkins didn't appreciate her help in running an estate he'd more or less controlled for most of his adult life. Jed could go to places where doors were closed to her, and do the things she was barred from doing because of her gender. She could not attend farmers' meetings, the corn exchange, or deal with the labourers.

She was aware that the pay rise she'd argued with Jed for the labourers still wasn't enough – was aware that there was trouble in the district, a direct result of the poverty. But in the first happy weeks of her marriage she lived only for Francis. The outside world was hardly allowed to intrude on that. After all, the muck was still spread on the fields, the earth was still tilled and the produce for market still grew.

Siana spent hours in the nursery playing with the son she adored. Goldie followed her around like a quiet little shadow, the girl grateful for any small attention paid to her. Daisy had attached herself to the Matheson girls. As a result, Daisy's manners had improved, though to Siana's mind, her young sister was beginning to think too much of herself.

That summer had a timeless quality about it. Deeply contented and steadied by her husband's influence, Siana used the time wisely, improving herself, educating herself and getting to know Maryse and Pansy a little better.

Nothing, she thought, could spoil the bounty life had brought her – not even the fact that she hadn't yet ferreted out who Jed Hawkins was courting.

Jed ran a finger under his stock to loosen it. A man of the land, he felt like a bumpkin aping his betters in his new suit of clothes. As clothes went, they were conservative. Donkey brown trousers were topped by a fawn jacket over a checked waistcoat. His riding boots were old and comfortable, but the leather was polished to a high gloss. On his head he wore a floppy country hat that had seen better days. He promised himself he'd discard it when he reached his destination.

Mounting the great black horse he rode, he headed

out, his forehead unclouded by worry. He touched his finger to his hat when he passed Siana, who was picnicking on the grass surrounded by the children and several servants.

Goldie leaned against Siana's side, whilst the young squire lurched across the grass as fast as his legs could carry him. Pansy Matheson, Daisy Skinner and his nurse were in hot pursuit. Jed grinned to himself. Damned if that Ashley wasn't the image of his sire, and already the women were dancing attendance on him.

His fine attire drew a roll of the eyes from Siana. He returned her enquiring grin with a mocking shake of his head. She'd know when he knew, and not a moment before.

He turned his face up to the sun for a moment. It had been a good year, for the seasons, the weather and the earth had worked together to yield a fine harvest. The usual supper would be laid on for the labourers, their bellies would be filled with as much food and ale as they could stand, and a fiddler or two would be hired for the dancing.

He'd also decided to pay a bonus for the farm workers this year, ten shillings for the overseers, five for field workers and labourers, and three for the women and those aged seventeen and under. He'd have to discuss it with the lady of the house, of course, but he knew she'd be delighted, for, whatever her wealth now, she would never be able to forget her humble beginnings.

Siana was a rare woman, with strength of purpose and honesty. Jed held the greatest respect for her. She had grown up in abject poverty, yet the need to put her loved ones above all others would prevent her heart from totally ruling her head.

Not that he would recommend the bonus from the goodness of his heart, either. The labourers were a dissatisfied lot, and Jed knew he'd get more work out of them next year if they thought they had something extra at harvest time to work towards.

He would suggest a raise in wages for himself, too. He deserved it, since he'd been forced to assume full responsibility of the estate. Although Siana Matheson was perfectly capable of running it, the mere fact that she was a woman meant she would be unable to enforce her authority if called upon to do so.

As for the doctor, he'd been brought up as gentry. Although Francis Matheson was a good, hard-working and well-meaning man, he'd never experienced poverty. The doctor had no idea of how the thought of the next meal kept a man working for a pittance, whilst he and his class lived off the profits.

To rise off the bottom level was hard, but once a toe-hold was made, a person with only half a brain would cling to it like ivy to a wall. As Siana had done – and himself come to that.

Now he was ready to advance further. If all went well and he'd read the signs correctly, come winter he'd have a wife and family to care for. He'd admired Elizabeth Skinner from afar and for a long time. Whilst Edward had still been alive Jed could not contemplate courting her, for his brother's prior claim on her was absolute. However, Edward's death had freed him from that obligation, and Jed now saw his way clear to offer for her.

Would Elizabeth have him, he wondered.

Elizabeth was gazing from an upstairs window when she saw the steward coming. He stopped behind a shrub, dismounted and removed his hat. She smiled when he shoved it inside his waistcoat and nervously smoothed his thatch of grey hair with his palms.

She'd known Jed Hawkins for a long time. A taciturn man, he'd always treated her with the utmost respect, despite her unconventional relationship over the years with Edward. She'd never understood his devotion to Edward until he'd explained it to her recently – in the longest speech she'd ever heard him make.

'When I was a youth, Edward came looking for me. He told me we shared the same father, and because of that he would offer me employment. Our kinship was never to be acknowledged, he said. It was not of his making, but by chance.'

'You must have been very young, then,' she'd said.

He gave a small smile. 'Only in years. Edward craved adventure, so we served in the army together, he as an officer and myself as his servant. He was very dashing and brave, and he put himself in danger to save my life when we were part of Lord Cathcart's assault on Copenhagen. That was back in 1807. He told me he'd had no choice, for I was valuable to him, the only man he could trust completely. I was proud to fill that need in his life, and have been loyal to him ever since.'

Elizabeth had known at once that Edward had used

Jed in the same way he'd used herself and Siana, holding them all hostage and manipulating them to serve him. Now his death had set them free and they would learn to live life without the need to consult him.

Elizabeth noted Jed's best suit of clothes, and watched him stoop to pick a posy of flowers from the garden bed, inhaling their scent for a brief moment. He resembled Edward a good deal, she thought, except a life spent mostly in the outdoors had given him a weathered look.

Jed had been a regular visitor of late, using the house she rented from Siana as an excuse to fix a slate here or there, or loosen a sticking window or inspect the pump. At her invitation he'd taken tea with her, awkward in the drawing room, his large hands cradling a delicate cup and saucer. Big as he was, there was an innate gentleness about Jed Hawkins. It was displayed in the way he held Susannah on his knee, or cradled the purring cat against his chest as he unconsciously stroked a finger under its chin.

She suspected that Jed was about to propose marriage to her, offering her the respectability Edward had never considered due to her.

She watched him proceed up the drive on foot, his horse following after him like a dog with its master. It was Edward's big, black old horse, the one which had carried him home so he could die in Siana's arms. Jed had always lived in his brother's shadow.

Mind made up, she turned to check her appearance in the mirror. She was dressed in serviceable dark blue taffeta. Her hair was not elaborately dressed, but tied with a ribbon at the nape of her neck. She thought of pulling it up under a cap, then shrugged. Jed would not be shocked by seeing her with her hair down.

He wasn't, but he noticed it, for his glance lingered on it for a moment and he smiled. He handed her the posy of flowers, but refused her offer of refreshment. 'Will you take a turn around the garden, Mrs Skinner? There is something I wish to say to you.'

'I thought I asked you to call me Elizabeth.'

'Aye, you did.' He didn't offer her his arm. Hands behind his back he ambled after her, saying nothing until they reached the garden seat.

'Would you oblige me by seating yourself?'

When she'd settled her skirts to her satisfaction, she glanced up at him. 'What do you wish to say to me, Jed?'

He drew a sheaf of papers from his pocket and ran a finger under his stock. Perspiration pearled his brow. 'I was wondering, with you being a widow with a young un to raise, and all, whether you would honour me by becoming my wife.'

The dear man had ignored her past relationship with Edward, mentioning only her widowhood. 'Yes, I would be honoured to accept.'

He stared at her for a moment, a puzzled frown concentrating between his brows, as if unprepared for such a swift answer to his proposal. He dropped the sheaf of papers into her lap. 'Before you answer, this is the sum of my worth. Apart from that which was strictly necessary, I have not drawn on my salary over the years, so it's accumulated somewhat.'

She handed the papers back to him, unread, tears

pricking at her eyes. 'Jed, your worth as a man has always been apparent to me.'

His breath expelled in a swift sigh. 'Then you'll accept me?'

'Didn't I just say so?'

'I thought I'd heard you wrong. A man is prone to doing that when he's seriously courting, for he goes around with his mind all of a pucker.' He smiled then, bending at the knees to occupy the seat beside her. 'I've always admired you, Elizabeth. I promise I'll care for you and Susannah always. You'll want for nothing whilst I have a breath left in my body.'

'I know we won't. You may kiss me if you wish, Jed.'

He stared at her for a moment, then he planted a kiss on her cheek.

She slid him a challenging glance. 'If that's the best you can manage I'll be compelled to reconsider.'

He stared at her some more, then he grinned. His eyes crinkled at the corners and the grin became a chuckle. Taking her face in his work-roughened hands, he gazed into her eyes for a moment. Then he kissed her mouth. It was a seductive, lingering kiss that promised much.

The look she gave him afterwards was assessing. 'You're not as innocent with women as you would have me believe, Jed Hawkins.'

One eyebrow lifted, and he shrugged as he said gruffly, 'I've known one or two over the years, but I've never proposed marriage to a lady before, and I wasn't sure how to approach it. I'm not a fancy man, so thought I'd ask straight out rather than go down on one knee and make a damned fool of myself.'

'You managed perfectly.'

'I guess I did at that. You accepted me.'

They gazed at each other and laughed.

'Will you tell Siana, or shall I?' she said.

He chuckled, as if the thought amused him. 'You'll be at the harvest supper next month. We'll tell her together, then. It's likely the little lady will give my ear the pointed end of her tongue, though, for she considers my business to be her business, and has been as curious as a cat with all my comings and goings.'

'And you've closed up like a clam, no doubt.'

His eyes went to her hair and he grinned. 'Your hair's like a tail of a fox in the sun. Can't say I noticed what a pretty colour it was, before.'

'Don't you dare play games with me, Jed.' Grabbing his hat from its hiding place she triumphantly dangled it from the end of her finger. 'What's this misshapen object?'

He gazed at it, his face a study of seriousness. 'Can't rightly say. Could be my hat, I suppose. It certainly looks like one I used to wear – until today.'

'You're a deep one, Jed Hawkins.'

He took her hand in his and said simply. 'I love you, Elizabeth. I always have.'

'Despite Edward?'

'I loved him too.'

'I know.' Her fingers entwined with his and she gazed up at him, wondering at her own depth of emotion and the easiness she felt in his company. 'You've always been twice the man Edward was, Jed. I'll be a good wife to you, I promise.'

She'd been too long without a man, and it wouldn't take much for her to fall in love with Jed Hawkins, for she was halfway there already.

She laughed with the joy of knowing it, because for the first time in her life she felt she'd been given the freedom to love another.

5

Elizabeth couldn't increase her bid any further. Picking up her gloves, she gazed at the agent. 'I'm afraid I've reached my limit. I cannot afford the price being asked for the Bainbridge premises now. They need so much repair doing to them, they're not worth it.'

'The price being *offered*, Mrs Skinner.' The snap of his ledger as it closed had a final sound to it. 'I'd have liked to tell you your tender was successful, but my duty is to the vendor. The agreement is being signed on Monday, and unless you come up with a better offer the matter is closed.'

She sighed. 'Would you mind telling me who's moving into the premises?'

The smile he gave was one of commiseration. 'Mrs Isabelle Collins. As you may have heard, she inherited the Prosser shop and cloth import warehouse in Dorchester when her father died. She's able to draw on its resources.'

Alarmed now, Elizabeth stared at him. 'But Mrs Collins doesn't sell groceries, so why would she want the Bainbridge building?'

'I believe she intends to sell general haberdashery and the fripperies so beloved by women. She will also sell patterns, fabric for gowns, and offer a complete dress-making service. As well, on the second floor there will be a department for children's clothing, unmentionables, sleep wear and perfumery. Everything ladies require, and that can be fitted comfortably under the one roof. Her customers will be spared the inconvenience of going from shop to shop.'

'That's exactly what I intended. The Bainbridge premises are situated right next to my shop. She will drive me out of business.'

'I'm sorry, Mrs Skinner. Perhaps you should consider moving your business elsewhere.'

It wasn't the agent's fault, Elizabeth realized. Shakily, she rose from her chair and picked up her bag. 'I must think of a way to dissuade her from selling the same goods as myself. An appeal for fair trading practices to be observed, perhaps.'

He came round the desk to open the door for her, apologetic, but firm. 'I wish you luck, Mrs Skinner. Although I shouldn't say it, Mrs Collins seemed to be a very determined young woman and I believe an appeal would fall on deaf ears. Perhaps she'd con-sider buying you out, though. She told me she was staying overnight at the Harbour Views boarding establishment tonight, so I expect you can find her there.'

Elizabeth knew she wouldn't be able to compete against such a large establishment, unless she could persuade Isabelle Collins not to stock the same goods. If that failed, she'd offer her the first option to buy her business. Once she got her capital back, she could always open up elsewhere.

She didn't want to close up altogether. Her shop brought her in a good income, and she now employed two assistants besides Peggy Hastings. Her original employee, Peggy had been promoted to buyer and manageress. Elizabeth spent most of her time at home now, caring for Susannah.

She and Jed hadn't yet discussed where they'd live after their marriage. Jed had managed the Cheverton Estate for a long time now. Elizabeth doubted if he would want to leave the comfortable house his living provided him with.

The thought of living closer to Siana was pleasing. In the first place they'd been driven together by need. Although they could have been rivals for the love of Edward Forbes, they'd ended up as friends, despite their age difference.

The confident young woman Siana had become was a far cry from the orphaned peasant girl who, forced to draw on her resources, had assumed the responsibility of her siblings and had wed the most powerful man in the district. Siana had been wed, widowed, and had become a mother, all in the one year.

Now Siana was wed to her true love, Francis Matheson, the respected doctor and a member of an aristocratic family headed by the Earl of Kylchester. Elizabeth wished them both all happiness.

She turned her mind back to Isabelle Collins. She would go and see her now, before her courage deserted her. The Harbour Views boarding house, the agent had said.

Isabelle had taken a room in the boarding establishment overnight. Expecting a visit from Elizabeth, she needed independent witnesses to observe any exchange that took place between them – and if need be, an alibi for herself. Her children had been left safely at home with her aunt, and Ben was being entertained by the husband of a seamstress at Bridport, and would spend the night at the inn there.

Isabelle knew how to act the lady when she had to, but she kept Elizabeth waiting for fifteen minutes before leaving her comfortable room at the back of the house to go to the drawing room. She asked her guest to be seated, then sent for lemonade, for it was a hot day and, for reasons of her own, she didn't want to appear inhospitable.

Taking a seat on the red plush sofa, Isabelle spread her skirts and gazed at her rival, envy spurting hotly through her. The scandalous creature looked cool and exquisite in her gown of green watered taffeta. Her glowing hair was topped by a straw hat decorated with wide green ribbons and an ostrich plume.

Immediately, Isabelle felt large and awkward in her salmon satin. Perspiration seeped through the taut fabric under her arms, making her itch. 'To what do I owe the pleasure of your visit, Mrs Skinner?' *For a pleasure it would be to destroy everything the woman had worked for.*

Elizabeth got right to the point, for even the thought

of asking a favour of this woman was repugnant to her. 'I believe you've bought the Bainbridge premises, with the intention of selling haberdashery.'

'Amongst other goods.'

'It's next to my own business premises. I wondered if we could come to some arrangement, so we don't poach each other's customers.'

'Ah, I see.' Isabelle gazed directly at her. 'Why are you in business, Mrs Skinner?'

Her visitor looked taken aback for a moment. 'To support myself and my child, of course.'

'Which is exactly why I'm in business. To support my family. I have no intention of pandering to a rival, or competing for trade.'

The creature cocked her head to one side, her blue eyes all at once speculative. Elizabeth sighed. 'No, I hadn't imagined you'd have any thought for anyone but yourself. Perhaps you would consider buying me out.'

Isabelle considered it for all of two seconds. Her smile was calculating. 'I have no need to. Two months after I've opened, you'll be closing your doors through lack of customers.'

Elizabeth lowered her voice when the other guests wandered in, a florid gentleman in sober black, escorting a rather meek-looking wife, but one of fine figure and refined features. 'It will take more than two months for the repairs to be completed. That place is a fire trap.'

Isabelle set the pitch of her voice up a little. 'My dear Mrs Skinner, I'm well aware of the fire risk. I've already instructed a firm of builders to start work later this month. I'll be open in time for the Christmas trade, with the addition of spirit lamps hanging in specially insulated holders from the ceilings, which is a safer method of illumination than having them standing on counters where they can be tipped over, or so I'm reliably informed by the engineer who has provided me with a certificate of inspection for the property.'

Leaving the lemonade untouched, her business rival stood. Though she was hardly a rival, Isabelle thought scornfully. Elizabeth Skinner wouldn't be able to compete with her. The woman's anger was well-controlled, but Isabelle noticed the fine tremor in her hands.

'I sell a specialized range of goods you'll be unable to procure, for I'll speak to my suppliers.'

Isabelle smiled at that. 'As for that, Mrs Skinner, you're too late. My orders are already being filled and I can offer the same range cheaper to the public. As for the . . . more *exotic* garments, I would not lower myself to sell anything so shameful. Should you persist in trading, I'll set up such a fuss that you'll have no choice but to close down. So, why don't you cut your losses whilst you still have some capital left? I'm prepared to buy your remaining stock at wholesale price, and take over your lease.'

'Never. I've worked too hard to give it away to the likes of you,' Elizabeth hissed. 'Why are you doing this? Is it revenge because Edward Forbes cast you aside?'

'Edward Forbes?' Isabelle gave a scornful laugh and said too quickly, 'It was I who cancelled the arrangement with him. I decided not to wed a man as corrupt as the former squire. No, it was not I who was cast aside.

It was you, his mistress and the mother of his illegitimate son. Edward Forbes didn't give you another thought once he set eyes on the Lewis girl, did he? And I was not prepared to share a husband with two females of bad reputation, however many airs and graces they displayed.'

There was a gasp from the woman on the other side of the room. The man in the chair turned to stare at them. Isabelle smiled to herself when she noticed the dog collar he wore. 'My apologies,' she murmured to them.

Looking stricken, Elizabeth Skinner headed for the door. 'I'll find some way of stopping you, just you wait and see.' She pushed past the proprietor of the establishment and a couple of delivery men, who had come to linger in the corridor outside the door.

Knowing the encounter couldn't have gone better for her purposes, Isabelle planted a seed in the minds of the witnesses as Elizabeth left. 'If anything happens to my premises, then I'll know who to blame,' she said, just before the door closed.

Holding a handkerchief to her face, she poked a finger into her eyeballs to make them water, then sniffled, 'I'm sorry you were witness to such an unpleasant scene. I had no idea she was coming to confront me. So distressing.'

The man made unctuous noises, the woman bobbed her head vigorously up and down.

'I've heard things about that woman and her establishment,' the proprietor, a pious and God-fearing woman past the age of attraction, muttered darkly.

Conveniently forgetting Elizabeth was only a Skinner by marriage, she added prophetically, 'Those Skinners were a bad lot. Blood will out!'

Thinking of her beloved stepson George, who was directly descended from the Skinner family, Isabelle only just managed to stop herself from giving the woman a slap as she continued with her damaging gossip.

'I heard there be comin's and goin's up at that big house she rents from the doctor's wife. And her with a young un and all. It's a disgrace, I reckon.' She patted Isabelle on the shoulder when she managed to summon up a convincing sob. 'There, there, my dear, don't let her threats upset you. That there woman be no better than she ought to be. It's her shop that should be burnt down, and good riddance to bad rubbish, if you asks me. She'll come to no good, that one. You mark my words.'

Blowing her nose, Isabelle emerged from behind the handkerchief with a martyred smile. 'But we mustn't be unchristian towards those of lesser moral value than ourselves,' she cooed. 'Rather, we must lead by example.'

'Quite so,' said the dog collar, for the subject of the conversation had intrigued him. The Skinner woman had looked so dainty and demure. He promised himself to pay a visit to her establishment at the close of day. Fallen women had always interested him and he wanted to observe for himself the nature of her sin.

'I feel a bit faint, I think I'll go and lie down,' Isabelle said, fanning her heated face with her hand.

'You do that, my dear,' the proprietor said, too familiarly. 'I'll make sure nobody disturbs you and I'll call you for dinner.'

The sales assistants were handling a last-minute rush when the man entered the shop. He saw no sign of the Skinner woman.

The shop windows were draped in black silk, out of respect for the late King William, who'd been called before his Maker just a few weeks earlier. He found the filmy material slightly frivolous for mourning, and fervently hoped that the young Queen Victoria didn't turn out to be equally indecorous. After all, she was only eighteen, which was young to shoulder the responsibility for a country.

Sidling through an unlocked door, he found himself inside a second establishment. He stared around him in wonder, especially under the long glass counter where a range of ladies' undergarments were displayed. They were made of the flimsiest materials, satin and laces, silks and cambric.

He crossed to where a figure of a woman's torso, stuffed with horse hair and attached to a wooden pole, stood. It was the shape of an hourglass and was clad in a corset of black lace over a frothy white petticoat. Atop the corset was a ruche of satin frills, then a stump of a neck, with a velvet ribbon around it.

He began to quiver. The thing was an abomination; it incited lust. He could feel it inside him, making him lose control. Leaning forward, he carefully placed his hands against the bosom of the torso.

'Is there anything I can help you with, sir? We're about to close.'

Breathing heavily, he turned to find a handsome woman gazing at him from a staircase. She was tall, modestly dressed in a grey gown. Her glossy hair was neatly arranged under a frilly cap with pink ribbons.

Shame welled up in him as she moved behind the counter and repeated, 'Can I help you, sir?'

He'd been caught touching, a caneable offence when he'd been in the schoolroom. Such an exquisite pain. On occasion he used the cane on his wife, a legal and fitting punishment, if the implement was no thicker than a man's thumb. But was that a gleam of amusement in the saleswoman's eyes? Hastily, he snatched up a small bundle of black silk. 'I'll take this.'

'Certainly, sir. Would you like some perfume as well, perhaps? Our latest fragrances have arrived from the salon of our perfumier in Paris today.' The perfumier being Josh Skinner, who'd bought a fat-bellied cod from a fishing boat that very morning. 'They sell very quickly.'

Paris, the city of sin. The cleric began to perspire and, nodding his head, frantically scrabbled in his pocket for some money as the woman wrapped the garment in a fancy grey and pink bag. The cost was extortionate. Shoving the bag in his pocket he backed away and headed rapidly for the door.

The two assistants were walking off up the road, giggling and laughing like young girls do. Their morals were being corrupted working in such a place, he thought to himself.

He thought of the older assistant, her eyes bland as she'd parcelled his goods. But he'd seen the carefully hidden amusement. She'd watched him touch the model, he was sure. He took the parcel from his coat and opened it, slipping the perfume into his pocket.

Blood flooded his face. He'd bought a black silk mask, looped cords and a little silk whip. All tools of a prostitute's trade. Surely a wife wouldn't lower herself to such abasement from her husband? His own wife was so meek and modest. How would she react to such treatment? The times he had caned her . . . he closed his eyes and swallowed. She had been amazingly pliable and eager to please afterwards. About to cast the devil's devices into the gutter, he remembered their cost and shoved them back into his pocket.

His lusts had been roused by the thought of using them. The hussy! No wonder she'd been laughing at him. His face burnt. That assistant needed to learn some humility, and he was just the man to do it. Women were born with the sin of Eve in their souls. They needed punishment.

Walking around the block, the man entered a narrow lane at the back of the shop. The door was off the latch. Making sure he wasn't observed, he placed his palm against the door and exerted pressure. The door swung silently open, revealing a dark passage.

Peggy had just finished counting the daily takings. Her employer was unusually late in picking her up. On Friday evenings she dined at Elizabeth's house, and they discussed business.

She wondered if Elizabeth had managed to get the premises next door. Remembering she hadn't checked the door to the lane, she pushed the money bag out of sight under the counter and made her way to the back of the shop.

Elizabeth would let herself in the front door with her key.

The back door was swinging open. Frowning, and vowing to chastise the assistants the next day, Peggy pushed the door shut and locked it. The passage was plunged into gloom. To her left was a cupboard under the stairs where they kept brooms and mops, to her right, a small, windowless room which served as a place of privacy. It contained a commode kept hidden behind a curtain, the bowl of which was placed outside at night to be emptied by a sanitary cart. On a table there was a ceramic bowl and a jug of water, the contents of which were drawn daily from the pump in the Bainbridge yard. Above it, a shelf held the bottles of spirits with which to fill the lamps, which were lined up next to the bowl.

As she moved back towards the shop Peggy heard a scuffling sound.

'Elizabeth, I'm coming,' she called out, hurrying forward. As she moved from the passage into the shop she had a quick glimpse of a shadowy figure. Something hit her from behind and she buckled at the knees.

'Peggy must have had late customers,' Elizabeth muttered to herself as she guided the horse down the High Street towards the shop, for she'd seen a man's figure slip from the shop and scuttle furtively off down the street.

The door was still ajar. Letting herself in, she closed it behind her. 'Peggy?' she called out.

A groan came from a small, pink velvet sofa, on which Peggy was lying. Her manageress rose groggily to her feet.

Elizabeth rushed to her side, her eyes wide with alarm. 'What happened?'

'Someone came through the back door and thumped me on the head, I think.'

'Are you badly injured?' Her fingers investigated Peggy's scalp and she grimaced. 'There's a lump on your head, but the skin's not broken.' She gazed nervously into the shadowy recesses of the shop. 'I saw a man leave as I came up the street. I'll have a quick look around, just in case.'

'Be careful,' Peggy warned unnecessarily. 'I'm all right now, I think. The back door is locked. I'll check whether he's stolen the takings. I hid them under the counter.'

As far as they could tell, nothing had been stolen.

'An opportunist,' Peggy said, ruefully fingering the lump. 'He must have panicked after he hit me, and ran away. How did your meeting with the agent go? Did we get the premises?'

'Unfortunately no, but I'll tell you about it over dinner. You can sleep at the house tonight so I can keep my eye on you.'

'I'm sure I'll be all right by myself,' Peggy protested. 'Whoever it was, they wouldn't dare to come back now.'

But Elizabeth wouldn't listen. 'I absolutely insist,' she said.

The two women left the shop together, making doubly sure the premises were securely locked behind them.

Minutes ticked by, then, inside the privacy room, a candle was lit. Isabelle lifted a bottle of spirits down from the shelf and, loosening the cork slightly, set it back up, but on its side.

Unlatching the back door, she stepped out into the lane. Soon, she was heading for the boarding house, slipping in the same way as she'd left, through a door in the wall of the shady back garden.

The proprietor nodded to her as she strolled inside the house. 'I hope you're feeling better, Mrs Collins.'

'Thank you, I am,' she said with a smile. 'A short sleep and a walk in the garden for some fresh air works wonders.'

Isabelle ate a hearty meal and, after a social game of cards with the other boarders, she went to her room and prepared for bed.

In the privacy room at Elizabeth's shop, the first drip of lamp spirit seeped through the loosened cork, providing a moist path along the lowest level for the rest to follow. It formed into a quivering globule and, growing too heavy to remain suspended, plopped to the table.

Another drop gradually grew in its place, then another. Soon there was a small pool of spirit on the table. Vapour rose from it. The candle flame flickered, an edge of blue grew to tease and flicker around it. Then suddenly the air around it whooshed into flame.

Just after midnight, an explosion was heard as the spirit bottles ignited. Roused from sleep by the noise, Isabelle smiled, then rose from her bed and went to the window.

The fire quickly turned into a conflagration which turned the sky red. People ran back and forth, a fire cart went by, pulled by a plodding black horse. No amount of pumping by the volunteers would extinguish that fire. It was a while before someone knocked at her door. It was the landlady. 'There's a constable waiting to see you, Mrs Collins.'

When he gave her the news she pressed a hand against her bosom and whispered faintly, 'She threatened to burn it down, but I didn't believe she would.'

'Who did, Mrs Collins?'

'Why, Elizabeth Skinner, of course.' Isabelle gazed around at her companion. 'Ask anyone here, they overheard everything.'

'Hellfire!' the cleric whispered, trying to hide his feverish excitement as he remembered his purchases. 'I must go up and comfort my wife, my statement can wait until the morning.'

Elizabeth and Peggy had been woken by the sound of the explosion, too. Trees hid the site of the fire from their view, but the red glow reflected over the water of the harbour.

'It's a big fire,' Peggy remarked.

'And seems to be in the centre of town.'

How big and how central, they were made aware of at dawn, when the constables came with their wagon and began to thump on Elizabeth's door.

Francis Matheson was about to depart his residence to visit his patients when Josh brought the cart up the carriageway at a fast pace. Susannah and her nursery maid were seated on the buckboard with him. A trunk was strapped to the back.

Throwing himself from the cart, Josh said frantically, 'Elizabeth's been arrested! She told me to bring Susannah to you.'

Siana gazed at him in horror. 'We must do something.'

'What's Elizabeth been charged with?' Francis asked him.

'Setting a fire. The shop burnt down last night. It took with it the old Bainbridge store next door, the one Isabelle Collins has bought. She and Elizabeth had put in competing bids for it.'

'But Elizabeth wouldn't have burnt her own shop down. What would be the point?'

'Isabelle intended to put her out of business. The constable told me that witnesses overheard her threatening to burn Mrs Collins's shop down.'

Siana poured scorn on the idea. 'It's ridiculous to imagine Elizabeth would do anything of a criminal nature. A mistake has been made.' Horror filled her eyes. 'What about Peggy Hastings? She sleeps over the shop.'

'There was a break-in earlier. Luckily for Peg, Elizabeth insisted she sleep at the house.' Josh helped the maid and Susannah down from the cart. Loosening the ropes, he heaved the trunk to the ground. 'Now I've got to find Jed and tell him. Any idea where he is?'

'*Jed?*' Siana said sharply. Her mouth pursed into a short-lived, but triumphant smile. Francis loved that smile, even mixed with the worry evident in her eyes. Usually, it meant she'd gleaned some interesting fact from a book. Francis could guess what she was smiling about this time, for his wife had been speculating on Jed's private life for several weeks now.

'Jed was in the stables a couple of minutes ago,' he said. 'If you're quick, you might catch him. He'll soon sort this nonsense out. It's a mistake. Elizabeth wouldn't do such a stupid act.'

Josh headed off at a run. Siana hugged Susannah before dispatching the nurse to the nursery with her, then she turned to him. 'Jed was courting Elizabeth? Why didn't it occur to me before?'

'Because sometimes you can't see past the end of your nose.' He ran a finger down its perfection, wishing he could nip the pert little end off and take it with him.

Her hand closed over his. 'Elizabeth might need expert legal help. Daniel's a lawyer, can you get in touch with him?'

Francis gazed reflectively at her for a moment. 'Josh is usually a step ahead of everyone. He's probably already done it.'

A fact which her brother confirmed a few minutes later. 'I've sent a message to Daniel, and I've hired

Oswald Slessor to advise her for the time being. He's much more experienced than Daniel.'

Seconds later, Jed emerged from the stables. Horse and rider came to where they stood. Jed's face was troubled as he gazed down at her. 'Elizabeth needs me. I must go.'

'Of course you must, Jed. I'm sure this mix-up will soon be sorted out.'

'I'll be at the infirmary later if you need me,' Francis told him. 'I'll drop in at the watch-house afterwards, see if I can do anything.'

Josh followed after Jed at a slower pace, relieved now the responsibility was handed to an older man. Despite the status that his rapidly expanding fortunes gave him, he was still in the process of emerging from adolescence.

'Give Elizabeth my love,' Siana shouted after them. 'Tell her not to worry.' But as soon as they'd gone from her sight, she burst into sobs. 'Poor Elizabeth.'

Francis slid his arms around her. 'I'm sure Jed will sort everything out. The notion of Elizabeth setting a fire is ridiculous.'

'Of course she wouldn't.' Siana gazed up at him, hope shining through the glistening tears in her eyes. Her bottom lip was trembling. 'Josh said there were witnesses.'

He pulled her close as she began to softly weep again. Francis wished he could stay with her for the rest of the day, but he couldn't. There were patients to see who needed him more. He consoled himself with the thought of the inner strength Siana possessed – a quality which had attracted him to her in the first place.

At the same time, he was thankful his workload had been lessened. Finding someone who was as qualified a physician as himself, as well as being a proficient surgeon, had been a stroke of luck. And Noah Baines had turned out to be a countryman by birth and nature, having been brought up in the neighbouring county of Somerset. Noah was five years younger than himself, a man with a propensity towards sea sickness, which had recently caused him to resign his commission from the Royal Navy.

'If I never set eyes on the sea again, it will please me mightily,' he'd said with a smile.

The appointment had lessened Francis's workload considerably, enabling him to spend time with his family.

Perhaps he could give Siana a small task to take her mind off Elizabeth's problems, at least for today. Opening his bag, he took out a bottle. 'Would you find time to visit Abbie Ponsonby at Croxley Farm today? Take her this blood tonic and make sure she's resting after her latest miscarriage. Impress on her the importance of avoiding pregnancy in the future.'

'I cannot go without Jed Hawkins in attendance,' she sniffed.

'Tell the groom to accompany you today. After the harvest supper we'll be able to relax a bit, for the itinerants will be gone from the district.'

Siana gave a small sigh as she turned her face up to be kissed. *At her own disappointment, perhaps?* Francis smiled to himself as he mounted his horse. Their inability to con- ceive a child wasn't a matter for concern so early in their marriage, and it was certainly not through lack of attention to the practice of it.

His mind turned to other things as he rode through an avenue of trees arching overhead. The leaves were just beginning to turn. In a month or so the tree limbs would be flaming with autumn colours.

Soon it would be winter, and his skills would be very much in demand. The onset of winter was always a busy time, but in the meantime he intended to enjoy the lingering remains of summer.

He hoped the weather remained fine for the harvest supper the following week. It would take place in the big barn, and besides the feast there would be a fiddler or two to dance to. Pansy and Maryse were looking forward to it with some excitement – and so was he.

Later that day Francis returned home to find a message from the Earl of Kylchester. Their brother, William, had fallen from his horse and broken his neck. William's affairs in Van Diemen's Land needed sorting out and since Will had left his entire estate to Francis, it was down to him.

I've secured you passage as ship's doctor on the Adriana, the earl wrote. *The ship sails from Southampton in ten days' time with a cargo of convicts. Its destination is Van Diemen's Land, an island situated south of the Australian continent.*

At least he would be here for the Cheverton Estate harvest supper, Francis thought. But he'd have to depart immediately afterwards.

*

They were readying themselves for bed when he told Siana of his almost imminent departure.

Her whole body assumed an aura of tragedy. 'But you'll be absent for months and months, Francis. How will I manage without you?'

He tried not to smile at her concern on that score. She was perfectly capable of managing without him for a while. 'In the same way that you managed before we were wed. I'll be back before you know it.'

'What will you do with William's estate? Can't you just put the sale in the hands of an agent?'

'William's debts have to be settled. As for selling the estate, I'll wait until I've seen it. My brother was very taken with the place. He describes the countryside in his letters as extremely beautiful, and very like England. Perhaps we could think about moving there.'

Astonished, Siana gazed at him. 'That's a silly suggestion. Why should we move halfway across the world to live in a strange place that resembles England, when we're already in England with our family and friends? Besides, who would look after Cheverton for Ashley if we left?'

'Jed Hawkins is perfectly capable of doing that.'

'Why can't you get someone to manage the estate in Van Diemen's Land, instead, for I do not want to uproot all the children. Prudence has promised Maryse and Pansy a season in London and they will be disappointed if it doesn't come about. Besides, I've heard there are naked savages there who throw spears.'

'We mustn't quarrel over this,' he said, trying not to grin when she stood on the tips of her toes to gently bite his ear, for what man could argue with such logic?

'There, I knew you'd see sense. Promise you'll be careful. I want you back in one piece, and I know I'll worry every minute you're away from me.' Loosening her hair from its pins she shook it free, then slid her robe from her shoulders. 'Tell me, Francis. Do you like me in this black satin corselette?'

So, it was to be one of those nights, was it? His mouth dried when she put two silk cords in his hands and purred. 'I have a fancy to be a slave to your passion, but only if that's your desire, too.'

His desire had no will of its own, for his imagination was suddenly running rampant and his urges following suit.

'Perhaps I'll be with child when you arrive home again.'

'And how will you manage that?'

Her chemise slowly slid from one shoulder as she partially turned her back to him. She gazed provocatively through the curtain of her hair and moistened her lips with her tongue. 'Tonight, I will make you my stallion. You have the reins in your hands.'

To which end, she succeeded. But the outcome of the passion he expended that night, whether potent or not, would remain unknown to him until he returned.

After hearing the sea tales of Noah Baines, he just hoped that the ship was sound, the captain sober and the weather was kind to them.

6

On the evening of the harvest supper, Pansy and Maryse hurried down the wide, polished staircase, their puppies chasing after them.

From the upstairs window they'd seen from the glow that the lanterns had been lit, and knew a pretty scene awaited them.

They were looking forward to the harvest supper, for they'd never been to one before. Maryse had dressed carefully in her new, dusky pink gown tied with a wide satin sash. Pansy wore a green and white checked skirt and a bodice with puff sleeves. Rosie had dressed their hair in a grown-up style with a centre parting and side ringlets.

They had visited the barn earlier, carrying a tray of biscuits apiece on behalf of the cook, whose plump arms hugged a round yellow cheese to her equally plump bosom. She'd set it on a side table with a sigh of relief.

The tables were arranged in a U shape, with a space left clear in the middle for dancing. Straw was strewn over the floor. Set to one side was a table containing kegs of ale and lemonade. The cook had allowed them to sample a glass of home-brewed ginger beer.

The sounds of jollity had increased over the last hour. Now it was time to join the estate labourers in the celebration. Maryse grinned at Pansy when, below them in the hall, they paused to watch their father and Siana exchange a kiss. The pair sprang apart when they saw the girls. Siana blushed a little, causing their father to grin at her.

He stepped forward to inspect them, making them turn slowly around. 'What beautiful young ladies my daughters are becoming. I'm going to miss you whilst I'm away.'

They hugged the tall, familiar figure close. He would be gone before they awoke, taken aboard Josh Skinner's coach. Maryse and Pansy were looking forward to seeing Siana's brother. Josh was a young man they both liked enormously, even though he teased them a lot. It was exciting to hear the coach horn as he galloped past, for Sam Saynuthin, the mute Josh employed, always blasted a greeting to them.

Josh was dropping off his passengers in Wareham before coming back to the supper. In the morning, he would pick up passengers at the terminal in Poole and change his horses for the run to Southampton.

'Here come the children,' Siana whispered, her eyes glowing with the love she felt for them. Tripping daintily and wide-eyed with excitement at being allowed to stay up so late, down the stairs came Goldie and Daisy with their governess. They would stay at the harvest supper for only a little while, then be brought back to the house and tucked into bed. Susannah and Ashley, who were too young to attend, were already fast asleep.

Susannah had settled into nursery life well, according to the governess. She'd mentioned her mother on a few occasions, but as she was kept fully occupied she was not given the time to dwell on the absence of her mother in her life. Francis had visited Elizabeth the day before, bringing back a note for Siana, which she'd read out loud, begging them not to worry about her. She said she was being treated well and was looking forward to being reunited with her daughter soon.

What a pretty pair of angels the younger girls were, dressed in white smocks over pale blue dresses, Maryse thought. Their eyes were different shades of blue and their hair a contrast of golden and copper curls.

'We can't wait for Josh any longer. No doubt he'll find us when he arrives,' their father said to them all.

The Matheson family proceeded two by two, following a track of glowing lanterns through the copse. Beyond the fall of light, the trees were mysterious shapes. The puppies, Spot and Victoria, trailed after them, their noses twitching at the unaccustomed night scents and sounds.

'Be careful of the tree roots,' their father advised, advice he should have followed himself, for he nearly tripped up with the next step he took. Siana began to laugh, which set the rest of them giggling, especially when he tried to bestow a stern look over his shoulder and tripped again.

Near the barn a couple of fires burnt. Over them, the carcasses of a sheep and a large pig sizzled and crackled as they rotated on the spit. The handles were turned by two sweating scullery boys who were red-faced from the effort. Trays of scrubbed potatoes waited to be placed in the ashes to bake, and pots of vegetables stood in a line.

Situated in the home meadow and hidden from the house by a wooded copse, the barn was decorated with cleverly woven sheaves of wheat and corn dollies, which had been fashioned by the village women and were designed to ward off evil spirits. Crusty loaves of bread, slabs of yellow butter, cheese and a pile of raw onion slices, steeped in a bowl of spiced vinegar, stood on a table to one side.

A cheer went up as the family entered the barn and took up the place of honour at the head of the table.

After they'd eaten, it was Francis's job to present the keg of scrumpy cider to the best itinerant team. Maryse watched with pride when her father made a small speech of congratulation to the winners. Her smiled faded when the keg was awarded to Henry Ruddle's team.

Henry Ruddle's eyes flickered towards her only once. He offered her a slight smile, one she ignored. Then he and his team went off, laughing triumphantly together, to consume their prize, no doubt. They stood in the doorway for a moment, heads together, five young men, two of whom she hoped never to see again. The laughter was drowned by the fiddlers as the dancing started. When she looked up again, Ruddle and his team were gone.

It soon became evident that this was nothing like the fine ball her aunt Prudence had described. Maryse enjoyed it nevertheless, enjoyed watching the weather-beaten estate workers grow more raucous and merrier as they swallowed tankards of ale and cups of meglathin, the local, spiced mead. Some quaffed cider from stone jars, smacking their lips in satisfaction.

The younger children were taken home to bed, pressing close to the nursery maid's legs and holding a corn dolly apiece in case Spring-Heeled Jack with his glowing red eyes and blue-flamed breath was abroad.

When enough alcohol had been consumed to relax the proceedings, the atmosphere became ripe in language and more abandoned in behaviour. Men pulled their women to the straw-covered space in the middle of the barn, skirts flared as heels were kicked up and the dancing began, if anyone could call the disorderly rumpus dancing.

When Francis pulled Siana to her feet she asked him, 'How was Elizabeth when you saw her?'

'In good spirits. I have written a letter of reference as to her character, and so has the Reverend White. They can't find any witnesses who saw her start the fire. And Peggy Hastings was with her when the explosion was heard.'

'Can I go and see her?'

'I'd prefer it if you didn't. I don't like the thought of you visiting the cells. Jed goes every day, so Elizabeth has a visitor to look forward to. He can deliver a letter from you. Now, stop worrying about her, for there's nothing more we can do.' He began to swing her around and soon they were laughing.

Jed Hawkins seemed to have temporarily put his worry about Elizabeth aside.

'Miss Matheson, would you care to dance with me?' the big man said, swinging Maryse off her feet as if she were a feather. Then it was a giggling Pansy's turn. Soon, the mismatched pair were lost in the jostling, stomping crush of dancers.

One of the fiddlers tripped over backwards. He lay with his feet kicking in the air, still playing the jig. Maryse laughed until her sides ached at the sight.

There was no sign of Josh yet. Maryse knew they'd shortly return to the house, for the company was getting too boisterous, and her father had to rise early to depart for Van Diemen's Land.

She looked around for Victoria and Spot. They were nowhere in sight. She wandered outside to look for the pups. The air had a balmy feel to it, the wind raising barely a sigh. Giving the occasional, excited yelp, the puppies were disappearing into the trees. They ignored her call.

There were many people about. Children romped on the grass and couples strolled arm in arm or talked together. She averted her eyes from a couple kissing in the shadows. To her relief, there was no sign of the youths as she set out to retrieve the dogs.

As soon as she entered the copse, the noise of the harvest supper was muffled. The silence was a little unnerving despite the comforting glow the lanterns cast, for beyond them was darkness, where a person could stand and observe those on the path without being seen.

Her skin prickled with uneasiness at the thought and she decided to turn back.

But then, over to her left, one of the puppies gave a prolonged squeal. She could see the faint glow of a lantern up ahead, and heard the sound of girls laughing.

'Victoria,' she yelled and, stepping off the path into the darkness, headed for the light coming from the lantern. After a few steps she caught her foot in a root. There was a sharp pain as her ankle twisted. She fell, giving a yelp of pain.

'Here, what be that?' a girl's voice said nervously. 'My pa will give me a walloping if he finds me here.'

'Last I see'd of your pa he were flat on his back, snoring like a pig in wallow.'

'I'm goin' anyway.'

Behind Maryse, came a snap of a twig in the bushes. Almost immediately, an arm came around her from behind, and she was dragged into a clearing lit by one solitary lantern. With a calloused hand tightly clamped over her mouth, Maryse was hauled upright and set on her feet. She groaned as her weight came down on her injured ankle, and slumped sideways against her captor. His arm tightened round her shoulder, held her fast.

'Who is it you've got there?' someone said.

'The girl from the field who thought herself too grand to pass the time of day with us. She tripped and fell right into my arms when I was havin' a piss. Look at her, she can't get enough of me.'

'What you goin' to do with her, then?'

'What do you bloody well think? She's beggin' fer it, ain't she, wandering about in the dark?'

The pups had set up a ruckus. Victoria ran off into the darkness squealing when somebody kicked her in the side. Spot stood his ground, giving puppy growls and snarls as he dodged and lunged at the feet. The feeble light revealed the shapes of five men.

'Let the girl go,' the one she recognized as Pethan said. 'She's no common maid and she's got trouble written all over her. Those country wenches will give us a jig or two for a coin.'

'You and every other cove with a coin to spend. This one's free of charge. She's clean, and as ripe a piece as I've ever set eyes on.'

Maryse tried to free her mouth to yell, but the youth tightened his hand and the noise became a frightened squeak. She struggled when his other hand cupped one of her breasts, which brought a rough squeeze for her trouble.

'I ain't goin' to be no part of this. Rape be a hanging offence and I like 'em to come willing,' one of the others muttered. He rose to his feet and began to walk away.

'She will be willing when I've liquored her up. What's the harm in having a bit of fun? 'Sides, she ain't going to tell anyone. They'd put her in a convent if she did, wouldn't they, my pretty one?'

'I'm going, too,' Pethan said. 'I reckon we can catch the girls up.'

'Take that dog with you, he might attract attention,' her captor grunted when another decided to follow suit. 'Strangle the noisy little sod, then meet us up at the road. I've got a lift arranged.'

Spot was picked up by the scruff of the neck and

tucked under an arm, still making threatening noises. 'He's a feisty little thing. I'm of a mind to keep him,' the other one said.

'Pass the keg, Silas,' the one holding her said. With a spurt of fear, Maryse recognized his voice. 'I'll give the girl a swig or two first. It'll loosen her up. Hold her nose while I get it down her neck.'

Heart pumping fit to break, Maryse nearly choked on the rough liquid as it was forced into her mouth. In the end she had no choice but to gulp it down, or drown in it.

When she was let go she scrambled to her feet and tried to run, but her ankle wouldn't support her weight. Her head beginning to swim, she fell to the ground with a screech of pain. The sound of Josh's coach horn faintly reached her ears as a rag was shoved into her mouth. Immediately, she began to gag on it.

'Blow the soddin' lantern out,' her assailant growled to his friend. 'I can find my thrasher in the dark, and we don't want to be seen.'

'Take the scarf out of her mouth first. If she vomits it might choke her.'

'Worse, it might choke me.' There was a moment of laughter, then the rag was removed. As she gulped in some air, her assailant's hands began to grope at her flesh. They were loathsome hands that pinched and squeezed and fondled her, before intruding into the secret places of her body. His breath whistled harshly through his mouth, his body became taut and a feral sharpness rose from him. Paralysed by fear, she could only whimper.

When she tried to cry out, a mouth covered hers and a tongue was thrust inside her throat. At the same time the weight of a body pinned hers down and her skirt was dragged up to her waist. The part of him that made him a man was swollen and rigid against her thigh.

Skin crawling, she found some strength to struggle, trying to claw at his face.

'Hold the wench down,' he growled to his companion and strong hands anchored her shoulders.

'Stop, please. You'll ruin me,' she pleaded.

'Don't take on so,' her assailant said, giving a chuckle when she moaned with fear. 'You've got to lose it sometime, and nobody will know it's missing 'cept us.' He clapped a hand across her mouth and she felt his muscles bunch.

Her scream was muffled by the hand as her thighs were shoved apart. He thrust roughly against her resistance and into her with a stabbing motion that ripped something inside her. She felt as though she was being impaled. At the same time, her body involuntarily arched upwards with the pain of it.

'That's more like it,' he said, his words slurring. 'I knew you'd like it.'

'Hurry up, Henry,' Silas urged. 'Someone'll be looking fer her before too long.'

Maryse began to struggle, but the man's weight, when combined with the brutal thrusting was relentless. Soon, her strength was exhausted and she could fight her assailant no more. His foul breath began to rush from his mouth in spurts, like a dog panting in the sun. Eventually, he gave a jubilant cry and a painful, sticky heat spread across her lower body. Then he went slack and the force of his breathing lessened.

'By Christ, that was tight and tasty,' he muttered, rolling off her.

Thank God it was over! But as Maryse tried to crawl away, she was dragged back down again. Whimpering with pain and shock, she lay on her back in the damp leaf mould as the second youth took his turn. Tears silently running down her cheeks, her body was unresisting now as the grunting and thrusting began all over again. Her only consolation was, this second time, it was over more quickly.

Afterwards, her chin was grasped between a thumb and forefinger and a voice said roughly against her ear, 'We haven't damaged you, so there won't be no bruising. It'll only be your word against ours, and we'll be long gone by morning.' A cold blade was laid flat against her throat. 'If you say anything about this to anyone, I'm goin' to do the same thing to your pretty little sister, only worse, 'cause I'll use this. Do you understand?'

When Maryse nodded, her chin was released. 'Make sure you do, then.'

'Where's the scrumpy?' the second one muttered. 'I've got a rare old thirst on me now.'

After a bit of fumbling there came the gurgle of liquid, and the sound of noisy gulping. Belching in a foul, self-satisfied way, her torturers stumbled off into the darkness, cursing as they tripped over roots.

Turning on her side, Maryse vomited, each violent spasm a reminder of what she'd been through. After a while there was nothing left to vomit. She crawled a short way, but found that she ached too much to carry on. She was shaking all over, her body reacting to the horror of the attack. She wanted to leave her body behind, to walk away from the dirty, soiled object it had become.

Her ankle had swollen, and her shoe had grown too tight for comfort. Curling into a ball, she nursed the hurt in the pit of her stomach, silently weeping. Then a wet nose nudged against her hand. Drawing the trembling Victoria against her, Maryse cuddled the dog close for the shred of comfort it offered her.

Presently, she heard someone whistling a tune. Still crying, and wondering if she'd ever stop, she called out, 'Josh!'

The whistling stopped.

'Josh,' she called out again, 'It's me, Maryse Matheson.'

'Miss Matheson?' and she could clearly hear the puzzlement in his voice. 'Where are you?'

'I'm over here.' She drew in a deep, steadying breath and tried to control the tremor in her voice. 'I've twisted my ankle and can't walk. Fetch a lantern and watch out for the tree roots.'

Soon, Josh appeared. He squatted on his haunches and gazed at her. His eyes glittered in the lantern light. 'Can you walk?'

'No. My ankle won't take my weight.'

'Then I'd better fetch help.'

She grabbed his jacket and said vehemently, *No!* Just help me back to the house, please.'

'I ain't sure it's proper for me to carry you, Miss Matheson.'

'*Please, Josh!*'

He didn't bother arguing with her a second time. 'Right, let's get you stood up first, then. Hold on to Queen Vic.' Hauled upright, she was swung into his arms. He strode back towards the manor, and when the house was in view, abruptly said, 'What happened to you?'

'I went into the copse after my dog and I fell.'

'No you didn't, luvvy. You smell of scrumpy and vomit and . . . and you're trembling fit to bust. Do you want to tell Josh about it?'

His tone invited confidence. Sorely tempted, Maryse thought of Pansy again, and shuddered. In desperation she almost shouted at him, 'I drank some cider at the supper and was sick. Then I tripped over a tree root whilst looking for my dog. That's the truth.'

'Don't take on so, Miss Matheson. There's no reason for me not to believe you, though I'll be surprised if your father does when he sets eyes on the state you be in.'

Thank God he didn't push the issue, but carried her into the house and up the stairs, saying to Rosie who appeared at his call, 'Fetch Miss Matheson some water so she can clean herself up. She's had an accident.'

Josh deposited her on a chair. 'I'll go and get your pa. Can you manage?'

She grabbed his sleeve. 'Yes. Tell him I've twisted my ankle, but it's not serious.'

Josh's silent contemplation of her brought panic

edging into her voice. 'Promise me you won't tell him anything else, Josh.'

Eyes calm against hers, Josh shrugged. 'What else is there to tell? I'll be about fifteen minutes.'

Longer than she needed to clean herself up, she thought gratefully, as Rosie came in with a kettle of hot water from the kitchen to add to the cold in the bowl on her washstand.

Sending Rosie off to fetch her some lemonade to remove the taste of her attackers from her mouth, Maryse hopped to the vanity, washed her face and hands, then sopped between her legs with a soap-filled sponge. She was sore and swollen, but nevertheless, she pushed the sponge up inside her as far as it would go, squeezing the water from it into herself, until the foulness of the men had been eradicated. Rinsing the sponge, she scrubbed savagely at herself, to make sure.

By the time Rosie returned, Maryse had removed her gown, pulled on her nightdress and returned to her chair. Bruised and throbbing, her ankle rested on a cushion.

Inspecting the grimy water, the maid's nose wrinkled. 'This sponge has blood in it.'

'A nose bleed,' Maryse lied, desperately attacking her knotted hair with a brush held in shaking hands. When leaves and dirt scattered on to her shoulders, to her consternation she burst into noisy tears, again.

'You're all of a tremble, my bonny,' Rosie said gently and, taking the brush from her hands, the maid applied it soothingly to her hair. 'You just relax and let Rosie fix things. There's some cool water left in the jug to bathe that sore ankle of your'n in. That was a right nasty fall you took by the looks of it.'

Within a few minutes Maryse's hair was brushed free of knots. The floor was cleared of debris, her soiled garments were bundled up and taken away to be washed. Rosie's mouth had pursed a little when she picked them up, but all she'd said was, 'I'll see to these myself.'

Maryse didn't care if they were burnt, for she knew she'd never wear the pink gown again. Seated in a chair in her robe, her swollen foot now soaking in a blessedly cool bowl of water, she slowly sipped at the lemonade Rosie had brought for her. But it seemed to have no taste, for the vileness of her attackers' breath still lingered inside her mouth.

Despite the warmth of the evening she was icy cold. Now and again tremors wracked her body. She didn't notice when Rosie tucked a soft shawl around her shoulders.

Out of her initial numbness had come the realization of the seriousness of her situation. The violation she'd suffered had rendered her unclean. Indeed, she felt so soiled and ashamed, she shuddered. She could scrub herself for a week and still the stench of the incident would remain with her. She'd also been cheated of becoming a wife or a mother, she realized. No man would want her now. Even if one did, the very thought of submitting to such attention again caused the nausea to rise in her.

She felt dirty, old and used – a far cry from the sprightly girl who'd stepped from the house earlier that evening. Would she ever laugh again? Her mouth might, but not her spirit. Would she learn not to cry? She took a deep breath to compose herself, knowing she'd have to. She would learn to keep the pain inside her, so nobody could suspect why she felt so sad.

So when her father, Siana and Pansy came hurrying into the room, their eyes full of concern for her, she saw clearly what else she'd lose if she confessed. Their respect, and the love she saw mirrored so clearly in their expressions, would be exchanged for pity – perhaps even disgust. Then there was the threat against her dearest sister, Pansy. How could she live, knowing she'd placed her in danger.

'Have you seen Spot anywhere?' Pansy wailed. 'He wandered off and I haven't seen him since.'

Maryse remembered one of the itinerant team saying he was going to keep him. Her bottom lip began to tremble, but she managed to get it under control. 'I expect he'll turn up in the morning. You can look after Victoria for me if you like. With my sore ankle, I won't be able to for a while.'

Pansy went off, happily cuddling Victoria against her chest. Siana turned to fuss with the bed, turning down the covers and plumping up the cushions.

'There are no bones broken, thank God,' her father muttered to himself, his fingers delicately probing the swollen flesh of her ankle. He looked up when she drew in a breath and winced. 'Does it hurt badly, my love?'

She nodded, tears coming into her eyes at his gentle tone.

'It's severely wrenched. Several weeks of resting it will

be needed to effect a cure. Siana, this ankle needs to be supported. Would you fetch some linen strips and bring my bag up? I'll measure out a weak dose of laudanum to ease the pain tonight, and I'll write a letter to Noah Baines and ask him to look in on her. One of the servants can drop it off in the morning.'

Maryse gazed down at her father's dark head when Siana had gone, then reached out to touch the streak of grey at his temple. 'I love you, Papa,' she choked out. 'Come back to us soon.'

He looked up then, uncertain, his grey eyes searching her face. 'Nothing will prevent me from coming back to you, my sweet and innocent Maryse. Your mother would have been so proud of the way her daughters are growing up.'

Would she, after what had happened? Alienated by the void she felt inside her, Maryse was no longer the child her papa knew and loved. Her innocence had been stolen from her. She was surprised he couldn't see the change in her written on her countenance.

It saddened her to deceive her father so, but she'd been given no choice.

'My dear Mrs Collins,' the agent, Simon Pullen, said. 'I thought the price for the property was agreed to. See, here is your signature on the offer. It's not the vendor's fault the premises burnt down.'

'Nor mine, Mr Pullen. My lawyer tells me that the original offer is not worth the ink it was written with now, for it hadn't been accepted by the vendor at the time of the fire. My amended offer is for the land only, which is worth only a fraction of what I was willing to pay before. Remember, I will have the added expense of clearing the site and erecting new premises. Besides, I have it on good authority that the place was insured.'

'But not against a deliberate act of arson.'

'Then your client should pursue Elizabeth Skinner. She has a large house she can sell overlooking the harbour. I might even make an offer for it myself.'

'The house is not hers. It belongs to Mrs Matheson. I believe it was a gift from her first husband, Sir Edward Forbes.'

Isabelle's eyes glittered at the mention of Edward's name. 'Then perhaps Elizabeth Skinner's son will make himself responsible for the debt. After all, he did marry an heiress of some considerable wealth.' Carefully, she laid some papers on the table. 'This will be the only offer I will make for the land.'

The agent's eyes narrowed when he saw the sum. 'It's beneath market value, Mrs Collins.'

'I've taken into account the loss of profit incurred whilst the rebuilding is taking place. I shall expect an answer by the end of the week, after which time I intend to purchase another property in a neighbouring town.'

'I will do my best, Mrs Collins.'

She stood, the black plume on her hat waving and bobbing as she shook the creases from her ruby skirts. 'If the purchase of the land proves to be successful I'll be looking to sell my property in Dorchester. I see no reason why you shouldn't handle both sales for me, Mr Pullen – if we can agree on a commission. Perhaps you could approach Mrs Matheson and see if she'd be willing to sell the property Mrs Skinner was living in.'

'Mrs Skinner hasn't been tried yet. She may need the house, afterwards.'

'I doubt it, Mr Pullen. The woman is clearly guilty, don't you agree?'

Summoning up a sickly smile, Pullen murmured a response commensurate with the situation, then preceded Isabelle to the door. Opening it, he bowed several times as she sailed through it. Back at his desk he gazed at the offer, shaking his head slightly. Isabelle Collins was an avaricious woman. If the evidence against Elizabeth Skinner hadn't been so convincing, he wouldn't have put it past his client to have started the Bainbridge fire herself.

Siana had no desire to allow Daniel free access to her home, but she couldn't prevent him from seeing his sister without good reason – though neither he nor his wife had shown any inclination towards relieving her of the responsibility of Susannah, which seemed slightly odd. Siana was glad of it, though, for Susannah was a perfect play companion for Ashley.

At least Daniel had brought his wife with him this time, but now Siana was obliged to entertain the woman, and just when she wanted to spend some time with Maryse, who'd become withdrawn since the harvest supper. Siana thought she must be missing Francis more than they'd anticipated.

Esmé had been silent when Daniel was present, but now he'd left the room she talked volubly about nothing of importance, which was slightly tedious. However, Siana leaned forward with interest when Esmé began to tell her what was going on.

'Daniel has given Peggy Hastings a week's notice to quit the house in Poole. Her employment no longer exists so she cannot expect to receive bed and board indefinitely. We intend to move into the house ourselves once Elizabeth has been sentenced.'

Startled, Siana gazed at her. 'You speak as though Elizabeth has been judged guilty already. Have you spoken of this with her?'

'My husband thought it better not to bother her with domestic matters. He persuaded her to give him power of attorney over her bank account this morning, and has transferred her funds into his own name. Daniel said there's no hope of release, for it is her word against several witnesses who heard her threaten Mrs Collins. Having control of Mrs Skinner's finances will prevent the insurance company from demanding reparation.'

'I see.' Siana's teeth worried at her bottom lip for a moment. 'Has he considered that Peggy Hastings might have nowhere else to go?'

Esmé's lips tightened. 'That is what workhouses are for. I'm quite sure the woman could find employment if she tries. Perhaps you could offer her a position as a maid.'

'I have no need for another maid, but perhaps I can recommend her to someone else,' Siana said thoughtfully, for Noah Baines had told her he was looking for someone to learn midwifery skills. He'd suggested it might be something Siana might like to consider herself, since she'd helped her mother through several births and had assisted the retiring midwife on occasion. Even Francis had approved of that suggestion.

Siana had considered it, but the local midwife was kept busy and she knew it would take up too much of her time – time she wanted to spend with the children. So she said to Esmé, 'Tell Peggy to come on Thursday. I can accommodate her in the servants' quarters for the time being.'

'Now, there is the question of your brother, Josh, which I'd like to bring to your attention.'

'Josh?'

'As you're aware, he still lives over the stables. He keeps very odd hours. Not that I'm suggesting there is anything wrong with that, considering the nature of Mr Skinner's business. However, should my husband take over the lease of the house, he'd prefer it if alternative accommodation was found for Mr Skinner.'

'Would he, now?' Siana tried to keep the anger from her eyes as she smiled, for it was obvious that Daniel had put his wife up to this. Did he still think of her as a naïve peasant girl he could manipulate?

'There is no lease between Elizabeth and myself. That's because we are friends and we trust each other. If Elizabeth is no longer able to reside in the house, I intend to leave my brother in it as caretaker until such time as she can return.'

Looking askance at her, Esmé blurted out, 'But Daniel said—'

'What exactly did your husband say, Esmé?'

Glancing past her shoulder, Esmé bit down on her lip.

'Only that we were once affianced, and that would most likely result in preferential treatment with regards to rent.' Daniel's eyes gazed darkly into hers as he came into her vision, his voice was ragged. 'Everything you've gained would be mine if you hadn't wed my father. I still love you, Siana. But since I can't have you now, it's about time you gave something back to me.'

When Esmé gave a tiny gasp he turned cruel eyes her way. 'That's what you wanted to hear me say, isn't it, Esmé? That I still love Siana in a way I can never love you.'

Siana shot to her feet. 'That's enough, Daniel! This is no place to rake up the past. I was young and impressionable then. Now, you mean nothing to me. You are paying both your wife and myself a disservice by even hinting at a relationship between us. You know it was not the case.'

He ignored her words, speaking as if only the two of them were present. 'The funny thing is, the estate could have still been yours if you'd waited for me. That boy upstairs could have been my son instead of my brother. Now I shall never have a son.'

Esmé burst into noisy tears.

Shaken to the core, Siana put a comforting arm around her and flung at him, 'Be quiet, Daniel, your behaviour is totally reprehensible. Esmé doesn't deserve this.'

'What Esmé deserves or doesn't is for me to decide.' His laugh gathered to it an edge of hysteria. 'Who would have thought my father would have lowered himself to marry an ignorant peasant girl, or that you would have become an old man's plaything.'

'Leave my house,' she said quietly.

'Your house!' he shouted. 'It's a house you cheated me out of. If it wasn't for you, Cheverton Manor would be mine.'

Esmé scrambled in her pocket for a small vial and, holding it out to him, begged, 'Take your medicine, Daniel. It will calm you.'

Grabbing it from her hand he threw it violently at the wall, where it exploded into tiny shards. The contents trickled slowly down the panelling.

Shocked, Siana stared at the damage, then back at him.

His expression became almost stricken as he gazed at her. *'Oh God! What have I done?'* Turning on his heel, he strode from the room.

Siana gazed dumbly at Esmé for a few seconds, then choked out, 'I had no idea he felt so hard done by.'

Sadly, Esmé said, 'He has been melancholy over it since we were first wed.' Wearily, she gazed around the room. 'The idea of dispossession cannot be dislodged from his mind. He is obsessed by it. It has become worse since he returned here.'

Siana stared at her with some bewilderment. 'What's wrong with him, Esmé? What's causing such erratic behaviour in him?'

Esmé hesitated for just a moment, then she folded her hands in her lap and stared down at them, twisting her wedding ring around her finger. Dully, she said, 'He suffers from melancholy. He has another dose of medicine in his pocket. I must go after him and make sure he takes it.'

Siana placed a hand on her arm. 'I'm sorry. Is there anything I can do to help?'

Eyes flickered her way, seething with ill-concealed dislike. God knew, Esmé had just cause to dislike her, Siana thought, but it was not of her making.

'You could sell him Cheverton Estate. He'd forget you then, for that's what his heart really desires.'

Siana's arm fell to her side. 'It's not mine to sell. It belongs to my son, Ashley.'

Biting down on her bottom lip, Esmé stood and walked swiftly away, making it obvious that no further explanation for Daniel's strange behaviour was forthcoming.

7

It took Francis a couple of days to adjust his balance to the ever-shifting liquid beneath the ship. The nausea Noah Baines had described eluded him, for his stomach gave him no trouble whatsoever.

That his eldest brother had signed him on as the ship's doctor gave him plenty to do. The sea air caused him to sleep deeply. He'd never been to sea before and the vast emptiness of the ocean and sky filled him with awe. Nothing remained still. The sea reared into hills that rapidly became chasms, sloped glassily sideways or erupted into slapping foam.

The skyscape changed. Clouds piled up on the horizon, or sometimes descended into thick mist to hover above the surface of the water. The ship sailed blindly in the clinging wetness. The rigging dripped and moisture streamed down the sails. Sometimes, the clouds were bruised, bleeding liquid gold as the sun went down.

The ship's owner and master, Captain McPhee, was a Scot. A man of grizzled and weather-beaten appearance, he'd been at sea since boyhood and stood on ceremony for no one.

The *Adriana* had once been a blackbirder, picking up slaves from the native traders of the fever coast and selling them on to the sugar plantation owners in the West Indies. McPhee, second mate on her at the time, had used a legacy to buy the ship from the previous owner. She'd served him well despite her age, and had rewarded his initial outlay with a profit.

Hard as he was, the slave trade had sickened him. Now the *Adriana* carried convicts, which wasn't much better except it was legitimate trade, so his conscience sat easier on his shoulders. He did his best to ensure that his prisoners arrived at their destination in as good a condition as he was able. The ship had made the journey to Van Diemen's Land several times before, usually with the lower deck packed tight and a complement of marines to take care of the cargo. McPhee never carried paying passengers.

'Och, I canna be bothered with all the bowing and scraping folks expect for their money,' he'd said to Francis when he'd gone on board. 'The convicts give me no trouble at all once they're made aware of certain facts.'

The contents of such facts were revealed to Francis the following day, when the sorry-looking prisoners were assembled on deck and given a taste of what was to come.

The weather was invigorating as the air, charged with the power of the wind, whipped foam from the crest of the waves to hurl it, hissing and stinging, at the bewildered scraps of humanity huddled together on deck. Above them, the sails bulged tautly and the rigging sang and snapped against spars and masts that creaked and strained.

'This is a tightly run ship,' McPhee bawled at them, his accent as thick as a lowland bog. 'It will remain that way. For your own good, you will be divided into groups, each of which will have a particular task. Rations will be issued each day and you will be expected to manage on what you are given. An overseer will be appointed for each group. He will communicate with the sergeant-at-arms on your behalf.'

He nodded at the sergeant, who took over the discourse. 'Your quarters must be kept clean at all times. Decks will be kept scrubbed. Males and females will not be allowed to fraternize.' A couple of the male prisoners groaned and the sergeant's eyes narrowed in on them. 'We have a physician on board. Disease or injury must be reported immediately. You will be allowed on deck in your groups to exercise, twice a day, for an hour each time.'

Captain McPhee made his authority known again. 'I'm a fair man, but let me warn you: if you cause me trouble you'll be either flogged, held in chains for the remainder of the journey or thrown overboard, depending on my mood at the time. Is that understood?' He smiled benevolently when a gasp went up. 'That's all for the present. Carry on, Sergeant.'

'Aye aye, Captain,' the sergeant said.

The captain's glance wandered to where Francis stood by the hatch, and he crooked his forefinger. 'Doctor, come with me. I wish to talk to you.'

Francis followed the captain down a ladder to his

cabin, stooping slightly between the decks, which were built to accommodate men shorter by a head than himself. He took the seat the man indicated, accepting the tot of thick and fiery rum offered to him. It had a kick like a mule. He grimaced as he added a fair amount of water, diluting it to his taste. The captain smiled at that, tossed his down neat, then poured himself another.

'Considering this is your first time at sea, you've found your sea legs fast, Dr Matheson.'

Francis nodded. 'I admit to being pleasantly surprised, though the ocean is more energetic than I'd imagined it would be.'

McPhee nodded. 'I wish to inform you of what to expect in the time we are at sea. It's necessary that I run a tight ship, and there are times when discipline has to be enforced. With you being a country gentleman and a member of the aristocracy, it occurred to me that accepting discipline might prove to be irksome to you.'

Despite the hostility he detected in the other man's voice, Francis offered a smile. 'I will try not to incur the need for you to enforce any.'

The captain made a humming noise in his throat. 'Have you ever witnessed a flogging?'

Frowning slightly now, Francis gazed at him. 'I've experienced most things, Captain. Which is not to say I approve of such punishments.'

'I'm not asking for your approval.' McPhee leaned forward, his eyes glinting. 'At sea, I'm the law aboard this ship. You are not above that law, Dr Matheson. Am I making myself understood?'

Did the man need to assert his authority in such a

way, Francis thought, the tips of his ears beginning to glow. His nod was cool. 'Perfectly. I won't interfere with your job, and will expect the same professional consideration.'

'Noo doubt,' McPhee purred. 'You should find your new appointment interesting and varied. You'll treat most common ailments. Broken bones, infectious diseases, dysentery, childbirth, even the clap.'

'I thought there was to be no fraternization on board.'

'Not between the prisoners, of course. But some of them are prostitutes, and no doubt will want to earn a favour or two from the crew. We are a long time at sea. It's customary for the officers to hire the women to look after them during the passage. Indeed, should you need a servant to keep your clothes and cabin in order, plus perform certain other duties when required, you're welcome to select a suitable female from amongst the prisoners. Looking after men comes natural to women, and keeps them occupied.'

'Do they have the right to refuse?'

'Noo, Dr Matheson. They're prisoners of the crown. I pride myself on being a good judge of character, sir. Am I right in thinking you're a fastidious man, a man who wouldn't break his marriage vows to consort with harlots under any circumstances?'

'You'd be right.'

'You'd also be a compassionate man, who'd put the comfort of other unfortunates before your own.'

'That's a correct assumption.'

'Then I have the very person in mind for you. She has worked as a maid. I'll tell the sergeant-at-arms to present her to you. You will have the right to refuse her, of course.'

Which, of course, he would. Francis bit down on his tongue as Elizabeth Skinner suddenly came into his mind. How would she weather such a journey if she was transported? But women were surprisingly strong when pushed to it. After all, she'd survived marriage to Tom Skinner and his horrendous beating of her.

'One other thing, Doctor. There are some professional dips amongst the prisoners. If anything is missed, report it to me, immediately.'

Francis nodded.

McPhee slid a key across the desk. 'The medicament chest contains the most popularly used physicks, purges, tonics and unguents, as you requested. If there's anything more you need, let me know and I will endeavour to obtain it on our first landfall. You may go now, Doctor. You know where the surgeon's dispensary is situated.'

Forewarned over what to expect if he transgressed and feeling decidedly uncomfortable about the lecture, Francis made his way to his compact, but surprisingly well-equipped domain. It would barely have served as a boot closet in Cheverton Manor. But it had been designed to make the most of the available space, with a surgical table that folded back against the wall, though he must endeavour to call it by its sea name – the bulkhead.

The family he'd left behind came into his mind. He didn't miss the manor. He wasn't entirely happy living in Edward Forbes's shadow, knowing the man had taken Siana's innocence for his own satisfaction. But that was Francis's own fault, for he'd failed to recognize his feelings towards Siana and had prevaricated for too long.

Already, he missed his family. The thought of them was a tightly held ache in his heart. He shrugged. And this, when his journey had hardly begun. His mind was assailed by a sharply pungent smell of warm, dark earth, of long shadows spilling across the Dorset hills in the hush of late afternoon. A vision of Maryse filled his mind, a girl standing on the very brink of womanhood. But his last memory of her had been of pain suffered, of her eyes brimming with tears.

His most recent memory of Siana followed. It was one of extreme loving. Her sighs had been ecstatic as her body had opened to him in the most giving and accepting of ways. Her hair had been tumbling to her waist in a riot of curls and her perfume . . . he closed his eyes for a moment, the subtle mixture of woods and wildflowers filling him with longing.

'I'll give you enough loving to last you until you return,' she'd said, the laughter in her eyes fading at the thought of their parting. But it hadn't been enough loving, for already his body was missing her touch and the ease she brought him. A smile touched his lips. Should an infant result from that last night together, he would be a very proud man. He adored his daughters, and wouldn't mind another, but he would like to have a son, as well.

There was a knock at the door. He turned to find a girl standing there. No older than Maryse, she had the same virginal innocence about her. Her frightened, heart-shaped face was smeared with dirt, through which paler tear tracks meandered.

The sergeant smartly saluted him. 'The captain sent the girl, Doctor.'

He stared at her for a few seconds, noting her youth and delicacy, the dark smudges under her eyes. She was under-nourished and poorly dressed. He drew the sergeant aside. 'What will become of her if I don't take her?'

'She's a sweet little piece. The first mate has already put in a bid for her.' The first mate was so gross in appearance and manner that Francis couldn't bear the thought of this vulnerable little creature being released to his care.

'She may stay.' He turned to the girl, smiling reassuringly. 'I'll expect you to clean my cabin, keep my clothes in order and help out in the dispensary. That's all.'

She stared at him, trembling and wide-eyed, whilst the sergeant departed, grinning to himself.

'You needn't worry,' he said. 'I have daughters your age. What's your name?'

'Fanny Perkins, sir,' she said, her voice low.

'And what was your crime, Fanny?' Francis couldn't believe a girl so young and delicate could have committed a transgression serious enough to warrant transportation.

'Murder, sir.'

'Murder! You killed somebody?'

'Yes, sir. My mistress's husband came to my room one

night and tried to force himself on me. I brained him with the wash jug.'

'Ah . . . I see . . .' Taken aback, Francis damned the captain's odd sense of humour.

Josh ran his hand over the flanks of one of the coach horses. 'What d'you reckon, Sam Saynuthin, should we give the nag a few days off?'

Sam grinned and vigorously nodded his head.

Josh didn't know how old Sam Saynuthin was. Younger than himself, perhaps, but his crooked spine and shuffling gait gave the impression of an old man. He could be fast when he wanted to be, but soon ran out of strength. Sam's face had a swarthy, gypsy look. His eyes were a muddy, greenish-brown with a perpetually defensive expression lurking in their depths. Dark hair sprang untidily from his head.

Although Sam had a tongue, Josh had only ever heard him grunt. The lad seemed to use his eyes as ears. His intense gaze never left a person's mouth when they spoke to him, and he always turned his head this way and that when they were in the street.

Sam had been close to starvation when Josh had found him. Someone had dumped him on the side of the road out of Wareham in the middle of winter and left him to die. His back had been covered with festering sores from the severe flogging he'd been subjected to.

Loading the misshapen lad on to his wagon, Josh had taken him home, to recover in the warmth of the loft over the stables of Elizabeth's house in Poole, where he resided. Josh had cared for him in the best way he knew how and Sam Saynuthin had recovered.

If the lad came with a name, Josh had never discovered it. One day he'd teasingly offered him one. Grinning with approval, Sam had copied it down on a piece of paper, at the same time making a sssss sound with his tongue. Since then Josh had attempted to teach him some letters, in the same way as Siana had taught him. How much he'd learned, Josh didn't know, but Sam often surprised him with his drawing ability and his knowledge.

Giles Dennings came out from the office he presided over, a ledger clutched in his hands. He looked entirely pleased with life.

Josh laughed. 'I know, we've made a profit again. But don't crow too soon, Giles. We'll need a couple of new horses in a month or two.'

'I've taken those into account.'

'I'll soon be able to buy a house to live in, will I, then?' Something which had always been his dream.

'You could afford to buy one now if you wanted.'

Josh nodded. 'But there wouldn't be enough left over to tide me over the lean times.'

'You wouldn't buy it with your own money. The bank would loan you the principal and you'd pay them some interest on the loan. Besides, you're not having any lean times. Money sticks to you like crap to the sole of a boot.'

Josh grinned. 'Getting mesself into debt is not for me, Giles. It's either cash, or nothing. There be security in knowing you don't owe folks.'

Giles Dennings sighed. 'How about you listen to me

for once, Josh. Your own money would still earn interest if left in the bank. There's a terrace of eight houses for sale in Smuggler's Lane. Two up and two down. They belong to old Bainbridge, and he's calling in his capital. I was thinking we could invest in those. Being centrally situated they bring in a good rent – more than enough to pay off any loan the bank held over them.'

'And what if people didn't pay their rent and we couldn't pay the loan payments – what then?'

'It won't happen, but it's simple. The property itself would be our collateral.'

'What does collateral mean?'

'It means we're offering something of equal value to cover the money lent. The bank will hold the deeds to the terraces until the loan is paid back in full, plus interest. If we default on the loan, the bank would sell the properties over our heads and take their money back from the sale.'

Giles Dennings was a canny fellow, who knew his way about finances. If he was willing to sink his money into such a scheme, so was Josh. 'So, it's like going to a pawn shop when you're hard up. If you can't scrape the money together to collect your goods, the pawn shop keeps 'em?'

Giles grinned to himself, knowing the bank wouldn't be at all impressed by the comparison. 'Exactly.'

'Sounds fair enough to me. When can we look at these properties?'

'This afternoon. I've arranged it with the agent, Simon Pullen. And we wouldn't have to chase up the rents, either. Pullen will do that for a small fee.'

Josh stared at him. 'I suppose you've arranged the loan as well?'

Giles's smug look told Josh it was in the bag. 'I've made enquiries in that direction.'

Josh grinned. 'I'll think on it after I've seen the properties. In the meantime, I'm off to see a man about a dog.' He shook his head, grinning to himself as he strode off. Smuggler's Lane, eh? He liked the sound of it.

Josh's business was conducted in a back room of the Hog's Head, where a fire roared up the chimney and the toddy was warmed with a red-hot poker drawn from the glowing coals.

The man he'd come to see was seated in the corner facing the door. They'd conducted business before, and the pair exchanged a smile. The conversation was brief.

'How many tubs?'

'A French score. Half-anker. Usual place?'

'There's been activity at Branksome. Make it the harbour.'

'Christ, you be takin' a risk, bringing it in under the noses of revenue men.'

Josh grinned. 'Not much of one. It's the dark side of the moon. I hear tell that most of the customs men will be goin' over Studland way tomorrow night, so it's a perfect time to be fishing on the mud flats.'

The man stood up to go. Money was exchanged in the process of shaking hands and the man left. His belly warmed by the rum, coat collar pulled up around his ears against the stiff wind coming off the harbour, Josh followed shortly afterwards, strolling leisurely back along the quay. The day was overcast and he could smell rain in the air. Perfect, he thought. There was nothing like a good downpour to keep people indoors.

About to pass the Customs House, he noticed two young boys larking about by the water's edge. The older of the pair shoved the younger one and he staggered backwards, his arms flailing at the air.

'Hey, be careful,' Josh yelled, but too late. The lad slipped on the cobbles and he tumbled backwards over the quay and into the water.

Shrugging out of his coat as he ran, Josh threw it towards the older lad, shouting, 'Fetch help,' as he leaped into the grey water. The cold robbed him of breath and he gazed frantically around him, just in time to see a head bob out of the waves. A mouth opened to scream, but it filled with water and the boy went under again. Josh dived after him. His fingers tangled in some hair and he hauled the lad to the surface.

'You're as lively as a bleddy eel. Keep still and stop yelling in my ear, will yah?' he said sharply as the kid began to thrash about and holler. When the boy quietened, Josh trod water for a few seconds. 'Good lad. What's your name?'

The boy's teeth had begun to chatter. 'J . . . Josh . . . ua.'

'Well, I'll be blowed. It's the same as mine. Here, put your arms around my neck and hold on tight whilst I get us to shore, young Joshua. And don't let go. Got it?'

When he reached the quayside, arms reached down

to pull the boy up. Josh was hauled up the same way. His eyes narrowed when he stood to find himself in the grasp of two uniformed men.

The lad was being tended by another man in uniform. His father, if the resemblance was anything to go by. The older boy had a scared look on his face – he was wondering if he was facing a strap across his arse, no doubt.

Josh gazed from one of his captors to the other, smiled and raised an eyebrow. 'Thank you for your assistance, gentlemen. You may unhand me now. How's the tyke?'

'My son is alive,' the third man said, hauling the shivering kid up into his arms and scowling ominously at his elder brother. 'How can I thank you?'

Josh shrugged, remembering his own savage floggings as a youth. He was too cold to hang around here exchanging niceties, especially with the revenue men. 'By going easy on the other lad, that's how. They were just two boys having a friendly tussle. It were an accident and the lad's had fright enough already, I reckon.'

He felt uncomfortable with three pairs of astute eyes fixed on him. Picking up his coat, he threw it around his shoulders. He had a set of visiting clothes back at the coach station, and a stove to cosy himself up to. 'You must excuse me now, gentlemen. I have a pressing need for dry clothes and a mug of something hot. Goodbye, young Josh. From now on, make sure you and your brother stay away from the water's edge.'

'I know your face, but what's your name?' the boy's father called out as Josh walked rapidly away.

He pretended not to hear him. He didn't see any sense in bringing his name to the attention of the authorities, however innocently – no sense, at all.

8

Four years transportation to New South Wales for a crime she hadn't committed!

Elizabeth gazed at the public gallery. Siana had a stricken look on her face. Next to her, Peggy Hastings was shocked and indignant. Jed had adopted his implacable look, through which nothing of his thoughts would filter to the outside.

Then there was Daniel, whose attempts on her behalf to secure a not-guilty verdict had been woefully inept. He seemed unprepared and had lapsed into a mumbling monologue of reference. Most of the words had fallen on deaf ears. He hadn't been able to meet Elizabeth's eyes as witness after witness was introduced and her background laid bare for inspection.

'Oh ar! I knows her, she was the mistress of the late Squire Forbes afore he wed that peasant girl,' a witness called Mrs Pawley said, her eyes avid with mischief. 'And her no better than she ought to be, if you asks me. But 'tis said there's no fool like an old fool, and there were some right goin's on up at that manor before Edward Forbes married, I can tell thee.'

'I object, your honour. This trial is not about the prisoner's morals, and the witness is slandering the memory of a man who used to employ her.'

'Objection upheld. Curb your tongue, woman,' the magistrate said hastily, for he'd been entertained royally at the manor himself on occasion, by Edward Forbes.

'If setting fire to a shop isn't bad morals, then what is?' Mrs Pawley had said, determined to earn the five shillings Isabelle Collins had paid her. 'And as the honourable defence is the old squire and the prisoner's by-blow, his own morals be suspect too. 'Tis bred into a bastard, see.'

'Shut up, you old hag.' Daniel had banged the heel of his hand against his forehead in a frustrated manner a couple of times before he'd seemed to gather himself together.

Elizabeth vaguely remembered the first witness as being the housekeeper at the manor. It was probable she'd be sentenced from the constant attacks on her character, not by any evidence presented of her maliciously setting a fire.

The reverend from the boarding house had come forward, his mouth crabbed into disapproval as he described his shock when he'd investigated the shop.

'You hypocrite. It didn't stop you buying some of the goods on sale, did it?' Peggy shouted from the public gallery, and was reprimanded by the magistrate for her outburst.

But not before the reverend turned the colour of beetroot. Had they but known it, he'd used the items he'd purchased on his wife to take note of the sinful excitations they produced. Both of them had been quite overcome by the moment, and the many other sinful moments thereafter.

Elizabeth's argument with Isabelle over the shop was brought up by the landlady of the boarding house, her words twisted out of recognition, so she was credited with an actual threat to burn down the shop.

'But did you actually hear the prisoner say those words?' Daniel asked her.

'I'm a God-fearing woman, young man. I have sworn an oath on the bible, so don't call me a liar.'

Taking out a handkerchief, Daniel mopped his brow and mumbled something.

'What did you say, sir?' the magistrate asked him.

'That I have a headache.'

The magistrate gave a sigh. 'You and me both. Do you have any more questions for the witness?'

'No, your honour.'

During her trial, Elizabeth had reached the conclusion that her son's character was not as steadfast as she'd once thought. Daniel was weak, when she'd always imagined him to be strong. She wished she hadn't given him power of attorney over her funds, and hoped he wouldn't demand the guardianship of Susannah.

This weakness was something his father had instinctively seen in Daniel – the reason Edward Forbes hadn't given him the responsibility of trustee for the young heir to Cheverton Estate. His illegitimacy seemed to weigh heavily on him now. Daniel bitterly resented being excluded, even though he'd been provided for.

She wondered how far he'd committed himself to her cause, for everything he'd said seemed to have hastened her towards the guilty verdict.

Isabelle Collins met her eye. Her stare was hard, her face gloating, for Elizabeth's shop was history and the new Collins Clothing Emporium was already under way.

Isabelle had set the fire, Elizabeth was sure of that now. It had been done out of revenge, but also for her own gain, and in a most cold and calculating way. But revenge for what? Because Edward Forbes had tossed her aside for someone he loved? Or was it because she was full of envy? She shivered. Isabelle Collins was an ugly woman, both inside and out. She never forgot a grudge. Elizabeth hoped Siana wasn't next on her list.

As she was led away from the dock, she turned her head to exchange a last, brief look with Jed. He smiled – a smile so reassuring she was able to manage one in return.

Elizabeth hadn't expected to see Jed again, but he was owed favours and was granted a few moments with her by one of the guards he'd helped in the past. As Jed approached, the guard discreetly turned his back and puffed contentedly on a pipe of contraband tobacco provided by Jed.

She was being held, along with some other female prisoners, in a sturdy stone building at Winterborne Farm. The windows were barred. It was a place lacking in comfort and full of draughts. From there they would be taken aboard ship on the morrow, and set sail that same day.

Glad to take a turn outside, even though the wind was bitter, Elizabeth keenly felt her lack of cleanliness when Jed drew her into his arms and held her close for a moment or two. She'd not bathed properly since her arrest and her hair was dishevelled and knotted.

He handed her a bundle from Siana, wrapped in a blanket. 'They wouldn't allow Mrs Matheson to come inside, but the guard said I could give you these.'

The blanket contained a drawstring bag. Inside, was a small sewing kit, some salve, a hairbrush, balls of soap and a leather-covered journal with a pencil. There was also a clean skirt of serviceable fabric, a bodice and a warm shawl. She wrapped the shawl around her shoulders immediately, for the day was cold. Best of all, there was a sketch of Susannah. Tears filled her eyes at the sight of it. Her daughter wouldn't know her when she returned.

'The mute, Sam Saynuthin, did it. That lad's right clever with the pen and ink.' Jed pressed some shilling pieces into her hands. 'You must sew these into the hem of your skirt, for they might come in handy as bribes for extra comforts.'

'Oh, Jed,' she whispered. 'What will become of me in that place, so far away from all those I love?'

'I won't be far away,' he said roughly. 'I'm planning to follow you to New South Wales as soon as I can book passage.'

'You'll leave your job at Cheverton Manor?'

'Mrs Matheson can manage the estate over winter.'

The smile he gave was slightly rueful as he said simply, 'If she was a man she could manage it permanently, for the earth is in her blood and she knows its ways and its wisdom. She feels change, that one, senses it, as if the wind is telling her something.'

A smile touched Elizabeth's lips at that. 'It's her Celtic blood.'

'The trouble is, the labourers wouldn't heed her, because she's a woman. Especially the itinerants. But I have someone in mind to run the place under her instruction. Until her husband comes home, at least.'

He had walked her around the trunk of a tree, which afford them a little privacy.

'Time's up,' the guard shouted out.

Jed's arms came round her. 'Keep yourself safe and strong during the journey, my love. Be assured, wherever you are, I shall find you.' With those words he slipped a band of braided gold on to her finger. 'This is my promise, Elizabeth. It's the best I can offer you under the present circumstances.'

'I'll treasure it until we meet again.' Tears sprang to her eyes as she caressed the love token. 'Give Susannah a kiss from me. Tell Siana to be careful of that Collins woman. She did this to me and can't be trusted.'

His glance touched against hers, the expression in his eyes enigmatic. 'Isabelle Collins won't have things all her own way. When seeds are scattered they have a way of taking root.

Now give Mrs Matheson a wave, she's waiting with the horses by the gate.' He caressed her cheek, then turned and swiftly walked away.

'Safe journey, my dearest friend,' Siana shouted out to her, tears tumbling down her cheeks. 'I'll look after Susannah as if she was my own, I promise.'

Elizabeth barely had time to blow her a kiss before she was prodded by the guard. She stumbled towards the building, her tears falling unheeded as the two people she loved rode away from her.

For several nights Siana had found sleeping difficult. Now, the sense of uneasiness in her was growing stronger, as if something momentous was about to happen.

This was not the momentary unsettling of rhythm associated with a change of season, but a sideways shift, which seemed out of sequence with the normal, forward momentum of her life. It had affected the people around her, people she loved. Elizabeth was on her way to a life of degradation on a scale she'd never experienced before. Her daughter, Susannah, left behind, was to be denied her mother's love.

For what purpose? A monument to the vanity of Isabelle Collins?

'There are rumours Isabelle Collins set the fire herself and blamed Elizabeth,' Josh told her the next time they met. 'The woman has asked me to supply her with French perfume. I've refused, of course. I couldn't trust her not to turn it back on me, so I'm not sticking my neck in a noose for the likes of her.'

'Be careful of her, Josh.'

'Isabelle Collins is nothin' to worry about.' He gave her face a thorough scrutiny. 'You look a bit pale to me, sis. How are you feelin'?'

'I haven't been sleeping well of late, that's all.'

'How's Maryse's ankle, now?'

'Her ankle has healed, but she's changed. She mopes around, hardly saying anything at all and bursting into tears at the least thing. She's lost her appetite, too. I was going to call Noah Baines in to see her, but she said she won't see him.'

'Perhaps she's missing her father.'

'No doubt she is. We're all missing Francis, but it won't be for ever, will it?'

'No, I suppose not.' Josh looked as though he was about to say something more. Then an uncertain look came into his eyes and he shrugged, obviously thinking better of it.

'The Countess of Kylchester is visiting at the weekend with one of her cousins. I expect that will cheer Maryse up.'

'Be careful she doesn't make things worse.'

'Why should she?'

'Because she's an interfering old magpie, that's why. The last time we met she kept sticking her beak into my business. Calls me Skinner, as if I was one of her bleddy servants instead of a businessman. "It be Mr Skinner," I says to her, and quick smart she boxes me round the ear, like I was some snotty-nosed brat. "Don't be impertinent, Skinner, else it'll be the worse for you," she says, all high-pitched and haughty.'

Siana began to laugh, for Josh had imitated Prudence perfectly. She had to admit, though, she wasn't looking forward to her overnight stay.

*

Prudence was slightly out of sorts, as usual, complaining about the weather, her servants, and the price of a hat she'd just bought, all in one breath and as soon as she marched through the door.

'The crown supports a peacock feather, a handful of ribbon and a silver crescent as decoration,' she said. 'It was poor value for the price demanded.'

'Did you purchase it?'

Prudence cast a puzzled glance at her. 'Of course. It's fashionable, and the colour of the ribbons and peacock feather suits my new gown perfectly.'

Pansy bounded down the stairs, her face wreathed in smiles. 'Hello, Aunt Prudence, how lovely to see you.' She aimed a wide smile at her cousin, exclaiming, 'Alder, you get taller every time I see you – and where did you get that growly voice from? I swear, you sound just like one of your father's hounds.'

Alder, pleasantly lugubrious in expression, wore a splendid moustache and side-whiskers, all of which lifted upwards with the smile he gave. 'Lordy, cousin, you grow more womanly every time I set eyes on you.'

'And I'd be obliged if you didn't mention the fact. Oh! Where did you get that awful set of whiskers from? It reminds me of hay on the end of a pitchfork.'

Alder wiggled his upper lip up and down. 'I cut them off a goat.'

Siana stifled a giggle when Prudence gave a snort, and said, 'Pansy, I do declare, you are as hoydenish as ever. Don't encourage the girl, Alder.' She stooped to offer Pansy her cheek to be kissed.

Pansy gave her a hug as well, to which Prudence

resigned herself with a martyred protest. 'Not so hard, my dear, you're crushing my gown.'

'Our little flower grows prettier every time I see her.' Alder, with a mischievous twinkle in his grey eyes, placed a kiss on her cheek. 'I think Pansy is such a jolly girl, mother.'

Pansy blushed pinkly and thumped him on the shoulder. 'Whatever you are learning at Cambridge, it seems to be having a bad influence on you. Stop teasing me, at once, Alder.'

He placed a hand over his heart. 'But I ain't teasin' you, Pansy, my dear. Every word I utter is sincere.'

'There you go again. I'll end up shaking you so hard that it will rattle your teeth from your head, if you don't behave yourself.'

'You most certainly will not, missy,' Prudence said. 'You can learn to accept a compliment from a young man with grace, and behave like a lady should.'

'Yes, Aunt Prudence.' Pansy made a face at Alder. 'Wait till I fetch my shawl, cousin, then you can come and tell me what you think of my horse, and practise your compliments on her. I swear she resembles Justina Parsons. Do you remember her following you around and making sheep's eyes at you last summer?'

Alder grinned. 'I can't say I do.'

Looking pleased with his answer, Pansy gave him a wide, untroubled smile. 'Did you know my puppy was stolen at the harvest supper?'

'Oh, bad luck,' Alder said, following her out.

'Maryse has given me Victoria to look after, instead. I hope she doesn't ask for her back . . .'

The countess looked after them, muttering almost to herself, 'I do think Alder is sweet on Pansy. Still, she could do worse. He will have a good living coming in when he's finished his education – and by that time he'll be ready to settle down.'

Siana gazed askance at her. 'Pansy is too young to know her own mind, let alone wed.'

Prudence gazed at her in a condescending manner. 'Your lack of breeding is not your fault, of course, but I do think the girl would benefit if I took her under my wing next year, for she needs to refine her social graces. Both of my nieces would benefit. I will discuss it with Francis when he returns.'

Siana tried not to feel slighted as she led the way into the drawing room. She might lack breeding, but that didn't mean she had no feelings. 'I'm aware my background isn't up to your high standards, but Francis might consider it rude of you to point it out.'

'My dear girl, why bring Francis into this when it's you who consider me to be rude . . . and I daresay I am.' Prudence sank onto the chair nearest the fire and sighed. 'There, I have unintentionally hurt your feelings and put you in a huff. For that I'm sorry, because I like you. The fact remains, Siana, Francis would want his girls to marry as advantageously as possible. Where is Maryse, by the way? Hasn't she been informed of my arrival?'

'She'll be down by and by. She wasn't feeling at all well this morning.'

'Missing her father, no doubt. Maryse always had a soft heart. She takes after Jane, her mother. No backbone, always moping about feeling sorry for herself. I don't know why Francis married a woman whose heart was less than robust.'

'Because he cared for her, I expect.'

There came a knock at the door and Maryse slid into the room. She dropped her aunt a curtsy, then seated herself on the sofa and stared into the flames of the fire. Her profile was so sad, Siana ached to comfort her.

Prudence gave her a puzzled glance. 'Have you nothing to say to your aunt, girl?'

Maryse looked up, her smile a vague shadow of its usual radiance. Her voice was lacklustre. 'I'm so pleased you've come to visit us, Aunt Prudence.'

'That's better. Now, I've some news for you. I've decided you're coming to us for a jolly Christmas with your cousins. And when your father returns, I'm going to suggest that you live at the hall with the earl and myself for a while. I'll have both you and Pansy measured up for a wardrobe for your season in London the year after. What do you say to that?'

The expression on Maryse's face became one of quiet desperation. Abruptly, she choked out. 'I can't . . . I mean . . . I don't want to, neither do I want a season, thank you.'

The few moments of silence were broken by an upward slide of the countess's crow-like squawk. Her eyes widened until they nearly bulged from their sockets. 'Don't want a season? What nonsense is this? You do want to make a good marriage, don't you?'

'I don't want to marry at all.'

'Goodness, you *are* a sad mope,' Prudence said, spots

of colour staining her cheeks in an effort to control her temper. 'Your cousins know all the eligible men and are planning to escort you to every event and ball.'

Maryse's voice rose to panicky proportions. 'I can't. I don't want to wed, not ever – and I don't want to go to London. I hate London.'

Instantly, Prudence became all prickling affront. 'Well, Miss Matheson, then I shall withdraw the invitation with regards to yourself. But you will not be allowed to ruin my plans with your sulks. I shall take Pansy by herself, and we shall have a merry time together. I shall not forget this insult, either. You will regret it when your sister makes a brilliant match and you are left to languish into the sorry state of spinsterhood.'

'I'm sorry, Aunt—'

'Precocious girl! Hold your tongue. You have said your piece. Your manners are too lacking to contemplate. You may leave the room, and I do not wish to see you for the rest of the time I'm here.'

Maryse began to weep. Siana crossed to where the girl sat and slid a comforting arm around her. 'It's all right, Maryse.'

'It's not all right. You're too soft on her, Siana. Francis would expect his elder daughter to seize this opportunity to marry advantageously.'

'Then she will wait until her father advises her of such on his return, for it's obvious she's not ready to wed.'

'Ready or not, she should snatch at an opportunity to marry whilst she is young, and before her looks fade. Especially so, since she has very little dowry.

Does she not want any children to comfort her in her old age?'

To which Maryse gave a large sob. Scrambling to her feet, she ran from the room. Her feet pattered up the stairs and a door thudded shut behind her.

Astonished, Prudence gazed at Siana. 'Good heavens! Whatever is the matter with that girl? I've never seen the like before. Is she sickening for some disease?'

Which was something Siana had no answer for, then.

Later that same afternoon, the Reverend Richard White called on Siana, his face grave. Luckily, the inquisitive Prudence was resting. Alder had ridden out with Pansy, and Maryse was sequestered in her room again.

When they had settled themselves, he fussed around with some papers in his hand, then told her, 'I'm the bearer of bad news, Siana. I have had a visit from a young friend of your father. I'm sorry to inform you that Gruffydd Evans has died.'

Siana folded her hands in her lap and thought for a moment of the tall, fiery old man with the white flowing hair who'd come into her life when she'd least expected it. She'd hoped to see him again, but had known in her heart that the meeting would never come about. Her father, a man she had known for only a short time, had been old and troubled. She hadn't known him well enough or long enough to grieve. Yet she'd learned to respect him despite his sin against her mother, for he'd been a true penitent who'd journeyed the length and breadth of the land to find her and seek forgiveness.

'So, his fire has finally gone out. I hope he's at peace now.'

'He seems to have found peace before he died,' Richard said with absolute conviction and allowed himself a small smile as he took a sheet of paper from his pocket. 'This is his last will and testament.

'I bequeath to you, my daughter, Siana Forbes (née Lewis), the earth and all its bounty to nourish your earthly body and the light and love of the heavens to replenish your spirit. I place within your keeping all my earthly possessions. I have listened to my voices, too, cariad. *I am with you always. May your pagan gods take my body into their embrace, and may Christ grant my restless spirit a true home.'*

Despite the moistness of her eyes, she couldn't stop the smile coming to her face, for her father had offered her a compromise at the end. 'He had so few possessions, and I already have his journey stick.' Her father's walking stick was carved with the name of every town he'd visited in his search to find herself, and her mother.

Richard pressed a small silver cross into her hand. 'You gave him this, I believe. It was something he treasured. His friend and fellow traveller, Marcus Ibsen, has come far to return it to you.'

'Thank him, from me.'

Richard fished in his pocket and came out with an elaborately wrought key. There was an address label attached. *Bryn Dwr.* 'This key opens the door to the house he owned in Wales. It has been empty for several years. He's provided a map of how it may be reached and on it has written, "Each heart needs to find a home, and yours might find one here."'

She suddenly wished she'd known her father better. 'One day, perhaps?'

Richard rose stiffly to his feet. 'Marcus will be my guest for a while if you wish to speak to him.'

'Yes, I would, if just to thank him. Perhaps he could call on me?'

'Of course. I didn't see Miss Matheson in church last Sunday.'

'Maryse was unwell.' Disguising the worry she felt over Maryse with a smile, she said, 'May I offer you some refreshment before you leave?'

'Much as I'd like to, it looks like rain, and my horse is as old and as stiff as myself. Besides, as I came in I saw Jed Hawkins. It appeared as though he wished to speak to you himself.'

Which turned out to be the truth, for the reverend had hardly departed when a knock came at the door. Jed was awkward and ill at ease when she bade him be seated, shuffling from one foot to the other.

'I'd rather stand, Mrs Matheson.'

'Stand then, Jed, and out with it. You look like a horse with the gripe. What's the problem?'

'I'll be leaving your service in a month.'

Her breath expelled with the inevitability of it. Everything was beginning to change around her as yet another thread began to unravel from her security. But it was one she'd prepared herself for. 'You're going to New South Wales to be near Elizabeth, then?'

He nodded.

'She needs to know someone's there for her. Whilst

this estate is in my hands, you will always have a job to come back to.'

'Lass, you will be unable to run it by yourself.'

'I know the land, Jed. I can handle this estate as well as any man.'

A smile touched his mouth at that. 'I'm aware of that, lass, but the labourers will take no notice of a woman, especially one who came up from their ranks. They'll resent you.'

'When Francis comes back, no doubt he will hire a steward on Ashley's behalf. Can you suggest someone competent enough to step into your shoes for the time being?'

Slowly, Jed shook his head. 'They wouldn't have your interests at heart. By spring you must have someone you can trust, long term, else the workers will rob you and your son blind. I have another suggestion – someone who might carry out orders on your behalf.'

'Who?'

'Daniel Ayres.'

'Daniel?' Shocked, she stared at him, slowly shaking her head from side to side. 'He's your nephew.'

''Tis a fact but I don't know if he's aware of it,' Jed said, in a manner that made her realize Jed had never given it much thought. 'Just hear me out. Daniel has the need to prove himself. He has friends amongst the landowners hereabouts and will be able to bargain for the best prices for the produce. To the peasantry, he represents his father in a way you never could.'

'You think he will take orders from me when he thinks I jilted him in favour of his father?'

Honey dark eyes contemplated her for a moment. 'You're strong enough to cope with that, and he has a wife now. Besides, your man won't be long away.'

'No, I don't suppose he will.'

'Daniel's legal training will easily secure him a position as a magistrate, which will ensure this estate retains some power in the district. This estate must remain a going concern until Edward's legitimate heir is of an age to take control. Lass, I wouldn't leave you if Elizabeth didn't need me more. Would you rather trust a complete stranger with the guardianship of Ashley's inheritance?'

Which was the most she'd heard Jed say at one time. It was obvious he'd thought this through very carefully, and had reached the best conclusion. She valued his advice because she knew he had Ashley's best interests at heart.

'Have you mentioned to Daniel that you're leaving the district?'

He raised an eyebrow. 'Apart from Elizabeth, you're the only person I've discussed this with.'

'I'll give it some thought.'

'But not for too long. Daniel will need to settle into the manor.'

She hadn't thought of moving out. 'But we can't all live here together.'

'You have other options. Your house at Poole is vacant.'

She hadn't given the Poole house much consideration, even though she'd recently been approached with regards to selling it. Not that she would sell it, and certainly not to Isabelle Collins, who she now despised. Head to one side, she gazed at Jed, this man whose depths she'd never been able to fathom.

'Elizabeth and I had some happy times together in that house – but it has unhappy memories too. My stepbrother died there.'

'Tom Skinner was scum. He's no loss, especially since he was there to kill Elizabeth. And even though Edward was critically wounded in her defence, his only thought was to return home to you.' He looked around him, his eyes sad. 'It was here he chose to die, in the place he called home and in the arms of the woman he loved.'

'I missed him for a long time.'

'I know,' he said gruffly. 'I realized then that you did love the man for himself, and not for what he could give you.'

'There was some of that too, Jed, for I had nowhere else to turn – he made sure of that.' She closed her eyes for a moment, recalling with sadness the untimely death of such a devious – and yet such a courageous – man. The house in Poole had been Edward's gift of love to her.

'I liked living in the Poole house,' she reflected. 'It's a comfortable size, and has plenty of room for the children, and their governess, too. Daisy and Goldie could go to the local school. So could Ashley and Susannah, later on – and it will still be there for Elizabeth to come back to.'

'If all goes well, Elizabeth will be making her home with me,' he said gruffly.

'Of course, Jed, and she's lucky to have you. I do wish

you'd call me Siana when we're alone.' She reached up to touch Jed's worn face, her heart lurching as she thought of Francis. 'I dare say Francis might prefer to live there too, for, although he has never said so, I know he dislikes living in this house, which has reminders of Edward in it wherever he turns.'

'As any man would.'

'I'm going to miss you, Jed. I will write a letter to inform Elizabeth of Susannah's progress and I'll pack a trunk for her that you can take with you, for her circumstances are bound to be poor. Do you have enough money?'

He shrugged. 'Edward paid me a generous salary, and I have savings. I thought to buy a small farm in New South Wales. I've heard you can get bonded servants from amongst the convicts and have made plans to have Elizabeth bonded to me as a landowner. That way, she'll be safe for the duration of her sentence.'

'I will ask the Earl of Kylchester to write a letter of character reference for you. It might prove to be useful to you. And I'm sure Richard White will furnish you with the same.'

'Thanks,' he growled, turning away.

'And before you go, Jed, if I do decide that an approach be made to Daniel, I will expect you to act on Ashley's behalf. He must understand that he's to consult with me on a regular basis, and any decision I make will be final, despite the trustees.'

'I will that.' He grinned. 'Just go easy on improving the labourers' lot, for the other landowners in the district won't thank you for it.'

She hesitated before saying delicately, 'Daniel has indicated that his feelings towards me have not yet been resolved. I'm uncomfortable with the thought of seeing him again.'

Jed's eyes darkened. 'All the more reason for you to move out of Cheverton Manor. You could employ an agent as a go-between if you feel uncomfortable.'

Her hands went to her hips. 'I cannot spend my life avoiding Daniel Ayres. He'll have to learn to live with it, and, if he doesn't, I'll ask Francis to deal with him when he returns.' Her eyes softened as she thought of her husband. 'Do you think he has reached Van Diemen's Land yet . . .?'

9

Preoccupied by the lack of a substantial reason for Maryse's melancholy, Siana had paid scant attention to her own body.

Vaguely aware she'd missed her regular cycle, because this had happened on other occasions, she paid it little mind. When the second cycle didn't appear she squashed the little niggle of hope she felt, for Ashley had made his presence known quite early in her first pregnancy, when she had suffered dizzy spells and faintness.

It had been then she'd realized she was in love with two men, her husband and Francis Matheson. She and Francis had kissed on the stairs and declared their love for each other whilst she'd still been married to Edward.

She'd decided she might wait for the third cycle to pass, so she wouldn't feel disappointed if her womb wasn't cradling a child for Francis. But this morning, as cold, pewter skies pressed against the window and a wild wind splattered rain against the glass – inside her, Siana could feel a glorious surge of awakening. This morning, she felt different.

Gazing at the blue canopy above her bed, she listened to Rosie bustling about, trying to discover why she felt different. A tiny smile tugged at her mouth. There was a slight queasiness in her stomach, that's why.

As her hands flattened against her stomach, the pulse under her skin throbbed strongly against her palms. Her little smile grew into a wide one and she pushed all doubts aside. *At long last!*

It was a disagreeable day, even for November, a day when the gods fought over territory. The air was as irascible as a colony of red ants after a child had stirred their nest with a stick. Thunder growled in the distance, a capricious wind puffed smoke down the chimney. There was danger in the air. Siana could sense it.

Upstairs, the attic door was rattling back and forth, something it hadn't done for a long time, for she'd had bolts fixed to the door to prevent movement. Someone must have been in there and forgotten to close them.

The queasy feeling in her strengthened into nausea. She began to perspire. Sitting up, she pushed back the bedcovers and swung her legs out of bed. Her head began to swim. Gulping, she staggered to the bowl on the dresser.

Rosie's arm came around her for support and comfort. 'Finally got yourself with cheil then, did you? I wondered when you missed your flux.'

Siana wondered at the lack of happiness Rosie displayed. 'It appears so.' But no amount of sickness in the mornings could spoil her own happiness, she thought. Nothing could.

She was proved wrong when Rosie handed her a

damp cloth to wash her face with. The maid drew in a deep breath. Words spilled out in a rush. 'I can hold my tongue no longer. Miss Matheson appears to be sufferin' from the same condition.'

Blood roared in Siana's ears and her eyes flew open in shock. Nausea forgotten, she gazed at Rosie and said stupidly, 'How can she be when she's unmarried?'

Rosie shrugged. 'I'm not saying she got that way willingly. Signs say different. She's been sick every morning for the last few weeks, the girl has. And weeping all the time. It could've happened the night of the harvest supper, when Josh carried her home. She reeked of cider. I thought someone might have got at her then. 'Twas her dress, see. Fair mucked up, it were, with blood on the skirt and muddied up along the back. The girl won't even look at it now, let alone wear it. She were shakin' like a leaf in the wind. Frightened witless if you asks me. The poor little moth. She's been off her food this last month, too. Eats hardly anything.'

This could account for Maryse's strange behaviour since the harvest supper. The thought of her being with child was too awful to contemplate – but contemplate it, Siana must.

'Dear God. Why didn't you tell me of your suspicions then?'

'I couldn't really, could I? Not with her father goin' away, and all. Her ankle was damaged, right enough, and I might have been wrong about the other – still might be come to that, 'cept I know fer a fact that things ain't right with her fluxes.'

'Have you told anyone else of your suspicions?'

Rosie shook her head. 'Demons with pitchforks wouldn't make me blacken that girl's good name. If she's been got at, she wouldn't have been willing, for she's not some forward wench who would smack and coddle with the village lads.'

Her own sickness forgotten, Siana's mind began to puzzle over it. Maryse had never shown friendliness towards any lad in particular, apart from her cousins, and—? Her stomach roiled and she gazed helplessly at Rosie. 'Not Josh, surely?'

Rosie, seemingly shocked by the thought, said in fierce defence, 'Josh Skinner thinks the world of young Maryse. Besides which, he wouldn't have had time. You should've seen his face when he brought her home – all of a thoughtful pucker, and angry at the same time, as if a haggling matter was goin' on in his head and he was decidin' whether to state his dark thoughts to someone, or not.'

'Thank goodness he didn't state them to Francis.'

'That lad ain't no fool when it comes to sensing the depths of folks and their doin's. He's like you in that regard.'

Rosie's remark about Josh made Siana think. She'd never considered Josh as anything more than her younger brother. But their mother's Welsh blood was part of him, too, so it was quite possible he'd inherited the same fey sense from their mutual ancestors. Not that he'd ever admit to it, for Josh considered himself very much in charge of his own destiny.

Josh was certainly capable. He hadn't leaned on her much since their mother had died and, accepting just a room over the stable at the house in Poole and food in his belly, he had managed to keep his independence. Although she knew little of his business affairs, she did know Josh was prospering.

She wavered between doubt and conviction. Of course Josh wouldn't hurt Maryse. She was ashamed of herself for even considering it. Indeed, she didn't even know if Rosie's suspicions were correct.

Yet, the more she thought about Maryse's current behaviour, the more likely the girl's condition became. Had it been a foolish act, brought about by ingestion of strong liquor? Worse – had she been raped? The latter seemed more likely.

Oh God! she thought, grappling with the enormity of this problem. Poor, sweet Maryse was trying to live with her hurt tightly coiled inside her. How frightened she must feel. Did the girl know what ailed her? It was more than probable, for although Maryse was young and unworldly, she was a country girl and the method nature used for procreation was both observed and absorbed from an early age.

She grabbed Rosie's arm. 'Promise me you won't tell anyone of your suspicions, Rosie. Maryse will become an outcast. Oh, God!' Her hand flew to her mouth. 'What will her father say when he finds out?'

Rosie muttered, 'Seein' as you've raised the question, some things are women's business and men are best off being kept in the dark about them.'

Astonished, Siana gazed at the maid, willing to grasp at any lifeline thrown to her. Practicalities took root in her mind. 'How can she carry an infant and give birth to it without somebody noticing?'

'It wouldn't be the first time such a thing happened. The doctor do be absent for several months. You take the girl away somewhere quiet and isolated, so she can birth the infant in secret. Course, you'd have to farm the cheil out when it be born. There'd be plenty of country folk willing to look after a bairn for the shillings it brings them, especially if it happens to be a lad who can earn his keep when his shoulders grow some strength. You and she be due at the same time, in June by my reckoning.'

Closing her eyes for a moment, Siana drew in a deep shuddering breath as she remembered having to farm out her brother and sister after their mother died, and the brutalization they were subject to as a result. She would find it hard to deceive the husband she loved over such a matter, too – but for the sake of Maryse, she would.

'I'll talk to Maryse after Pansy has left for her visit with her aunt and uncle. Her condition can be kept hidden until spring. If we let my happy event be known, it will draw attention from hers. By that time, we will have moved into the house at Poole. I know hardly anyone there, so if we go away for the birth, our absence will be less conspicuous – though I shall inform the countess of my trip and ask her to keep Pansy with her longer.'

They exchanged a conspiratorial glance, then Rosie grinned. 'Your eyes tell me you have somewhere in mind. Out with it, then.'

It would take some planning, but if Maryse was

indeed with child, at least she had somewhere to go where nobody knew them.

'Would Wales be far enough away, d'you think . . .?'

It was obvious to Francis right from the start that he and Captain McPhee would never get on. As a result, he avoided the captain's company as much as possible.

The weather had been tolerable during the voyage. Now, its many moods no longer held his interest to any great degree. He'd treated the unwilling passengers for the usual complaints. But despite the exercise and fresh air afforded to the convicts, he'd watched some of them suffer. The overcrowded conditions, poor nutrition and hygiene had worsened complaints that were usually mild by nature.

They had anchored in Sydney Cove for repairs, because the ship had been taking water for several days. With no time for a proper overhaul, and with the captain eager to discharge his human cargo, some caulking was hastily replaced and they were on their way again.

By this time, every one of the convicts was infested with body lice, and most of them with intestinal worms. Francis had treated festered wounds inflicted by the cato'-nine-tails, a barbaric weapon which flayed the skin from the backs of both recalcitrant convicts and crew alike.

He meticulously recorded each case, but avoided making adverse comments, for the log was inspected by McPhee on occasion, and Francis didn't want to inflame the man's uncertain temper.

As they grew closer to the journey's end, the food became rancid and the water fetid, so there had been several cases of dysentery.

Recently, they'd crossed an expanse of water named Bass Strait, a churning, unpredictable maelstrom, across which enormous walls of water moved without purpose, unless that purpose was to collide and create mayhem. Several of the convicts had sustained broken limbs, and were now kept below.

After a total journey of five months, plus six days out from Sydney Cove, Francis was heartened by the sight of an island. But it was not their destination. The next evening, the long dark mass of Van Diemen's Land was sighted on the horizon, and the sailors set up a cheer.

'We'll keep the land in sight on the starboard side and should round the peninsula and sail into harbour tomorrow evening,' the captain informed them at dinner the same night. 'But we're shipping water again and there are heavy seas under us, so keep vigilant, gentlemen.' He gazed at Francis with a grudging smile to match his praise. 'Not a soul lost during the passage, Doctor. Well done.'

But although none of them knew it at the time, those words proved to be too much of a challenge to fate.

Francis's downfall – and saviour, as it turned out, for if he hadn't been on deck at the time to raise the captain's ire he wouldn't have survived – came in the form of Fanny Perkins, the young girl he'd taken under his wing.

Discovering the loss of some scissors and a needle and

surgical thread for stitching wounds, he duly reported it to the captain. A subsequent search of the female quarters revealed the instruments hidden amongst Fanny's possessions. She'd been using them to patch a ragged skirt.

'Ten strokes of the birch,' Captain McPhee said, staring hard at the girl, who stood trembling between two marines.

'Fanny is only a child,' Francis protested. 'She intended to return the instruments before we anchored.'

The captain's eyes flicked up to his. 'Are you attempting to usurp my authority, Dr Matheson?'

'I'm asking for leniency in this case.'

'I am being lenient, Doctor. The punishment for this crime is usually fifty strokes. Back off, I have a ship to run and the weather is worsening. This is not some simple serving wench. The lassie murdered her master in his bed.'

'It was my bed, and he was forcing himself on me,' Fanny protested, then she began to sob. 'I'm afeared, Doctor.'

The captain nodded at the sergeant. 'Carry out my order.'

Francis placed a hand on his arm. 'Show her some mercy, Captain.'

For a moment, Francis thought he'd made an impression, for the man hesitated. Then he gazed down at his hand.

Francis removed it.

The eyes that came up to his were like angry wasps. 'Mercy, is it? Now there's a concept. Perhaps the proud

170

aristocrat would be willing to take the lassie's punishment upon his own shoulders.'

Francis looked at the weeping girl. She was too thin,
and the cane would lay her sparse covering of flesh open
to the bone. This could be one of his own daughters, and
he couldn't allow her to undergo such punishment. He
inclined his head in agreement. 'Aye, I'll be willing to do
that.'

'Twenty strokes, then, Sergeant. It might teach the
good doctor to be more vigilant in his duties, as well
some humility.'

Ten minutes later Francis found himself tied to one of
the open hatch covers, his back bared. A couple of the
marines gave him a sympathetic glance, but most of the
crew were being kept busy in the rigging as the ship
battled her way through the capriciously rough seas.

The convicts were in their quarters, the solid hatches
had been battened down, to keep the seas from pouring
into the holds. Fanny had been sent below with them.

The ignominious birching was carried out in front of
the officers, without ceremony, and efficiently fast by the
sergeant himself, who nearly lost his footing when the
ship crabbed sideways on a couple of occasions.

'Put some effort into those strokes, Sergeant,' the
captain bawled.

'A pox on the Scottish bastard,' the sergeant cursed
under his breath.

The fact that Francis stopped himself from crying
out with each stroke was sheer bloody-mindedness.
He hadn't been caned since childhood, and couldn't
decide which was worse, the embarrassment of it, or

the pain. He decided it was pride as his fury rose with each stroke.

The thin cane brought fire to the surface of his skin, which eventually became one big area of raw pain. He grunted as the next stroke brought blood welling. Sweat beaded his brow despite the cold wind. Mercifully, the beating stopped on the count of twelve, when the deck was swamped by a wave and the ship nearly keeled over. There was a loud crack when she sluggishly righted herself.

'Cut him loose,' the captain shouted. 'About your duties, men, the ship isn't responding to the wheel. Lower the mainsail, she's taking too much strain.'

Taking advantage of the confusion, Francis pulled on his shirt and jacket, but was knocked off his feet by a roll of water over the deck. Below him, he could hear a babble of screams and cries coming from the convicts.

The ship spun broadside to the waves. A second wave surged over them, plucked him from the deck and carried him high on its crest. It dumped him just as easily. Tossed and turned in foaming turbulence, Francis surfaced several hundred yards away from the ship. Fighting to haul some air into his lungs on the next crest, he discovered the *Adriana* was floating keel up. She appeared to have broken her back, and was in the process of being splintered and crushed by the roll of the breakers. In contrast to the air, the water was powerfully cold.

Cresting a wave and about to slide down a truly terrifying slope of water into an abyss, he saw the ship's boat coming up to meet him. The breath left his body as they collided. He managed to clutch the side and haul himself painfully into the bottom of the little craft.

Flimsy though it was, when compared to the awesome might of the ocean, Francis was thankful for the solid wood beneath him. When he found the strength to look again, the *Adriana* had gone, leaving surprisingly little debris, in an empty sea, in a wide horizon.

He tried not to think of the drowned convicts and crew as he drifted at the mercy of the mountainous waves. He hoped Fanny hadn't suffered. And although his back throbbed from the whipping he'd taken, the pain served to remind him that he'd survived. The salt water, no matter how badly it stung him, could only be beneficial, for it would prevent infection settling into his open wounds and help them to heal.

Presently, night fell. The wind keened like a banshee over the dark, shifting water. The night was black, the moon a thin scimitar slicing through the clouds. His body bitterly cold, Francis had never felt quite so alone.

He'd seen people die from the cold, falling asleep and slipping peacefully away. He struggled to stay awake, trying to conserve as much warmth as he could by exercising his arms and legs. Finally, he fell into a fitful sleep.

When he opened his eyes it was to see a gull perched on the side of the boat. Its head was cocked to one side as it observed him through bright eyes. It squawked in alarm when he sat up, flying into the sky to glide gracefully amongst the air currents.

He looked around him, flicking his dry tongue over even drier lips. There was a large island to his left, and he was between that and the shore. Although his navigational knowledge was almost nil, from the remarks he'd overheard on board he realized that if he didn't make landfall he could easily sail on past Van Diemen's Land.

During the day he sighted two ships under sail, but they were too far away for him to attract their attention. That night he drifted a long way and when he woke the shore was closer. It was too far to attempt to swim to it, but in any case the shoreline was formidable in places, and he wasn't foolhardy enough to even try. He was aware that the current was edging the boat nearer to the coast, and tried to keep his optimism high.

The next day, the weather and seas calmed. He spent the hours knowing what hunger, cold and thirst felt like, despite the heartening warmth from the sun. The third night seemed to be endless. He saw a tiny flicker of light on shore, a small comforting beacon. It meant another human being was near. But the light was suddenly extinguished. The whisper of hope it had afforded him changed to despair.

'No!' he shouted out and, giving in to his fears, he laid himself down in the black womb of the night and curled in on himself.

Waves breaking on the shore and the raucous sound of gulls, jerked him awake. Bright sunlight squeezed his eyelids into a painful squint. Through the squint he observed a balm of green vegetation, which stretched into a halo of misty light.

'Heaven,' he whispered, overjoyed to think there was such a place after a lifetime of doubting.

Then he was engulfed by the flurry of water and was hurtled towards the shore. Sand grated under the keel, the boat canted sideways and was broached by a wave. He floundered about in the shallows in panic before rediscovering the wit to lift his head from the water.

Crawling on to bleached, bone-white sand, he flopped face downwards, laughing and crying until his throat was too sore to continue. So much for his great discovery! Light-headed from lack of food, he rested for a while, his body absorbing the sun's warmth.

After a while he allowed himself to think. He needed food and water. Water was no problem. He could see a trickle of it dampening the face of a rock. The terrain looked rugged, but at least he had shoes on his feet, kept in place by the stirrups on his trouser bottoms. He marvelled that they'd stayed there throughout his ordeal.

Francis rose, staggering a little from his weakened state. Wandering to a rocky outcrop covered in oysters he smashed them open with a rock. He knelt and, inserting his tongue into the rough shells, sucked them dry. They slid, wondrously cool, down his throat.

Gulls flew threateningly around him as he headed inland, as well they might, for he was in a predatory mood and their nests were not well guarded. The eggs he found had an oily taste that made him gag. He swallowed them down with water, which trickled over rocks into a pool. It was the sweetest he'd ever tasted.

The deeper he got into the terrain the more dense the vegetation became. He stumbled across a place of great beauty, where water gushed down a mossy sheet of rock to pool in a natural basin set amongst ferns, before becoming a brook heading towards the sea. Trees stretched upwards, higher than he'd ever seen in his native land, as if competing for a place in the sun.

He took his fill of the cool, sweet water, lapping it up like a thirsty dog then, running a hand over his salt-encrusted whiskers, he began to laugh with the euphoria of just being alive. Washing the blood from his shirt, he hung it on a branch to dry and, after fashioning a bed out of the fallen leaves, he lay painfully on his side, covering his body with his coat for warmth, then fern fronds for protection against biting insects. Closing his eyes, he fell into a deep and untroubled sleep.

He dreamed of Siana, of her sweet face, of her smile. She was standing on the hill overlooking the sea, her father's carved walking stick clasped in her hand. How enticing she was. He moved closer to her, to discover she was crying. Suddenly, she raised the stick and poked it in his chest.

The pain of it made him gasp, and brought him awake to discover it was a rifle barrel positioned over his heart. A uniformed man stood over him.

'What is it?' he mumbled, his eyes widening as another man jerked him to his feet. Automatically, he struggled against the grip of his handler.

A rifle butt smashed against the side of his head.

When Francis next woke, his head was splitting, and he found his wrists had been manacled together.

'What the hell d'you think you're doing?' he shouted.

'A merry dance you've led us since you escaped, Philip Piper,' the soldier grunted. 'I shouldn't be surprised if you didn't get another flogging for your trouble.'

Francis offered him a hard stare. 'You're making a mistake. I'm Francis Matheson, youngest brother of the Earl of Kylchester, and I'm a doctor by profession.'

The two exchanged an unbelieving laugh. 'With stripes like that on your back, d'you think we was born yesterday? A doctor now, is it, and an aristocrat and all? Well, we all know what a con man you are, Piper, but this time you ain't tricking spinster ladies out of their savings with your silver tongue.'

'I suggest you check with the shipping agent. I was aboard the *Adriana*, which overturned in heavy seas, and sank.'

The second man pushed him forward. 'Your scheming won't work on us, so shut your bloody trap else we'll shut it permanently for you. It wouldn't take much for me to put a bullet in your gut and leave you to rot. It'll be Port Arthur for you, now, and glad to see the back of you.'

Francis decided it would be judicious to keep his explanations for their superior officer as they began to lead him away.

10

Maryse, still in her nightdress and bare feet, stared despairingly out of the window. She felt as if she'd been sculpted from stone, like the marble angel that kept watch over her mother's grave in the churchyard.

She hoped death would come to claim her, too. Soon, her condition would be discovered and she wouldn't be able to stand the shame. They would bury her next to her mother. Odd, since the woman was a stranger to her. Would they recognize each other in heaven, she wondered.

Maryse had stopped eating, hoping that the sickness would no longer plague her and the unwanted life growing inside her would die. She felt empty and light-headed from hunger, but far from being weak, she was attacked by sudden surges of restless energy.

Her glance went from the letter on the mantelpiece to the copse outside the window. She shuddered. There was a slight incline down to the edge of the copse – which at this time of year was a place of shifting shadows, gloomy with rain, bruised and wind-lashed foliage and long, grey, clutching branches.

Beyond the trees, a bank of cloud boiled purple and grey. Now and again, lightning shafted down. A handful of miles across the hills was the sea. The storm would have provided a turbulent surge of seaweedy waves to smash against the cliff face.

Soon, her misery would be over. She could sneak down the back stairs, which hardly anyone ever used. But then she would have to find the courage to pass the spot where she'd been attacked. She managed a faint smile and said aloud, 'It won't matter, for they're long gone. After they used and discarded me they left without a second glance and didn't give me another thought. Nothing can hurt me now, or ever will again.'

To Maryse's troubled mind, the solution she'd reached was completely rational, even heroic. Fetching a cloak from the cupboard she drew it around her shoulders and headed towards the door.

She encountered Pansy in the corridor – Pansy who was packing for her visit to Aunt Prudence. It was something Maryse must be excluded from. Victoria was at Pansy's side, for her dog had turned away from her now, preferring the livelier company of Pansy. Maryse squashed a flicker of remorse as she remembered the jolly times she and her sister had enjoyed at Kylchester House. But it was no good indulging in self-pity.

Pansy smiled tentatively at her. 'May I borrow that blue gown of yours to wear at Christmas, your second-best one?'

Engulfed by a sudden rush of love for her sister, Maryse stopped to give her a hug, and a smile so brilliant it made her cheeks ache. 'You can have anything of mine that you wish. Give aunt and uncle and the cousins my love, and beg Aunt Prudence not to think too harshly of me. I love you, Pansy.'

With that she was gone.

Puzzled, Pansy stared after her sister as she headed for the back stairs. Where on earth was she going at this time of morning? She thought about Maryse's odd behaviour as she entered her room. Her sister had suddenly become a stranger to her, and was definitely no fun to be with.

Pansy was looking forward to Christmas at Kylchester and was eager to see her cousins, especially Alder. But she wished the whole family had been invited. If their father hadn't been absent, they would have been. She didn't like Siana and the children to be excluded.

Throwing open her sister's closet door she pulled the blue dress from the rack, then noticed with bewilderment what lay behind it. Maryse's best gown, the new pink one that she'd worn to the harvest supper. Taking it down, she stared at it in horror, goosebumps racing up her arms. It had been slashed into ribbons with a sharp knife or a pair of scissors.

Crossing to the window she gazed across the grounds. Maryse was hurrying towards the copse, her nightgown billowing in the wind, her hair hanging loose and streaming out behind her. Discarded, her cloak was a dark huddled shape on the grass.

For a moment, Pansy was so taken aback that she couldn't quite believe what she was seeing. Without a cloak, her feet bare, there seemed to be a strength of purpose to Maryse's stride as she disappeared into the copse. What was her sister about?

Fear clutched at the furthermost reaches of Pansy's heart when she saw the letter addressed to their father on the mantelpiece. Holding the ruined garment against her, she snatched it up and began to run towards Siana's room.

'She wouldn't have had the time to come this far,' Rosie said, when they reached the top of the hill. Hand against her chest, the maid was panting with the effort of running.

The sky was dark and ominous, the air vibrating with tension. Lightning sheeted through it, licking the undersides of the clouds with flickering, incandescent tongues.

Siana took off her cloak and tied her skirts into a knot. 'If she went through the copse she's heading towards the cove. Go back to the house, Rosie. Fetch some warm boots and a dry cloak for Maryse, for she's wearing only her nightgown. Wait for us in the shelter of the copse, for I don't want anyone to see her in the state she must be in. I know these hills and can go faster without you.' She took off after the girl, running like a fox after a hare.

It had been a long time since she'd been up here, alone. The wild sky filled her eyes. Exhilaration tore through her as the tough coastal grasses bent beneath the hiss of wind to flay at her ankles. She chased through it at a comfortable lope, her breathing fast, but not unpleasantly so.

'Let Maryse suffer no harm,' she pleaded, to whoever

might be listening. 'She's the heart of my heart and has been punished enough.'

More than an hour slipped by before Siana saw the girl up ahead. She narrowed the gap between them. The cliff top sloped steeply towards a drop into the sea, as if a giant had thumbed the edge of a lump of bread dough.

Maryse's head was bent in despair as she battled against the wind's resistance. She was spent, staggering as she placed one foot in front of the other. But the sea was so close now, the drop over the cliff sudden. The smell of sea salt lured the girl on as it sharpened in Siana's nostrils.

All too clearly Siana heard the breakers pounding against the cliff face. Maryse thought she had nobody to turn to, and intended to end her life. Siana's heightened senses brought mental pictures of Maryse's body broken on the rocks, with too great a clarity for comfort.

'Maryse,' she called out, but her words were snatched up by the wind and thrown mockingly into her face.

Just then, lightning forked down from the sky to stab into the earth. There was a great booming noise. Small rocks were split asunder, the smell of sulphur filled the air and the earth hissed.

Thrown backwards by the blast, Siana's scalp prickled as she staggered to her feet again. She sucked in a mouthful of heated air and her heart began to pound. Ahead of her, the grasses were scorched and smoking. Her blood ran cold. It was if a barrier had been placed between herself and Maryse. On the other side, her quarry was a slight, curled-up shape huddled against the ground. Her hands pressed over her ears,

Maryse was screaming, her voice high-pitched with terror.

There came a pause, all fraught and stretched. Siana's ears vibrated with the warning of it. Her nerves were a discordant pluck inside her. She hesitated, knowing the danger of ignoring her intuition. She gazed at Maryse, so small, helpless and frightened, caught up in this primitive meeting of elements.

'You can't have her,' she yelled angrily, and stepped forward. The lightning had made a devil's brew of the earth itself. The heat from the cinders singed her ankles and the leather soles of her boots smouldered, bringing an acrid scent to her nostrils. The air crackled around her, sparking the hairs upright on her arms and neck.

The danger seemed to retreat before her determination. Suddenly she had an ally. The sky opened, sending rain sheeting down to extinguish the fiery coals. The ground hissed and steamed as she ran across it. The smell of soot and burning reminded her of another time, another fire, and of her dead mother. There were forces at work beyond her control, Siana could feel her mother's protective spirit surround her as she stooped to the troubled girl.

'Thank you,' she murmured to all the gods when she heard Maryse give a great, gulping sob. She gathered the trembling girl against her and rocked her gently back and forth. 'My darling girl, I think I know what ails you. Tell me about it so I can help you through your trouble.'

Maryse sobbed as if her heart was broken for a few

moments, then, miserably, she choked out. 'How can I even speak the words when I feel so soiled. I cannot even stand to look at myself in a mirror because my reflection condemns me.'

Siana brought Maryse's face round to hers. 'You can speak them to me. Then they will not hurt so much. And I'll look after you, Maryse.'

'Can you take the infant from my womb?' she cried out in anguish.

Siana shook her head. 'Would that I could, but such a path is fraught with danger, and your life is precious to those who love you.'

She brushed the wet strand of hair back from Maryse's face. 'Will you tell me who fathered the infant and how it came about?'

'Fathered it? If only I knew, for there were two of them.' Words of unimaginable horror began to tumble from her mouth as she told of her rape in the copse.

Siana hugged the girl tight as she emptied herself of the horror of it, whilst the rain pounded down to soak them both to the skin. 'It's all right, my dearest, you're not alone any more. We'll make our plans together. Nobody need know, for I'll take you away and will help you through this time. Your secret will never be known and the babe can be placed with a foster mother at birth.'

She tipped up the girl's face and gazed into her wounded eyes, knowing this was not the time to tell Maryse of her own good news. 'You do know you won't be able to keep this infant, don't you?'

Her Matheson eyes hardened and the girl gave a long,

drawn-out shudder. 'I don't want to even see it, let alone touch it.'

Maryse had been forced into womanhood the hard way, Siana thought, as she helped the girl to her feet. How much this experience would affect her was hard to tell. It might strengthen her, or do exactly the opposite. Only one thing was certain. When Francis returned, his elder daughter would no longer be the child he'd left behind him.

Removing her boots, she bade Maryse slide her feet into their warm depths. Her toes curled into the wet blades of grass. It had been a long time since she'd gone barefoot and, although it was cold, she enjoyed the feel of the earth under her feet.

She jumped when a cloak was dropped around Maryse's shoulders, intruding on their privacy. Siana pushed in front of her stepdaughter to offer protection as she turned.

The intruder stood before them now.

Of medium height and build, he was well-muscled. He wore a robe of coarse brown material of the type worn by men of holy brotherhood. An abundance of loosely curled dark hair fell to his shoulders. His fine-boned face was slightly gaunt, as if he'd known hunger. It would have been unremarkable had it not been for a pair of dark, enigmatic eyes that revealed the very essence of him to her.

Siana had neither seen nor heard him approach, and she wondered how much he'd overheard. He was not from these parts, yet, although they'd never met, she knew him. As the danger in her mind receded, she offered him a smile. 'You're Marcus Ibsen, are you not?'

'That's my name.'

'Thank you for bringing me news of my father.'

'I'm only sorry it had to be sad news, Lady Forbes.' Inclining his head to one side, he chuckled. 'Your father said I'd find you running like a hare with the wind. He was right.'

She smiled. 'It's Siana Matheson, now. I've been widowed and have married again.'

'Ah, a conundrum. I don't know whether to offer condolences, or congratulations.'

'We will take them as said.'

The rain eased to a drifting, fine drizzle as they gazed at each other in silent contemplation. Maryse came to her side and Siana slid a comforting arm around her when she plucked restlessly at her sleeve. She gave no explanation for her stepdaughter's odd attire.

'This is my stepdaughter, Maryse. I must get her back home. Will you come back and take refreshment with us, Marcus Ibsen?'

'I will, for I was on my way to visit you.' He offered Maryse his arm. 'You're too young to be tired of living, so I can only think you lost your way, for the sea makes a restless bed. Here, lean on me. When you tire I'll change into a donkey and carry you on my back.'

After a moment of hesitation, Maryse gave him a faint smile, and Siana was pleased that she sounded calmer now. 'Yes, I did lose my way, and I think you would make a nice donkey. Thank you, Mr Ibsen.'

As if it had been thwarted of its prey, the storm passed out to sea and rumbled away into the distance.

The three of them headed slowly back towards the copse, where Rosie waited for them.

By Christmas, Jed Hawkins had gone, leaving a big gap in Siana's life.

Peggy Hastings, secure in her new position as midwife in training, had been offered accommodation in Francis's former residence, by Dr Noah Baines. There, Peggy would be given the opportunity to learn the business of attending to wounds and dispensing medicines.

'Mrs Hastings will sleep in an attic bedroom and will share the housekeeper's sitting-room and chores when she's not kept busy assisting the midwife,' Noah Baines explained carefully. Siana thought the arrangement might develop into something more, for the pair had a way of looking at each other, as if each was taking the measure of the other – and it would certainly solve the problem of where Peggy would live when Daniel and Esmé moved into the manor.

Christmas was celebrated with a church service. The Reverend White delivered the same sermon he'd preached the previous two years. He looked flushed and tired. From habit, Siana seated herself in the Forbes pew. Daniel and Esmé sat beside her, suitably attired for their new role as master and mistress of the manor.

On the other side of her, the children were arranged, with Ashley and Susannah in the charge of their nurses. Maryse sat between Daisy and Goldie to stop them arguing with each other, as they were wont to do at the least provocation. The household staff took up the seats behind them.

Siana inspected Edward's memorial window. It was a splendid affair with Saint George, clad in his shining armour, lancing a fearsome dragon through the heart. A long, red flame curled from the dragon's mouth and stopped within an inch of a maiden's breast. Looking suitably virginal, the maiden's eyes turned upwards towards heaven. Idly, as the sermon droned on, Siana wondered how the dragon had managed to tie the knots in her bindings. Then she noticed Maryse was looking at it too, and her sad expression stated exactly what was going through her mind.

Although Marcus's presence wasn't obvious, Siana could sense him nearby. Her glance moved around the church, seeking him out. Her search stopped at a stone pillar supporting the roof. He was standing behind it, partially concealed. Their eyes met and she felt like laughing out loud when he winked at her.

Afterwards, she invited him back to the manor for the Christmas feast, for he was good company. He explained that Richard White was unwell, and needed him to stay a while longer. Indeed, it turned out that the reverend did, for he was taken ill with a fever and was confined to his bed that very same evening.

Siana vacated the manor a week later. Daniel and Esmé moved in as tenants on the same day.

Daniel was unable to hide his jubilation as he swaggered up the front steps.

Siana called the staff together to introduce them to their new master and mistress. Most of them, like Maisie Roberts, the head housekeeper, knew Daniel from the past.

Esmé, assuming a regal bearing, gazed critically over each member of staff and talked in a high-pitched, carping voice, about expecting service and cleanliness from them. Afterwards, she looked the place over, her mouth pursed and spidery as she made pointed comments about refurbishing it.

To Siana, handing Cheverton Manor over to another mistress – no matter that she didn't entirely like living in the place herself – rankled. She tried not to sound sharp when she said, 'The house is perfectly comfortable as it is, Esmé. Kindly remember that the estate belongs to my son. I will not permit you to change it in any way.'

Daniel smiled slightly as he engaged her glance, a suggestion of hauteur in his eyes. 'Cheverton Manor will not change. It will remain as I remember it from my childhood days.'

The altogether specious statement served to place Siana as an outsider. She gazed dispassionately at him. Daniel was beginning to run to fat in a way his father had never done.

The pair had not offered to care for his sister, and made no comment when Susannah came downstairs with her nurse. When Susannah smiled at the sight of him, he kissed the child's cheek in a perfunctory manner. 'I'll visit you and Ashley often,' he promised.

Not too often, Siana thought. Inclining her head, she said firmly, 'I'll be pleased to entertain you and your wife on occasion, Daniel. We must set a day in advance, so neither party will be inconvenienced.'

His forehead crinkled into a slight frown. 'We'll meet often over estate manners, will we not?'

'On recommendation, I've decided to engage an agent to convey my instructions to you until my husband returns. The agent will also bill you for expenses incurred on Susannah's behalf, such as wages for her nursery maid.'

'Susannah's expenses?'

'Why yes. You do have power of attorney over your mother's account, I believe. Elizabeth would not want her daughter to go without.'

His face mottled red as he mumbled, 'Of course, but the insurance company is pursuing me for damages incurred by my mother for setting the fire. You could always dismiss one of the nursery maids. I'm sure the other one could manage both children by herself.'

But Siana knew she'd need the nursery staff when she took Maryse to Wales, so she gently shook her head.

Esmé stepped forward and took Daniel's arm in hers. 'You mustn't worry about your mother's debt, Daniel. You're not liable.' Smiling falsely, Esmé turned towards Siana and said firmly, 'Mrs Skinner's assets were tied up in stock, which was burnt to ashes in the fire. There was very little in her bank account. One would have thought, when you agreed to foster Susannah, you would be taking the burden of her expenses on your own shoulders.'

So the woman was tight-fisted. Siana didn't insist, for she was well able to support Susannah. And she had enough on her mind, with Maryse, without absorbing any more of Elizabeth's problems. Gathering her flock of children together, she inclined her head and shepherded them out to where Josh waited with the coach.

With them came Rosie, the children's nurses and Miss Edgar, the governess. Their riding horses and baggage had been sent over earlier.

Siana didn't look back as they bowled down the drive. Perhaps, now, she wouldn't be reminded of Edward Forbes at every turn. But with the handsome little squire seated on her lap, she knew she could never forget his father. She smiled a little as she kissed the top of her son's head.

The interior of the coach smelled peculiar, a mixture of leather, polish and body odours. It wasn't as comfortable as the Cheverton carriage. When they reached the road, pitted as it was with potholes and slicked with mud from the recent rain, it dipped and swayed alarmingly, making the children shriek with laughter and cling to their nurses. They, in turn, gritted their teeth and clung to the straps.

The journey to Poole didn't take long. Although Daisy and Goldie had been there before, the sight of the harbour and ships still made their eyes widen. Ashley stared at the bustle through solemn eyes, absorbing the new sights and sounds, his thumb jammed firmly in his mouth. Susannah bounced up and down excitedly when she saw the house, as if she'd remembered it was her home, and she expected her mother to be there, waiting for her.

She was to be disappointed.

Still, the house was beautiful, set as it was halfway up the hill with a view over the backwaters of the harbour. Here, at Poole, Siana intended to turn this house into a comfortable and loving home for her husband to return to.

When Maryse slid her hand into hers, she turned to smile reassuringly at her. But first, she must help this beautiful stepdaughter of hers through the traumatic times ahead.

11

Ben Collins was on his way to Poole to bank the weekly shop takings when the thirst came upon him. Usually, Isabelle came with him. But today he was on his own, for his wife hadn't been feeling well and had called for the doctor to attend her.

When he walked into the inn and heard the patrons gossiping about her, colour rose swiftly to his face.

'I heard it said that Isabelle Collins set that shop fire herself, and blamed Elizabeth Skinner for it.'

Turning the speaker round, Ben thumped him soundly on the snout. The youth's nose collapsed with a satisfying crunch. Blood squirted. 'My wife didn't set no shop fire,' he roared. 'You say one more disrespectful word about her, and I'll be after thee with more than my bleddy fist.'

The other drinkers in the bar fell silent, for Ben was known to be a brawler when his dander was up. The victim's two brothers gazed at each other, then stepped forward, beefy arms folded over their chests. One of them said, 'You'm better bugger off back home, Ben.

You ain't one of us no more and we don't want you drinking with us.'

Setting his money bag on the table, Ben began to remove his jacket. 'I've got as much right as any of you to drink in this inn. Anyone who says different, can step forward.'

Ben had just got the coat off his shoulders when a pair of hands slapped against each ear. He went down backwards when a foot tripped him, arms trapped in his jacket, his ears ringing. A foot was planted in his stomach, weight applied.

Hard eyes stared down at him from a round, ruddy face. 'This be my inn, Ben Collins. I says who has the right to drink here and I ain't about to let the likes of you to smash it up, so don't you go startin' any trouble.'

'Well, you tell 'em to stop talking about my wife.'

''Tain't my place to tell a body what he can and can't talk about. Robbie was only telling us what everyone else is saying, that the Skinner woman paid the price for your wife's crime.'

When Ben began to struggle, the pressure on his chest increased. 'No. You be still and listen, for there's more. It ain't right that a man shouldn't know what's being said about his own wife. In certain quarters it's said she was responsible for Hannah Skinner's death.'

Ben could hardly remember his first wife, the woman who'd given birth to his son, George. He recalled now the raw-boned slattern he'd first married with some surprise, for he rarely thought of her. He'd taken her in wedlock because he was tortured by an unnatural need that caused him embarrassment if it wasn't seen to regularly.

Hannah hadn't turned out to be much of a wife in that way, or much of a mother, come to that. He'd felt only relief when she'd died. It had meant he could wed Isabelle, a woman who had attended to his needs from the very first moment they'd met, and with much enthusiasm.

Ben's brow furrowed into ridges. Things came slowly to his mind, but once they were there it took a lot to shift them out. The manner of Hannah's death had been odd. Someone had run over her head with a cart and left her lying in the streets, like she was a piece of old rubbish. The constable had questioned him about it at the time, asking him where he'd been when Hannah had been killed.

'I can't rightly remember, sir,' he'd said, truthfully and respectfully, for he'd never deliberately broken the law, except for burning the odd haystack or two in protest over low wages. Not that he needed to do that now, for he had Isabelle, and Isabelle had money.

Isabelle, taking no nonsense, had fixed the constable with a stare. 'Mr Collins was at the warehouse with me,' she'd said, which was wrong, for she'd left him at the warehouse alone and gone off to the shop.

But Ben hadn't remembered that until a long time afterwards. A right scolding mouth, his woman had on her at times, he thought resentfully. When he'd told her what she'd said to the constable was wrong, she'd flown at him in a temper, smacking him back and forth across the face and shouting, 'You great, daft oaf, are you trying to get us hanged for her murder? Hannah is dead and buried and can stay that way.'

But now, Hannah had risen from the grave to haunt him. Why else would they be wondering about it?

Uneasily, Ben shook his head from side to side, trying to clear his brain. Isabelle had got scared on his account, and she'd lied most like. But she'd let on that she'd maimed Squire Forbes's favourite mare out of spite, taking advantage of a haystack firing to smash its fetlocks with a stick she'd found in the church. A right to-do there had been about that, at the time.

He muttered, almost to himself, 'Isabelle wouldn't kill anyone.'

'That be all right then, don't it? But at least you know what's being said, now. If it do get to the ears of the authorities they might ask questions, and best you be prepared for that.' Another foot came down across his throat, halfway choking him. His victim stared down at him, his broken nose dripping blood. 'You should enter that woman of yours in the County Fair. I reckon she'd beat all the other sows to kingdom come.'

The laughter was raucous.

Giving a roar, Ben made a grab at the leg pinning him down. But his arms were trapped in the sleeves of his jacket. The pressure on his throat increased, cutting off his air. His eyes began to bulge from their sockets.

'We don't want to hurt you, Ben, but my brother has the need to give thee back what you gave him, for it were a coward's punch, thrown before he had time to defend hisself. Now, Robbie be small, on account of he was the runt of the litter and ain't growed into his manhood proper yet.'

'Excepting his dangler. I hear tell all the maids be after pulling a length of that un,' somebody shouted out.

'When he ain't pulling on it hisself, that is,' said another.

Robbie's face turned bright red when everyone laughed. 'Aw, shuddup.'

His brothers waited until the laughter died down. 'Now, will you take your punishment and leave peaceable, like, Ben? Or are we going to beat you into a pulp before we throws you out? You knows you can't take us all on.'

Ben reluctantly nodded.

A few minutes later he was lying face down in the dirt, blood dripping from his nose and one eye puffy and closed. The money bag lay beside him, coins spilling out across the ground. He scooped them back into the bag. Isabelle would give him hell if he lost any. As he staggered to his feet, the horse turned its head to gaze down at him.

'What you looking at, then?' he said. 'Ain't you seen blood afore?' Perhaps it had. Perhaps this was the horse and cart that had done for Hannah that day in Dorchester. But the old horse was saying nothing. As it usually did, the animal farted in his face as he clambered on to the buckboard.

'Dirty bugger,' Ben muttered and flicked the reins.

The men inside the inn laughed as they watched him move away, shaking his head from side to side.

'That's given Ben Collins something to think about, ain't it? Who started that rumour about his missus?'

'Jed Hawkins mentioned the old squire suspected her of having a hand in the slaughter of Ben's first wife. And although he didn't say she started the fire, Jed did say Isabelle and Elizabeth Skinner were both bidding for the shop premises. By hook or by crook, Isabelle was determined to have it all. It didn't take much to work it out, did it?'

'A nasty one to cross, that Isabelle. If it wasn't for Ben, she would have thrown that aunt of hers out of her house long ago. There's no love lost between them. Caroline isn't much older than Isabelle, but she's one to mind her tongue.'

'Has to, else she'd be out on the street.'

'That Isabelle has been after revenge since the old squire tossed her aside for Siana Matheson. He made a fool out of Isabelle, the old squire did, on account of Elizabeth Skinner being his doxie.'

'If rumour is to be believed, both women were his doxies.'

'Not the one who's married to Dr Matheson now. The squire broke her on their wedding night. My Millie used to help with the laundry, and she saw the bridal sheets. Edward Forbes brought a right rosy blush to the girl's cheeks by all accounts.'

'I heard that Isabelle Collins went to the house the women lived in, as bold as brass, demanding they be evicted.' The landlord shook his head and grinned. 'Edward Forbes gave her a right earful, I'll wager. Now the doxie's son is running the estate. I dunno.

Them fancy folk have strange ideas sometimes.'

'And a right gent that Daniel Ayres thinks he be. He'll give us something to think about if'n we don't get the pastures prepared for the sowing of spring wheat, peas and beans, and make sure the bull is put to the cattle. By heck, I never expected to see the old man's bastard running Cheverton Estate.'

'Daniel Ayres won't notice what's what. He wasn't brought up on the land, so he's a bushel short of a brain when it comes to farming. Won't get his hands dirty. He don't take after his father on that one.' The speaker gazed at the landlord. 'Ale all round.'

'Let's see the colour of your money first.'

A couple of silver shillings were thrown onto the bar. 'They fell out of Ben Collins's bag. I reckon he can afford to to stand us a round or two.'

The landlord slid the coins off the counter. 'Poor old Ben. I'd rather have no money than service that great cow of his.'

'Oh, I dunno. I met a carriage driver once who caught them going at it in the woods. He reckoned Ben was built like a stallion. And she was as juicy as a ripe pear and couldn't get enough of it. The driver reckoned she sucked him in, balls and all.'

As they all began to laugh, the speaker scratched his crotch, thinking of his own wife. Her skin was as weather-beaten as an old gourd, her udders so long and stringy from suckling infants she could tuck them under the waist of her skirt. He gave a rueful smile. She'd been a right little beauty once.

*

Daniel Ayres stood in his father's old chamber, a fine room at the front of the house with a commanding view over the estate. His father's personal servant had been reinstated to his former position, but now served him instead.

In the adjoining room, the windows were barred. The room had belonged to Patricia, his father's first wife. She'd become insane after her infant had died. Siana had slept there too, during her marriage to Edward, within easy reach when the man had needed to expend his lusts.

The room was empty now. Daniel would not allow anyone to sleep in the bed once occupied by his one true love. Esmé had settled herself in a grand room on the other side of the house, as far away from him as possible. She was not fond of his attention.

He closed his eyes, imagining the green-eyed woman who had always remained just beyond his reach, accepting his father's caresses. Had she enjoyed the touch of Edward Forbes's hands against her flesh, his mouth against hers or his thighs astride her hips as he plundered her depths? Had she arched towards him to beg for more, and cried out in the ecstasy of the moment – or had she been like Esmé, cold and unresponsive?

How he hated his wife. She'd been out visiting today, enjoying her role as lady of the manor as she patronized shop assistants, gushed to her equals and fawned over her betters. She had been all sweetness before their marriage, leading him on with smiles and flattery. How quickly she had lost her attractiveness. She was late with his medicine tonight. It had been prescribed for his constant headaches, but it also dampened his desire.

Thinking of Siana brought that desire to the surface. He could feel it, throbbing in his groin, gathering momentum. His hand closed over the powerful hardness of it.

He softly swore when a knock came at the door. 'Come in.'

It was the maid Esmé had engaged at the hiring fair, a pretty little thing with lustrous dark eyes and bobbing brown curls. He'd watched her go about her duties, self-conscious in his presence, her hips swaying just that little bit extra when her mistress wasn't around. She had a knowing look about her and carried a tray in her hands. 'The mistress sent me with your medicine, sir.'

'Set it on the table and come here. I want to talk to you.'

She came to stand in front of him, bobbed a curtsy and slanted him a flirty gaze from under her lashes before she straightened. He gazed at her full red lips, at the pink tongue that flicked out to moisten them. 'What's your name, girl?'

'Florence, sir, though most people call me Florrie.'

He traced his finger over her bottom lip, took her hand and placed it against his rigidity. 'Well, Florrie, how would you like to earn yourself an extra coin or two?'

Her eyes hooded over slightly. 'I'll lock the door then, shall I, sir?'

From his closet, Daniel brought forth a silk chemise he'd found behind Siana's bed. Bunching it in his hands he pressed it against his face and inhaled her musky perfume before handing it to the girl. 'Put this on.'

He took his time with her, touching her intimately. Not that she minded. The maid displayed sluttish tendencies, for she'd cried out with the sudden rush of pleasure he afforded her. He was pleased by it. He liked women to be responsive to his needs.

So he bade her go on all fours, like a dog, and he stood behind her, the length of him inside her as his fingers caressed underneath, bringing her nipples jutting against his fingertips through the silk, and sliding them downwards until he divided her cleft to touch the erect little bud. She gave little yelps of excitement when he teased it.

'Do you like that?'

'It do make me feel right wicked,' she said, trembling in her pleasure.

'We might as well enjoy that wickedness, then.'

A few moments later a knock came at the door, causing him to pause in the activity he was indulging in. 'Daniel, are you in there?'

'What is it, Esmé?' he said, annoyed by the interruption. 'I'm resting.'

'Have you seen Florrie?'

'Florrie?'

'The maid I sent to you with your medicine.'

Palms grazing against her nipples, he began to slowly thrust in and out of her, another woman's image in his mind, enjoying the way the maid tried to stifle her moans of pleasure.

The doorknob rattled. 'Why is this door locked, Daniel? Are you all right?'

How sharp Esmé was. How he would love to make her watch, and see the shock on her face. 'Let me be,' he growled, 'unless you're here to provide some wifely duties. Are you, Esmé?'

Florrie giggled.

After a moment of tense silence, Esme whispered, 'Don't forget to take your medicine.' Her footsteps pattered away.

Daniel began to laugh. 'The mistress has no interest in being a wife today, it seems. Will *you* be my wife for today, Siana?'

'My name be Florrie, sir.'

'It will be anything I want to call you,' he snarled. Grabbing her hair, he pulled her head back so she was forced to look up at him as he savagely impaled her. 'Do you understand, you peasant slut?'

It was a dark night, thick with cloud. Josh was out in his boat. Sam Saynuthin was trawling the grapple and keeping a sharp eye out for the revenue men. But there wouldn't be anybody about tonight. There was a big push on to capture a gang of smugglers over Lulworth way after one of the revenue men had been killed in a shoot-out the previous week.

Even if they saw him, Josh knew he and Sam were a familiar sight on the harbour. Mostly, the smugglers worked in gangs. A pair of lone crab-catchers wouldn't rate a second look, he reckoned, as he hauled in a dripping crab basket.

The pair shivered as a cold wind keened over the black water, which reflected back the lights on the shore as rippling, glistening lines. They could send a man into a dream state if he stared too long at them. Dreams he didn't want, for he was not like his sister, who was wise in a womanly intuitive way. Siana's house was up there on the hill, shining as brightly as any of them.

He felt warm as he thought of his sister. She'd done right well for them since his parents had died. She'd be tucking little Daisy and Goldie into bed now, telling them a story she'd made up, just as she used to tell him stories when he'd been small. He was pleased she'd moved back to Poole. He liked being around her and the kids. And she was growing a bit plump, so there was another one on the way by the looks of her. The doctor would have a nice surprise to come home to.

When Francis did return, Josh had decided then might be time for him to move out. He might move into one of the cottages in Smuggler's Lane when one became vacant. Now he'd learned from Giles Dennings how interest and money worked together, he knew he could have anything he wanted. He'd set his sights on building himself a new house.

He already had the land, a handsome acre overlooking the sea at Branksome Chine.

He'd bought the acre with the stash of accumulated cash made from smuggling. His smuggling activities were something his partner, Giles Dennings, knew nothing about. He never would either, for Giles was an upright and honest man, who wouldn't want to be associated with something illegal.

Josh was still designing the house. As he described what he wanted, Sam Saynuthin drew it on a sheet of paper. When it was exactly how Josh wanted it, he was going to take it to an architect to draw up a proper plan. It wasn't as big as Siana's house, but it would be comfortable enough.

Josh began to wonder if he needed to smuggle any more. So far he'd got away with it, but the revenue men, aided by the Royal Navy, had become more vigilant over the last few months. If he was caught by them he could easily be killed, or pressed into the service. And if the smuggling gangs got hold of him no explanations would be needed. He'd be found floating in the harbour with his throat cut.

Josh grinned. He'd miss the excitement of pitting his wits against the authorities, though.

Sam Saynuthin's grunt brought him to the alert. There was the gleam of a lantern bobbing over to the left. At the same time the grapple caught at something underwater. The tubs of brandy were tied together along a rope, which was anchored by stone sinkers to the sea bed. It took some time to haul up and remove the sinkers.

The choppy water slopped over the side of the boat, soaking them through as they headed carefully for one of the channels into the backwater. Josh swore when the clouds thinned to reveal a half-moon riding high in the sky. There was enough danger of exposure from the light it cast to make his ear sing with tension. Of late, he'd been getting these uneasy feelings inside him, like someone was watching him. It made the hairs on his arm prickle and he wondered if he should heed what his intuition told him, which was to abandon the illegal trade as soon as posssible.

The tide was out. Rolling the contraband brandy across the mud flats was easy, loading it on the waiting horse and cart, hard work. Twenty half-anker kegs, containing approximately eighty-five gallons of spirit, was worth well over a hundred pounds in profit to him. They fitted into the bed of the cart exactly.

Over them, he placed a false floor, then piled his crab baskets on top. The contents would be cooked over a brazier on the quayside, for he'd handed over the cockle and crab business to Sam, so he could earn himself an independent living. He sent the mute off to his bed in the coach station. He'd have no trouble getting rid of the brandy, he thought, as he set the cart in motion. All he had to do was deliver it to his regular customers.

It didn't take long to empty the cart. Josh sighed with relief when the last barrel was bought by a barber surgeon. The man watered it down, bottled it, added a few herbs and sold it as a miracle cure for everything. Placing the proceeds of his night's work in a small canvas satchel, Josh strapped it in a space under the box that served as a seat.

By crikey, he was cold! He would be glad to get home to his cosy bed above the stable. But as he was about to set the horse in motion, a figure strode out of the shadows in front of him and yanked the reins from his hands. A gun was held against his head. 'My name is Henry Weaver.'

Josh's heart flapped in his chest like a stranded eel.

'Shit! What the hell are you after? I ain't got no money on me.'

The man stepped back into the dim light cast by the lantern, the gun held steady at arm's length. His face was familiar. 'You keep your stash under your arse, Skinner.'

Josh nearly groaned out loud. Of all the bleddy luck! To get caught just as he'd decided to give up the trade.

It was the revenue man whose brat he'd pulled from the harbour. It wouldn't hurt to remind him of it. 'Oh, it's you, sir. You gave me a right turn. How's the young tyke, these days? I hope his ducking didn't do him any harm.' He shrugged when the man didn't answer, decided he might be able to talk his way out of this. 'You don't have to keep the pistol on me, Mr Weaver. I'm not armed and I'm going about my lawful business.'

The gun was lowered. 'Lawful, it ain't at this time of night, lad. I've been watching your activities of late. Since you brought those tubs ashore tonight I could've placed you and your rig under arrest at any time, and had enough evidence to hang you with. I could also have blown a hole in your head a moment ago, and nobody would've been the wiser.'

That accounted for the uneasy feeling he'd had earlier that evening. Josh didn't see much sense in lying, so nodded, interested to find out why he hadn't been arrested. 'May I ask why you did none of them things, Mr Weaver?'

'I know the adventure of smuggling appeals to someone of your age, for I did it myself once or twice. Take heed, though, it's a hanging offence, and there ain't no adventure in that. A hanged man's eyes bulge from their sockets, his face turns purple and his tongue hangs out. The rope stops the air getting into the body, see. And a man craps in his trousers as he jerks about trying to reach the ground with his feet afore he dies, so the last thing he smells is his own shit. But that ground is just out of reach, and the more a body struggles the tighter the noose gets. A most undignified and painful way to go.'

Josh's eyes widened. 'It doesn't sound peaceful, for sure.'

'Think on, lad. If I catch you at it again you'll be apprehended.' He jerked his head towards the hill. 'If you want to make old bones, bugger off home, consider my debt to you paid in full and mark my soddin' words. You won't hear them twice.'

'Thank you, Mr Weaver,' Josh said hastily. 'I won't need to.'

'Consider yourself warned then, lad. From what I've heard, you've worked damned hard for what you've got. The fact that you're still alive is a testament to your cunning and luck. But the luck will run out before too long. Ask yourself if the game is worth the risk.'

That notion alone was enough to make Josh's cockiness disappear. 'Thank you, sir. I will consider your advice most carefully.' Clicking his tongue, he set the horse in motion, determined to reform in his ways.

Henry Weaver watched him go, a smile inching across his face when Giles Dennings detached himself from the shadows. 'Will that put the fear of God into him, Giles?'

'Thanks, Henry. I can breathe easy in my bed now. I don't think my young partner will be tempted to stray from the straight and narrow again. I'm in your debt.'

'No, Giles. I owed the lad for young Joshua. It was a brave thing he did, jumping in the harbour after him, and I'll never forget it. Now, I'm off home to my bed. I suggest you do likewise.'

The pair shook hands and parted.

Never in his imagination had Francis thought he'd live in a such a grim place as Port Arthur penal settlement. Never had he felt so helpless and despairing.

Despite his protestations of innocence, the authorities had chosen not to believe he was any other but the escapee, Philip Piper. He'd received a second flogging, much more severe than the caning Captain McPhee had dealt him. It had taken a long time before the agony of that had healed. His back would retain the scars for the rest of his life.

In the past, he'd always observed poverty from the outside, looking in. Now, manacled at the ankles, covered in lice and unimaginable filth, his stomach hollowed from hunger, Francis experienced it first-hand.

The wooden prisoners' barracks were set into the side of a slope. The convicts' berths were separated by low partitions which afforded no privacy, and allowed free pass to illnesses passed on by infected breath. Lung complaints were common.

It was true. There was no honour amongst thieves. Every scrap of food was fought for, whether rancid or not. He'd learned to fight for his share with the rest of the pack, snatching it and stuffing it down as fast as he was able.

He'd lost weight, but not muscle, for being part of a convict team, clearing bush was a labour which had made him strong of body. How long his strength would last before malnutrition took its toll of him was another matter.

Here, as an inmate of the notorious Port Arthur penal settlement, where discipline was rigidly enforced, the niceties of life were abandoned in the need to exist from moment to moment.

Francis was not ashamed of his behaviour. In a few short weeks, the authorities had reduced him to little more than an animal. He was innocent of any crime and must put himself first, do anything to survive – even lie and cheat. He tried not to weep as he remembered his family, for to weep was a sign of weakness in this underclass he inhabited.

Had Siana received the letter he'd sent from Sydney Town, he wondered. He imagined the children standing around her, listening whilst she read it to them, telling them of his life aboard ship and the bustling port called Sydney that he'd explored. He imagined her sweet face, her trembling, sensuous mouth, the mysterious forest-green darkness of the eyes he so loved. Would he ever see her, or his children again?

He drew in a deep, shuddering breath. He must not lose hope. He'd requested to see the prison commandant, who was reputed to be a fair man. Francis had been waiting for several weeks to see him. Some convicts had been waiting for several months.

Waking up was always a chore. Sometimes he forgot he was no longer waking a free man, but a convict. By his reckoning, it was early April. In England, rain would come softly in showers to drench the massed daffodils. He took a deep breath, his nostrils seeking in vain for their elusive scent.

All he could smell were the foul vapours of waking humanity, with their sweating, corrupt flesh, farts, coughs and curses. He was just as foul himself. One of them, in fact.

Unexpectedly, a hand dropped on his shoulder. 'Commandant will see yer this morning, Piper.'

Francis shot upright, cracking his head on the berth above. He stroked his matted beard, muttering, 'He can't receive me looking like this, I'm filthy.'

'Yes, your lordship, so you are. Shall I ring for your servant to come and shave you? Perhaps he could bring you a clean suit of clothes, as well.' The man went off, chuckling to himself.

The prison commandant, Charles O'Hara Booth, was a lean and upright man. A receding hairline, side-whiskers and dark, straight eyebrows, made his face appear long and gaunt. He didn't bother looking up from the paper he was studying.

'State your business with me, Piper.'

'I'm not Philip Piper, sir. My name is Francis Matheson. I'm a doctor, and I was on the *Adriana* when she sank. I was washed ashore, and was arrested by mistake for—'

'Yes, yes, I have your statement here.' The commandant looked up then. 'You were recognized from the wanted poster as Philip Piper, confidence trickster, petty thief, and an absconder from the work gangs.'

'I'm a physician and surgeon by profession, and a land-owner.'

The commandant turned a wanted poster his way. 'Are you denying this is you?'

Francis stared at the likeness. 'I admit, it looks like me, but—'

'Take him back to the barracks. Give him fifty lashes first, for his impertinence.'

'My eldest brother is the Earl of Kylchester,' Francis said, resisting as the guard tried to march him away, 'and my second brother is Admiral Augustus Matheson of Her Majesty's navy.' A second guard stepped forward and took him in an arm lock.

'For God's sake, man, you have a reputation for being fair-minded,' Francis shouted as they began to drag him out. 'Surely you can check my veracity.'

The commandant held up his hand. 'You say you're a doctor?'

When Francis nodded he said to one of the guards, 'Fetch the Assistant Colonial Surgeon.'

When the prison doctor arrived, Charles Booth told him, 'This man is attempting to make me believe he's a physician and surgeon. Perhaps you could determine how much knowledge he possesses, in my presence.'

The assistant surgeon grinned, for it had happened before. 'With great pleasure. Under whom did you study your profession, Doctor?'

'Sir Astley Paton Cooper.'

The prison surgeon's smile faded. 'Ah yes . . . but most

people would have heard of him, no doubt. Can you tell me of Edward Jenner's contribution to medicine?'

'He injected pus from a cowpox pustule into a patient and discovered what's thought to be a preventative for smallpox.'

There were more questions, then the surgeon asked him, 'Have you ever performed surgery?'

'On many occasions. I have my own country practice in Dorset.'

A surgical instrument case was placed on the desk. 'Can you name these?'

'Syringe, forceps, scalpel, trepanning drill -'

'I think that's enough.' The surgeon nodded towards the commandant. 'I wouldn't rule out that this man is in possession of medical knowledge, but it could have been learned from a book. In fact, I would suggest I examine him further by observing any practical skill he may possess.'

'You mean you've decided you'd like to have him as an assistant, Doctor.'

The assistant surgeon grinned. 'He seems to be a cut above the others I've had.'

'Then keep a good eye on him, for I'll hold you responsible should he abscond again.' The commandant nodded to the guards. 'The order for fifty lashes is rescinded. Make sure Piper is scrubbed clean of dirt and deloused before he's taken to the hospital. He stinks.'

'My name is Francis Matheson, sir.'

'Not until you can prove it, it isn't.'

'How can I prove it?' Francis shouted as he was hustled away.

Sir Charles drummed his fingers on the desk when the door shut behind the convict. 'He speaks well and seems to be well educated.'

'You think there may be some truth in the tale he tells?'

'I'm dubious. Piper has a reputation of being able to talk himself out of any situation. The *Adriana* did go down about the time he was caught. The stripes on his back are more indicative of a truer tale, though. A ship's captain might flog his crew, but I doubt if he'd flog a fellow officer and surgeon. It's not gentlemanly conduct.

'However, I'll bear it in mind, in case the opportunity arises to prove it one way or the other. In the meantime, you can do with the help. If nothing else, helping his fellow man might influence his rehabilitation when the time comes. I'll make enquiries as to the land he says he inherited from his brother.'

But Francis was forgotten when the next petitioner was brought in.

'Thomas Webb, sir. He was caught stealing food from the kitchen, sir. First offence.'

'Then we must make sure he doesn't do it again. Fifty lashes and bread and water for a week. Take him off kitchen duty and put him to hard labour . . .'

12

It had been hard to leave the younger children behind. There had been tears, not the least being those shed by herself at the wrench of being parted from Ashley, who, as he gave her a kiss and waved her goodbye, bestowed on her the gift of his father's smile.

'How can I possibly forget him when you remind me of him every day, you little wretch,' she said, turning back to snatch one last hug. Susannah, determined not to be left out, demanded one too.

Daisy looked sulky, and Goldie was tremulous at the parting.

'I'll be back before you know it,' Siana told them, giving them both a kiss.' She would have taken them with her, but she couldn't risk Maryse's secret getting out, and they were of an age to be aware that something was amiss. She comforted herself with the thought that they were in good hands with the governess. She'd left Miss Edgar in overall charge, and with the two live-in nursery maids under her, plus two house servants and a gardener/stable hand who came in on a daily basis, the house was well staffed.

Josh had agreed to move into the house whilst she was away. The children loved and trusted him, and would not miss her so much if they had him to turn to.

She had sent a note to the Countess of Kylchester, explaining that she was with child, would be visiting her property in Wales and would remain there for the birth. She added that Maryse would accompany her, and requested that Pansy remain in the charge of her aunt.

It had suddenly become imperative to leave. Even a tightly laced corset and a voluminous skirt could not conceal the fact that Maryse was rapidly losing her waistline. She no longer went abroad, confining herself mostly to her room again. Even so, she was forced to wear a high-waisted gown to disguise her state.

As for Siana, she wore no stays and emphasized her stomach by wearing a frilled peplum at the waist, which made her pregnancy appear more advanced than it was. Thus, it drew attention to her own state, and away from that of Maryse. But she couldn't risk staying any longer.

With a minimum of luggage, and with Rosie complaining at every turn, the coach, with Josh at the reins and Sam Saynuthin by his side, set out for Bristol. There, they intended to stay the night before transferring to a boat that would take them across the Severn Estuary and into Wales. Josh had reserved rooms for them at a coaching inn. Siana had not thought past that, for her directions were sparse at that stage.

It was a fine day, the occasional showers refreshing for the horses. But the rain was not heavy enough to churn the road into mud. The trees were cloaked in the freshest of spring green and daffodils bobbed cheerfully in the darkest places of the woods for as far as the eyes could see.

Rosie's head craned this way and that when they drove through Cheverton Estate. 'It be a bit quiet in the fields, I reckon. They should be spreading manure, sowing oats and barley, and planting the mangold-wurzels, potatoes and flax. I hope that Daniel Ayres knows what he be doing.'

Siana smoothed her hands over her stomach. She had not lost interest in estate matters. But as much as she was looking forward to the birth of her infant she was dreading the birth of Maryse's. Her mind fluctuated between elation and despair, and had no room in it for business. Her agent was a friend of her first husband. A magistrate, he was also a trustee, and named in Edward's last will and testament as one of those who would administer the finances of the estate on behalf of Ashley, his legitimate son and heir. She trusted him to know what he was doing.

'I expect he does know,' she replied to Rosie now, 'for the estate managers advise him.'

'There goes Mr Ayres on Jed Hawkins's great horse. That horse ain't as young as he used to be. Lord, look how he put the poor creature to the fence. He thinks he cuts a fine figure like his father did, but that there Daniel Ayres be going to seed by the look of him. His stomach be bulging over his trousers.'

Siana didn't bother glancing up from her perusal of Francis's letter which had arrived the previous day. His description of the sea voyage and of Sydney Cove was interesting, but more interesting to her, he wrote, '*I miss you every moment of every day. When I return, I'll never allow myself to be parted from you again.*' Such sentiment was precious to her, for Francis was not a demonstrative man by nature. Though she didn't doubt his love for her.

She caressed her stomach again, smiling with glee. He would be overjoyed by the gift she had for him on his return. Folding the letter, she slid it into her pocket.

'I don't envy that wife of his, either. I hears tell . . .' Rosie glanced sharply at Maryse. 'Well, never mind what I hears tell. 'Tis only gossip and not worth the breath of it. Though that Mrs Ayres be a sour thing, and getting old before her time, like a dried-up stick of rhubarb.'

Rosie kept prattling on until, at last, she ran out of breath and fell asleep. Siana exchanged a small smile of relief with Maryse. At least the girl could manage a smile now. Once this was over she hoped that Maryse would soon become her former sweet self, and none would be the wiser.

Rosie had made enquiries, a letter had been sent, arrangements made. The infant would be fostered out to a farmer who lived near Monmouth, with enough money to raise and educate it. Siana was using a false name, so they could never be traced. She intended to tell Maryse that the infant was stillborn.

Josh kept up a steady pace, changing the horses at Andover. Soon they were in Bristol, where they would take a boat from Avonmouth across the Severn Estuary to Chepstow, then up the River Wye into Monmouth.

'I'm sorry I can't take you any further, but I'm a driver short and have to get back for my regular runs,' Josh told them. 'You'll be able to ask directions and pick up further transport at the inn. I'll be here to pick you up when you return, as arranged.'

Much to Siana's surprise, she ran into Marcus Ibsen as they were about to board the boat. The smile Marcus gave them all was warm. 'Mrs Matheson, I'm pleased to see you again. I trust you are well.'

She introduced Marcus to Josh, who looked him over carefully, taking his measure before deciding he liked him. He extended a hand. 'How do you do, sir.'

Marcus nodded, then inclined his head at Maryse. 'Miss Matheson. We meet in the oddest places. You look well.'

Maryse blushed, unable to meet his eyes. Remembering, no doubt, the circumstances under which they had first met. 'Thank you, Mr Ibsen, I am,' she whispered.

Marcus turned away from her, pretending not to notice as her blush subsided. 'Am I to take it that you're going to your father's house, Mrs Matheson?'

'Why, yes, we are, for a short time.'

There was a slight awkwardness, then Marcus chuckled. 'I must confess, I'm going to the same place. I have some goods stored there, and intended to stay for the summer to carry out necessary repairs.'

'Oh, I see.'

'It will not cause you any problem, I hope, Mrs Matheson. With your permission, I can move into the shepherd's cottage. It's sufficient for my needs. It would be better if you had someone there who knows the lie of the land and can fetch and carry for you, for you will need to purchase food and –' his glance flickered momentarily to her stomach '– you may require help. The house is in a fairly isolated position and I have some medical knowledge.'

'I thought there would be a town nearby.'

'Monmouth is twenty miles away. There is a village within a five-mile distance,' he said gently, 'but it supports nothing but cottages for the villagers, most of whom are self-sufficient. Usually, I take flour and tea, and I hire a cow, purchase some laying hens, then walk to the farms to buy meat and vegetables every week. Though if we are lucky the vegetable plot will provide us with some, for I planted seeds before I left. There might be a hardy hen or two which survived the snows of winter and the hungry foxes. They will be tough, but can be used for the pot.'

Siana laughed. 'You would slaughter the poor creatures after they survived all that? Is there water?'

'More than you'll ever need. There is a spring. The countryside is very hilly. Steeper, perhaps, than the hills you're used to at home.'

'I don't like the sound of it,' Josh said. 'I'll try and find you somewhere else to stay.'

Maryse surprised Siana with her firmness. 'No. I want to go where there are no people to bother us. If Mr Ibsen is willing to help, and is going there anyway, I can see no reason why we should have to find somewhere else.' Maryse placed a hand over hers, and her voice took on a tiny pleading note that wrenched at Siana's heart.

'Siana, didn't you want to see where your parents were born?'

Siana knew only too well the motive behind Maryse's reasoning. As far as Maryse was concerned, Rosie and Josh were the only people who were aware of her plight. For some reason, she was willing to trust Marcus, though it was hard to judge whether he guessed the truth or not. How brave the girl was. Maryse didn't want to risk being exposed, and Siana couldn't fault her for that.

She bestowed a bright smile on the girl. 'You're right, Maryse. I do want to see where my parents came from.' She turned and gave Josh a hug. 'There's no need for you to come across the estuary, then. Mr Ibsen seems to know the lie of the land, and is perfectly capable of looking after us. I'll be grateful to have him living close by.'

When the others turned aside, she took the opportunity to whisper in Josh's ear, 'I'll feel better if I know you're there for the children. Our mother would be so proud of the way you're growing up – and your dad too. For though he wasn't much of a father to me, he was proud to have you as a son, Josh. He'd be prouder still to know what you've made of yourself.'

Josh, a flush spreading across his cheeks from the praise, gave her a quick squeeze and whispered, 'Look after yourself, sis.' Then he was gone, Sam Saynuthin at his heels.

And so it was settled.

They had been travelling for the best part of the day.

Maryse looked as exhausted as Siana felt when they stepped onto dry land.

Monmouth proved to be a town of great flourish as old jostled with the new. The streets were dominated by mail coaches, but they proceeded in a smooth flow through the recently built Priory Street, which itself ran alongside the steeply sloping banks of the Monnow. Priory Street acted as a tributary to Church Street, or so Marcus told them.

He gave a running commentary on everything as they passed, following a man with a hand-cart piled with their luggage. Marcus travelled light, a canvas bag slung over his shoulders.

There was a huge ditch crossing Monnow Street, part of the fortifications of what was believed to be a Norman settlement. There were pleasure gardens, which, it was said, the preacher John Wesley sometimes visited. Opposite, were the ruins of a Benedictine priory, built in honour of Geoffrey of Monmouth.

Siana's senses were heightened by the ancient environment she found herself in. She breathed it in like a hound on a scent. It was strange to be in a town so steeped in history, and a bloodthirsty one at that. From the castle tower dominating the hill, to the river running through the town, she could feel a response to it quivering in her veins.

The town faded into the background as her blood suddenly stirred with that of her ancestors. Her mind brought an impression of fierce, wild-eyed men wielding their swords against the English invaders. The heaving, twisting bodies and screams of dying men and horses were all too real, as was the smell of the river, choked with their bodies and running red, like a sunset of spilled blood.

Then it was gone. Feeling nauseated, she slumped weakly against a wall, perspiration soaking her face as she asked out loud, '*Why?*'

Rosie let out a squawk, like an agitated hen watching a fox make off with its chick.

In a moment, Marcus was by Siana's side. 'This has all been too much for you,' he said. 'You will rest tonight whilst I arrange transport for us.'

'We are delaying you,' she protested, but he would have none of it.

'I am not delayed.' His dark eyes searched the depths of hers, as slowly he quoted,

'"*To everything there is a season, and a time to every purpose under the heaven.*" You have the sight.'

'You see too much,' she answered crossly. 'Who are you, Marcus Ibsen?'

'A fellow traveller, a friend you can trust and lean on.'

She believed him, so she leaned on him.

They stayed at the Queen's Head Inn, which was situated across from a new-looking methodist church. When she woke, Siana was quite recovered and ready for the journey ahead.

Seven sturdy Welsh ponies stood patiently in the charge of a man of few words. Two of them were packed up with their luggage, the rest stood waiting to be mounted. Except for thick sheepskins tied around their middles, and rope halters, the animals were unsaddled.

Rosie stared at them for a moment, her mouth pursed, but she said nothing as she resignedly scrambled astride the back of one, giving an aggrieved sigh.

A little while later, dressed in travelling clothes and sturdy boots, and with a hurried breakfast of potato pancakes fried in bacon fat sitting warmly in their stomachs, they were heading along the valley towards the foothills of the Black Mountains, shrouded in mist, some twenty miles away. The saturated soil beneath them sucked at the ponies' hooves.

Clouds scudded overhead, there was the smell of rain in the air. Contentment wrapped Siana in a warm blanket, for the valley was lushly green, nourished by the Monnow river which flowed through it towards the sea. The landscape was rugged and dominating and, for all its serenity, possessed an air of danger. Here, the people had learned to live within the scope of the land and had not attempted to tame it, for it was obvious they would fail.

'We'll be lucky if we escape a drenching before the day is over,' Maryse said, but for the first time in months, her eyes were shining with excitement and she wore a fine smile on her face.

How beautiful she is today, Siana thought. Marcus turned to look at the girl too, responding with a grin that deepened the lines defining his cheeks.

Siana had asked Marcus who he was and had been told only what he'd wanted her to hear. Which was not very much. His simple robe did not make a simple man of him. He was a complex, enigmatic man.

She would ask him nothing more. That was the

only way she reckoned she would learn anything about him.

They took the last, and steepest leg of the climb on foot, spreading the luggage between the sturdy ponies to lighten their load. They rested a while before the last stretch, sitting by a stream that slid noiselessly between the rocks. The guide went on ahead. Twenty minutes later he came back down.

Marcus took him aside, money changed hands. There was also an exchange of words in a language unfamiliar to Siana. The man slid her a sideways glance. Their eyes met for a moment and she saw the curiosity in them.

Siana rose to her feet after he'd gone. 'What did he say?'

'He agreed to bring over a cow and some hens in the morning. We shall have to make do tonight.'

'. . . about me?'

'He asked if you were Gruffydd Evans's daughter. I told him, yes, and he expressed surprise that you had come here.'

'Why should he be surprised, when it's my father's home?' She shrugged. 'The house must be nearby, for he was not gone for long.'

'It's just over the next hill.'

The house also clung to the hill. It was nestled into the side, a rambling low stone building that afforded a view of the English Border towns. Fortressed behind by a rocky ridge fronting it, the land fell gradually away to a tumble of rocks that led down into a valley.

Fed by a spring, which trickled into a rock pool, a flow

of water, the thickness of a man's arm, splashed from one rock to another, to disappear amongst a lushness of watercress, ferns, moss and bright rainbows. The spring looked as if it had been there for ever, and probably had. 'Why didn't my father live here?'

'He felt he didn't deserve to.'

'Did he deserve to?'

Marcus shrugged. 'Can a man truly know what is in his own heart? We must each live by our own tenet.' He pushed the door open. It was fashioned crudely from thick wooden planks and secured by a bar; the wind had cracked the surface into tiny splits and splinters. 'We leave it unlocked, for if a man is lost in the mountains, especially in winter, he may seek shelter here.'

'Why did my father give me the key, I wonder?'

'It was a symbol. It's a very old key. He found it hidden behind a loose stone in the fireplace. Gruffydd carried it with him to remind him of his ancestors.'

'Then I must put it back where it belongs.' She gazed at the carving over the stone lintel. 'What does *Bryn Dwr* mean?'

'*Bryn* means hill, *Dwr* means water. Roughly translated, the house is named "Hill of the Water". Though not far from here there is a cave containing a pool. That's called *Gwin Dwr*, which means wine water. There's a legend attached to the place. One day I'll show you the cave and relate its history to you.'

Inside the house was a long room, sparsely furnished, with a large and threadbare, hand-hooked rag rug on the floor. There were no windows, only openings in the stone with wooden shutters to guard against the elements. A huge stone fireplace dominated one wall, the chimney piece surmounted by an exquisitely carved wooden cross.

Siana gazed up at it. 'Is that my father's work?'

'Mine, but the tutor was your father. I was snowed in the winter before last. It kept me occupied.'

'You do fine work.'

He seemed pleased by the compliment, for he smiled and said, 'It was a labour of love.' He walked from room to room, throwing the shutters open to let some air in. 'Nobody has been here since my last visit.'

Through to the back was the kitchen, with an open fireplace on which to cook. There were cast-iron pots, china and cutlery. Four rooms led off the kitchen. Three contained two beds apiece with slat bases and sheepskins to serve as mattresses. They looked very uncomfortable. The fourth was stacked high with trunks and household goods, such as tubs and brooms.

Rosie tutted as she picked a sheepskin rug off one of the beds and shook the dust from it. 'This looks as though a dog has made a bed out of it. It'll be full of fleas, if you asks me.'

Siana snatched it from her and threw it out through the nearest window. 'Then stop shaking them round the house, else we'll all be scratching all night.'

Rosie rummaged around a bit and came up with a tub. 'I'll have to wash them sheepskins afore they can be used. I'll get the fire lit first, and clean the place up a bit.'

Siana rolled up her sleeves. 'I'll go and gather some firewood and explore the vegetable garden.'

'What can I do?' Maryse said helplessly, for she'd

been cared for by a housekeeper since birth and was unfamiliar with most household duties.

Marcus spoke up. 'You can help me, if you like. There should be some clean straw in the stable and there are some palliasses and rugs in one of the trunks. You could find them, and anything else you think might be useful. Then you can help me fill them and sew up the ends. I'm sure you're more proficient with a needle than me, Miss Matheson.'

Maryse looked slightly self-conscious at the praise. 'I will do my best to be useful.'

By sun-down, they had clean beds, and a meal of thick potato soup flavoured with smoked bacon and watercress to look forward to. Siana had made bread, cooking it in the ashes, so a thick crust formed. It had been a long time since she'd performed such a task and she enjoyed the fruit of her labour, especially since it had been produced in such a primitive kitchen.

Candles were lit, and Marcus rolled up his palliasse and rug.

Siana smiled at him. 'I went to see the shepherd's hut you intended to sleep in. The floor is covered in dung and the roof has caved in. Would you like one of the bedrooms? Maryse and I can sleep together in the bigger one.'

'Thank you, Mrs Matheson. Having inspected the hut myself and drawn the same conclusion, I've decided to sleep in the barn until I complete the repairs. The hayloft is quite clean. Good night, ladies. I hope your slumber is undisturbed.'

Which indeed it was, for the exercise and fresh air had

tired them so much they fell asleep the instant they laid their heads down.

It was an unseasonably warm day. Isabelle Collins had hired a brass band for the opening of her Emporium. Bunting was draped around the building, softening the rawness of the new, red brick.

Inside, standing behind the counters and dressed alike in severe black serge skirts with drab pleated smocks over the top, her shop assistants waited to serve the rush of customers who would flood into the shop after the ceremony.

Her glance ranged over the small crowd. But there seemed to be no customers – not customers who mattered and had money to spend, at least. Unless one could count a ragged army of urchins marching up and down to the band, and their poorly dressed mothers who'd come to listen to the music. Goodness, why didn't these women take some pride in themselves?

Isabelle had invited the Mayor to be the guest of honour at the grand opening of her shop, but the man had declined, saying he had another engagement. She'd then invited her bank manager, but with the same result. Then the Reverend White was asked, followed by Dr Noah Baines and on down through the town council to the lesser public servants until she was left with only a strutting little police constable – and he was late!

Fuming, she stood there in the sun, the tiered and flounced purple silk gown she'd had specially made for the occasion hanging damply against her back. She seemed to be getting thinner lately, a fact she welcomed.

Her bonnet, which was trimmed with dyed feathers and ruched ribbons, was wilting in the humidity. Dying for a pee, she pressed her thighs together tightly.

Ben stood beside her, his hands clasping those of their children. He'd changed towards her of late. Oh, he still did his duty by her, but sometimes she caught him looking at her, like a stupid donkey, his eyes all sad. And he'd begun to criticize the way she spoke to people in her employ.

'People have feelings, Isabelle, so don't you do anything like that again,' he'd said to her the other day.

As far as Isabelle was concerned, she didn't pay them to have feelings, so they could keep them to themselves. There was something else troubling her. She could feel a lump growing inside her womb, and thought she might be pregnant again. But something wasn't quite right about it. She still lost blood every month and her back ached. Sometimes she was so tired she stayed in bed all day and let Aunt Caroline look after everything.

The employees worked better when Ben asked them to, for he was polite to both men and women alike, and they liked him. The children behaved better when they were with him, too. The truth was, the great gawk-hammer didn't have a mean bone in his body unless he had a drink or two under his belt.

Lord, she was tired of standing here, though a few people were turning up now, attracted by the music. Josh Skinner and the deformed mute who dogged his steps were standing at the back. Now, *there* was someone who was doing all right for himself. Obviously there was money in transport, lots of it.

The mute had a sketching block in his hands. She shuddered and turned away when he looked her way. Ugly beast! He was drawing the scene. Well, she wouldn't mind a copy of the occasion and would pay him a ha'penny for it afterwards, if he wanted to sell it.

George was scuffing the toes of his new shoes against the pavement. 'Behave yourself,' she hissed, and he poked his tongue out at her. Alexandra giggled.

She managed a smile for her daughter when she saw the constable coming along the road. He was driving the horse-drawn wagon they used for transporting prisoners. She hoped his speech wasn't going to be too long-winded. But his superior officer was with him, and he had some papers in his hand. Perhaps he was going to open the shop instead.

What the hell are they up to, she wondered, for the pair had driven the wagon straight up to her.

When the constable climbed down from the wagon and held up his hand, the music trailed to a stop. His superior officer unrolled a piece of paper and began to read, 'Mrs Isabelle Collins, you are charged with the wilful murder of one Hannah Collins, whose head was crushed when she was run over by a cart—'

Isabelle's blood ran cold. She shouted out before he finished reading the charge, 'It's a lie.'

'There was a witness,' the constable informed her.

'No, there wasn't. It were too early in the morning and nobody was about—'

She could have screamed when the two policemen smiled at each other.

The onlookers began to clap their hands and jeer as she was grasped by the arms and bundled into the wagon. She caught Ben's glance. He was staring oddly at her, as if seeing her in a completely new light.

'I didn't do it, Ben,' she shouted out in desperation.

He came up to the bars of the wagon and said quietly, 'I ain't so stupid as you think, just a bit slow at figuring things out. And you set the fire at the shop as well, so that poor Elizabeth Skinner would suffer for it, didn't you?'

'What if I did?' she said defiantly. 'I can't be tried for that, can I?'

'You be a wicked woman, Isabelle.'

'It strikes me that you're listening to people's lies, Ben Collins. The Skinners are scum and should be wiped off the face of the earth.'

'What have the Skinners done to you that you be so set against them? My George was born to a Skinner woman. He hasn't done you no harm. I'm not going to let you call him names when you feels like it. His own mother did enough of that.'

'Then someone did you a favour when they flattened her head.'

Tears filled his eyes. 'It better not be you, then, our Isabelle. You've got a wicked tongue on you sometimes, and a nature to match. I don't want no murderer for a wife, and for the cheils' sake I won't take you back if you be found guilty.'

'You won't be able to take me back, stupid. They'll probably hang me.'

He thought for a moment or two. 'If that happens, I

reckon the business will become mine, with me being your husband and all.'

The force of the expletive she gave caused pressure on Isabelle's bladder. Then, the indignity of it . . . she peed herself.

13

In Cheverton Manor, Esmé entreated her husband, 'You must talk to Dr Baines about your condition, Daniel. Your headaches are getting worse.'

'All I want is some peace and quiet. Why don't you go and stay with your mother for the summer?'

Esmé's eyes filled with tears. 'You haven't taken your medicine.'

'It makes me tired.' Daniel picked up his hat and jammed it on his head. It was the tallest he could find and was difficult to keep on. 'I've got some business to discuss. I should know today if I've been appointed as a magistrate.'

'You are supposed to be managing the estate. I was talking to Mrs Ponsonby from Croxley Farm the other day. She said our crop was planted too late, and we'll be lucky if it's ready to harvest before the autumn rains come.'

'She should mind her own business. Being a magistrate is an important part of managing the estate. It brings respect. My father before me was one, and he managed the estate as well.'

'He had a competent steward. The farm labourers are taking advantage of you.'

Daniel turned and slapped his crop against his hand, trying to hold on to his temper. 'Stop meddling in estate business, Esmé.'

'If it doesn't pay its way we will be replaced when Mrs Matheson's husband comes home.'

'It's not your estate, so why should you be so concerned?'

Her lips pressed into a narrow line. 'It's not yours either. It belongs to your brother. You're supposed to consult with Mrs Matheson's agent over capital expenditure.'

Daniel scowled, annoyed by her reminder of his status. 'Leave Siana out of this. I consult with the trustees who, in their turn, advise her. I would like nothing better than to consult with her personally, but she's gone traipsing off to Wales.'

'And all her words about calling on each other have come to nought, for I've never received an invitation to visit. Anyone would think she imagines she's a cut above—'

'Don't say another word against her,' Daniel warned.

A malicious look came into Esmé's eyes. 'I've been given to understand that Mrs Matheson is with child.'

The shock Daniel felt was nothing compared to the upsurge of anger which followed it. It should be his child Siana was carrying, not Francis Matheson's. Was there no end to the punishment she intended to inflict on him? The anger was replaced by self-pity. Siana would love him again. All he had to do was match the man his father had been. One day, she would come back to him. When she did; she would never escape him again.

He turned his back on his wife and left her without a word of farewell.

Outside the house, the day was warm and humid. It made the sore that had broken out on his neck itch. Resisting the urge to scratch it, Daniel ordered the black gelding to be saddled and brought round. It sidestepped as he tried to mount, dragging him several yards with one foot in the stirrup. 'Hold the damned thing still, will you?' he shouted at the stable boy, his dignity in shreds.

When he was settled in the saddle he gave the animal a touch of the crop. It surged forward, squealing with the unexpectedness of it. Daniel managed to keep his seat, but only just, as he fought to get the animal under his control. It needed a good run. He started off at a canter, then put it to the gallop, whipping at its flank to urge it on, clearing hedges as he'd seen his father do. Soon, the ginger went out of the horse and it began to foam. He waited until its breathing was laboured, then slowed it down. 'That'll teach you to try your tricks on me,' he said with satisfaction.

It had been a long time since he'd been into Dorchester. He jingled a bunch of keys in his pocket as he passed the house where he'd grown up. From an adult perspective, it seemed less grand than his childhood mind had made it, but it was pretty, built as it was of pale Portland stone and with its small-paned bow windows and pink roses rambling over the porch.

He intended to make it his place of business, with a

little pleasure thrown in when the mood took him, for it was big enough to entertain clients in. He wouldn't tell Esmé of his plans, though, for she'd only interfere.

It was market day. The place was crowded with wagons, people and street vendors. Chickens clucked, sheep baa'd and horses neighed, their stench ripe in the warmth and attracting a swarm of flies.

Soldiers of the Queen's Own Dorset Yeomanry strolled through the crowds, the silk plumes on their hats waving high. They drew the glances of the women, so handsome did they appear in their uniforms. Their presence also reassured the businessmen, who felt threatened by the occasional outbreaks of civil lawlessness brought about by the Chartist movement.

The trouble had increased since the Tolpuddle transportee, George Lovelace – now pardoned for his part in forming a union – had returned to publish his manifesto on the persecutions experienced by the Dorchester Labourers, *The Victims of Whiggery*. Victims, was it? The Cheverton labourers did as little as possible for their pay, Daniel reckoned.

Throwing the reins to a lad touting for business on the street and instructing him to cool his horse off, Daniel strode into the Antelope Hotel. Allowing his eyes to grow accustomed to the change in light, he looked around him, smiling when he saw the man he'd come to meet. Calling for a tankard of ale to quench his thirst, he shouldered through the crowd and took a seat beside him. 'Well, Oswald?'

Sir Oswald Slessor, magistrate, entrepreneur and wool merchant, a man with his fingers in many pies, smiled slightly and patted his pocket. 'Your appointment has been confirmed.'

It was as Daniel had expected, for several palms had been greased in the process. The estate trustees were a voracious bunch, honest only just past the length of their fingertips. Good business sense, they called it.

'You will need to be sworn in, but I promise you that your first case of real importance will prove to be interesting. It's a woman called Isabelle Collins. I believe she was to be wed to your father at one time.'

Daniel's hand jerked and ale spilled on to the table. 'What crime has the woman committed?'

'You haven't heard? She's charged with the murder of Hannah Collins several years ago. The deceased was married to Isabelle Collins's husband at the time.'

'And you expect me to remain impartial? Good God, man! Isabelle Collins was the cause of my mother being transported for a crime she didn't commit.'

His companion's forehead creased into a frown. 'You were appointed to the bench because of your connection to Sir Edward Forbes. You will be expected to examine the facts put before you in a fair and proper manner. It wouldn't do to remind people that your mother is a convicted felon, especially since the magistrate who heard the case has considerable influence.'

'Gossip has it that Isabelle Collins set that fire herself.'

'I know. Regrettably, for I liked your mother, that case has been tried and the defendant declared guilty. I have to say, Daniel, that the verdict was due partially to your ineptitude in properly cross-examining the witnesses at the time. To make up for your inexperience, a light sentence was handed down. You should have kept me on to defend her. For your own good, it's best not to point fingers of blame, or suggest that your mother was unfairly dealt with.'

Daniel swallowed his ire. 'Of course, sir, I understand.'

'I hope you do, Daniel. Be discreet and doors will open to you. Do you have premises in town?'

Attacked by guilt, Daniel murmured, 'There's a house in the upper end of West Street, where I was raised. It's been tenanted since my father's death, but has recently been vacated. I'll use that for my chambers and occasional residence, when I'm not at Cheverton.' He checked the gold hunter watch he wore. Once his father's, he'd discovered it in a drawer in the bedroom. It was engraved with the Forbes crest and kept perfect time. 'In fact, I'm expecting an interior decorator in an hour, to discuss its refurbishment.'

'Good, I'll send my clerk round there with the details of the case when you've settled in.' Slessor nodded. 'The charge is based on a series of drawings made by a deaf mute who witnessed the crime, and the evidence of the arresting constables. It's a case of the defendant's word against theirs. Good luck with it. People will be watching you on this one, so make sure you're well prepared.'

A little time later, Daniel wandered through the empty house of his childhood, an interior designer in tow.

'Will your wife be living here, sir?' the man asked him.

Trying to sound more modest than he felt, Daniel implied instead of lied. 'My residence is Cheverton

Manor. This house will be my professional offices. I'd like ivory embossed wallpaper in this room. And some comfortable chairs and a desk with accessories. What do you think of rosewood?'

'A good choice, sir. May I recommend leather for the seating? Two wing chairs would be welcoming for either side of the fireplace, where you might wish to share a brandy or two with a client in the winter. Leather suggests power and opulence, and it doesn't show the dirt easily.'

Daniel, who'd been toying with the idea of velvet, smiled a little. 'Yes, I was going to suggest leather myself. We'll need a *chaise longue* to accommodate the ladies' skirts.'

'Ah yes, skirts.' The man looked up from his notebook, an oily smile on his face. 'May I ask if you'll be needing a maid, sir?'

'You have someone in mind?'

The man's eyes narrowed a trifle. 'I know of one or two females who may be suitable. What is your preference?'

'I prefer someone young. They're much more . . . *adaptable* than older women. On the slim side, with dark hair and green eyes, if possible.'

The man smiled. 'I know someone exactly like that. A pretty little thing, too. She has just turned sixteen and is an orphan.'

'Is she . . . *a good girl?*'

'Of course, sir. She has lived in the workhouse dormitory for several years, where my brother and his wife work. They keep a good eye on the girls in their charge. There will be a small handling fee for the girl's release.'

Wasn't there always! 'I want someone who is willing, and able to *socialize* with my guests, on occasion.'

The man held his gaze. 'The girl will be made aware of what her duties will entail. She will need clothing suitable for the occasion, you understand? Will you require a bed, sir?'

'Certainly,' Daniel muttered, grinning to himself. It would be convenient to have a girl on the premises.

By the end of the day, Daniel had spent a great deal of his young half-brother's inheritance, including the fee charged by a house of easement in a back street – where the wondrously talented Jasmine had once resided. The slut had given him a dose of the clap in his youth, but luckily it had cleared up quickly. Jasmine was long gone, now.

But, as he said to the trustee, when the man questioned the amount of money he'd spent, 'The Dorchester house needs to be kept in good order. And who better to keep it in order than the little baronet's closest blood kin?'

Which reminded him. Perhaps he ought to go and see his siblings one of these days. But he might wait until Siana returned home, so he could see for himself if she'd given birth to an infant.

It was almost dusk when he set out for home. A couple of snifters of brandy had cured his headache, and his mind was clearer than it had been in months. He was looking forward to his dinner, too.

He passed the thresher on the way home, a pile of

rusting junk. He should ask the blacksmith if it could be repaired. He shrugged. The labourers would only wreck it again, as they had when his father had first bought it, regarding it as a threat to their employment – although they seemed a lazy lot of swine, who didn't want to work, anyway.

He supposed he must do something about the estate one of these days. It was inconvenient, Jed Hawkins up and leaving so suddenly to run after his mother. Had Daniel been properly informed about the work involved in running the estate, he would have insisted that a proper steward be hired. Now, they couldn't afford one.

'I love your mother and we intend to be wed,' Hawkins had told him. 'I'm going to follow her to Australia and look after her whilst she serves her sentence.'

That had been a surprise to Daniel. He didn't know whether he approved of the liaison or not, but at least she'd be less of an embarrassment if she was respectably married.

It had been Esmé who'd prudently made sure his mother's money was placed in his care. Not that there was much of it left now, for he'd lost a great deal of it gambling and, so far, had not recouped his losses. His luck would turn, eventually.

Daniel's mount seemed reluctant to move. 'Come on, you damned nag,' he cried out in frustration and slashed it across the rump. It bucked, throwing him to the ground, where he sprawled in the dust. The horse turned to stare at him.

As he rose to his feet, a red mist seemed to surround

him. Grabbing the horse by its rein he lifted his crop and brought it down hard across its back. It began to squeal as he thrashed at it, but Daniel couldn't stop. Soon, welts appeared on its back and blood trickled from its wounds.

When he'd exhausted his temper he saw that a small crowd had gathered. Ignoring them, Daniel scrambled into the saddle and rode the gelding as hard as he could, until the breath was a harsh rattle in its throat. Then he slowed it to a canter. For the rest of the way the horse behaved beautifully, proving to him that it just needed a firm hand. Throwing the reins to a waiting servant, he strode into the manor, his mood foul.

Esmé was in the drawing room when he went in. She looked up, her face tight and drawn. 'You were gone a long time,' she accused.

'Was I?'

Her nose wrinkled. 'You smell of horse.'

How unpleasant she was. 'Why did you marry me, Esmé?'

She appeared taken aback for a moment. 'You know why, because I love you.'

'Then why don't you show it?'

'I . . . don't know what you mean.'

'Yes, you do.' He crossed to where she sat. 'A man needs comfort from his wife. You offer me none.'

Her faced coloured. 'You know I'm unable to bear children.'

'A fact you and your parents conveniently forgot to inform me of before we wed. You've changed since then, the softness has gone from you.'

She turned her face away, murmuring, 'That's because you're cruel to me, Daniel. You mock me in company, torture me with your love for another man's wife and . . . *entertain* one of the servants under my roof.'

His finger found the niche under her chin and turned her face around. 'I do it because you show me no love.'

She tried to twist her head away when his mouth covered hers, but he kept her there whilst he kissed her. She began to gag.

Withdrawing, he gazed at her for a moment, a sneer twisting his face. Then he back handed her across the face – not hard enough to physically hurt her, but to show her who was in control. Giving a yelp, she cringed away from him, then stared up at him anxiously. The fear in her eyes was entirely satisfying. He realized he'd always been too soft with her.

'You've forgotten to take your medication,' she whimpered.

'I'll decide if I've forgotten to take it. I'll expect you in my room tonight,' he said, and turned and walked away from her, slamming the door behind him.

Esmé knew she couldn't refuse him. Steeling herself, she waited as long as possible before she presented herself to her husband, hoping he'd be asleep.

But he wasn't. 'Now,' he said, smiling meanly at her. 'We must do something to loosen you up. A little brandy, perhaps,' and he slopped some into a glass.

'You know I don't drink spirituous liquor, Daniel.'

'You don't do anything.' He surveyed her from head

to foot, the dowdy grey gown and prissy cap she wore were designed to repel his advances. 'D'you know, I've never seen you naked. Take your clothes off, let's have a look at you.'

She gasped. 'No, Daniel. It's indecent.'

'I'll decide what's indecent.' His fist bunched the material of her gown. 'Take it off or I'll beat you.'

Trembling, her fingers went to the buttons. She stood there, her body exposed to his critical glance, her hands covering herself as best she could. He came to where she stood, held the glass to her mouth and tipped it. 'I don't want to hurt you, Esmé. Drink. I've put my medication in it, so you'll be nice and relaxed.'

She obeyed, choking on the fiery liquid, hoping it would make her unconscious so she wouldn't have to experience what he intended to do to her as he reached out for her.

But it didn't make her unconscious. It relaxed her muscles, so she was powerless to stop his debauchery of her, even if she wanted to. The loathsome contact of his lips and hands seemed to go on for ever. She couldn't find the energy to cry out when he hurt her.

He swore horribly when he remained unaffected by her. Finally, he withdrew from her. His lips curled as he delivered the final indignity. 'You wouldn't be able to find employment as a whore, for there's nothing about you designed to arouse a man.'

Her love for him teetered on the edge of hate as she dredged up a modicum of spirit. 'Daniel, there's something wrong with you. What are those sores on your neck? I'm calling in the doctor tomorrow.'

His eyes narrowed as he stared at her, then he began to laugh.

'Stop it,' she whispered, backing away from him, her gown clutched in front of her in defence. 'I'd starve rather than let you touch me like that again.'

The laughter stopped as abruptly as it started. 'Would you, indeed?' he said.

From time to time, supply outnumbered demand for prisoners in New South Wales. So, after a long and frustrating wait in port, the ship carrying Elizabeth was turned around to head across Bass Strait for Van Diemen's Land.

In the women's quarters, Elizabeth lay head to foot with two other prisoners. 'Five more days,' she said wearily. 'We're already into May. Will this journey never end?'

'I hope there's a doctor at the other end. I think I've got the clap.'

'Share and share alike on this ship, I reckon,' the other one muttered. 'Sometimes, I wonder if the game is worth the coin.'

They had shared the same bunk since they'd left England five months previously. Both of her companions were London prostitutes with raucous laughs and very little sympathy for someone like Elizabeth.

'You're a fool if you don't take the opportunity to earn a few comforts from the crew,' one of them said, and the other laughed.

'Parson's daughter, ain't yer? That must account fer it.'

Neither of them had found the small cache of coins or the ring Jed had given her, which were sewn into the hem of her skirt. They'd pawed through the rest of her possessions, however, taking anything they thought might be useful to them. Elizabeth had been powerless to stop them.

Slim to begin with, Elizabeth had lost weight, for as the journey had progressed the food had spoiled, and most of the time her stomach had rejected it. Her flesh was sunk into shadows under her cheekbones, her eyes were weary. Her menses had ceased too, something she was grateful for, because the smell of women who couldn't tend adequately to their own hygiene was rank enough already. Sometimes, she thought it might be nice to die.

The flame of her hair still burnt defiantly, though. For the sake of convenience she kept it braided. But it was infected with lice, as was her body.

As usual, she spent a fitful night. Morning brought her the opportunity to snatch some fresh air. Carefully, she leaned against the door jamb, a reeking night bucket in her hand, trying to find her balance on the bucking deck, so as not to spill her burden before she got to the side of the ship and emptied it overboard. Perhaps she would throw herself after it, for she didn't think she could stand the conditions she'd found herself in for much longer.

She'd heard that their destination was The Cascades, the female factory in a town called Hobart. Rumour said it was already overcrowded, so she wasn't expecting much. The air smelled wonderful after the closeness of the women's quarters, and the breeze was brisk and invigorating against her skin. The clean smell made her dizzy for a moment. Finding the opportunity she tottered to the side and stood upwind, throwing the contents of the bucket into the sea. Seagulls dived as it dispersed and she gave a little shudder. Then she saw it. Land! They were sailing parallel to it. Thank God, thank God!

She forgot dying. Instead, she thought of Jed Hawkins, a good man who loved her enough to offer her the respectability of his name. She thought of Susannah too, who was being cared for and loved by another. Then she thought of Daniel, her son.

Why hadn't she noticed the weakness of his character before? What had driven him to trick her out of her money, then betray her in court? Somehow, she would survive this. She would demand an explanation from him. Her spine straightened. No, she most certainly would not give in to despair now. She had too much to live for – and Jed would not be too far behind her.

Suddenly, a wave reared up in front of her, as grey as dishwater and flecked with little pieces of brown seaweed. The deck canted and she lost her balance. Tumbling over and over she slid into a hatch, then somersaulted down some stairs. There was a crack as the bone in her shoulder snapped, and the pain of it made her scream. Her head flopped against something unyielding and hard, and the day became dark and quiet.

When she woke, Elizabeth didn't know where she was. She was not on the ship, for the restless motion of the past few months had ceased. She felt rested, but her head throbbed and her tongue was so dry it clove to the roof of her mouth.

For a moment, she imagined she was in her own bed and was waking from a dreadful dream. Then she felt the thrusting pain of her shoulder and knew she was fooling herself. She lay there for a while, trying to make sense of the alien sounds. The click of a door latch, the clanging sound of tin against tin and the low, muffled grumble of a man's voice.

Opening her eyes was a slow process. The penetration of light pained them and the lids seemed to be glued together. Finally, she managed it. She could see that she was in a room with high windows.

She groaned with the thumping ache of her head. A man came across, stared down at her. 'Ah, you're awake.' He held up some fingers. 'How many?'

Her sight was blurred a little, but she could get by. 'Three. Where am I?'

'The female factory in Hobart Town. Let me take a look at that head.'

Someone knocked at the door and it opened. A minute later there was a shuffling sound. 'I've brought Piper, sir. The boys gave him no trouble. Do you want my report now, sir?'

'Unshackle him. I need him to help process the new female prisoners, and would prefer to hear the report from him, first-hand.'

There was a metallic rattle of keys in the background as the man's fingers kneaded firmly at the sore spot at the back of her head. 'Hmmmm,' he said. 'The skull could be fractured.' He turned his head slightly, speaking to someone behind him.

'How did you find the lads at Point Puer?'

'One of the boys nearly died from the flogging he received from one of the warders. It was too savage and he wasn't fit to begin with.'

His voice was gruff, but Elizabeth thought it vaguely familiar.

'It happens occasionally. Blood poisoning, was it?'

'Aye, I suppose you could call it that. I'd call it attempted murder. The boy is only nine years old and he was flayed to the bone.'

'I'll talk to the warder. At least the lads have been separated from the adult convicts, now. That's progress. And if I were you, I'd keep opinions like that strictly to yourself, for it won't bring you any favours. Come round here, man, I'd like to see what you make of this. This female fell down a hatch on the ship bringing her here. She sustained a fractured collar bone and a heavy blow to the head, and has been unconscious for several days. In that time the swelling has subsided a bit, but she's fevered. She's just regained consciousness.'

Gentler fingers probed at Elizabeth's aching head. The man's eyes were preoccupied as he felt the swelling. His hair was dark, grey at the temples, and unkempt, as was his beard. He wore some coarse prison garment, but it was clean. Another convict, she supposed, but what was he doing in the female factory, and why was he examining her?

'There's no discharge from the ears. The swelling is localized and should subside of its own accord. I would say she suffers from severe concussion of the brain from the force of the blow.' He didn't look at her directly. 'Are you having any trouble with your vision?'

'It's blurred a little.'

'That should clear up in a day or two.' He turned to the man in charge. 'The patient should rest for several days with her arm in a sling to allow the collar bone to knit, and a strict eye should be kept on her recovery from the coma.'

'And the fever?'

'Not serious. An infection caused by parasites, I'd say. She should be deloused and kept isolated, in case she's been bitten by the fleas of plague-carrying rats.'

Elizabeth watched him give a faint grin when the other man took a step back, holding a linen handkerchief in front of his nose. It smelt faintly of lavender.

'Good. Exactly what my diagnosis would have been. I'll make a doctor out of you before your sentence is served, Piper, just see if I don't. You seem to have an aptitude for it.'

'It's extremely good of you to say so, considering I'm already more qualified than yourself,' he said, his manner so dry that Elizabeth stared hard at him.

Where did she know his voice from? She put a hand on his arm, made a noise. He looked directly at her then, and he frowned. His eyes were grey, like those of . . .? Was she dreaming? 'Francis?' she whispered. 'What are you doing here, and why is that man calling you Piper?'

251

His mouth stretched into a smile that was totally recognizable. 'Elizabeth? Oh, my dear, you've lost so much weight I hardly recognized you.'

'I could say the same for you.' Tears began to tumble from her eyes. 'I was afraid I'd never see those I love again. Now, I see your dear, familiar face, and it gives me hope.'

The other man stepped between them, his eyes sharp as he gazed down at her. 'Am I to conclude that you know this prisoner?'

'Of course I know him. He's Dr Francis Matheson, and he's wed to my dearest friend.'

'I see.' The assistant surgeon looked agitated as he turned towards Francis. 'In view of this development, it seems I have urgent business to attend to with the commandant. In the meantime, you will be separated from the female prisoner and placed in charge of a warder. No doubt, the commandant will want to question her and there can't be any suspicion of collusion between you. You understand, uh . . . Piper?'

'Matheson,' Francis prompted, a smile splitting his face apart. 'Dr Francis Matheson.'

The assistant surgeon grinned. 'Ah, yes . . . well, that remains to be proved, *Doctor*.'

Elizabeth could have sworn she saw tears glinting in Francis's eyes when he whispered, 'Thank you, Elizabeth. I'm for ever in your debt. How long is your sentence?'

'Four years. But you, Francis . . . it's obvious you've done nothing to warrant being held here. I will swear on the bible as to your character if it will help to obtain your release.'

But Francis wondered. The commandant was a cautious man, not easily convinced. He would probably demand proof, not just take Elizabeth's word for it.

As it was, Francis was granted a conditional pardon by the prison board, which meant he was a free man, but couldn't return to England until his innocence had been proved.

He stayed in Hobart as the guest of a Quaker family until Elizabeth was well enough to travel, then having nowhere else to go, he had her assigned as his servant and set out for his brother Will's property. All they had was a spare set of clothes and a blanket apiece, provided by the prison. The Quaker family had provided him with food for the journey.

Will's property was set in hilly, wooded country, a day's journey north of Hobart, and another day to the east. It was a long walk, through rugged country. They slept in the wild, their rest disturbed by strange barks and snuffles, and a procession of small animals that shuffled through the undergrowth.

Francis was pleasantly surprised by the property, which consisted of a low, sprawling house built of wood, several cabins and some stables. Land had been cleared around the house, trees had been felled and horses grazed on the lush grasses. It was isolated, surrounded by thickly wooded country.

They were greeted by a man holding a rifle. 'Name your business.'

'I'm Francis Matheson. My companion is Elizabeth Ayres.'

'Assigned?'

Francis nodded. 'My guest, nevertheless.'

The man stared hard at him for a moment or two, then relaxed and held out his hand. 'You have the look of your brother. I'm Bart Stowe. This is my wife, Jean. We own the adjoining property and were partners with your brother in a logging business.'

Francis bowed to the worn-looking woman. 'Your servant, ma'am.'

She blushed, her hand going to her hair in an unconscious feminine gesture. 'Our eldest son worked for William. He's been looking after the place since Will died. You'll find it in good order.'

'I'm indebted to you. Why the gun?'

'It's wise to take precautions. The logging is done by assigned convict labour. Sometimes they escape and band together.' Bart Stowe gazed around him, calling out, 'You can come out now.'

There were three sons, strapping young men of various ages. A girl named Emmy smiled at Elizabeth. About eight years of age, she resembled her mother with her dark eyes and brown hair.

'I'll show you the house,' Jean said, smiling at Elizabeth, for she seemed genuinely pleased to have some female company, and the fact that Elizabeth was an assigned convict didn't seem to bother her. The two women walked towards the low building, talking together, Emmy skipping after them. The action seemed so normal after their former hardships.

Young though she was, the girl reminded Francis of his own daughters. He blinked away his tears as he was filled with a great yearning to see them again.

14

The old woman came to the house called *Bryn Dwr* late in the afternoon. Nobody observed her arrival. Siana found her seated on a stool outside the door, her face turned to the east, where the long shadows cast by the mountains reached towards the border.

It was old that face, her skin a lacework of lines, like cracked glaze on a piece of delicate antique porcelain. Her eyes were milky, her hair fine white strands escaping from under a white linen bonnet, topped by a high-crowned black beaver hat tied by a ribbon under her chin.

Her black gown, a lace collar its only decoration, hung slack on her wasted frame. Her boots were old and scuffed, but sturdy. Siana had worn worse.

'Can you offer an old woman a glass of water?' she said, her high fluting voice making the hairs on Siana's arms stand on end.

Fetching her a cup of water, Siana took the stool beside her whilst she drank it, excitement churning in her, for she recognized herself in the old woman's face. Finally, she said, 'I bid you welcome, Great-grandmother Lewis.'

'You know me, then?'

'As you know me. Megan is dead now.'

The woman's hand touched against hers, her fingers as soft as a butterfly alighting on a flower petal. 'How did my Megan name you, girl?'

Taking the cross from her neck, Siana placed it in the woman's palm. Her crooked old fingers ran lightly over it and she smiled. 'Siana, is it? She named you after me, then. I thought she would.'

'Will you stay?' Siana said, trying to hide to sob in her voice.

'Until they come for me . . . and they will, for by now they'll know I have gone, and where. They're unsettled, knowing you are here, for you remind them of their own sin.'

Siana made a small, angry sound in her throat. 'I have the right to be here. My father, Gruffydd Evans, left me this house.'

The old woman spat on the ground. 'Gruffydd Evans. Your father, is it? A way with words, that man, and a soul of blackness. The devil entered his soul in the womb and he was born with a flaming tongue and a dark caul. He is not worthy of this place and it rejected him. It is the *Gwin Dwr*, the place of the virgin souls.'

'I don't understand. What's the significance of *Gwin Dwr*?'

'During the time of the border wars the men hid their young daughters from the marauding English soldiers.

When the soldiers discovered their hiding place they dragged them out and used them for sport. Afterwards, their throats were cut and they were thrown into the hidden pool yonder. Their blood turned the water into wine.'

Marcus, seated on a log and whittling on a piece of wood, smiled to himself, for the red colour of the water was caused by iron oxides leaching from the rock.

Maryse had come from the house to listen. Staring at the women, her eyes intense, she asked her. 'What's the rest of the legend?'

Great-grandmother Lewis slanted her head towards Maryse. 'Little one, only those who have been truly sinned against can drink of the *Gwin Dwr*. But they must have the courage to enter the pool too, so they can be cleansed of their sin inside and out. The water is bottomless and the spirit of the virgins will drag down those who are impure of mind.'

There was a moment of silence when the wind stopped its sigh, the hens their clucking and the stream its rill. There was a moment when the glow of the sky was dimmed and the world stopped. A great dread filled Siana, and all she could hear was the primitive beat of the earth in her ears, and the softer rhythm of her heart, frail in comparison.

Then all became as it was before.

Great-grandmother Lewis took Siana's face between her hands and kissed her mouth. Her breath was scented with camomile flowers. 'Do not fear now you've come face to face with the Welshness in you, Siana mine. The gods of the earth demand a reckoning for the favour they bestow. There will be a hard price exacted for the legacy Gruffydd Evans tried to give you, for nobody can own this place, and that he would deny.'

After the others had gone to their beds, they talked long into the night, the old woman in a comfortable chair and Siana seated at her knee. She told the old woman of her mother, Megan Lewis, and of her own life since she'd died. It was hard to remember Megan now as being a mother to her, alive and loving, though it was not so very long ago. The anger in her voice told of her rage for the manner of her mother's passing. 'Her life was one of degradation, and her end reflected it.'

'So it was written in the smoke. But Megan's at peace now and you have your own journey to make. The first man you married . . . did he satisfy the pagan side of you?'

When Siana gave a soft laugh, the old woman chuckled. 'My own man had the wickedness in him to please a woman, too, for he knew of the secret desires a woman rarely reveals. It's good when the body is satisfied as well as the heart.'

Siana felt the stirring of her own body. 'And it's hard to live without both.'

'Pah! A woman need not follow the rules set down for her by men. She is the soul of the earth and can satisfy her desires as easily as a man. She just has to pick the right man and be careful not to involve her heart.'

A mixture of shock and excitement stirred in Siana. She couldn't imagine ever being unfaithful to Francis. 'How old are you, Grandmother?'

Her question was rewarded by a toothless smile. 'As

old as the earth is young. Now we've met, I can go to my rest. But you will see my face in every flower and blade of grass, reflected on the surface of the pond in summer and flying in the air with the wings of a butterfly.' She reached out to caress Siana's face, her fingertips silky upon her skin. 'There's bonny you are, *cariad*, just like your mam. There are sorrows for you to face, but you are possessed of a strong mind and heart.' She hesitated for a moment, then said quietly. 'Last night I dreamed of ripples widening on a pool.'

'What is the meaning of the dream, Grandmother?'

The old woman gave a shiver. 'I know not, *cariad*. We shall talk about this no more.' Folding her hands into her sleeves, her head nodded forward and she fell asleep.

'You're lying; you do know,' Siana whispered to her as she tucked a blanket around her, but she received no answer.

They came for the old woman the next morning, an upright man of weathered appearance and a thin, dried-up stick of a woman, who stared at Siana with both curiosity and dislike in her eyes.

She didn't deserve such hostility from a stranger, family or not. Siana calmly held the woman's gaze until it was turned aside.

'Begone, girl,' the man said. 'We do not want you here.'

'Your authority is not recognized by me, Grand-father, for even though I was not born at the time, you lost my respect when you cast my mother from your hearth.'

'She was a sinner.'

'And you're a hypocrite, for you do not practise that which you preach. My mother and I would have died from cold and hunger if another hadn't taken us in.'

'Be careful, girl, lest you be sent on your journey like your mother was.'

He was a hard man, but she wouldn't yield to his bullying ways. 'I will stay here until I'm ready to leave. I have a pistol inside. If you come here spouting your threats again, I'll shoot you through your miserable black heart. Now, get off my property and don't come back.'

Her lie must have sounded convincing, for his face paled and he took a step backwards. The old woman spat angry words at him in their native tongue and he remained quiet.

Siana exchanged a hug with her great-grandmother. Tears fell from her eyes. 'I'm so glad we've met. You'll always live in my heart.'

The woman gently touched her wet cheeks with her finger. 'Walk with my love, *cariad*. Stay strong.' As she turned away, they both knew they'd never meet again.

As the trio walked off down the hill, the mist poured down over the mountain from above, shrouding the land in a clammy whiteness which hid them from Siana's sight. Shivering, she returned to the house.

The three women were comfortable living in *Bryn Dwr*. Marcus shared the meals they cooked. He brought firewood, helped carry water for their baths, and spent time in their company.

Sometimes, he disappeared into the hills above them for a day or two, coming back with a leg of pork, a flitch of bacon or a side of mutton.

Often, he sat with them in the evening, conversing on many subjects, for he was a learned man. He drew Maryse out of herself, making her laugh, all the while keeping his hands occupied as he carved an intricate design of twisted ribbons, hearts and flowers into a piece of wood.

He found repairs to carry out, too. A wall from which the stones had tumbled, a hinge hanging on a door, a slate or two misplaced by the wind on the roof.

The women shared the work of the house between them. Maryse seemed to enjoy the simple domestic chores that fell her way. She learned to pluck and dress a chicken, milk the cow, skin a rabbit, cook a stew and bake a loaf of bread. It was a time of waiting, of companionship. She and Siana worked together in the vegetable plot. As their friendship deepened, so their hands grew dirty and rough. Neither of them cared.

Maryse never mentioned the child she was carrying, nor complained about the burden her body had become. But one night the girl woke Siana from slumber. 'My time has come, I think,' she said, her voice unemotional

And that time had come early. The girl's stoicism during her ordeal surprised Siana. Hardly a sound passed her lips, though the labour went on for a day and a night. It was as if she was doing penance for her sins. Perspiration flooded her body, which was too rigid with the effort to lend itself to a comfortable birth. She gave a low, wild moan of painful release as she finally expelled the infant from her body.

The boy hardly made a noise as he entered the world, just gave a little whimper as if he'd resigned himself to his rejection in the womb. As he closed his eyes and slept, Siana's heart went out to him. He was a handsome, robust child. To be abandoned by his mother with an uncertain future to face and with no name to call his own, seemed too cruel a fate. Yet she couldn't blame Maryse, who'd suffered so much that it wasn't her fault that she could never love her child.

The girl wouldn't look at her infant, but turned her exhausted face away and murmured. 'I don't want to know anything about it, what it is, or where it goes. I must face the future as if this had never happened, but I can never become any man's wife, now. To do so would be to deceive him.'

Siana knew she couldn't farm the boy out without satisfying herself that he'd be cared for adequately. She told the lie she'd prepared, but even to herself it sounded false. 'The infant is dead, Maryse. He was too small to survive for long.'

Maryse said nothing, but Siana knew she'd swallowed the lie, because she'd wanted to.

She signalled her intention to Rosie before the child could wake and make his presence known. Rosie nodded. Wrapping the child in a square of linen, Siana took him outside.

Something about him reminded her of Francis; the set of his mouth, perhaps. He opened his eyes. They were marbled with the Matheson grey. His hair was a sparse, dark patch as he automatically turned his head this way and that, trying to nuzzle against her breast like a puppy.

Her breasts, ready with their bounty for her own infant, sensed the call of him. They throbbed and wept milky tears as he sucked against the flimsy barrier of her bodice. The unbearable contentment of the sensation was hard to stand when the future of this innocent was uncertain.

She blinked her tears away when Marcus came down the hill, an enquiry in his eyes.

'The infant is a boy. I have told Maryse that he died. If he's to survive, I must take him to where he will be raised, at once.'

'You cannot walk all that way when the birth of your own infant is so near.'

She smiled a little at that. 'The farmhouse is ten miles this side of Monmouth. I have the endurance to walk there and back, and my baby is not due for another two weeks.'

Marcus sighed. 'I cannot let you go alone, you might fall or lose your way.'

'I'd appreciate your company, then. Hold the boy whilst I pack us some food to eat on the way.'

The day was fair, the way downhill was easy. She swapped their food for the child and, wrapping the infant in her mother's shawl, tied him against her chest. She tried to fight the feeling of pity the thought of his future kept raising in her, especially when she caught sight of their destination, a grim-looking stone farmhouse in the distance. His life would be hard there, if he survived his childhood.

Then the farmhouse was obscured as they descended into a line of rowan and wild cherry trees. She stopped as a sudden thought occurred to her. There were lots of unscrupulous people about. Would his foster parents allow him to die of starvation once they had the purse?

She eased her back with her hands, letting Marcus go on ahead. It had started to ache from the exercise. She would stop for a short rest when they emerged from the wooded area. She was carrying her child low, so it was not really a cumbersome burden, but she'd not walked this far for a long time.

They'd reached the slope down into the valley and were about to emerge from the trees, when, without warning, the water cradling her own child came rushing from between her thighs to soak her skirts. Immediately, the pressure of the infant's imminent birth became apparent to her.

'Marcus!' she called out to the figure up ahead.

He came back at a run, gazed at her soaked skirts. 'I'll fetch help from the farmhouse.'

'There won't be time.' He took the boy from her, placing him, still asleep, gently on the ground in his shawl.

Siana fell to her hands and knees, her stomach muscles convulsing with the urgent need to expel the infant. Fifteen minutes later her daughter slid from her, complete with the afterbirth. The child was stillborn, her body floppy and mottled blue. She'd been strangled in the womb by her own umbilical cord. Nothing Siana could do could revive her. Distressed, she cuddled the infant against her heart.

'Breathe for me,' she cried out, her heart set to break as she called her the name she'd chosen for a daughter. 'Live for me, sweet Elen.'

She gave a small, keening cry when Marcus took the tiny, limp body from her and placed it to one side – though she knew it must be done.

'You must look after the living,' he said gently, filling her empty arms with the boy.

The other one opened his eyes and seemed to stare at her, then a small, frustrated whimper came from his mouth as he nudged against her breast.

Her eyes filled with tears. But she didn't protest when Marcus loosened her bodice and placed the boy's mouth against her swollen breast. A miracle happened as his mouth closed around her. The love she'd held in store for the child of Francis, was suddenly and inexplicably transferred to his grandson. Yes, she could raise this child as her own, and nobody need ever know.

The infant was strong in his desire to feed, his suck one of desperation, as if he knew he needed to bond to the source of her love, as well as sup of her mother's milk, if he was to survive. Instinct gave him the need to reassure himself that he was wanted.

'You greedy little piglet,' she scolded, torn between laughter and tears when he belched loudly. She knew she would give him everything he needed then, and so did he, for he fell into a contented sleep.

Marcus buried the baby girl in the protective shadow of a wild cherry tree, placing stones over her grave. 'Do you need to say words over her?' he asked, as they stood looking down on it. Above them, a lark began to sing, as if her infant's soul had become a bird.

'May the womb of the earth goddess nurture my daughter, Elen,' Siana murmured, trying not to cry. It was sad that the result of her love for Francis must be left in such a lonely grave. But her daughter's tiny, peaceful face would remain a precious memory she'd hold close to her heart.

'And may the daffodils and lilies celebrate her resting place and reflect her purity every spring,' Marcus whispered.

'You have a good heart, Marcus. Thank you.'

'Not always.' He gazed down at the sleeping boy child, his eyes bleak. 'Did Miss Matheson tell you the name of the man who assaulted her?'

'There were two of them. Itinerant labourers. She could only recall their first names, but I looked them up in the estate ledgers. One was called Silas Barton, the other, Henry Ruddle.'

'They should pay for their crime.'

Alarmed, she gazed at him. This man held the happiness of the people she loved in his hands. 'For Maryse's sake, promise me you will never mention this to anyone. You mustn't go after them – but those men will be made to pay for their sin one day.'

'They most certainly will.' When Marcus gave a tiny sliver of a smile Siana shivered, for there was something slightly chilling about it. 'I understand your fears. But you can trust me, absolutely. I would die myself, rather than do or say anything to upset you or your stepdaughter. Are you recovered enough to walk?'

'I will need to attend to myself first. Perhaps you would allow me a few moments of privacy whilst I go to the stream.'

The stillborn child had been delivered easily and cleanly. Siana washed herself, then tore some strips of linen from her chemise. Filling it with the spongy moss that grew along the bank of the stream, she folded the linen over, fashioning a sling to secure it firmly between her legs and round her waist. It would absorb any moisture and keep her comfortable.

Afterwards, they ate the bread, cheese and apples they'd brought with them, and headed slowly back up the slope towards *Bryn Dwr*. The path was stony and steep, as if the hills had already begun to reject her. But she must stay another two weeks, at least, so she and Maryse could both recover from the birth of their children.

Then she would depart, and she would never willingly come back here again. The travellers could have the place. Eventually, the mountains would reclaim it. Welsh by ancestry she might be, and the pull of the place was strong, but these dark and mysterious mountains had no hold on her heart. The soft green landscape of Dorset did. The sooner she could sit at her own hearth again, the safer she would feel, and the better she would like it.

Two weeks later they were ready to depart. Marcus disappeared down the hill, to reappear the next day with the man leading the string of Welsh ponies.

But when they'd packed the luggage, Maryse was nowhere to be found.

Marcus smiled in reassurance. 'I think I know where she is. I'll go and fetch her.'

The cave of *Gwin Dwr* was reached by an opening of two boulders half buried in the hill and leaning against each other.

Maryse shivered as her eyes adjusted to the dim light. Beneath her, roughly hewn steps circled down to a pool of dark water. Shrugging from her clothes, she left them in a heap and, clad only in her chemise, carefully made her way to the bottom.

She found herself on a flat rock. Cupping her hands, she bore the water to her mouth and drank it down. It was a rusty brown rather than red, with a sharp, salty taste to it, like blood when she sucked a pricked finger. Remembering the legend, she shuddered.

The pool was bottomless, the old woman had said. She stared at the still surface, imagining herself clean and free of sin. But she must not be afraid. She sat on the edge of the rock and, finding her courage, slid off it into deep water. It was bitterly cold against her warm body, as if the source of the pool truly was the tears of the virgins, released from the frozen heart of the mountains above her.

Under she went, floating down and down into numbing darkness. Then something brushed against her ankles, as if caressing fingers had tangled in her chemise. They held her fast.

She tried not to panic and fight it, though her chest burned from holding her breath in. Her head and ears began to throb, and she prayed the *Gwin Dwr* would let her live. Finally she could hold her breath no more. It broke from her mouth and nose in a stream of silver bubbles and floated up into the gloom.

Suddenly she floated free. She began to drift upwards, until through the water she could see a faint light. As she emerged through the surface into the cave she sucked a deep, harsh breath into her lungs.

He was waiting on the rock for her, the man with eyes of darkness who could see into her soul. Even in the dim light she could see the anger in their depths.

'You needn't have worried,' she said, light-headed with the relief of her survival. She took the hand he offered, rising from the water when he turned his head away, her chemise clinging to her shivering body.

'I was watching the bubbles rise. I thought I might have to dive in and rescue you. There are tree roots that can trap you under the water.'

'Were you afraid for me?'

'Terrified.' Smiling now, he handed over her clothing, then turned his back to her whilst she dressed herself. Afterwards, he braided her damp hair, his fingers swift and sure. When he followed her up the steps and into the sunshine, it struck her as odd that she hadn't felt embarrassed by his closeness.

She turned her face up to the warmth of the sun for a few seconds, sighing with pleasure. 'The *Gwin Dwr* was so cold.'

'I know. I was fool enough to bathe there myself, once.'

'Had you sins to wash away, then?'

He chuckled. 'No doubt I have gathered more to me

since then, and will do so again.' He held out the carving he'd been working on. 'It's time for us to leave, but before we join the others, I want to offer you this gift.'

'It's exquisite,' she said, her finger running over the intricate work. 'What does it represent?'

'It's a Welsh custom, a love spoon. The man carves it for his sweetheart when he calls on her, as a token of his esteem.'

Her heart leaped, then crashed. The bowl of the spoon was heart shaped. Two hearts, their initials carved on them, were caught by a twisting ribbon threaded with flowers in the talons of an eagle. She blushed and averted her eyes, holding it back out to him. 'You know I cannot accept such a gift.'

'You've been in the *Gwin Dwr*. That took a great deal of courage, for you offered yourself to the mountain to be cleansed, when it might have claimed you.'

'It's only a legend.' But she remembered the gentle fingers holding her captive under the water for a short time, and she shivered.

'You're too young to close your heart to love, Maryse.'

It was the first time he'd called her by her first name. It tripped softly and tenderly from his tongue, making her afraid again. 'I'm not worthy of it.'

'You judge yourself too harshly.'

She tried to retreat behind formality. 'I regret, I cannot allow myself to accept your offer, Mr Ibsen. Though I do believe I could have enjoyed the nomadic life you lead.'

Laughter glittered over the dark surface of his eyes.

'One day, when you are a little older, I'll appear before you in a different guise. Perhaps you'll be dazzled by me. Do not discard me so easily, Maryse. Keep the token as a symbol of our friendship. I hope you will think of me now and then, and remember me as a man who holds you in the highest esteem.'

'I will certainly remember you with . . . affection.'

'Thank you for that.' Taking her hand in his, he placed a kiss in the palm before leading her down the hill to where the others waited.

Rosie looked slightly sour, as if she'd like to have told her off for delaying them. Siana was smiling down at her new son, who was wrapped in her mother's old shawl and snuggled as close to her heart as he could be. Her smile widened when she looked up and saw Maryse. Although she struggled against it, Maryse experienced a small moment of regret for her own lost infant.

But though she might never experience motherhood, she could be a good and loving sister. The new member of the family was a dear little thing. His only resemblance to Siana that she could see was his sparse patch of dark hair. The Matheson look was strong in him.

She placed a kiss on his forehead and laughed when his skin wrinkled into a frown. 'My brother looks so much like dear Papa, especially when he frowns. When will he be given a name?'

Siana exchanged a quick glance with Marcus before she answered her. 'I thought, perhaps, that you'd like to choose one for him before we leave.'

Feeling honoured, Maryse gazed up at the house. 'I think he should be called Bryn, after the house, because he was born here. And Francis after Papa, who will be so proud of him when he returns.'

'Bryn Francis Matheson. A good name for a son. I like it.'

Maryse's hand closed over the spoon in her pocket and she slid a shy, wondering glance at Marcus, who had turned away to check the luggage. He was making sure it was evenly balanced and comfortably placed on the ponies.

Was it possible this man could show an interest in her, knowing what he did? Or was he just trying to make her feel better about herself?

As they descended from the hills, she decided it was the latter. She was pleased to think he didn't truly love her, because he was a good man who deserved someone better.

As they'd returned early, Josh wouldn't be waiting for them at the appointed place. Instead, they secured seats on one of the fast mail coaches out of Bristol.

'Where will you go now?' Siana asked Marcus just before they boarded.

'To Cambridge to complete my studies.'

Her eyes widened a little at that. 'I hope we will see you again?'

Glancing past her to Maryse, he gave a little smile. 'My intention is to visit you in the future, for my heart remains with your stepdaughter.'

Lightly touching his cheek with her fingertip, Siana

whispered, 'Then I will try and keep you alive in her memory.'

The door was fastened, the whip cracked over the horses' heads and they set off, their speed becoming a cracking pace when they cleared the city.

A few hours later they were passing through Cheverton Estate. Siana gazed with dismay at the corn fields. It was a poor crop this year, the wheat ears looked sparse, and the field should have been much higher.

There were two months to go before the harvesting started, but unless the summer lingered into September it would not bring in any profit.

But she couldn't worry about it now, for she was longing to see her home and family again.

It was nearly dark when they reached Poole, just in time to hire a carriage to take them up the hill. Home had never looked so dear to her.

Maryse went to her room, fell into her bed and went straight to sleep.

Ashley and Susannah were both asleep. Siana gazed down at them, wanting to sit and watch them sleep until morning. They remained blissfully unaware when she kissed their flushed cheeks.

Daisy and Goldie were almost asleep, but they shed their sleepiness as soon as they saw her.

'Mamma,' Daisy whispered, and the pair raced across the room together, hurling themselves into her waiting arms.

'I've missed you so much.' She hugged them close,

then after a few moments led them through to her bedroom to introduce them to Bryn.

Being made comfortable by Rosie, Bryn was red in the face, punching at the air and giving impatient cries, for it was way past his feeding time.

'He's ugly,' Daisy said, 'and he smells.'

Goldie gave her a dirty look. 'So do you.'

'I do not. You do, and your hair is horrid, like carrots.'

Fists settled on hips. 'Well, I like him.'

'I like him better'n you do, even if he is ugly.'

Bryn started to yell, and the argument ceased when the two girls gazed at each other and grimaced.

Siana tried not to laugh. 'Back to bed, the pair of you.'

They went, united in a common cause, Daisy stating, 'I'm not going to have any babies when I grow up.'

'Nor me. They're too noisy. Mamma must have got him from Wales.' Goldie's voice dropped. 'He has a tail, like Ashley.'

'That's 'cause he's a boy. All boys have tails, like puppy dogs. Anyway, we're not supposed to talk about it. Miss Edgar said it's not nice.'

The door closed and, after a while, silence settled.

Bryn stopped squawking when Siana placed him against her breast to suckle. She was exhausted from the journey. By the time she'd finished feeding him, Rosie had taken the dust sheet off the cradle she'd left ready. Bryn was full to the brim, and already asleep when she tucked him into it.

Rosie took a letter from her pocket, handing it to her. 'The maid gave me this letter for you. It's from the Earl of Kylchester. She said the servant told her to give it to you as soon as you returned.'

It was addressed to The Hon. Mrs Francis Matheson, and affixed with a seal. She smiled at the formality of the aristocrats.

Dear Madam,
It is my unpleasant duty to inform you that the Adriana, *the ship on which your husband took passage to Van Diemen's Land, sank with the loss of all crew and passengers on—*

The letter fluttering from her hand, Siana gave a cry of anguish, buckled at the knees and slid to the floor . . .

15

It was Josh who delivered Siana's message to the Earl of Kylchester. A footman carried it on a silver salver into the drawing room, where the earl was in the company of his wife.

'Tell the messenger to wait whilst I read it, there might be a reply . . . Good God!' he exploded, a few minutes later.

Prudence lifted her head. 'What is it?'

'I tell the girl her husband is dead and she denies it. "*I do not feel it in my heart that Francis has left me,*" she writes. Doesn't feel it in her heart? What superstitious nonsense is this?'

'Her words are not meant to be taken literally. She simply means she doesn't want to believe such a thing has happened to Francis, yet. In time it will sink in.' Prudence set aside her needle and cast a critical eye over the tapestry she was working on. 'Pansy tells me that Siana thinks oddly, at times. It comes from her Welsh forebears and I believe it is called "the sight".'

'Does she, by thunder? She would have been burnt at

the stake for that a few decades ago. I hope she isn't filling my nieces' heads with nonsense.'

'Siana has more sense than to do that. Does she mention the infant she was carrying?'

'She's been delivered of a son, which means there is someone to inherit the property William left Francis in Van Diemen's Land. Augustus is about to depart for the colony in his official capacity as admiral. He said it helps to show the British flag now and again in these God-forsaken places. I will tell him to transfer the property into the boy's name, and to appoint a manager until he comes of age. He may wish to run it himself in the future. If not, the property can be sold at a profit.'

'What's the infant's name?' Prudence said a little impatiently, though she was used to her husband leaving out such important items of news.

'Bryn Francis Matheson. Hmmm, an odd first name for a boy. I've never come across it before.'

'It sounds like some outlandish Celtic name. Does Siana mention Maryse?'

'She reports that the girl is in good health. Maryse sends her felicitations to us both and hopes to find us well when we next meet.'

The message met with Prudence's usual snort. 'The girl's disposition must have improved since last we met. She was most unpleasant in her manner to me. I've been thinking that perhaps we should take Francis's girls under our wing permanently. Being brought up by a member of the lower class cannot be good for them.'

The earl appeared to think the notion over. 'We must tread carefully and remember that Francis considered

Siana good enough to raise his children. He was no fool. They are fond of her, I think. Siana was also wife to Edward Forbes, who had a good eye for a woman.'

'Rumour had it that he had too good an eye. His indulgence in the matter of marriage was unexpected, although she learned how to conduct herself properly under his tutelage, in the main. It certainly improved her standing in the community.'

The earl grinned. 'Stop sounding so disapproving. Most men would have applauded Forbes for his taste. The girl will come to accept Francis's death, in time. Perhaps she'll wed again, for she's young to be widowed for a second time, and is a fetching little piece. I know a couple of fellows who are waiting to take a snap at her.'

Prudence led the subject back to safer ground, for her husband had neither agreed nor disagreed about their nieces, which meant he was open to suggestion. 'As you know, I have always wanted a daughter, so I should certainly like to have the girls here and arrange good marriages for them.'

Her husband leaned forward and patted her hand, a gleam of interest in his eyes. 'We could produce a daughter between us, yet. You are not too old.'

Prudence was appalled at the thought of being got with child again, for although she appeared to be still fertile, she was now past forty. 'You must be careful of your health,' she murmured, thinking she must be careful of her own. Her husband was still inclined to come to her bed in order to prove his potency, even though there was a widow he visited on a regular basis.

She sighed in annoyance when he squeezed her thigh,

recognizing it as a signal for her to expect a visit from him. He was a randy old goat at times.

'I'll visit Siana on the morrow and argue our case for having the girls turned over to our care,' she said. 'No doubt Pansy will want to see her sister and her new brother, so she can come with me in the carriage. If they are agreeable, and I see no reason why they shouldn't be, I'll bring both the girls back with me.'

Knowing how intractable his wife could be about such matters, the earl decided to go with them. 'I'll accompany you; I've not visited the house in Poole, and should like to see my new nephew for myself, for he may need support in the future.'

They were in the garden. The refreshments and niceties were over. Now they'd got down to the real reason for the unannounced visit.

'Live with you?' Despite her grief over her father's disappearance, Maryse tried to hide her dismay as she caressed Bryn's silky hair. 'But it would mean leaving my brother. I don't want to leave him, and I thought I'd made my intentions regarding marriage clear.'

'I don't want to wed, either,' Pansy said staunchly, trying not to laugh when Ashley, seizing an opportunity when the nursery maid's back was turned, snatched Susannah's doll from her hand and dashed off across the lawn with her in hot pursuit.

Pansy loved being part of a big family and her tiny new brother was a delight. But she knew her aunt Prudence would accuse her of being disrespectful to her father's memory if she laughed out loud. The edge had gone from her grief a little. Due to her aunt's relentless nagging over the past few weeks she had been forced to train her tears to come only at night. Aunt Prudence had so many rules and regulations, one couldn't be oneself even for a moment of grief.

Pansy had been delighted to see Siana again. Her stepmother had held her in a long, warm hug and whispered, 'My darling, Pansy. We've been so dull without you, and have missed you so much. I'm so glad all of Francis's children are together again.' Siana's words had made Pansy feel loved and wanted, so she was all choked up inside and couldn't do anything more useful than cling to her stepmother and hug her back.

As much as she loved her aunt, Pansy had found it hard living with her. Being on her best behaviour all the time was wearying, especially since that behaviour never proved good enough.

And the attention of her cousin Alder had proved to be more tedious than she remembered. She liked Alder a great deal, but was not ready to commit herself. Indeed, the fact that everyone thought a marriage between them was inevitable was becoming quite irksome – as if she herself had no choice in the matter. Her father wouldn't have pushed her into marriage, however advantageous it was. Oh, why did she have to grow up?

She intended to talk to Siana about it when they were alone and she had the chance, and to Maryse, who seemed to have recovered from the mysterious malaise she'd been suffering from before her trip to Wales.

She moved to where Maryse sat, cuddling their brother in her arms, gazed down at him and smiled. 'I want to do something useful before I settle down. Perhaps I can teach the children of the workhouse their letters and numbers, for surely it would improve their lot.'

Although the remark had been meant for Maryse's ears alone, the countess answered.

'Being a wife and mother is useful too, Pansy. I think you'd agree that Maryse looks quite at home with a child in her lap, almost as if she was mother to Bryn herself.' Maryse stiffened, but didn't look up. 'Besides, you would be exposed to squalor and disease. Philanthropy is a male trait, rarely indulged in by a true lady, and then only from afar and with a certain amount of con-descension, otherwise the recipients of charity will take advantage of one's good nature. The poor are usually rude-mannered, and rarely grateful.'

Pansy gasped, and both girls gazed at their aunt through shocked eyes.

Prudence shrugged, aware she'd made a *faux pas*, but unable to imagine what it could be. 'Oh, I'm not referring to you girls, since you are of good birth. Your relatives will never allow you to go hungry and will provide you with opportunities for your future. You must reconcile yourself to that and be grateful. Besides, you only have a small dowry, so will not have the means to support yourself. Marry you must, and you will marry well if I have anything to do with it, as befits your father's status.'

Pansy joined Siana and took her hand in hers. 'Papa

would not have insisted we marry before we were ready. He loved us too much.'

Maryse added a trifle absently, 'And he wouldn't have allowed you to insult his wife in such a manner, either.'

To which the countess snapped, 'I'm not referring to Siana, as you well know, missy. She's a sensible girl, and wouldn't have taken anything I said personally.'

Siana thought the countess had held the floor for long enough, and made her presence known. 'I accept you may have spoken without thinking, Prudence, and meant me no insult, as you often do.' She gently squeezed her young champion's hand. 'All the same, I enjoy the company of my stepdaughters and would be unhappy if you remove them from my care, as would Francis. He gave of himself to others with a good heart, and would applaud Pansy's choice to do the same.'

Prudence expelled an aggrieved sigh. 'There, you have taken the snit. Why am I always so misunderstood? I am only trying to do what is best for his children.'

'I like living with Siana,' Pansy murmured, her voice becoming mutinous.

'Kindly be quiet. Your likes and dislikes are immaterial.'

Siana's stubborn streak surfaced. Prudence was squabbling over the children like a dog with a bone, instead of listening to their wishes. Wasn't it hard enough that they might have lost their father? Prepared to fight to the death for them now, she got to her feet. 'Their wishes will never be immaterial to me.'

Prudence glared at her. For the first time Siana saw how truly lacking in compassion the countess was.

The earl, as if sensing the situation was about to take a turn for the worse, intervened, holding up his hand for silence. 'Don't say another word, my dear, for it seems to me that my nieces have made their wishes perfectly clear.' He bestowed a smile on them. 'You shall live here if that's your preference, for I can see that you're well cared for. I ask only that you indulge your aunt in a season or two in London, though, so she can bring you out. It's a long-planned-for event on her calendar. I don't wish her to be disappointed.'

'Hrummph!' Prudence snorted, taking a swipe at a wandering bumble bee and knocking it to the ground before crushing it underfoot. 'Exactly what I was about to suggest myself.' After all, she thought, once the girls were in her care, there was nothing to say she must return them, for they were not Siana's children.

Siana smiled when the two girls gazed at each other and nodded. Coming from the earl, it was almost an order. And really, it didn't matter what plans they made. Francis was still alive, she could feel it. One day he would return to them.

It was cold. Frost spread across the ground, a full half-inch thick. Snow coated the slopes and peak of Mount Wellington, towering in the distance. The horses, wearing their rough winter coats, were dark shapes pushing at the tussocks with their noses as they foraged for feed.

Francis was thankful for his brother's thick jacket – for all of the clothing in William's cupboard in fact. Some shirts had gone to Elizabeth, who'd managed to fashion two thick skirts for herself out of blankets, plus a jacket and boots out of sheepskins.

The property was well set up, the comfortable accommodation supporting serviceable furniture made by his brother and embellished with a crude attempt at carving.

It surprised Francis that William, a former army officer, had proved to be so resourceful in matters of husbandry. He had obviously come well provided with household goods, for there was no comfort lacking, except perhaps furnishings that a woman would add, such as cushions and fancy ornaments. William's rifles were hung over the fireplace, oiled and cared for, ready to load and use.

Books were stacked tidily on a shelf over a desk containing writing implements and business ledgers.

There was enough to eat, too. Vegetables had been planted and there were cabbages, carrots, beans or potatoes to eat, as well as mutton, eggs and poultry.

His brother was buried in a small fenced-off area on the other side of the hill, his resting place marked by a wooden cross.

'I said a prayer for Will's soul, though he didn't set much store on praying himself,' Stowe, his new neighbour had remarked with a grin, when he'd shown Francis the grave site.

Francis had grinned at that, too. When they were small, their father had remarked to the bishop once, after they'd made a nuisance of themselves during the service, 'With six sons in the family, I should be able to spare one of the two younger pups for service in the church.'

To which the bishop had answered, 'It depends on which of them shows a better aptitude for religious studies. I could turn either one of them into a fine parson.'

Something Francis and Will had vowed never to be. From then on they'd tried to outdo each other in devilment and unruly behaviour, lest they be the chosen one, the verbal sparring often ending in fisticuffs – until they'd gained enough wit to know better and had become the best of friends.

Empty niceties didn't seem to matter in this part of the world of make-do. By his own standards, he and Elizabeth were an odd-looking couple, but no odder than their neighbours. Supplies of luxury goods such as clothing and materials were hard to come by, and expensive.

Although he was living on the property he'd inherited, his brother's bank account was inaccessible until proof of his identity was established. To this effect, he had written a letter to his eldest brother, the earl, before they'd left Port Arthur, and another to Siana, reassuring her of his survival in case she learned of the shipwreck through other means. He just hoped the prison commandant had dispatched them.

Word had got round about his doctoring skills, though. Soon he was called out around the district for a variety of ailments and ills. Sometimes, it was an animal he treated, a favourite dog with its side ripped open, or a horse with the colic.

He had few instruments at his disposal. A couple of knives, ground down and sharpened to a thin blade, a pair of pliers, a sail-making needle and strong thread, and a pair of small scissors offered to him by Elizabeth.

He gave of his skills willingly, but often his visits brought reward, a piglet for a dislocated shoulder, a piece of salted beef for a case of chicken pox and some home-made wine for pulling a tooth – with a warning to be careful not to chip the bottles, and return them when empty. The wine tasted vile, had a kick like a mule and provided him with a foul hangover.

Francis wondered what Siana was doing as he swung his axe. He thought of her and the children almost constantly; missing them was a nagging ache in his heart. Knowing they were there to go home to in the future kept him optimistic, though. He felt the shock run up his arm when the axe split the log of wood in two. He'd never worked so hard in his life, but he enjoyed the new-found strength in his muscles.

Although he liked the countryside he found himself in, he didn't have much interest in estate management, so intended to return to his family in England as soon as he was able.

He didn't know quite what to do about Elizabeth, however. She'd been released into his care, but he had no intention of being parted from his family for four long years whilst she served out her sentence, unless it proved necessary. He couldn't just abandon her, though. Elizabeth had endured her ordeal to a certain extent, but her mental health seemed frail. She suffered from melancholy now and again, didn't eat enough and rarely smiled. Francis often heard her crying during the night and sometimes feared for her sanity.

'What's troubling you, Elizabeth?' he asked her one day.

Her eyes filled with tears. 'I'm scared, I've been scared since I left England.' She shrugged. 'I think I'm suffering from a dose of self-pity but I never expected to end up in a place so far from my family and friends.'

Her admission touched him. 'We are bound to feel melancholy from time to time. You mustn't give up hope, my dear. Four years will soon pass. And you told me Jed was coming.'

'It's not the time I resent, though I'll be a stranger to Susannah when I return. As for Jed, men often say one thing and mean another. But even if he does follow me out here he'll be looking for me in New South Wales.'

With her background, she was not without cause in her remark about men, Francis thought. But Jed Hawkins hadn't struck him as being superficial. As Jed had proved by his deeds in the past, he was loyal in his relationships and if he'd declared himself to Elizabeth, the man would do his best to discover her whereabouts.

'I'm sure Siana will keep you alive in Susannah's memory. Your daughter was in good health when I left. Siana has kept her nurse on so she has someone familiar to look after her. Also, she has Ashley as a companion.'

'I don't know how I can repay Siana for her kindness, for I signed my bank account over to Daniel. I now believe it was a mistake to do so.'

'Why is that?' he asked gently, for now Elizabeth was

unburdening herself a little, he knew she could only benefit from sharing her worries with another.

'The suspicion that Daniel might have betrayed me is troublesome. He made no real effort to defend me at my trial.' She gazed helplessly at him, tears running down her face. 'I try not to have these black thoughts, Francis, but they seem to crowd in on me at times.'

Francis, who'd always considered Daniel to be a singularly shallow young man, hadn't known how to answer that. Awkwardly, he said, 'I'm sure Daniel defended you to the best of his ability.'

'Then his ability is not as great as I thought it to be.'

'Sometimes we expect too much of our children, Elizabeth. Now, I've been called into town to attend a difficult childbirth. Would you like to come with me? The trip might cheer you up.'

She gently declined, with some excuse about cleaning the house. But as he rode away she was staring bleakly out of the window.

Having safely delivered the child, who was in a breech position, Francis was about to leave the residence when he noticed a green taffeta gown decorated with a lace collar, thrown over the back of a chair.

The woman he'd attended was a seamstress by trade. The gown was much too small for his patient. Although loathe to part with it, he fished his brother's silver watch from his pocket. 'Would you be willing to part with that gown? I have this watch I can give you in return.'

'Take the gown in return for my son,' she said, gazing at the healthily bawling infant in her arms. 'I was making it for my sister, when she ran off to marry a soldier who was going back to England. It won't fit me and the hem still needs turning up.'

Elizabeth smiled and cried at the same time when she set eyes on the gown. 'Thank you, Francis. It's so kind of you to think of me.'

'Of course I think of you, Elizabeth. What are friends for, if not to support each other in times of adversity?'

Elizabeth stitched it around the hem, but she didn't wear it. She'd seemed more cheerful since he'd given it to her, however, as if the gown had made her feel more womanly.

Francis was whittling down the woodpile that afternoon, when the eldest of the Stowe boys came galloping in. Stowe was lucky to have three fine, strong sons to help him farm his land, Francis thought.

'I've come to warn you. There's a stranger heading your way. I heard him asking for directions in town.'

'What was his name?'

'He didn't say, just gave me a long look that plainly told me to mind my own business.'

Elizabeth came out onto the verandah, the ghost of a smile on her face. 'What did the man look like?'

'Can't rightly say. He was a big man, not young, but tough-looking. He had a way with him I wouldn't want to cross.'

'Can you remember the colour of his eyes?'

'I didn't really notice, on account of he had an old brown hat pulled down over his forehead. I'll hang around in case he causes you any trouble. It might be a good idea to load your rifles.'

'There's no need,' Francis told him. 'It sounds like a friend of ours from England. Was he on foot, or horseback?'

'Foot, and he had a trunk hefted on his shoulders. He was carrying it as if it weighed nothing at all. It will take him an hour or so to get here.'

It couldn't be anyone else but Jed, Elizabeth thought, her heart beginning to sing as she went back inside.

Taking a steaming kettle through to her room, she washed herself all over, including her hair. She gazed at her protruding ribs, wishing she hadn't become quite so thin, before donning the green taffeta gown Francis had brought her and drawing a shawl around her shoulders. Jean Stowe had given her the garment, the wool spun and woven from her own sheep. Fetching the brush Francis had given her, one of a pair owned by his brother, she brushed her hair dry in front of the fire. When she finished, it lay in bright, foxy ripples about her shoulders. She tied it at the nape of her neck with a ribbon of taffeta cut from the hem of her gown.

Extra potatoes and carrots were added to the mutton stew and, deciding to make dumplings as well, she prepared the dough and chopped a cabbage into pieces.

Stoking up the fire, she went outside again, taking a seat on the verandah.

Francis threw the axe onto the woodpile, smiled and complimented her. 'You look lovely, Elizabeth.'

'Thank you, Francis.' She wished she had something to occupy her hands as she gazed down the hill. 'What if it's not him?'

'It is him. See, just coming out of the trees.'

And there he was in the distance. Jed Hawkins, coming up the hill with his long stride, the box held on his shoulder with one hand, bag and bedroll on his back. Nervously, she gazed at Francis, smoothing her dress down and patting her hair. 'I knew he'd come.'

'So did I.' Francis drew on his coat, stretched and said casually as he headed for his horse, 'I promised Bart Stowe I'd go and take a look down his throat. It's been giving him a bit of trouble. Give Jed my apologies at not being here to greet him, won't you? I'll be back in time for supper.'

She nodded, then came to where he stood and gave him a hug before he could mount. 'Thank you for everything, Francis.'

Disentangling himself from her arms, he chuckled. 'I hope Jed didn't see that. He might get the wrong idea.'

'Not Jed. He's a man with faith in himself and in others.'

She watched Francis ride away, then turned to gaze at Jed again. He'd put the trunk down and was seated on it, taking a rest.

'Jed,' she shouted and waved to him.

Snatching the hat from his head he pushed it inside his coat and stood up, his hands smoothing at his hair. They stared at each other for a few moments across the distance. Elizabeth could feel herself smiling all over. Her love for Jed was suddenly an all-consuming thing. She picked up her skirts and began to run, jumping over tussocks and rocks like a young girl.

He strode forward to meet her, snatching her up in his

arms as she hurled herself at him. 'Oh, Jed, I'm so glad you've come. I've missed you so much.'

'You're as skinny as a rat's tail,' he muttered to himself. 'I'll fetch that Francis Matheson a good clout for not feeding you better than this. He should know better, him being a learned doctor and all.'

She was laughing and crying at the same time. 'You most certainly will not, Jed Hawkins. Without Francis, I'd be dead by now. He's been worrying himself sick about me, and him with troubles heaped high upon his own shoulders. Now, set me down and let's get up to the house. There's a pot of stew cooking over the fire with extra dumplings. I've got so much to tell you, not the least of which is about Francis.'

Jed looked around, his golden brown eyes speculating on the countryside as he backtracked towards the trunk. 'It's good country. There's plenty of water, and the climate is milder than in England, I've heard. How much of it belongs to Francis?'

'In three directions, as far as the horizon, then twice as far again. Back from where you've come, you've been on Matheson land for at least an hour.'

'And most of it's uphill.'

'That depends where you're coming from or going to.' She curled her fingers around the handle of the trunk. 'Can I help you with it?'

He laughed at that. 'By rights you should, for the trunk is from Mrs Matheson for your own good self. She's promised me a thump should it go astray, even though it only be full of women's fripperies, and such.' He picked up his bag and blanket, handing them to her. 'Here, you can carry these, for they looks to be more your size.' He swung the trunk onto his shoulder again and they set off up the slope towards the house.

'Jed,' she said after a few minutes, for she was panting for breath. 'Slow down a bit. This bag's heavy.'

He gave her a sideways glance, noting her glowing face. He grinned, and reckoning he'd have to look after her a bit, came to a stop. 'Here, I'll carry it on my other shoulder.'

Whilst they were arranging that, she happened to look up at him. He was gazing down at her, a happy, idiotic expression on his face.

Love for him seeped up through her body, setting her heart to giving odd little skips and thumps. This was something she'd never felt before, something rich, warm and utterly contented. Jed was a man who accepted her past without censure – a man she could depend on. Tears glistening in her eyes, she cupped his face in her hands, went up on her toes and kissed him with all the tenderness she could muster. 'There, that's better.'

'Not when both my hands are occupied, it isn't,' he grumbled, though his eyes were filled with laughter. 'Now, out of my way, woman. I'm starving, and can smell the stew from here.'

There was a letter from Siana for Francis, entrusted to Jed, just in case he ran into her husband. One particular piece of news cheered him immensely.

My dearest Francis,
I have some wonderful news for you. You are to become a
father again. Our child will be born in June.

June! It was August now, so the infant would have
already been born. Francis savoured the thought, grinning to himself, wondering if it was boy or girl as he
gazed at Jed. 'Was Siana well when you left?'

'Oh, aye, and as smug as a cow belly-deep in clover.
Said to tell you she thought it were a girl she was
carrying.'

He remembered Siana's strange, fey sense. She'd
known Ashley would be a boy. Would she be right
again and give him another daughter? He shrugged.
'As long as the infant is born healthy. How were my
girls?'

Jed hesitated for a second or two, then he smiled. 'Mrs
Matheson takes good care of them.'

'Yes, she would.' Francis folded his letter and put it in
his pocket after committing the basics to memory. He
intended to read it fully, later, in private.

Jed cleared his throat. 'There is something you should
consider, Dr Matheson.'

'What is it, Jed? And do use my first name. This is not
a place to stand on ceremony.'

'If the ship you were sailing on went down, Mrs
Matheson might have been informed of the fact by now.
She might believe you have perished.'

'It had occurred to me. I've sent a letter to both her
and my brother informing them of my survival, and
asking my brother to find some means of furnishing the

commandant of Port Arthur prison with tangible proof. That is all I can do.'

'Would it be of help if I told the commandant you are who you say you are?'

'I doubt it. He is a cautious man, and my resemblance to the felon called Piper is too great. He wouldn't take Elizabeth's word for it.'

Jed nodded then glanced at Elizabeth, who was happily going through the contents of the trunk and had just exclaimed, 'Look, Siana has sent me some embroidery to do. And there are pieces of fabric I can make a quilt with.'

She'd received a letter from Siana too, with news of Susannah. With the arrival of Jed and the unexpected gift of the trunk, both her appetite and mood improved.

Jed grinned comfortably at Francis, saying quietly, 'Would there be a preacher man hereabouts? I'm of a mind to wed that woman.'

Elizabeth gazed up at him, her eyes shining, a wide smile on her face. It had been a long time since Francis had seen her so happy. Love seemed to have transformed her.

'A preacher makes occasional visits to the town. Put yourself on the list at the blacksmith's shop, for there will be other weddings and christenings to be officiated over on his next visit. In the meantime, you must seek permission from the authorities and have Elizabeth assigned to you. For as soon as I can, I'm returning to England.'

He gazed from one to the other and smiled. 'There's a bible in the desk. If you would care to exchange vows over it, it will be my pleasure to act as your witness. That's what most people do here, and we can record the marriage in it.'

Jed gazed with some uncertainty at Elizabeth, who calmly nodded.

The next day, as Francis listened to the pair exchange their vows, he remembered his own vows to Siana. A stab of despair hit him when he thought that if his letter to Siana had gone astray, she and the children would be mourning his death.

16

September arrived, still bathed in sunshine, and voluptuously ripe.

Someone who looked closely might have discovered it to be too ripe. Apples with perfect skin housed maggots in their core. Chestnuts fell to the ground and split open. The haymaking was complete, but the hay had been stacked badly on the staddles, so mould was forming at the base of the ricks.

The Cheverton fields still hosted the corn crops. To a casual glance the wheat was ready for harvesting. But although the seed had fattened a little, the crop looked sparse to anyone with an experienced eye. An abundance of field mice were busy consuming more than their usual share.

Suffering from a fit a temper, Daniel called the overseer to the house. 'Where are the field labourers?'

'Can't rightly say, sir.'

'You can't or you won't?' Daniel slapped his crop against his hand in a threatening gesture. 'If it rains I shall lose the crop, and if I lose the crop you'll be flogged. Tell them I'm off to the bank to withdraw their wages and if they don't get on with their work, they won't get any.'

Muttering resentfully to himself, the overseer, a solid-looking man nearing fifty years, moved off. 'Flog me, would you? I'd break the crop over yon bleddy back, then piss on it, first, you young bastard.'

Damn them, Daniel thought. Most of the field labourers had worked on the estate for years. They should know better than himself how it was run. To make matters worse, he'd been forced to dismiss most of the house servants, for they'd been spying on him on behalf of Esmé. Well, he'd solved that problem, as he solved the problem of his wife. It was peaceful without her snooping around the house!

He thought he might take a ride over to Croxley Farm to ask Rudd Ponsonby's advice. Then he might call on his godfather. At least the Reverend White would lend him a sympathetic ear.

His head ached badly today. And the sores from his neck were beginning to spread up into his scalp. He wondered if he should consult with the doctor again. But no, Noah Baines would only prescribe some foul-tasting elixir or another, the same as the high-priced fool in London had. It always made him feel lethargic, and dulled the pain only a little.

'Did I feed Esmé today?' he said out loud, and glared at the stable boy who stared at him with his mouth open. 'What are you looking at, boy? Fetch my horse.'

Esmé had begged him to set her free the last time he'd visited her. Damn her, he thought, his conscience troubling him a little. If she hadn't nagged so much he wouldn't have locked her in the barred room in the first place.

Sweating slightly, for the day was warm and humid, he pulled out his handkerchief and mopped his forehead whilst the stable boy scurried to fetch his horse. Mounting, he headed out to the road. For a moment he hesitated, trying to remember what his plans were for the day. It wasn't the trial; that was next month. Ah, yes, he was going to visit Croxley Farm, then his godfather.

Tomorrow he intended to visit his half-siblings, for he'd heard Siana had returned from Wales. She had given birth to another son, by all accounts, and she'd been widowed. He smiled at the thought. Perhaps now she would come home to where she belonged. He would welcome her children, and perhaps she would bear a son for him, too.

He began to feel better as he headed off towards Rudd Ponsonby's. Once things were cleared up in his head, he always did.

The tenant farmer had several sons who worked side by side with him. Daniel liked Rudd, who always called him squire. Abbie Ponsonby and her girls were always respectful towards him, too. He'd taken a liking to Barbara, the eldest one, a tender little piece of about fourteen years. She was high-waisted with long legs and big, dark eyes, and her breasts were jutting little buds against her bodice. She'd blushed when she'd noticed him looking at them. He felt in his pocket. He'd brought the girl a brooch to wear, one of Esmé's. It was silver, fashioned in the shape of a blue enamelled bow.

'Rudd and the boys be ploughing the muck and clover

in,' Abbie told him, fussing around like a hen. 'And the two young uns are off-colour today, but they be sleeping so they won't be a bother.' She turned to Barbara, all flustered. 'Serve the squire some cake and tea and keep an ear out for the young uns while I fetches your father from the field.'

Daniel watched the girl bustle back and forth. She was growing out of her gown. Her breasts strained against it, and her limbs were tanned from the sun. He brought out the brooch for her to inspect, smiled at her. 'See what I've brought for you, Barbara. Come over here and I'll pin it to your gown.'

''Tis a right pretty bow,' she said, coming to stand in front of him.

'You're a pretty girl.' His mouth dried as he pinned it to her bodice, his knuckles brushed against her sweet, hard nubs. Sliding his arm around her waist, he gently drew her down onto his lap. 'A nice gift like that deserves something in return.'

When she hung her head he fitted a finger under her chin and, lifting her face up, smiled at her. 'What shall it be, Barbara? A kiss? Or will you allow me to tickle you?'

She gazed dumbly at him, her eyes slightly wary. 'I ain't tried kissin' no boys, sir, though I be tickled sometimes by my brothers.'

'Kissing is pleasant, you must try it,' he urged, and gently kissed her. Her mouth was slightly open so he penetrated it with his tongue, delving into its depths, which were moist, but not unpleasantly so.

When he finished he gazed at her. 'Did you liked being kissed?'

'Kissin' be right fancy, sir, but not as good as a tickle.'

'Ah,' he said, 'like this?' Slowly, he slid his palms up to her breasts and, cupping them, rubbed his thumbs over her nipples. They'd grown since he'd last seen her and nestled in his palms like a couple of plump, nesting robins.

Her face turned red and she mumbled, 'Not 'zackly.' The girl didn't quite know what to do, so remained sitting there on his lap as he fondled them, with her face turned away. Her buttocks were firm against his thighs. When he spread his knees slightly, her thighs opened too, and her plump little venus opened against his nudging member. 'Do you know what that is, Barbara?'

'Yes, sir, I see'd a big un like that on a stallion, once,' she said, and began to giggle. 'It were nearly touching the ground. Something be wrong with the horse, though, fer it were all lathered up and squealin' at the mares.'

He chuckled and whispered, 'Would you like to touch mine?'

Just then Daniel heard Rudd and his wife talking as they came into the yard. There followed the clank of the pump handle.

The girl leaped from his lap like a scalded cat, saying breathlessly, 'I think the kettle be boiling, sir.'

'It is, indeed.' So was he. The slut had known exactly what she'd been doing. Hastily, he placed his hat on his lap, keeping it there until his state became less conspicuous.

Rudd left his dirty boots outside the door, slipping into a pair of clogs his wife held out to him. Daniel stood, taking the work-roughened hand the man extended in a brief shake. Despite Rudd's hasty wash, he smelled of cow dung and sweat, causing Daniel's nostrils to pinch.

'Good morning, squire,' Rudd said as his glance went to his daughter, still red-faced and trying to stifle her giggles. 'Where did the brooch come from, Barbara?'

'Squire gave me it. It be a pretty thing, ain't it?'

Daniel shrugged. 'It's a trinket I found in my pocket.'

'Then I expect it belongs to your wife, sir. No offence meant, sir, but my Barbara had best give it back, for Mrs Ayres might miss it and accuse her of stealing it.'

'Very well,' Daniel said sulkily, holding his hand out for it. 'I meant no harm.'

'Of course you didn't, sir.' Daniel was steered into the best room, still furnished as his mother had left it. The house was spotlessly clean and smelled of polish. He took the winged chair, sitting with his legs slightly apart in the same stance his father had always adopted, his arms extended, his hands cupped over the knob on his cane.

'Now, how can I be of assistance to you?' Rudd said, turning a frown towards his daughter, who'd followed them in. 'Go and help your mother with the tea things.' When the girl hurried off, he added, 'I'd be obliged if you didn't bring the girl gifts, squire. Barbara be a foolish cheil at times, and I don't want her gettin' ideas above her station.'

'It was nothing to make a fuss about. Don't give it another moment's thought. Actually, I've dropped in for this quarter's rent,' Daniel informed him, deciding not to ask this jumped-up labourer's advice after all.

'The rent's not due until the corn's been sold, and it's usually paid to the agent. Wheat's fetching a good price this year, I believe.'

A cry of alarm came from upstairs. Footsteps thudded down the stairs and Abbie poked her head inside the door, her face screwed up with worry. 'The pair of them be running a high fever, our Rudd. And Eddie has broke out in a rash. I think the doctor be needed.'

'Don't get yourself all in a pucker, woman,' Rudd soothed. 'Barbara had a sore throat the day afore yesterday and it came to nuthin'. Still, if you be worried, send the girl on the donkey to fetch the sawbones. Tell her to take the short cut past the old cottage, and if she dawdles I'll put the strap across her back when she gets home. I don't know what's got into that girl lately, but she allus seems to be in a daydream.' Daniel was the recipient of a meaningful look. 'I can't spare any of the boys, we've got too much to do before the weather breaks. Was there anything else you wanted to discuss with me, sir?'

'Come, man, surely the work can wait for half an hour or so. Let's pass the time of day whilst your good woman feeds us.' Perversely, Daniel relaxed back into his chair, wasting the man's time as he consumed the refreshment he was offered. He was enjoying the power he had over the tenant as he watched the farmer champ at the bit.

Eventually, Daniel picked up his hat and smiled benevolently at them. 'I'm on my way to visit my godfather, the Reverend White. I'll give him your kind regards, shall I?'

Abbie dropped him a curtsy. 'That be very nice of you, sir.'

After their unwanted guest had gone, Rudd gazed at Abbie. 'There be something not quite right about Daniel Ayres. His eyes be shifty, and I don't trust a man who can't look at you straight. He ain't like his father, that's for sure. Edward Forbes might have been hard when his dander was raised, but he knew the land.'

Abbie shivered. 'I heard tell that he has his wife locked up.'

Rudd laughed, squeezing her cushiony rump as she bustled past. 'Now, don't you go getting in a fret over gossip, else trouble will visit us. I'd be lockin' *you* up if you was as skinny as that there woman of his. A man likes a nice warm handful to cuddle up to in bed.'

Abbie chuckled. 'You keep your hands to yourself, Rudd Ponsonby, and your other bits. You know what the doctor said. No more cheils.'

'He'll think differently when he weds and has Peggy Hastings to whet his appetite, for she lost her youngster at birth and has the need inside her for another.'

'She be a bonny girl, that one. Folks round here won't forget how that Mrs Matheson helped her out, either. There's a woman who doesn't forget her roots. A pity she isn't running Cheverton Estate for the little squire, for I reckon the labourers would heed her more than Daniel Ayres. They don't like the way he looks at their wives and daughters.'

Suspicion brought worry to his eyes. 'D'you reckon he was eyeing up our Barbara? She was blushing like a beetroot and giggling fit to bust.' Rudd frowned. 'When that maiden comes back you tell her I want to talk to her. I want to know 'zackly what that Forbes by-blow was up to with her.'

'Thank goodness he was goin' in a different direction,' Abbie mused.

But Daniel had doubled back. Dismounted, he was waiting to intercept Barbara outside the old cottage.

Taking a hold of the donkey's reins, he brought her to a stop and held a silver coin under her nose. 'How would you like to earn a shilling for yourself, my dear? You'll be able to buy some pretty ribbons for your hair at the market.'

Barbara's eyes began to shine. 'I be going to fetch the doctor, sir.'

'It won't take up much of your time.' His hands spanned her waist. 'I'll give you the pretty brooch, as well. I know of a perfect place where you can hide it, in a hollow oak tree in the woods behind Croxley Farm.'

He took the brooch from his pocket and, laughing, held it out to her as he walked towards the cottage shell. 'Come in here, there's something I want to show you. A sweet little ferret which needs a burrow to hide itself in.'

'I ain't daft. I know what 'e be after. My dad said I've got to keep meself for when my true love comes along.'

'Your dad won't know. Besides, I am your true love. Why else would I bring you a gift? Come, Barbara. I'll take you to the manor and give you a pretty gown afterwards.'

Unable to resist the lure of the gown and brooch, she

followed him in, her hand closing around the trinket when they stopped.

Five minutes later she began to cry, a loud wailing noise that got on his nerves. 'Shut up, will you.'

'But you be hurtin' me, sir.'

'You stupid little slut,' he shouted, placing his hand over her mouth. 'It's your own fault, you shouldn't have led me on.'

The girl struggled and moaned against his hand as he finished his business, then sank her teeth into it. The little whore! Rage filled his body and his head began to throb with it. He wanted to cry out with the unrelenting pain squeezing at his head.

Incensed, he dragged her upright and punched her. She flew backward and hit the ground, her neck giving an ominous crack. The brooch fell from her hand.

Daniel stared at the girl. She was limp. The weight of her head made it hang at an unnatural angle over a stone, her eyes were staring, her mouth hung slackly open.

'Oh God, she's broken her neck,' he muttered, adjusting his clothing. He stared at her a moment longer, wondering what he should do. Make it look like an accident, he thought.

He carried her out to the lane, placing her in the same position, her head over the same stone. Unconcerned, the donkey munched the grass at the side of the lane. Eventually, the animal would return home and someone would search for her. They would think she'd fallen from the donkey.

Mounting his horse, he turned its nose towards his

godfather's house. He hoped the reverend had some laudanum, for his head was aching so much he could hardly think straight. It would be best not to mention the still figure of the girl on the road.

By the time he reached the rectory, he'd convinced himself that there had been no fault on his side.

That same night, another of Abbie Ponsonby's children died, from a convulsion brought on by scarlet fever.

Siana wasn't pleased when Daniel turned up alone, and unannounced. He looked tired, she thought, and agitated. Walking from window to door, his fingers twined and twisted unceasingly, making her feel uneasy.

'Black doesn't suit you,' he said abruptly.

At the Countess of Kylchester's insistence Siana had adopted black in mourning for her husband. Still, she couldn't bring herself to believe Francis was gone from her. He had been too alive and loving, giving her so much of himself in the short time they'd been wed.

There was a calm sense of waiting inside the real her, that other self who was wise in the ways of the earth. If she had to, she would wait for Francis until the end of time. She would see him again. And when that happened, she hoped they would never be parted. In the meantime, she had their family to care for.

Abruptly, Daniel stopped in front of her. 'I'm sorry to hear about the demise of Francis. He was a worthy man in every sense of the word. You and the children are welcome to make your home in the manor with me.'

'Thank you, Daniel, but that won't be necessary.' The

smile she gave him was serene, despite the turbulence of her thoughts. 'Won't you sit down?'

'I'm restless these days. I like to pace.' He turned to gaze at her. 'I believe you've been delivered of a son.'

She drew in a deep breath. 'Bryn is over three months of age now and he has the Matheson looks. How is Esmé?'

'Esmé?' He passed a trembling hand over his forehead. 'Ah, Esmé . . . yes, she is well, I think. She's visiting her parents.' He began to pace again. 'Will my sister and brother be long?'

'Their nurse will bring them down shortly. It's a warm day, we can take refreshment on the terrace together and they can run around and enjoy the fresh air.'

He stopped his pacing to gaze down at her, chewing on his lip. 'I suffer from headaches, Siana. The doctor in London gave me some medicament to take, but though it calms me down, it makes me melancholy. I've stopped taking it.'

'You should consult with Dr Baines, he may be able to prescribe something better.'

'Perhaps I will. Sometimes, I imagine I've done horrifying things, then I can't remember what they were. Sometimes, I think I'm going mad.'

'I'm sure you're not.'

She was sure he was! There was an air of unpredictability about him, something that wasn't quite right. He wouldn't meet her eyes and kept trembling. Unease grew in her and she was relieved when she saw Josh coming from the stables, for she didn't want to be left alone another moment with Daniel.

'You *are* staying for a while, aren't you, Josh?' He caught the plea in her voice, and nodded. Kissing her cheek, he offered his hand to Daniel, then seated himself, crossing one long leg over the other. 'I hear your corn hasn't been harvested yet.'

'The field labourers should have started on it today.'

Siana frowned. 'It's a little late in the year, isn't it, Daniel? If it rains, you'll lose it.'

'The weather's holding up so far.' He sounded truculent.

'But it's been humid for the past two days and clouds are massing on the horizon out to sea. If the wind pushes that onto shore, there will be a storm.'

'I told you, it's being taken care of,' he said shortly.

They moved onto the terrace when the refreshment arrived, the atmosphere strained and awkward. The children came down a few moments later. Ashley and Susannah had seen so little of Daniel they were hardly aware of their connection with him. He lifted them onto his knees to be kissed but they were boisterous after their rest and Daniel grew impatient with them when they wriggled to get away from him. The pair soon lost interest in him, joining Daisy and Goldie, who were searching through the grass for the last of the summer daisies to make chains with.

Daniel watched Ashley, his eyes hooded over. 'It's hard to believe someone as young as Ashley owns Cheverton Estate. Has provision been made in case he doesn't survive his childhood?'

A cloud moved over the sun and Siana shivered. 'Your father made his wishes clear in his will.'

'Ah, yes . . . I'd forgotten. I must look at it again. Where is it?'

'Where he left it, in his bureau.' She wished Daniel would leave. His strangeness unnerved her and she didn't like tempting fate with talk of death. How could Daniel have changed so much in such a short time?

Bryn, brought down for a brief inspection, received only a cursory glance. Maryse and Pansy were polite to Daniel, but he was hard to converse with as his attention skittered from one subject to the other.

Pansy got bored with playing the lady and involved herself with the smaller children. Maryse, uncomfortable in Daniel's presence, begged to be excused after a short while. She went back indoors to practise on the piano.

Josh stayed until Daniel made a move to go, then said, 'I'll accompany you into town, if you like. I've got business to attend to. I believe you're the magistrate trying Isabelle Collins for the murder of my sister, Hannah.'

Daniel nodded. 'A cut and dried case. I'm looking forward to it.'

Josh gave a short bark of laughter. 'Hannah was a miserable cow. Your father had a warrant out for her arrest when she died. She slaughtered most of the livestock at Croxley Farm out of spite, then sold it to the butcher.'

Blood filled Daniel's face at the mention of Croxley Farm, but his colour receded, leaving his face ashen when Josh added, 'I hear Rudd Ponsonby's eldest girl has been killed.'

'She was thrown from a donkey and broke her neck,' Daniel stated with absolute conviction. 'I had a meeting with Rudd, and the accident happened just after I left the place, I believe.'

'Like hell, she did! When her mother laid her out there were signs that the poor kid had been got at. The bugger who dunnit tried to make it look like an accident. Abbie Ponsonby be out of her mind with grief. That same night, one of her other youngsters upped and died of scarlet fever. Doc Baines has quarantined the place to stop it spreading.'

Shocked, Siana stared at him. 'Poor Abbie.'

Leaving his refreshment untouched, Daniel hastily scrambled to mount his horse. 'I must be off. I have urgent matters to see to.'

'I intend to call a meeting of the trustees next week. Your attendance will be expected,' Siana said before he left, but she didn't tell him she was going to insist that a competent steward be appointed for the estate.

Daniel didn't answer. Relief filled her when he headed off down the carriageway at a canter and she turned to Josh. 'Thanks for keeping me company.'

'Any time, sis. That man's wound up so tight he's set to explode. You shouldn't allow him to visit without his missus on his arm. A right piece of scrag end she be now, though, and a face as long as a yard of pump water.'

'When he comes here uninvited to see Ashley and Susannah, I can't just tell him to leave. Besides, his wife is away visiting her parents.'

'A fat lot of attention he paid Suzie and Ashley. It's you he came to see. He couldn't keep his bleddy eyes off and I don't like what I saw in them. You want to be careful of him, Siana. There be rumours about him, and none of them be good.'

'When are rumours ever good?' With a shock, she noticed how manly her brother had become. He was tall, lean and wiry and walked with a long, loping stride. His pale blue eyes were inherited from the Skinner family, as was his hair, darker now than the straw colour of his childhood. She reached up to run a palm over his chin and, feeling the rasp of whiskers, grinned. 'Well now, shaving your chin, is it? You'll be telling me you've got a sweetheart next.'

His grin widened. 'I'll be telling you nothin' of the sort. And you can keep your nose out of my courting when I gets meself a girl. Besides, I'm only seventeen and have no intention of getting wed for quite a few years yet.'

'Then why are you planning a house with five bedrooms for yourself?' she teased.

Josh shrugged. 'A house is an investment. When it's built, it'll bring me in a good rent from the nobs. They like a bit of space around them, for they ain't used to huddling together like fleas in a cat's armpit. When I get around to moving in meself, someone else's money will have paid for every brick.'

Siana laughed. 'You were always a pinch-penny, Josh Skinner.'

'I'm just careful with my money. 'Sides, where else can I put my family when they come to visit me? You and me have gone up in the world, our Siana. We ain't used to sleeping five to a bed no more. I've got things to learn afore I takes me a wife, too. Giles Dennings is teaching me to write and do numbers, so nobody cheats me. The numbers is easy to understand and he's making me keep a set of books for practice. When I get to be a bit older and I knows a bit more, he said I can apply to join the businessmen's institute.' He choked out a laugh. 'Ma would turn in her grave if she could see us now.'

'More likely, she'd pick up her skirts and dance.'

Josh jerked his head towards their sister. 'When are you going to tell our Daisy that you're not her ma?'

'I don't know, I haven't given it much thought. When she's Maryse's age, I suppose.'

His nod displayed his dubiety. 'Just so I knows, in case I puts my foot in it. I reckon you know what you be doing, but our Daisy might not thank you when she finds out you've been lying to her for all these years.'

'I haven't lied, Josh.'

'But you haven't told her she's not your daughter, so that's the same thing, ain't it? She knows I'm her brother and she knows you're my sister. One day she's going to figure things out.'

Feeling unsettled, Siana's glance went to the children romping in the garden. Daisy was beautiful with her blonde hair and blue eyes, though she was a handful, at times. Goldie's hair was spun from pure gold. She was a quiet little girl for most of the time, but her wit was more than a match for Daisy.

Susannah was a dainty copy of her elegant mother, Elizabeth. She'd settled in well with the family, and it was going to be a huge wrench when her mother reclaimed her. Then there was Ashley – her beloved Ashley, the little squire, the child of her womb. He was a charmer with his soft dark curls and beautiful smile. How she adored him. He'd be a wonderful elder brother for Bryn.

She scooped him up in her arms as he ran past, kissing his neck and blowing into his curls so he giggled and wriggled in her arms.

Josh grinned. 'I remember Ma doing that to me. It's been over five years now and I still think of her every day.'

'So do I.' Siana smiled softly as she reminisced. 'Ma used to say, "I love this skinny little lad of mine so much I could munch his toes off him," and you'd wriggle your toes and scream with laughter when she'd put them in her mouth.'

Their laughter faded as they shared a glance and Josh said gruffly, 'I miss her something cruel at times, Siana. I don't know what I'd have done without you to turn to. Sometimes you say things she used to say, and you remind me of her so much.'

She ruffled his hair, happy to share this moment in memory of their mother. 'Our ma loved us, Josh, she'd have wanted us to look after each other.'

Immediately she thought of Bryn, born of a vicious attack to a girl scarcely out of childhood – a vulnerable girl, an innocent who had known nothing but gentleness all her life.

If the facts were brought to light, otherwise decent people would condemn Maryse, and consider Bryn as human rubbish. Well, he was worth something to her, she thought fiercely, and she would bring him up knowing that worth. Besides herself, only Marcus Ibsen knew the truth about Bryn's parentage, and he would keep his silence.

She hoped the pair who'd attacked Maryse rotted in hell for their act.

Marcus Ibsen's pilgrimage was over. He was in his uncle's London house.

There had been a feast on his return. It had surprised him when he'd been able to don his old persona like a snake climbing back into its skin. The other him, with its ancient instincts, passion and darkness, would claim him from time to time, he knew.

'I have decided not to follow in my father's footsteps and take up a career as a minister. I'd find the vocation too constricting,' he'd informed his uncle on his return. 'After I finish my studies, I intend to buy a small country estate with my inheritance. There, I will pursue further studies, play the philanthropist, travel from time to time, and eventually take a wife for myself and produce some offspring. I hope you approve.'

'Heartily,' his uncle had told him. 'Having a bishop for a father was difficult enough for someone with your questioning intellect and you've never pretended to be a total believer.'

Marcus was not the same man who'd left his uncle's house two years previously. He'd found what he'd been seeking, a sense of self. That self had been revealed to him, but not by the preacher, Gruffydd Evans, who'd indulged in self-pity and dramatics. It had been revealed by his daughter, Siana, a woman of strength and acceptance, whose soul had opened to his at that meeting on the hilltop.

He would never believe that meeting was chance. He and Siana Matheson had been destined to meet and the reason for it became clear to him at *Bryn Dwr*.

Marcus had fallen deeply in love with Maryse, a girl hardly out of the schoolroom, who'd been violated in the cruellest way and imagined herself unworthy and unclean as a consequence.

He'd never thought love could hurt so much or bring out the need to protect in him. How brave she'd been, and how lucky to have Siana to guide her at her time of trial.

He would have taken the infant as well, brought him up as his own. But the child would have been a constant reminder to Maryse, and besides, Siana Matheson had needed the unfortunate infant herself.

Deep down, Marcus knew Siana would need Bryn again in the near future, for he'd sensed something around her. She'd denied the fates that day on the cliff top. She'd risked her life for Maryse, and the infant she carried. She'd defied the elements to snatch Maryse from the jaws of death, and he'd aided her in that. There would be a reckoning, there always was. But would it be her reckoning, or his?

'*"To everything there is a season, and a time to every purpose under heaven,"*' he murmured. '*"A time to be born, and a time to die . . ."*'

He'd felt such rage at *Bryn Dwr*. Not because the girl he'd grown to love had been despoiled, but because she would always fear that she might encounter again the scum who'd hurt her.

"*A time to plant, and a time to pluck up that which is planted.*"

He wondered what the perpetrators of the crime were doing now.

His eyes sharpened and his mouth stretched into a thin smile as he quoted, "*A time to kill, and a time to heal . . .*"

17

Daniel hadn't turned up for the meeting of the trustees, which was held in a sumptuous conference room on the second floor of the bank building. All the men were getting on in years, corpulent to varying degrees, and patronizing in manner.

'Mr Ayres is preparing for the Collins case,' Albert Sedgewick said and, although he didn't state it, he went on to make it perfectly clear that the late squire's widow shouldn't meddle in Cheverton affairs. 'I'm quite sure Mr Ayres has his brother's interests at heart. Besides, everything is approved by the board, which was appointed by your husband, the late squire.'

'I'd like to see the account books, Mr Sedgewick.'

They all appeared affronted by the suggestion. 'My dear, Mrs Matheson,' another of them said, 'that's quite impossible at the moment. They're in Dorchester.'

'But the bank is here, so why are the books in Dorchester?'

'They're being independently audited by an accountant, a common practice applied to trusts. It keeps the trustees honest.' They gazed at each other with

319

indulgent chuckles, like naughty boys with secrets. 'Rest assured, the estate properties are being maintained as they should be.'

'The land isn't being worked properly. When I spoke to Mr Ayres last week he assured me harvesting had started. It hasn't. I believe the labourers spend more time in the inn than in the fields. Poor as it is, that corn crop needs harvesting immediately. If nothing else, it will sell for stock feed. I want a competent steward appointed to manage Cheverton. Is that clear?'

'Mr Ayres has a signed contract. We cannot break it without good reason, and without incurring penalties.'

Siana stood up, for she wanted to get home to her elder son, who'd been unwell that morning. She gazed at them all with as much hauteur as she could muster. 'Mr Ayres is incompetent. Is that good reason enough? Any penalty the estate had to pay him would be compensated by a decent harvest next year, no doubt. I intend to see those account books, gentlemen. As soon as the audit is finished, have them sent to my house. Otherwise, I'll appoint a lawyer to act on my son's behalf.'

They didn't bother lowering their voices as she left. 'Matheson's widow is a fetching little piece,' one of them said. 'No breeding, of course, which is why Daniel dropped her in the first place. His father wasn't so fussy. But they say there's no fool like an old fool, and she soon had Edward twisted around her finger.'

'I'd happily twist *her* around my finger,' another said coarsely, and they all began to laugh.

Her mind churning with a mixture of anger and

disgust, Siana slammed the door so hard the whole building shook.

It began to rain as she made her way up the hill. Still seething and wishing she had the power to loosen the hold these self-indulgent and smug men had on her life, she didn't register the significance of it until she turned into the carriageway. When the rain became a downpour she realized with dismay that Cheverton's corn crop was now lost to the estate.

Leaving Keara at the stable in the care of the outside man, she picked up her skirts and made a dash for the house, tumbling through the door pink-faced from exertion and anger.

She was met by Miss Edgar in the hall. 'Master Ashley's fever has worsened. Josh has gone to fetch the doctor.'

Everything else left Siana's head. Throwing off her cloak and hat she ran to the nursery, taking the stairs two at a time. Bright spots of colour splashed her son's cheeks, his eyes were glassy and bright from the fever. 'Mamma,' he whispered and, crawling into her lap, snuggled against her body, his thumb in his mouth.

Tears filled her eyes as she smoothed the damp strands of hair from his forehead. 'The doctor will make you better,' she whispered.

It was not Noah Baines who came, but the physician from town. His examination of Ashley was thorough. As soon as he'd finished, Ashley clung to his mother, whimpering, then his eyes closed and he fell asleep.

'Hmmm,' the doctor said. 'Has he been in contact with other children recently?'

'Only his sisters and brother.'

'And they're healthy?'

She nodded.

'I see.' He touched the back of Ashley's arms where small, ruby-coloured patches had appeared. 'I'm very much afraid he has contracted the scarlet fever. This rash is typical of it. There has been an outbreak of the disease at Croxley Farm. Have you visited there lately?'

'No . . .' Her eyes widened with fear. 'But we recently had a visitor who had.'

'You must expect the other children in your household to become ill as well, Mrs Matheson, for they've been exposed to the infection.'

By nightfall, Ashley's rash was widespread. By morning, it became obvious that Susannah had caught the disease, too. By the end of the week, Daisy and Goldie were struck down, then Bryn.

Fortunately, Maryse and Pansy had already survived a mild dose in their infancy.

The disease hardly affected Bryn. It left his appetite unaffected, and he still demanded to be fed on time. The girls began to recover quickly, but not so Ashley. Despite Siana's efforts to cool him down, his temperature soared and he drifted in and out of delirium. Following the normal pattern of the disease, the skin peeled from his tortured body. But unlike the girls, Ashley developed weeping sores.

The doctor shook his head. 'I think the boy has a secondary infection, for he should be showing signs of recovery by now. Keep the sores free of pus and apply this salve. It will soothe them.'

Siana took her son to her own room, leaving him only when necessary. She had an armchair brought in so she could sleep next to him. She was there to comfort him when he woke, crying out and sweating and twisting in his sheets. But nothing she did would lower his fever, and he would begin to convulse. His suffering pierced her to the heart.

None of Josh's entreaties could drag her away from his side, so he stopped trying.

She remained there for two weeks, during which time Ashley seemed to grow weaker minute by minute.

'My beloved son, my beautiful gift from Edward,' she whispered in his ear, her heart a mixture of despair and dread. 'I love you so much.'

Even though they were still recovering from the fever, Siana was aware that the usual exuberance of the girls was muted. The maids talked in hushed whispers and she wanted to cry out in protest, 'He's not dead yet, and I refuse to let him die.'

But there was an awful inevitability about it. Siana could feel Ashley's life being gradually withdrawn from her. Her heart railed against it as she ignored her intuition, for she couldn't bear the thought of life without him. Only the vain hope that he would survive sustained her through those dark days.

Something woke her that night. She sat up to see the moon send an incandescent slant of light across the room. Eyes open, Ashley was gazing at her. He gave her a faint smile, whispering, 'Mamma.'

Hope leaped like a tiger in her breast. For a heartbeat they gazed at each other, then his face contorted and he began to convulse. Fear shot through her. She gathered up his jerking body, holding him close to her as she entreated, 'My beloved boy, don't leave me.' But she knew her prayers were in vain, for the gods had given her that one precious moment of recognition as a gift.

The convulsion stopped as suddenly as it had started, leaving Ashley lying limp and heavy in her arms. There was no rise and fall of his chest, not even a sigh of breath. The house was hushed, as if everyone in it had stopped breathing at the same time. Even the clock seemed to have stopped its tick.

An anguished and silent scream was trapped within her throat, swollen with unshed tears. Siana kissed her son's pale face. She felt as if her heart had died along with him. She wanted to die, too. There were scissors in her sewing basket. Laying her son on her bed, she crept along the corridor and down the stairs to fetch them, carrying them back.

Her finger touched against the pulse in her wrist. The scissor blades gleamed in the moonlight. All she had to do was open the veins and the life would drain from her, not cruelly like Ashley's had but gently, so she'd go to sleep and die with him cradled in her arms.

She took the body of her beloved son in her arms and laying back against the pillows, placed the point of the scissors against her vein, closed her eyes and exerted a gentle pressure.

In the other room, Bryn gave a loud, demanding cry. 'Damn him!' she cried. Her breasts, which were aching from their bounty, flooded her bodice at the mere thought of being relieved, as if they too had heard Bryn cry out. He wasn't even her child, she thought rebelliously. Why hadn't he died instead of Ashley?

She squashed the traitorous thought. Yes, he was her child. She'd made him so, and she couldn't change her mind now. So she couldn't die yet, however much she hurt. There were others relying on her. She burst into loud, tormented sobs.

There was a touch on her arm. Goldie was there, trying to comfort her. The girl's arms stole around her neck in a hug as she placed a sweet, loving kiss against her cheek. 'Don't cry, Mamma. God took Ashley's soul away on the moonbeam to be an angel.' The girl traced a finger over Ashley's soft cheek. 'I'll wake Rosie up. She can help me look after Ashley, and you can feed baby Bryn. We'll wash him, and I'll find some nice clothes for him to wear. Then I'll say a prayer for him.'

'You're far too young for such a sad task,' Siana sobbed.

But Goldie wasn't. She coaxed Ashley from Siana's arms, laid him in his bed and lit a candle from the night light. 'Go, Mamma, before Bryn wakes everyone else.'

Thus, Siana was parted from her beloved child to give succour to another, the demanding little cuckoo in her nest. Although her heart was set to break, she knew she had to be strong now, for she had no choice.

The rain, torrential for days, eased to a relentless drizzle that morning. Siana was adamant. Ashley would be buried in his rightful place, in the Forbes plot with his father.

The children had been left at home. They were still in quarantine, though their recovery from the fever was assured. Maryse and Pansy offered their support by asking to accompany her. Their faces were tense and pale from the enormity of this second recent tragedy in their lives. Siana wondered if any of them would ever laugh again.

But she had to be strong, for the children looked to her for support, and she couldn't fail them.

Josh was driving them in a plain, black carriage. They followed after the hearse, pulled by four dark horses which walked at a pace seemly for the solemn occasion, the plumes on their heads bobbing.

The road was slick with mud, deep in parts. The horses' plumed heads nodded with each step, water slanted off their broad backs.

Ashley's small coffin was clearly visible through the glass sides. Siana couldn't take her eyes off it. It was draped in a black silk cloth with a fringed edge, a cross embroidered on top in gold silk.

Sir Ashley Forbes, Bt. Her little squire. He'd never been aware of his importance. He'd just been loved and loving, like any mother's son.

They were passing the little squire's estate now. The corn was beaten down to a pulp by the rain, the gardens were unkempt, the haystacks mouldering. Water flooded across the road from the stream. Daniel had allowed the debris to build up. The cellars would be flooded.

Just as they were passing the gates the Forbes carriage came out, driven by the stable boy to join the cortège. The painted coat of arms was scratched. Siana caught a glimpse of Daniel gazing from the carriage window. He had no right to ride in his father's carriage as if he was lord of the manor. He had no right to come to the funeral when he'd brought into her house the disease which had killed her son.

Siana hadn't invited anyone to the funeral, not even the trustees of Ashley's estate, who clearly disdained her. Still, there they were. But she had no need of them now, and intended to dismiss them as soon as she could. Then she would give Daniel notice to quit, too.

There were estate workers there as well, caps in hand, pinch-faced and grey-looking from constant hardship. They should be in the fields, preparing them for the next season. It was hard to believe she'd been the same as them once, before Edward had allowed her to escape such poverty.

The earth was relentless as it followed its own seasons of birthing and dying. It accepted her son into its sodden depths without remorse, pulling him into its crumbling womb and closing over him before he'd hardly lived.

The Reverend White's voice droned on. Siana stood on one side of the grave, arm in arm with her step-daughters, taking comfort from them. If they hadn't been with her she didn't think she could have borne this.

On the other side stood Daniel Ayres, fleshy-faced and arrogant. He was surrounded by the trustees, dressed all in black and hunched into their collars like a collection of sodden crows. Daniel's dark eyes were upon her, defiant and relentless. When had he become her enemy?

She turned her face up to the sky's drifting tears, felt their coldness against her skin. I'm sorry, Edward, she thought. Here is our little squire, now committed to your care. Had you lived to see him, you would have delighted in his existence.

Her face felt as if it had been carved from stone. What would she do now? Sell the estate, perhaps, for Edward Forbes, having no legitimate heir but Ashley, had covered this eventuality in his last will and testament. She shivered. It was almost as if he'd known it would come about. The estate had now become hers to do as she liked with. It was a poor exchange.

When the reverend finished, she accepted his condolences and turned to follow after Josh and the girls. Daniel stepped into her path. 'Wait, Mrs Matheson.'

'What is it, Mr Ayres?'

'I thought you should know. I intend to challenge my father's will.'

Blood rushed to her ears and her reaction was too swift to be stopped. Her palm cracked across his cheek. 'You're an insult to your mother. I've lost my beloved son and not only do you make a mockery of his funeral, but you inform me of your intent to pick the meat from his bones before he's cold in his grave.'

Nerves twitched in a grotesque dance across his cheeks as people turned at her raised voice.

He moved closer. 'Not only will I have the estate, I'll have you as well, Siana, whether you like it or not.'

Siana pushed him away from her. 'Over my dead

body.' Overhearing, Maryse gave a distressed cry and Pansy gasped.

'Perhaps that could be arranged, too,' he said, his eyes boring into hers, a pulse beating furiously in his jaw. Siana's throat dried as, for the first time, she felt physically endangered by him. But her eyes never left his, and, eventually he shifted his gaze away.

Moving between them, Josh growled, 'Get out of her way, Ayres. I'll knock your bleddy head from your shoulders, else.'

There was no doubt that he meant it, for his fists were clenched and his body was tightly coiled with fury. She had never seen her easy-going brother so incensed and placed a warning hand on his arm, for Daniel probably carried a weapon.

Her adversary stood aside, his tension reaching out to capture her as she moved past him. What had happened to the fine young man she'd once known, her first love? Only she hadn't loved him enough, for she'd wed his father instead, a man who had flattered and dazzled her.

But her heart had belonged to Francis since the moment they'd met, and only to him. Where was he now, the man she loved? He couldn't be dead, he couldn't! It would be too cruel. But as each day was born without word, her convictions were being sorely tested.

The next day, Siana consulted with Josh's partner, Giles Dennings. He expressed his willingness to look over the estate books if she could get hold of them, but he also recommended that she consult with a lawyer. 'Sir Oswald Slessor is about the best around here.'

But when she saw him, Oswald Slessor gave an indulgent chuckle. 'My dear lady, I wouldn't dream of prosecuting a fellow magistrate. Mr Ayres has the sympathy of most of his colleagues, so the verdict is bound to go in his favour.' He reached across his desk and patted her hand. 'Edward lifted you from the gutter and educated you, my dear. Be grateful for your house in Poole and your allowance. Why don't you come to an agreement with Daniel over this, for he's indicated that he's agreeable to you keeping those assets.'

This man seemed to know a lot of her business. She gave him a tight little smile. 'It seems I must find someone less biased towards his own gender and profession to represent me, then. As for your assumption that I come from the gutter, I'll require an apology for that remark. A man with any breeding at all wouldn't have made it.'

Actually, it was a perfectly accurate statement. Her first husband had rescued herself and Daisy from a ditch after a mule had shied and tipped them out of the cart it had been attached to.

'My sincere apologies,' Slessor said, his face reddening with embarrassment at being reprimanded. 'It was merely a figure of speech.'

He sounded contrite, so she nodded. 'If Edward had wanted Daniel Ayres to have Cheverton Estate, he would have left it to him in his will. I certainly wouldn't have contested it, if those had been his wishes. I intend to take this matter to the House of Lords, if necessary.'

Slessor shrugged and rose to his feet. 'I doubt if you'll

find anyone in the profession willing to risk their living over this.'

All the same, after she'd gone, Slessor's conscience pricked him. Despite what he'd told Siana, it was not an open and shut case. Daniel's erratic behaviour of late was worrying a few people. He was reckless at cards, spent freely, and paid very little attention to his marriage vows. In fact, Daniel's extramarital preferences were slightly suspect, too, for they involved very young girls thrown by circumstance into prostitution.

Mrs Matheson had lost both husband and child recently, and the self-indulgent Daniel Ayres was turning out to be less of a gentleman than Oswald had first thought. He frowned and, removing a cigar from the humidor, slowly inhaled along its length before clipping the end from it. He would see how Daniel handled the Collins's case on the morrow, and, if need be, he would recommend someone from out of town to advocate on Siana Matheson's behalf.

Isabelle Collins had already decided on her strategy. Ben had told her that Daniel Ayres was to be the presiding magistrate. This was a man with an axe to grind on his own behalf. She would play dirty and use it, causing as much mayhem in the process as possible. She couldn't rely on her lawyer. The man had turned out to be a fool, for he'd advised her to plead guilty.

The court was crowded and, as she was taken to the dock, some of the onlookers hissed, booed and called out insults.

Daniel Ayres looked self-conscious when he came

in. His eyes bulged a bit, so in his stupid wig, he resembled one of those flat-faced spaniel dogs with flapping ears.

Ben was sitting at the front with her aunt, Caroline. He was smart in a new suit and waistcoat. His hair was parted in the middle and he'd grown a moustache.

Aunt Caroline was as plump as a partridge. In a dark blue gown and matching bonnet, she looked quite handsome, though. How old was she, Isabelle wondered. Twelve years older than herself, perhaps. Young enough to marry and give birth if anyone wanted her.

Isabelle felt sick and was growing more tired by the day. She'd lost weight since she'd been in prison, mainly because she couldn't swallow the awful food. Her gown hung on her like a sack. The child she carried inside her was painful. It occurred to her that it might be dead, for this was nothing like her other pregnancies. She would have found some way of getting rid of it if she'd been at home.

Ben looked suitably nervous and overawed by the occasion. She sighed, wondering why she'd fallen in love with such a fool. Because he'd genuinely admired her and filled a need in her, she supposed. She'd enjoyed him too, but she'd wanted none of that lately, either. He wasn't one to have his need denied, though . . .

Isabelle's eyes narrowed slightly when he exchanged a smile with Caroline. How simpering she was when she was around Ben. Ben needed someone to think for him, not to rely on him, and he needed . . .

She jumped when a gavel thumped. 'Isabelle Collins, you are on trial for the murder of Hannah Skinner. What is your plea? Guilty or not guilty.'

Before her lawyer could speak, she said loudly, 'Not guilty, your honour. It was an accident. Hannah Skinner sprang at me with a knife. I was trying to escape her clutches and—'

'Sit down and be quiet,' her lawyer hissed.

She flicked him a glance. 'You be quiet.'

The gavel banged down again. 'You will restrict your comments to answering the questions when they are put to you.'

'Yes, your honour.' She drew in a deep breath, irritably shaking off her lawyer's hand. 'I wish to make a statement to the court.'

'Which is?'

'I object to my case being heard before your honour, on the grounds that your mother is the notorious whore, Elizabeth Skinner, who was transported for the crime she falsely accused me of committing. I believe you will unfairly penalize me for that.'

Daniel Ayres's mouth fell open as the courtroom erupted into an uproar. He didn't know quite what to do, so banged his gavel several times on the bench. Eventually, calm was restored.

'If you carry on with these accusations, you will be charged with contempt of court.'

'I'll plead guilty to that charge, for I hold nothing but contempt for the likes of you. I demand another magistrate.'

'Your demand is denied.' Daniel Ayres turned to the

prosecution, mopping the sweat from his brow. 'Do you have any witnesses?'

Her lawyer stood, gathered his papers together and stalked from the court.

She must tell Ben not to pay his bill, thought Isabelle.

Sam Saynuthin took the oath by spitting on his palm and slapping it on the bible when the official read it out.

'What have you to say?' Daniel asked him.

'He ain't got nothing to say, for the poor little bugger be dumb,' Ben said out loud, and the onlookers began to laugh again.

Sitting at the back of the court, Oswald Slessor grinned at that, even though the spectators were walking all over Daniel. The young man was having a baptism of fire. It would test his mettle a bit, but that was all to the good if he could get it under control. Oswald hadn't enjoyed a case so well in a long time. But if it got too much out of hand he would intervene.

Daniel thumped his gavel for silence again. Forgetting he was wearing a wig he ran a shaking hand through his hair. The hairpiece was dislodged and flew across the desk to thump onto the floor like an overweight seagull.

'Shut up, else I'll have you all arrested,' he roared, taking the wig from a court official and jamming it back on his head. He glared round at everyone until the ensuing hubbub died down, and gathered his dignity together as best he could. 'Let us proceed.'

But nothing proceeded as he'd imagined it would. Suddenly the door to the courtroom was pushed open and Rudd Ponsonby stood there, a constable at his shoulder.

'I've brought the law to arrest you, Daniel Ayres. It was you who attacked and killed my young un, and her only just turned fourteen. I found that brooch in the cottage, the one I made her give back to you, and she had a shillin' in her pocket.'

'A shilling she exchanged for her services. The girl was a slut and deserved all she got.'

The spectators booed and hissed at that.

'No, sir, she was not. You took her innocence, killed her, and tried to make it look like an accident. You be a wicked man and my Abbie is sufferin' real cruel. To hell with you, Daniel Ayres. I'm not going to let you get away with it, however high you think you've risen in the district.'

Daniel's face suddenly blanched. Clutching his head with both hands he rocked back and forth. 'I didn't mean to kill her, it was an accident, I swear.'

'Like mine was an accident, you murdering bastard,' Isabelle screamed out, seizing the opportunity. 'You ain't fit to judge me.'

'*But I am.*' The trial had become a farce. Oswald Slessor strode to the bench, signalled to the court officials, then turned to Isabelle. 'Close your mouth, woman, or you'll be gagged.' Within seconds, Daniel was hustled from the bench to a back room.

'The court is adjourned,' Oswald said calmly to the clerk. 'Set another date for the trial. I'll hear it myself.' He gazed at Rudd Ponsonby and the constable. 'You two, wait there until I'm ready for you.'

Isabelle was dispatched back to the cells. The court was cleared of unnecessary spectators. Rudd Ponsonby was questioned, the evidence inspected. Not that Oswald needed to. Daniel Ayres had damned himself with his own words.

'It seems there are grounds for an arrest,' Slessor told the constable, and slowly shook his head. 'A mockery has been made of this court today, gentlemen. Rest assured, justice will be done.'

Daniel didn't wait to be arrested. Felling the court official with a heavy book, he fled outside and, mounting his father's great black horse, took off out of town.

As soon as he left Dorchester, he forgot the debacle he'd left behind. His headache was replaced by a sense of elation. People gazed as he went by, high on his horse, the squire of Cheverton Estate. Everything was his, the fields, hedges, trees and flowers, every stick, stone, man, woman and child – even Siana. When she came to him he'd keep her safe, a sweet bird, caged in her room. His brow wrinkled. But he'd have to dispose of Esmé first. And he had to get to Siana before they did. Putting the horse to hedges at a frenzied gallop in his urgency, he drove it forward, relentlessly kicking its sides when it began to flag.

The horse made a gallant effort, but the last hedge was too much for him. A vessel in his great heart burst just as he'd cleared it. Daniel rolled clear as the beast thudded to the ground, convulsing in its death throes. Eventually the spasms stopped, the gelding's eyes lost their brightness.

'Damned animal!' Daniel screamed as the gelding

rolled towards him and he was forced to scramble out of the way.

Esmé didn't know how long she'd been in the cellar. Two weeks, she thought. She couldn't remember when she'd last eaten. It was daytime, for she could see a chink of light coming through the keyhole.

At least it had stopped raining. She gazed at the patch of dark water on the floor and shuddered. The flood water had reached her chest at its height, for the table had floated during the night and she'd rolled off into its murky depths.

Damp and cold, disgustingly filthy, her hair hung in matted lengths. Worse, she'd soiled herself several times and was so weak she could move only with great effort. Her throat was so sore she couldn't speak, either. Not that she had anyone to talk to.

The last time she'd set eyes on Florrie, the maid had turned up wearing Esmé's favourite gown and her jewels. Flaunting herself, she'd taunted, 'I'm the mistress of the manor now, but we be going to London town in a day or two so I've brought you some food.'

The girl had given her some bread and cheese to eat, but the rats had smelt it. They'd come from everywhere, swarming all over her, fighting with each other to get at it.

The only thing keeping Esmé alive was the brandy. It warmed her body, helped her sleep and allowed her to escape into pleasant fantasy from time to time. She had to survive this and escape, for Daniel would need her to look after him when they came back.

She intended to lock him in the same barred room he'd kept her in, and hire a couple of strong manservants to care for him. It would be easy to keep him happy, by pandering to his belief that he was the squire. If she could become Siana Matheson, she would do that too, for she loved her husband and would do almost anything to win his regard back – even that!

He was obviously insane. The London doctor had warned her his condition would deteriorate. 'Besides the headaches, your husband will harbour strange ideas and behave erratically,' he'd said. It had seemed kinder not to tell Daniel of the suspected tumours in his brain, for she'd been assured the medication would keep his headaches under control.

She took another sip of the brandy. There had been no noise outside for a couple of days now. There had been a flurry of activity back then. She'd tried to shout, but she'd only managed a painful croak. Nobody had heard her. Most of the servants had left, or had been dismissed. No footsteps echoed overhead, as if the place had been abandoned. Perhaps Florrie had left too. Funny, how she didn't feel hungry now. She ached all over, though.

Eventually, night arrived. The blackness became blacker, the cold, colder. The brandy did its work and she fell into a stupor, curled up on the table.

For the next four nights, she dreamed of Siana Matheson.

18

The dream woke Siana again. The woman was calling her from the darkness, her voice coming from far away. There was an odour of dampness and mould in her nostrils.

'Who are you?' she whispered, anguish rising up inside her, for she didn't want to lose the thread joining her to this woman, 'Where are you?'

There was no answer. She tried to sleep, tried to escape from the despairing thought that came with each dawn. Ashley was gone from her. Her arms hugged his memory against her as she relived the feel of his skin against her lips and his small boy smell.

Bryn interrupted the moment of grieving. He woke, eager for his breakfast, gloriously alive, his legs kicking in energetic spurts at the blankets and his fists punching the air as he raucously proclaimed his right to attention. He made her laugh, her cuckoo child. Red-faced and gulping noisily at her breast, he took hardly a breath, lest it ran out before he'd taken his fill.

His nursery maid came in just as Siana finished feeding him, when Bryn was lying on his back like a damp, fat puppy, his mouth stretched in a windy grin, totally relaxed. He stared up at her, his slate-coloured gaze stating, *All is right with my world when you're here for me.*

'You stink, but I love you,' she said softly, grazing her mouth across the warm, satiny skin of his cheek. The child took her mind from Ashley, forcing her to live in the present, as if fate had designed him for exactly that purpose.

Bryn snatched a handful of her hair, then belched milk from the side of his mouth. It ran into the creases of his neck.

Beyond the curtain the sky was pale grey, as if the clouds were full of the grieving tears she'd shed. But at least it was dry, for the rain had been unrelenting of late.

She wondered where Daniel Ayres was. Despite everything, she hated the thought of him being hunted down like a rabid dog. She ought to write to Elizabeth, inform her of her son's disgrace. She didn't know where to send such a letter, though. She decided to put off the task until he'd been apprehended and dealt with. Perhaps that would be when spring came, bringing life to the earth to dispel all the sadness.

'Shall I see to him?' the nursery maid said, when Bryn began to hiccup. There was a short-lived tug-o'-war for possession of her hair before he was borne away, giving contented coos and chuckles, like a dove in spring.

Siana swung her legs out of bed and went through to the nursery to exchange a hug with the three girls and check on their progress. She was not looking forward to the Sunday service, but she must attend as it was All

Souls Day and the reverend was saying a special prayer for Ashley.

She preferred to think of Ashley's soul as a shining flower that would blossom every spring in the daffodils she'd planted on his grave, like her little Elen, buried high on a Welsh hill.

Grey-faced and defeated-looking, Daniel's godfather, the Reverend White, stumbled through the service. He looked as though he no longer believed in God.

Afterwards, he accompanied Siana to her mother's grave, where she was going to place a wreath of ivy and glossy dark green leaves.

'My name is Skinner and so is Josh's,' Daisy suddenly said, and stared up at Siana, her eyes questioning.

Siana didn't need Josh's finger in her back to know the time had come. She sighed, hoping the girl would understand. 'This is our mother's grave, Daisy. Your papa and baby brother are also buried here.'

'But you're my mamma.' Tears pricked at Daisy's eyes. 'I don't want Megan Skinner to be my mamma. I want you to.'

They were standing on layers of decaying leaf mould with water oozing through from the waterlogged ground underneath. Siana had sturdy boots on, but the hem of her gown was bedraggled and mud-stained.

'Our mother loved us all, Daisy. She didn't want to leave us. Before she died, she said, 'Look after my sweet little Daisy for me. Tell her I love her.' So I became your mamma for a short time.' When Josh's lips twitched at her embroidery of the truth, she elbowed him in the ribs.

341

'But now you're growing up, I hope you'll like having me for a sister, instead.'

Daisy gazed at Goldie. 'Only if I can still call you "Mamma".'

'Your mother has been watching over you from heaven, I expect,' Richard White said, wearily.

'My mamma watches me from heaven, too,' Goldie said, darting an uncertain look at Siana, 'and she hasn't got a name like yours has.'

'Why hasn't she got a name?'

Goldie shrugged. 'I don't know.'

'When your mother died, there was nothing on her to say who she was. So I took you home, and when I married, we gave you our name,' Siana told the girls.

'We could give your mamma a name.' Such a suggestion when coming from Daisy startled Siana, especially when she added, 'We could call her Mary Joseph after Jesus's mamma and papa.'

Hands on hips, Goldie slanted her a superior glance. 'Don't you know anything? Jesus's papa was called God.'

'Well, we could call your mamma Mary God, then.'

Head to one side, Goldie was clearly considering the idea. Siana tried not to grin. 'I think that's a lovely idea, but Mary Matheson might be better, then she'll have the same name as Goldie.'

Daisy aimed a cool look her way. 'I want to be called Daisy Matheson then, otherwise it's not fair.'

Siana hastily gazed at Richard, who'd made a strangled sound in his throat, and now had a suggestion of a smile on his lips. 'There's nothing like a child to restore one's faith in the almighty,' Richard said, although there was sadness in his tone.

Far too many souls had been harvested of late as far as Siana was concerned. Her glance strayed to the left, where her son's resting place was marked with a new, bright angel. The Forbes garden was full. Her son, the last of the true Forbes, had taken his place beside his father. Odd how the fenced-off Forbes area had been calculated to the exact number, as if someone had known the dynasty would end with Ashley.

There was no room for Daniel there. He would be alone in death, set apart by his illegitimacy, his envy and intrigues come to nothing. She couldn't find it in her heart to despise him now. He was ill. She only had room for compassion, despite the horrible crime he'd committed.

With a tiny sigh she wondered where her Francis was. If he were alive, surely he'd be home by now? But she couldn't imagine him dead and drowned, for every time she tried to believe it she could feel the living thread between them, strong, taut and pulsing with her heartbeat.

And where was Esmé, she thought. Something began to niggle in her head. What if the rumours she'd heard were true? Daniel's behaviour had been strange of late. She tried to dismiss the thought but, as the prayers proceeded, unease grew in her to such an extent that she knew she could afford to ignore it no longer.

When they reached the church gate, she turned to Josh. 'I feel uneasy about Esmé not being here. I'm going to stop off at the manor just in case there was any truth in those rumours.'

'Perhaps you'd allow me to accompany you, Mrs Matheson,' offered Noah Baines, who was standing nearby, talking to Oswald Slessor. 'I understand the place has been abandoned by the servants.'

Oswald Slessor had also overheard. 'You shouldn't go there alone in case someone has taken advantage of the situation to force an entry.' That someone being Daniel, she supposed. 'Perhaps you'd allow me to accompany you, as well. And I'd like to represent you in the other matter.' His eyes assumed a shamed look. 'At no charge, of course, since I was wrong about the suitability of Mr Ayres.'

She smiled a little, for a man who could apologize when his pride had been dented was rare. 'That matter has settled itself, I think, Sir Oswald. The trustees would not dare back his cause now.'

'In one respect, but I believe you'll find that the estate capital has been depleted by extravagant expenditures. Mr Ayres has run up certain debts.'

Alarm pricked her. 'I'm not responsible for Mr Ayres's debts.'

'Many of them were charged against the estate, I believe.'

'And the trustees sanctioned them.' She drew in a deep breath, but remained calm. It was no use panicking until she knew the worst. 'Very well, Sir Oswald, you may act on my behalf. My brother's partner, Giles Dennings, has offered to examine the books and receipts. I'd be grateful if you'd consult with him in this matter. Excuse me for a moment.' She turned to the Reverend White. 'I'm so sorry things turned out this way, Reverend.'

'Daniel isn't bad, Siana. He's ill. Esmé told me in confidence that he had tumours growing in his brain. She thought it better not to tell him, or his mother, and intended to nurse him at Cheverton Manor. She wouldn't have abandoned her husband, whatever the circumstances.'

There was an involuntary, sceptical snort from Noah Baines, but his eyes gave nothing away.

'I realize Daniel is ill, but we must bear in mind that he's killed someone, Reverend,' Siana reminded him as gently as possible. 'There have been rumours. I hope they are nonsense, but we're going to Cheverton Manor on the way home to look around. Will you come with us?'

He nodded. 'I'll fetch my horse and follow you. It's a large house to search. By the way, a young man from London has been enquiring about you.'

'What was his name? Did he say why he wanted to see me?'

'Sebastian Groves. He seemed a nice young man, but didn't elaborate. I directed him to Josh at the coach company.'

She wanted to grin as Richard White walked away, thinking it funny that her younger brother was now regarded as head of the household by these men. As if she didn't have any sense of her own.

The carriage containing the children was sent off home, for Oswald Slessor had offered her the use of his.

They searched barn and stable first. Someone had fed the horses, and they had fresh straw. 'The stable boy is still here, I imagine,' Siana told them. 'He was an orphan and would have had nowhere else to go except the workhouse.'

As they walked towards the house Siana glanced up at the attics. For a moment she was puzzled, then she saw that someone had removed the portrait of Patricia Forbes, Edward's first wife, from the window. It struck her as an odd thing to do.

Cheverton *was* a big house. It took over two hours to search Siana's former home. It was cold and gloomy without the servants, as well as being dirty, bitterly cold and very empty in the main living areas. Liquor bottles and empty glasses littered the drawing room. The grates were full of cold ashes. Dust coated every surface and mouldy food was strewn over the kitchen. Esmé's room had been ransacked, her clothes thrown about. Her jewellery case stood open and empty.

There was no sign of recent occupancy. In fact, the place looked neglected, and rather sad. Fear gripped Siana. 'Esmé wouldn't have allowed the house to get into this state. And she wouldn't have left Daniel whilst he was ill,' she mused. 'Also, wouldn't she have taken the jewellery case as well as her jewellery?'

'So, where is she?' Noah said.

Closing her eyes, Siana reached into her mind to recall the details of her vivid dream. 'Where are you?' she murmured, and a strong stench of slime and mould filled her nostrils. Bottles came into her mind, rows of them. The cellar! Her eyelids snapped open. 'We haven't looked in the cellar,' she cried, and she picked up her skirts and hurried downstairs.

There were two ways down. A door from the outside, and the one that led from the scullery. The internal door was locked but the key was still in the door. Water and debris reached halfway up the stairs, blocking their way. Siana had never seen the water so high.

They found the outside key hanging on a nail. Water gushed over the door sill when Josh pushed it open and wet-slicked rats scurried over their feet. Fetid air enveloped them, causing an involuntary movement of hands over pinched nostrils. A thick film of slime and grey mould lay over everything. The movement of the water set the table rocking. There was a bundle of mildewed rags on it. It gave a faint groan.

'Oh God!' Siana breathed, horrified when she realized what it was. 'How could he have been so cruel.' Turning away, she strove to compose herself when Noah Baines wedged himself down the steps and strode, chest deep, into the water. Now was not the time to break down.

'See if you can find the stable boy,' she said to Josh. 'He must be around somewhere.'

They took Esmé into the house, where Siana helped Noah strip the clothes from her body. They wrapped her in a warm blanket. She was so emaciated, her bones were clearly visible, her skin was wrinkled like that of an old woman and she was covered in festering sores and mould. Noah Baines doubted if she'd survive the ordeal she'd been through and said dolefully, 'The infirmary is already overcrowded.'

347

'She's survived so far,' Siana told him fiercely. 'If she can be removed to my house in Poole, I'll look after her myself. I can put her in the little sitting room downstairs; it's warmed by the afternoon sun. She will be given constant attention and all the nourishment she needs.'

'She'll be unable to swallow solid food, if anything at all. Her lungs are congested. It's hard to tell whether it's consumption or pneumonia.'

'Then I'll feed her nourishing broth, a spoonful at a time until her stomach *will* hold solid food. I'll try and make her live, Dr Baines.'

He nodded. 'It will be better if she's kept isolated until we see how her condition develops. Wear a scarf over your nose and mouth as a precaution. I'll brief Dr Pelham, and he can keep an eye on her on a daily basis between my visits. He's a good physician and I'm thinking of forming a partnership with him as soon as your husband's estate is settled. I would like to buy the house I rent, if possible, for when Peggy and I wed.'

Siana opened her mouth, then shut it again, thinking it might be wiser to keep to herself her belief in Francis's survival. If her husband did prove to be dead, then his house would belong to his daughters, and she intended to advise them not to sell it.

'I'd prefer to discuss this at another time, Noah. I'm not ready to dispose of my husband's assets.'

Noah nodded, resignation in his eyes, for he'd raised the issue several times before. 'Don't allow your children near Mrs Ayres until a proper examination has been made and a diagnosis reached.'

'How could Daniel do something terrible like this? Can't the brain tumours be cured?'

'I've consulted the patient records your husband left in my care. I believe Mr Ayres was misdiagnosed by the London doctor and is suffering from a disease commonly associated with low morals. It is incurable, and often leads to insanity.'

'You mean he has syphilis of the brain?'

Noah looked slightly taken aback. 'Ah . . . you've heard of it, then?'

'I'm not some drawing-room flower,' she retorted, then chuckled, 'though I try to be on occasion.'

'And succeed most admirably, Mrs Matheson.'

'What about Mrs Ayres?' Despite her assertion, she went slightly pink. 'Would she have caught the infection from her husband?'

'Quite possibly. It's hard to diagnose at the moment. If she recovers I will certainly raise the issue with her. Sometimes the disease takes a little while to make its presence known.'

Josh knocked at the door, to tell her the stable boy had been found hiding in the loft. The boy was trembling when he was brought before her.

'Where are the servants?' she asked him.

'Gone, the master kicked them all out long afore he fell off his horse. He rode that gelding too hard, that he did, for the beast was gettin' on in years and was all of a lather when he died. That Florrie. Her who said she was goin' to be the mistress of the house, found the master after his accident. They packed their bags and left real quick before the constables came lookin' for him. Tole me not to go to the house because it be haunted by a ghost.'

'There's no ghost.'

His eyes grew large and fearful. 'There *do* be a ghost, missus, I hears it moaning in the cellar sometimes. It gives me a right fright.'

'But you didn't run away.' She ruffled his tawny hair. 'You're a good lad, thank you for staying to look after the horses. What have you been eating?'

'Same as the horses, missus. A bit of hay, some oats and some chestnuts I picked in autumn. But I fetches meself some eggs from the hen house sometimes and boils them in a kettle over the fire, and I tickled a trout from the stream and necked one of they hens. I didn't mean to steal them, though, missus. But I was right hungry and the hen were the old scrawny one. 'Twas hard to chew on her, right enough.'

Siana managed a smile. 'It's all right, you won't get into trouble.' She gazed at Josh. 'Can you find room for the horses until I sort something out?'

'If I can be so bold, missus, there be no need to take them away,' the lad said in alarm.

'I can stay here with them and look after them, if that be a proper respectful way to ask, and I can keep an eye on the place. 'Tis better than the workhouse here. I have a nice warm blanket to sleep in, and the coachman gave me some boots to wear and a coat. He said he be over Wareham way with his sister until the Candlemas hiring fair comes along, but if the horses be taken sick I must fetch him.'

Siana exchanged a glance with Josh, who nodded. 'I'll

see if I can persuade the coachman to return here in the meantime.'

'The horses miss him, though they be right good company even if they do fart a lot. And that there ghost doesn't bother me none, as long as I don't go near the house. Then it groans and gives me such frights I be fair mazed, so I have to run away and hide, all of a tremble.'

'The ghost has been sent on its way, so you needn't worry any more on that score again,' the Reverend White said. 'And you must allow me to give you a meal each day. All you need do is present yourself at the kitchen door. I'll tell my housekeeper to expect you.'

'Thank you kindly,' the boy said gratefully. 'And if you wants anything done in return I be happy to oblige thee, sir.'

They lifted the skeletal Esmé into Oswald Slessor's carriage. The magistrate promised to swear out a warrant against the maid, Florrie. When they reached Poole, Noah Baines left them briefly to alert the local doctor to the situation.

By the time the two physicians returned, Esmé had been washed and put to bed. Siana had been tempted to wash her lank locks, as well, but had decided to wait until she was stronger.

Her eyes had opened for a couple of seconds, but they'd been unfocussed and she'd just groaned.

'Everything will be all right now, Esmé,' Siana had soothed. 'I'll look after you and soon you will be strong again.' The milk she trickled into the woman's mouth had been accepted and swallowed. To Siana's relief she managed to hold down the liquid.

'Good,' Noah muttered when she told him. 'Give her a few spoonfuls every hour.' He shook his head. 'A bad business, this.'

To Siana's relief, Esmé regained consciousness the next day, although she was too weak to feed herself, and slept for most of the time. Within a few days, however, the colour began to creep into her cheeks and her skin showed signs of improvement.

One day, Siana was spooning broth into her mouth when Esmé's hand touched her wrist. Painfully, she whispered, 'Where's Daniel?'

'I don't know. He's being sought by the authorities.' Briefly, Siana told her why, for the woman deserved to know the truth after what she'd been through. 'I'm so sorry.'

Tears squeezed from the corners of Esmé's eyes. 'Daniel's ill. It's not his fault and I don't want to live without him.'

Bitterness filled Siana's heart and, although she struggled to keep it under control, she couldn't quite manage it. 'Stop being a martyr. Your husband violated and killed a young girl. He also tried to kill you. He's gone off with the maid, taking your jewellery with them. Daniel is a greedy, shallow man, who doesn't deserve your devotion. If you intended to sacrifice yourself for him, you should have done so in the cellar. I refuse to let you die whilst you're under my roof. Do you understand?'

Esmé didn't speak to her for two days, then on the third day she squeezed her hand. 'I don't really want to die. What will happen to Daniel when he's caught?'

'Noah Baines will probably certify him as insane and he'll be sent to a mental institution.' She kissed Esmé gently on her cheek. 'Now, do you feel strong enough to leave your bed and get into a bath tub? It will make you feel better, and Rosie will wash your hair for you. I've received word that your parents and sister are coming to visit you as soon as they can get here.'

'But they're in the villa in Italy.'

'When they were informed of your plight they decided to return to England. When you are fit to travel they will take you home with them, for you cannot return to the manor.'

Thankfully, Esmé's chest infection proved not to be as dire as Noah Baines had feared. Her cough lasted for five weeks, but eventually the infection subsided and she gained a little weight. She had developed a craving for brandy, though, and although Siana often found the decanter empty when she rose in the morning, she didn't begrudge the woman the comfort of it after all she'd been through.

'You'll have to be careful in the damp weather, for the lung infection could flare up again,' Noah told Esmé three weeks later, 'and I have explained about the other malady, although you show no signs of infection at the moment. Both Dr Pelham and I are in agreement. You can be discharged into the care of your parents now. They have hired someone to look after you, and intend to take you to Italy in the spring. In time, you should recuperate fully.'

For several reasons, Christmas and the start of the new year had not been celebrated as well as they should

353

have been. It was nearing the end of January when Esmé departed. Siana wasn't sorry to see her go. They would never be friends. But she was glad the woman's life had been saved, and Siana wished her well.

Then Giles Dennings visited her with more bad news.

'I've inspected the account books. I'm sorry to be the bearer of ill tidings, but in my opinion, unless Cheverton Estate is placed into a productive situation almost immediately, within a year it will be bankrupt.'

The next season's crop would be lost if she was not careful.

Siana had no choice but to visit Rudd Ponsonby and ask for his assistance.

'I'm sorry to intrude on your grief, Rudd, but could you manage Cheverton Estate, as well as Croxley Farm, until I can employ a steward?'

'You've been grieving yourself, lass, and the land and season gives no quarter. I've allus been willin' to offer a helpin' hand to a body in need. Nothing you did was responsible for the tragedy that visited upon my home, so don't you fret none about that.'

''Twas the Lord's will,' Abbie said. 'He'll make that man pay for his sins. Aye, my Rudd will give you a hand. The men will listen to him.'

'Best you address them yourself as owner of the manor, though,' said Rudd. 'Tell them the truth. They'll respect that, even from a woman.'

So a meeting was called for the next day in the grounds of the manor. The workers were slightly shame-faced, but truculent all the same. Arms folded over their chests to keep the cold at bay, their mouths steaming as they talked loudly in their rich, rolling dialects, they stamped their feet up and down like a herd of skittish horses huddled together for warmth.

Siana stood on the top step where she could be seen, Rudd Ponsonby and Josh beside her. Rudd shouted for silence. 'Hush, you lot. The missus wants to talk to yer.'

'The corn harvest was ruined last season,' she said. The men hunched into their shoulders and shuffled their feet, but they were listening. 'I've known hunger myself. How will you feed your children if the estate is allowed to fail? I cannot afford to give you what you haven't earned. You took your wages, gave little in return and still you do nothing. You must return to work. The roads and drainage systems need attention and the fields must be prepared for this year's crop. The stream needs to be cleared of debris, for already it has flooded the manor cellars and will waterlog the fields if we're not careful.'

'Why should we work when there's no squire to work for?' somebody shouted out.

Her hands went to her hips, her chin lifted. 'Because I own the estate and am telling you to.'

'You're no better'n us for all your airs and graces,' somebody else shouted out. 'Why should we take orders from thee, woman?'

'I'm the one paying your wages. If you prefer not to work for me you can leave and go elsewhere – and you can do it now.' She gazed a challenge at them. 'Those who intend to stay can give their names to Rudd

Ponsonby, who has agreed to oversee the estate until I can hire someone with suitable qualifications.'

The men muttered amongst themselves for a few moments.

'Cheverton Estate is in trouble, for Daniel Ayres and the estate trustees nearly ruined it with their incompetence.' She saw no reason not to lie a little, for what she forecast would soon come to pass as the flies gathered over the corpse. 'I've had several offers to buy the land – from gentlemen who seek to pay me far less than its worth, and who would use their own labourers to work it.'

The men gazed at each other in consternation and began to mumble again.

'If I'm forced to sell it cheaply to them, you, your wives and your children will be knocking on the door of the workhouse.' She looked around, reminding them softly, 'Being poor and homeless in winter is not an enjoyable experience I promise you, for I've suffered it myself.'

'What if we goes back to work and you sells Cheverton? What happens to our jobs, then?'

'There is more likelihood of you retaining your employment if the estate is being worked. If the land remains neglected you'll surely be dismissed by a new owner, for he'd not employ workers who have proved they are idle. Nobody would.' She exchanged a glance with Rudd when mutterings of consternation reached their ears. 'The choice is yours. If you wish to start work and earn your wage, inform Rudd Ponsonby. If you intend to leave, vacate your cottages and be off my land by the end of the week, please. And a sorry day it will be to see any of you go. Good day to you all.'

She nodded to Josh, who had become her permanent escort whilst Daniel was still at large. Though Daniel would be long gone from the district if he had any sense left. As they headed towards the carriage, the men began to gather around Rudd.

When Siana and Josh arrived home, it was to find Ben Collins waiting for them, cap in hand.

'How can I help you, Ben?'

''Tis like this, missus. I went to see a lawyer fella. He tells me that folks is against Isabelle because of the shop fire business.'

'My sister has done nothing to encourage such talk,' Josh said.

Ben nodded at Josh. 'Isabelle said that Hannah's death were an accident. Hannah came at her with a knife, and she slipped under the wheel of the cart. Isabelle got in a fair maze, and took the fright.' He looked troubled. 'The lawyer fella said it be a hanging offence if she be found guilty.'

'I don't see how we can help,' Siana told him.

'You knows the magistrate. Isabelle wants you to tell him that she'll make it worth his while if he sentences her to transportation instead of hanging.'

'We can't do that, Ben. It would be dishonest to try and bribe a magistrate.'

'Josh Skinner, you've done many a dishonest deed in your life. I remembers a time when you used to run messages for the dissenters. What about the squire's trout, and the smuggling? My son George be your own kin. D'you want to see him motherless?'

'He survived losing Hannah, didn't he? 'Sides, poaching a few trout ain't the same as killing someone. You'd have a hard time proving I'd done anything wrong.'

Ben stood his ground. 'Hannah was a slattern who was no bleddy good at being a wife or a mother. I should know, I was married to her.'

'That doesn't mean Isabelle had the right to kill her, Ben.'

'It were an accident, I tell thee.' He stood up, his face sad. 'Isabelle is a fine woman, and clever with it. She be a real woman, she be. Though she was wrong in what she did, I can't let her hang, especially since she be with child. It ain't right to punish the child inside the mother as well. It ain't right at all when the infant be partly mine.'

'I'm sure they won't do that, Ben,' Siana told him, for Josh was looking a bit fierce. 'They'll probably postpone the sentencing until the child has been born. I'll write a note to Sir Oswald Slessor asking for leniency, and explaining the reason why. That's all I can do.'

'Thank you, missus,' he said humbly, 'and if I can persuade Isabelle to own up to the fire, then perhaps Mrs Ayres can be pardoned and set free. Though Isabelle can be mighty stubborn when she wants.'

But that didn't come about, despite Ben's efforts.

Isabelle worked herself up into a fury and Ben found himself on the wrong end of a tongue lashing. 'If it wasn't for the likes of Siana Matheson and Elizabeth Skinner, I'd have wed Edward Forbes and become the owner of Cheverton Estate. Instead, I got a worthless dolt like you. I'd rather die than accept help from that damned peasant woman, you fool. The fire is over and done with, so don't you dare mention it again. Nothing can be proved because all the evidence was burnt. Anyway, do you think them magistrates are going to make donkeys of themselves by saying they was wrong in the first place?'

Ben gazed at her through wounded eyes. 'What about our baby, Isabelle?'

'It'll bring me some sympathy from the jury, I suppose, and the only witness they've got is that Sam Saynuthin. He can't talk and is so ugly nobody will believe him. Besides, everyone knows he's a friend of Josh Skinner. He'll do anything Josh tells him. And once I gets free I'll find some way of making them all pay, just see if I don't.'

Everything Ben had ever felt for Isabelle fled. He was forced to face the uncomfortable truth. Her heart was black with scheming and she didn't care for anyone but herself.

But Isabelle's plan miscarried. Oswald Slessor ordered a physician to examine her. There was no pregnancy evident.

The jury, put off by her aggressive manner, her interruptions and her attempts to discredit the mute witness, who had produced an amusing set of caricatures showing exactly what had occurred, pronounced her guilty.

Oswald Slessor didn't like handing down the death sentence, even when it was justified. He deliberated for a moment, remembering the letter Siana Matheson had sent him. She was a pretty little thing, and compassionate. He approved of the way she'd taken Daniel's wife in, when the man had robbed her blind.

He'd lost his own wife several years previously and had never thought of remarrying, until now. Perhaps when she'd finished mourning her husband . . .? In the meantime, he could make himself useful to her.

His thoughts came back to the present as he gazed at the sullen face of Isabelle Collins, a woman he heartily disliked. But he couldn't let that influence his judgement.

Her husband was sitting in the court, a simple, but honest fellow. There was another woman with him, an older relative to judge from her resemblance to the accused. Two children nudged against her sides.

Obviously, they'd been produced to evoke the jury's sympathy. It hadn't worked on them because of the rumours concerning the shop fire and Elizabeth Skinner. Oswald had never believed in Elizabeth's guilt, but Daniel's ineptitude had ensured that his mother had been found guilty. That couldn't be undone. He could make sure the Collins woman didn't profit from her maliciousness, though.

Should she be sentenced to death? She certainly deserved to be dealt with harshly. But the children did weigh on his conscience. How could he be responsible for her death, especially since Siana Matheson's plea had been couched in such pretty terms?

The children would have someone to care for them, though. The female relative was holding a comforting arm around each of them. He was glad of that, for the doctor's report would remain confidential.

He cleared his throat and banged his gavel on the bench. Before he could change his mind, he said, 'Isabelle Collins, you have been found guilty of the crime of murder. You will be taken to the house of corrections, and there you will remain for the term of your natural life.'

Isabelle Collins hurled threats and abuse at him as she was led away. The onlookers began to clap and cheer.

They were not to know the woman was already under a death sentence from the tumour growing inside her womb, and her natural life would be over in a few weeks.

19

An imposing figure in his dress uniform, Admiral Matheson was piped ashore. The gangplank of Her Majesty's ship, *Turlington*, provided a small bridge from the ship to the shore of Van Diemen's Land.

The admiral was well pleased with his tour of the remote southern colony, and was impressed with the way it had progressed.

Convicts and freemen alike worked shoulder to shoulder, laying the foundations for a future nation. There was already an air of permanence about the places he'd visited, solid buildings were being erected and commerce had commenced.

Representing the young queen was a privilege, as it had been with regard to her predecessor. She would be pleased to read his favourable report, for rumours concerning Governor Arthur's treatment of the native population had reflected badly on her.

It had been explained to him that the natives were now safely settled on Flinders Island. The fact that the island was rather remote, situated as it was in Bass Strait, hadn't escaped his notice. He'd been assured that they'd survive there, though.

Of all the places Augustus had visited, this island was the most reminiscent of England in its verdant landscape. He looked forward to a pleasant stay in Van Diemen's Land.

A year younger than his older brother, the Earl of Kylchester, Augustus possessed the same grey Matheson eyes. They were hidden by his heavy lids, hooded from the constant need to shield his eyes from the sun. His face was handsome, although weathered from a life spent mostly at sea. Upright in bearing, he was muscular, lacking paunch, and silver-haired.

The admiral had never married. Although he greatly admired the female form and had left several broken hearts behind on various shores, he preferred to seek his comforts ashore when he could, rather than be an absent husband. He'd observed that to be a state which often led to trouble for the couples concerned. Sometimes, to his own satisfaction, though, he attracted the favours of sea widows, who were easy to woo and win.

Part of the Battle of Trafalgar fleet as a midshipman, Augustus Matheson had served under Lord Nelson on his last, fatal engagement – one that had brought the British fleet victory. That had been thirty-four years previously.

A band on shore struck up, playing the national anthem with excruciating gusto. The band consisted of a bugler, two fiddle players, a fife and a drum, none of whom seemed to have a sense of harmony. Augustus tried not to wince, for he was fond of music. The musicians were doing their best, no doubt. They just weren't doing it together.

Face grave, he stood to attention, saluting the flag whilst they tortured his ear drums.

Now, he'd turned fifty and this was his last voyage. He understood he was to be honoured with a knighthood, followed by a posting to the admiralty. Augustus intended to find himself a wife, a socially aware female, competent enough to run the house he owned in London whilst providing him with companionship and comfort. He had in mind the sister of a younger colleague – a widow woman without means, but of comely appearance.

When the anthem stopped he stepped forward to accept the official welcome from the governor. He made his own short speech, bestowing on the populace warm greetings from the young Queen Victoria to the far-flung and obedient subjects of her budding colony.

Then came a fine dinner with selected guests, held in his honour and with all the pomp and circumstance with which the citizens of Hobart Town could honour his position. And – what could be more charming? – they'd provided him with a most delightful dinner companion, who later took his arm and paraded him round the room to make introductions.

He found himself cornered by the commandant of Port Arthur Prison, and reluctantly excused himself from the diminutive Arabella Bascombe, who stood at exactly the right height for him to view the twin charms of her decolletage without it being noticeable.

'My husband has been on the mainland for several weeks,' she thought to inform him.

'We must talk again before the evening is over,' he replied, kissing her palm and gazing ruefully into her glistening brown eyes for a moment. Her lips twisted into a small, secretive smile and she gracefully inclined her head.

He was looking forward to rumpling the fair Arabella's petticoats.

The prison commandant was Charles O'Hara Booth. 'I hesitate to take up your time with what could be a trivial matter, sir, but I have a letter addressed to your brother, the Earl of Kylchester, and wondered if you'd be good enough to deliver it on your return to English soil. Also, another addressed to a Mrs Siana Matheson. I didn't want to send them on without verifying that the man is who he says he is.'

Augustus took the letters and read the name of the sender on the back. 'Good God! These are from my brother Francis, who went down on the *Adriana*.'

'You recognize his hand, then?'

'We don't often write, so I couldn't swear it was Francis's hand. How come you by these?'

'I believe the man who wrote them to be an impostor, a prisoner who goes by the name of Piper, amongst others. Piper is a confidence trickster of some skill. The man who wrote the letters greatly resembles the wanted poster. He was apprehended in the bush without means of identification. He . . . Piper, claims to be Francis Matheson, a physician and surgeon.' The man shrugged. 'His doctoring skills are not without merit, but he has scars on his back from a flogging, which throws a great deal of doubt on his claim!'

'My brother Francis is a fine physician.' Augustus felt quite agitated at the thought of his brother being considered a convict, and especially that he'd been flogged. 'Why do you consider this claim to be counterfeit?'

'It's common for escaped prisoners to claim they're someone else, and there are plenty of barbers who practise as surgeons. Besides, where would he have received the first flogging?'

'You mean you flogged him for a second time?'

'A standard punishment for recalcitrant prisoners. It teaches them who's in charge.'

'I would be recalcitrant if I'd been unjustly detained. In this case, you may have flogged an innocent man. There is only one way to find out. I shall visit your prison and inspect this man for myself.'

'He's not at the prison, Admiral. I afforded the man the benefit of the doubt and made sure he had a ticket of leave whilst I investigated his claim. I've sent him to work the property he claimed to have inherited from William Matheson.'

'That's good of you,' Augustus said curtly, but he couldn't really fault the man's reasoning. 'I'd intended to settle the Matheson property whilst I was here, anyway. Would you be good enough to furnish me with a horse and directions?'

'I'll furnish you with an armed soldier, as well. I never take anything for granted, and this man might prove to be dangerous if cornered.'

They arranged to leave early in the morning, so

Augustus bade his host goodnight. He discovered Arabella Bascombe lingering in the hall, arranging to depart. He took her cloak from a servant and slid it around her shoulders, murmuring. 'A happy coincidence. I was just leaving myself. I've enjoyed your company tonight, my dear.'

'Thank you, Admiral.' Her eyes came fluttering up to his. 'Perhaps you'd care to show me around your fine ship before I return home. My carriage will wait.'

His fine ship was an Albion class 11, built of good British oak more than forty years previously. Her commander was a first-class seaman who ran a tight ship and was a credit to the service. Augustus intended to mention him in dispatches.

'It will be my pleasure. Most of the crew will be seeking entertainment ashore and the ship will be quiet. I have a bottle of wine we can share.'

Three hours later, Augustus sent the woman home in her carriage, escorted by two marines. He had a smile on his face, for she'd proved to have a passionate nature.

The watchkeepers grinned at each other when the admiral playfully pinched the lady's arse as he handed her into the carriage.

'Naughty, Admiral,' she said, giving a little squeal and striking him on the shoulder with her fan.

They were still grinning when he strode back up the gangplank. He winked at them as he went past, giving a sigh of satisfaction.

His servant already had a bowl of water and soap ready. He set about washing his genitals. When they left port he'd have the ship's surgeon examine him for disease, as a precaution, for you could never totally trust a woman with loose morals.

Francis saw the two men coming and called out to Jed, 'Two men, they're both in uniform. Soldiers, by the look of them.'

'Stay in the house,' Jed said quietly to Elizabeth and, loading a rifle in case it was needed, stood in the shadow of the verandah.

Leaning on the gate, Francis watched the uniformed men come closer. A puzzled frown touched his face. He hadn't seen his brother for a few years, but he could almost swear it was Augustus. *It was!*

'Gus?' he shouted, striding jubilantly forward, a smile broadening on his face. 'What the devil are you doing here, so far from the ocean?'

Dismounting, the admiral winced as he cupped his crotch and made the necessary adjustments. 'Put a ship under my arse any day, my balls are black and blue from bouncing on that horse.' He carefully looked his brother over. 'I can safely inform the commandant he was wrong. You are certainly not Philip Piper.'

Francis was too overcome to speak as they hugged each other, making a great show of back-slapping to hide their emotion. Finally, they pulled apart.

'You can't imagine how glad I am to see you,' Francis said. 'I've been here for almost two years.'

'I have a good idea, for the prison commandant filled me in on what's occurred. You can't blame him for being careful.' Augustus grinned. 'You and Will were always trouble when you got together. He'd be laughing now if he knew you'd been mistaken for a convict.'

'Knowing Will, he probably arranged it before he died,' Francis said drily. 'I'll go back to Hobart Town with you. If you vouch for me I'll have access to William's account, and can book passage on the first ship going to England. I sent a letter to Ryder, explaining the situation, and also to my wife, but I've heard nothing back.'

Augustus took the letters from his pocket. 'They haven't been sent. As far as the family is concerned, you're dead, and I'm here to settle William's estate.' He chuckled suddenly. 'You wouldn't know, of course, but your delicious little wife has presented you with a son.'

'A son?' A smile spread across Francis's face as fierce pride swelled inside him. He shook his head, bemused by the thought of having a son. 'He'd be seventeen months old now. What did Siana name him?'

'Bryn Francis Matheson.'

His brow wrinkled. 'Bryn? An odd name.'

'The name's Welsh, I believe. The infant was born there.'

'Ah, I see,' Francis said, when he really didn't see at all. Siana had an unhappy history with her Welsh kin, so why she'd chosen to be in Wales at that particular time, he couldn't imagine. 'I must get home to them as soon as possible.'

'You will, Francis, you will. You'll be the guest of the Royal Navy. We sail in a week or so, for the western part of the continent. The west is a difficult place to settle, for its climate is hot and dry. They have requested more convicts, for the existing settlers are short of labour. As soon as I've finished the flag waving and the ship is provisioned, we shall set sail for England with all speed.'

He flicked a glance at the soldier, who was tending to his horse and pretending not to listen. 'Trooper, I'd be obliged if you'd go back to the commandant when you've rested and taken some refreshment. I'll write him a letter, and if I were you I'd stand out of earshot whilst he reads it.'

'Yes, Admiral,' the soldier said, and grinned.

'Now,' Augustus clapped Francis on the back, 'introduce me to your companion at the house.'

'His name is Jed Hawkins.'

'I didn't mean the watchful, silent one with the loaded rifle, I meant the small one with pretty red hair, who's hiding herself behind the shutter.'

Francis chuckled, his brother hadn't changed. 'Sorry to disappoint you, Gus, but that lady is Mrs Hawkins. If you look at her the wrong way, no doubt Jed will rip your bruised balls out by the roots and choke you with them.'

'I would that,' Jed growled.

'That would be a pity,' said the admiral with genuine regret, 'for I'm very fond of my balls.'

As Siana had predicted, she received several offers for Cheverton Estate. Most of them were an insult, and were curtly refused. Two offers were upped considerably, but still they were not high enough to tempt her to sell.

With Josh still in attendance, she went back to the manor. Gathering up all of Daniel and Esmé's belongings, she dispatched them to Esmé's parents' address in London. Let them deal with it, for Daniel was not her responsibility.

Packed into sealed boxes, the papers pertaining to estate matters were stored in the library, for she didn't know what else to do with them.

She managed to track down her former housekeeper, Maisie Roberts, two manservants, a gardener and maid. She persuaded them to move back into the house, with the promise of reference of service to the new owner, when the manor was sold.

An army of village women were set to clean the manor from top to bottom for the shillings it earned them. Dust sheets were thrown over the furniture.

Outside, the gardens were made presentable, the stream cleared of debris, the potholes in the road filled. The flood in the cellar had subsided a little, enabling Siana to empty the cellar of wine. Some of it had been spoiled by seepage. The bottles above the tide mark were loaded into the carriage and transported to her house in Poole.

Wondering about the state of the foundations, she consulted with an engineer. The remaining water was pumped out, the cellars inspected.

'The foundations are solidly built,' he reported back, 'and a little dampness from time to time won't damage them.' But he recommended that the stream be dredged and deepened so the flow was diverted past the house in times of prolonged rain, not under it The work cost her a fortune, but the house received certification as to its soundness.

Thanks to Rudd Ponsonby, the fields were being worked again. Edward Forbes would have approved her industry, and the constant activity stopped her thinking about Francis.

She sold several pieces of monogrammed silver to finance repairs to the outbuildings, farming machinery and stock. Thanks to Josh, she received a good price directly from a silversmith, who intended to melt it down and rework it.

Maryse and Pansy came to the house to help choose what should be sold. The pair ran about like a couple of excited children at being back at the manor, bringing life to the place.

'I always loved living in this house,' Maryse said a trifle wistfully.

'Me too,' Pansy agreed, giggling as she slid down the banister. 'We stood at the top of these stairs and watched Papa kissing you, once. You blushed and sprang apart when we made our presence known. It was the night of the harvest supper, do you remember, Maryse?'

Maryse lost her smile. 'I don't remember much about that night, except I tripped over and hurt my ankle.' Abruptly, she changed the subject. 'Wouldn't it be lovely if Papa hadn't gone down on that beastly ship after all, and he walked through the door, right now!'

They all gazed in the direction of the entrance, quiet for a moment. Tears coming to her eyes, Siana whispered for the hundredth time, 'Perhaps he managed to swim to shore. He could be on his way home to us.'

'You only say that because you want it so much,'

Pansy flung at her almost angrily. 'Aunt Prudence said it's your Welshness, and you shouldn't fill our heads with such nonsense. She said we should get our mourning over and done with and get on with our lives.'

'What does Aunt Prudence know? I'd rather believe Papa was coming home than believe he is dead.' Maryse's glance went to the portrait of Edward Forbes. 'Siana knew when Edward Forbes was going to die. Rosie told me. She said it amazes her just thinking about it.'

'Everything amazes Rosie,' Pansy observed, taking Siana in a fierce hug that would have horrified Prudence. 'I'm sorry I was so mean. I miss Papa so, but you've had much more to bear, for you lost your child, and your first husband too.'

Memories flooded back to Siana. Edward's portrait still hung on the staircase, overseeing his domain. Time had made him look different to her. The attraction and excitement he'd always represented had faded, as though the scales had fallen from her eyes. She stared at the painting for several minutes, trying to imagine being naked in his arms, bending herself to his will, loving him. But she could only bring Francis to mind. Ashley's death had ended the Forbes family line, now it seemed as if the ghosts had moved out too. Just as she thought that, something creaked in the upper levels of the house. She shuddered as she thought of Daniel.

Cheverton Manor was a moderately large house which would need constant maintenance into the future. As such, it would be a drain on her finances, especially since Daniel had squandered much of the capital. Siana had already sold the Dorchester house, and had returned most of the expensive furnishings to the provider, at a loss.

She gave Pansy a hug in return, pleased that the girl had snapped her out of her melancholy. Sentiment had no place in her life. She had a family to provide for, and must put them first.

She was pleased, therefore, when two days later, Oswald Slessor told her he had a likely buyer for the place.

'He's from London, a man who describes himself as a scholar and a gentleman of means. He's looking to settle in the country.'

'What is his name, Sir Oswald?'

'I don't know, for he's dealing through an agent, John Taggart. His client said he won't consider buying the place without meeting the owner. He suggests Thursday would be a good day for him to look it over, for he intends to call on friends in the district then. The agent's message said his client would like to meet us there at eleven o'clock. Unfortunately, I'm presiding over the quarter sessions. Can someone else accompany you?'

It fell to Josh to provide her with an escort. 'I've got to go to Dorchester anyway, so I'll leave you there and pick you up on the way back. Keep one of the manservants with you when you show him around.'

The day was cold, but dry. At Cheverton Manor there was a fire lit in the drawing room. The staff had been warned in advance, and were dressed formally. The clock with the blue enamel and gilt face ticked time away on the mantelpiece. It was a pretty timepiece, one she hadn't really looked at before. Everything seemed strange to her. The house was as alien to her now, as it had been to the impressionable peasant girl she'd once been – the girl who Edward had fallen in love with and woven his schemes for.

The client was late. She hoped she hadn't wasted her time. Then she heard a light carriage approaching at a fast trot. She resisted the urge to answer the bell, for she'd posted a manservant in the hall, and he would do his job.

There was a rumble of voices, a knock on the drawing-room door. She turned as it opened, a smile on her face. Her eyes widened at the sight of the figure standing there, her smile faltering. 'Marcus Ibsen?'

Amusement came into his eyes, warming their depths.

Her glance swept from his fine leather boots to his dark trousers and velvet-trimmed top coat, then up to his tall top hat. On his little finger he wore a gold ring set with a ruby. He looked exceedingly elegant. She chuckled when he swept the hat from his head and bowed.

'At your service, Mrs Matheson. I succeeded in surprising you, then?'

'I'm totally amazed by the transformation. Where is your robe? I formed the impression that you were a monk.'

'I was never a monk, though I was considering following my father into the Church of England before I decided the profession was not for me. You could say I was a pilgrim when we last met.' Taking her hands in his he kissed both her cheeks. 'You're wearing mourning, Mrs Matheson. Have I come at a bad time?'

'I've lost my son, who was the heir to this house. And they tell me my husband has drowned on his journey to Van Diemen's Land.'

Their eyes formed a connection. 'You cannot bring yourself to believe it, can you?'

She shook her head. 'If he was dead, surely I would know it in my heart.'

He tucked her arm into his. 'It was you who taught me to believe in my instincts. I'm sorry your son died. How are your other children?'

'They are well. Bryn thrives. He is a confident and delightful boy who has kept me sane through the trials I've experienced of late.'

'I'm pleased. Tell me, how is Miss Matheson?'

'Pensive at times. Her heart still bruises easily. But she has hidden strength and is proving to be more resilient than I thought her to be.'

'Tell me about her whilst we inspect the house and outbuildings. Then when you leave, I will follow you home and, with your permission, will renew my acquaintance with her. Shall we start at the top and work our way down?'

The attic door was still firmly bolted. She was reluctant to enter, for she remembered a time she'd been locked inside with only the portrait of Edward Forbes's first wife to keep her company. She told him, 'This door used to rattle so badly in the wind that you could hear it in the library. When I lived here, once it slammed shut and trapped me inside. Francis rescued me.'

Her skin prickled. This house had never really welcomed her, now she was stirring up painful memories and the ghosts were coming back to life. She felt better when his body came between her and the door. 'There is no need for me to inspect the attics.'

They turned aside and headed down the stairs, wandering from room to room. 'I'd like this house to go to someone who will run the estate as it should be run, Marcus.'

'A man has been hired to assess the land on my behalf. Should he find it productive, he'll be offered the job of managing the estate. I intend to get my hands dirty and learn the ways of farming first-hand. I will need to look over the books, too.'

'Sir Oswald Slessor has them. The farmlands of Cheverton Estate are fertile. But for a while the estate was badly mismanaged, so the books will average very little income over the past two years. You will have to look at previous years to get a true picture of its potential. However, the labourers are back in the fields. Next year the estate should produce its normal profit.'

'I will take that into account.'

'Your man has only to ride to Croxley Farm to see how fertile the soil is. I have Rudd Ponsonby, the tenant farmer, acting as steward at the moment. In return, I have promised that his rent can be retained by him for three years. It is an agreement of trust, and I expect it to be honoured should you decide to buy.'

He nodded, stopping to contemplate the portrait of

Edward Forbes on the way down. 'There are tied cottages, I believe.'

'The village of Cheverton Chase is a little dilapidated. The trustees of my son's estate wouldn't let me improve the cottages to any great extent. I've done the necessary repairs with the money available to me, though I was forced to sell some of the silver from the house to pay for it. Those sales have been recorded on the inventory and all items bore the Forbes family crest.'

'Which someone outside the family will not need. You use common sense, and know a great deal about farming.'

'I grew up on the land. The estate is debt free, at least, but it needs a man to run it and I have my family to raise. I have my house in Poole and investments which provide me with an allowance. The trustees could not touch those, thank goodness, but I'm paying estate wages out of it at the moment, as well as maintaining my family.'

'Thank you for being honest, Mrs Matheson.'

'You won't find a better estate,' she said fiercely. 'My first husband, Edward Forbes, knew and loved this land. It was his life's work.'

He turned to face her. 'Rest assured, I have every intention of making it my own life's work if I purchase it, and so far, the house suits me.' They moved on. 'Shall we haggle much about the price?'

'I'd not like to haggle with you, Marcus, you're much too astute. Your agent can negotiate with Oswald Slessor instead. Be warned, I've already turned down several offers.'

He chuckled. 'I'll make you a fair offer, I promise.'

As they left the house Siana felt as though she was being watched. She gazed back at the manor. The light from a pale winter sun reflected on the windows, presenting her with blank eyes, like those of a blind man.

Then the sun went behind a cloud. Standing at the attic window was the figure of a woman. Her heart lunged and she gasped.

'What is it?' Marcus said, taking her arm.

'Nothing,' she replied, and gave a shaking laugh, for she'd just realized. The figure was the portrait of Edward Forbes's first wife, Patricia. It had been moved again, the servants must have been up there.

They visited the stables and were strolling through the copse to the barn when he suddenly stopped. 'Was it here, where it happened?'

She didn't pretend not to understand. 'Yes, over to the right.'

'They will pay for the deed, those men.'

His voice was curiously flat and her mouth dried up. 'Will they? Would you . . . seek retribution?'

She couldn't free herself from the shadowy darkness of his eyes. 'Do you think I'm capable of killing them?'

'Yes . . . no . . . I don't know, Marcus. There is something of the hunter in you.'

His grin had a rawness to it. 'I don't know whether to be flattered or not. Given the circumstances, would you kill them for their crime?'

She thought for a moment, but couldn't reach an answer. She shrugged. 'I don't know.'

He slanted her a glance, slightly speculative. 'You have more wisdom than I'll ever have.'

'I know.' She smiled at him, diverting his attention from the darkness of his thoughts. 'You're all passion, Marcus, though you conceal it well. Shall we go up on the hill?'

There was a strong wind blowing in from the sea and Siana could smell the salt in the air. Her black gown flattened against her legs, her cape fluttered and her bonnet pulled against its ribbons, as if it wanted to leap from her head and fly away. Birds tumbled and wheeled against clouds as white and as billowing as the sails of a ship.

She closed her eyes, thinking of Francis, apart from her, but part of her. Life and love should be celebrated, not mourned. The love she felt for her husband overflowed into a dangerous exhilaration. Pulling the bonnet from her head she tossed it high into the wind and smiled at Marcus.

He chased the hat as it bowled over the land, his dignity lost in the exertion of the boyish scramble and chase. He brought it back to her dented and dusty and was still laughing when they turned to go back to the manor, his eyes berry bright. 'I could easily love you, Mrs Matheson.'

She remembered Grandmother Lewis telling her that the act of loving could be enjoyed for itself alone. And Marcus would be wild and tumultuous and leave no room for thought. They would scorch each other. Once tasted, he'd be a fever in her blood for ever. It would be easy, too easy to encourage such closeness, for her connection with Marcus was strong and she missed the physical contact she'd enjoyed in marriage. But he could never capture her heart, for it belonged to Francis, and she could never love anyone else as much.

'But I love Maryse, and I love her father even more.'

He offered her his arm, his manner more formal than it needed to be. 'My apologies, Mrs Matheson. I was carried away by the mood of the moment.'

Her answer brought the laughter back into his eyes. 'Yes, I know, Marcus. So was I . . . almost.'

Maryse was in her room when the carriages arrived. As they came closer she sensed something familiar about the man in the two-seater. Then he glanced up.

Her heart gave an uncomfortable lurch. It was Marcus Ibsen! Colour raced into her cheeks then drained away, leaving her feeling giddy.

Opening her jewellery box, she removed the finely carved wooden spoon he'd made for her, with its hearts and profusion of ribbons. Her fingertips knew every curve and delve as she traced over their initials carved into the hearts. He'd made it especially for her.

Marcus had declared his love for her in the *Gwin Dwr*, the cave of the wine water. She remembered standing wet and almost naked before him. How natural that had seemed at the time. Her cheeks began to burn and she placed her hands over them. She hadn't asked him to love her, hadn't done anything to encourage his attention.

When one of the maids came up with a message to say there was a visitor, she panicked. She couldn't face this man who'd looked into her soul and knew how soiled and worthless she was. Indeed, she had never thought to see him again.

'Tell my stepmother I'm unable to come down, for I'm feeling unwell.' As soon as the maid left Maryse began to cry, allowing the tears to flow unheeded down her face.

Siana came up in a little while and, taking her in her arms, rocked her back and forth like a baby. 'You must not think so badly of yourself, my dearest.'

'How can I face him?'

'You must learn to, for Marcus has decided to buy Cheverton Manor and is looking forward to entertaining us.'

And although part of Maryse rejected him, another part rejoiced that he would be close by.

'Dry your tears and come down to take refreshment with us. Pansy, Daisy and Goldie are there, so you'll not be alone.'

'But I'll look a fright.'

'Wash your face with cold water, then. We shall tell him you have a slight cold. I'll wait for you.'

They went into the drawing room together. Marcus rose to his feet. Maryse could hardly meet his eyes as she curtsied. 'Mr Ibsen. It's so nice to meet you again.'

'Thank you, Miss Matheson,' he said, his voice silky, the gleam of amusement in his eyes undisguised. 'I'm honoured you were able to overcome your indisposition on my behalf.'

He'd seen right through her. She wavered between

outrage and feigned ignorance; chose neither. She would not allow him to goad her into a reaction.

'The honour is mine, sir.' Taking a seat in the corner of the room, she picked up her embroidery and concentrated on her stitching, aware of his eyes on her from time to time.

'Cheverton Manor is a lovely house. When will you be moving in?' she asked, when she was used to his presence again.

'Not until July. I thought I'd spend some time in London. But I'll be down from time to time to inspect the refurbishment.'

'Perhaps we'll run into each other whilst you are there.'

'I will make it a priority.'

Maryse inclined her head. She had caught a glimpse of herself trapped in the dark mirror of his eyes and the scales had dropped from hers. She'd seen a woman, not a girl, and had realized with a mixture of dismay and excitement that she'd left her childhood completely behind.

20

Early in 1840 the Collins business interests went bankrupt.

Josh Skinner and Giles Dennings bought out the mortgage, acquiring the building and the family house for considerably less than its true worth. All the bank wanted was for its loan to be covered.

Ben decided that without Isabelle pushing him, he wasn't cut out to be a businessman. He hired himself out as a man of all trades and found plenty of work.

Caroline, having a little money of her own, bought a cottage in Wareham and took up the trade of dressmaking.

Her maidenly dreams were brought to fruition when Ben, surprising her in her chemise one night, placed his considerable arousal in her hand for her inspection and rubbed his palms gently over her bosoms.

It was something Caroline had been secretly dreaming of for years, so she didn't protest when he pushed her onto the bed and spread her thighs apart. They wed as soon as possible and within the month, Caroline found herself with child.

Josh hired an architect to convert the Collins building into several smaller shops, with offices over the top.

'Shop and office premises are in short supply,' he told Giles. 'We'll soon earn the money back, from the rents.'

Word got round and, by March, the building was fully tenanted.

Josh kept a suite of corner offices for themselves. Their door boasted gold lettering:

Skinner and Dennings
Property Development

'We should sell the coach business whilst it's still a going concern,' Josh told Giles, self-consciously stroking the moustache on his upper lip, as if testing the thickness. 'I was in Dorchester yesterday and Charles Castleman let slip that there be plans afoot to build a steam train railway from there through to Southampton.'

'Since when have you been rubbing shoulders with solicitors?'

Josh grinned. 'I happened to be leaning on the bar in the Antelope at the time, chatting to the innkeeper's daughter. We'd best sell quick, before word gets out. Besides, the coaches and stock are getting tired. Property, that's what we should buy into. I don't want to go back to digging fer cockles. I'll drop a few hints into the right ears, it'll save us the cost of advertising.'

It didn't take long. Before the week was out they had an offer from a rival coach company, who bought the business lock, stock and barrel.

Any doubts Giles might have harboured, fled. Josh Skinner had the Midas touch as far as he was concerned.

After Isabelle Collins's trial, Sam Saynuthin's caricatures had been printed in the newspaper. They'd asked for more. His fame had spread and he was approached by a publisher to do a series of illustrations for a London magazine. Josh negotiated a better fee for him, and took ten per cent commission.

Siana chuckled when he told her. 'You're a miserly wretch, Josh. All that work Sam's done for you and you haven't paid him a penny in wages.'

'Sam had a roof over his head and food in his belly,' Josh said practically. 'What's more, I gave him the cockle business.'

'Anybody can dig for cockles, Josh Skinner.'

'He didn't know that.' Josh grinned. 'Now don't get yourself in a schoolmarm mood. I'm going to allow Sam to live in one of the Smuggler's Lane properties for nothing. He can do some of the repairs, keep an eye on the tenants and earn money from his drawing on the side. What do you think of that?'

'I'm overwhelmed by your generosity,' she said faintly.

'By the way, someone made an enquiry about you at the coach office a few weeks ago. It were a man.'

She gave a little gasp. 'Surely not Daniel Ayres?'

'No, it weren't him. They'd have recognized him, for there be wanted posters pinned up in the coach house. This'n had red hair and was called Sebastian Groves. They didn't know you'd sold Cheverton, so they told him you was living at the manor. He said he'd call on you next time he came to town.'

April, and rain drifted in on a soft, scented wind that promised a summer of glory.

Siana, filled with the urges of her nature, felt caged in by the house.

Maryse and Pansy had gone to London to be with their aunt, Pansy filled with exuberant excitement, whilst Maryse exhibited nothing but dread.

'Try and enjoy yourself,' Siana told her. 'You're young, and your aunt means well. Besides, your father would not want you to be unhappy.'

'Then I'll try to be happy, for him, but that doesn't mean I'll wed myself to someone I don't love.' Maryse reached out, touching her cheek rather pityingly. 'Do you still think Papa will return after all this time?'

Siana's faith in her own intuition was beginning to waver after two and a half years absence. She sighed. 'I just can't bring myself to believe he's dead. Perhaps I never will.' She gazed down at her drab skirts and said ruefully, 'Since I don't really believe he's dead, I can't understand why I'm in mourning. I hate black.'

'Because Aunt Prudence would be scandalized otherwise, and because it keeps suitors at bay. Sir Oswald is madly in love with you, you know.'

'Much good it will do him,' Siana said darkly, then laughed. 'I shall follow my own dictates from now on, but will cling to my pagan belief for a little while longer, for I loved your father too much to let him go yet.'

'It must be nice to be able to love somebody so well,' Maryse said a little wistfully.

She kissed the girl gently on the cheek. 'Go and finish packing, Maryse, my dear. The carriage is coming for you soon.'

'I'll miss them,' she thought later, as she watched the Kylchester carriage convey the girls far away from her side. She just hoped Prudence wouldn't kick up a fuss again, when it was time for them to return.

The next morning, she donned a simple skirt of moss green topped by a lighter green bodice. Drawing her mother's shawl around her, she tied her hair in a long braid. Immediately, she felt better in body and spirit.

She was driven by a deep yearning, for she knew not what, and walked into town to try and persuade Josh to drive her out to the country.

Dressed in a smart pair of striped trousers, a black coat and grey cravat, Josh told her, 'I can't drop everything on a whim. Giles be introducing me to some important people who might send some business our way.' He caught Sam Saynuthin's attention, and said, 'You've got nothing much to do, Sam. You can drive Mrs Matheson around today, if you would. You'll like that. Take the small carriage. I won't be needing it. And don't give her any of your cheek.'

Sam grinned, then opened the door for her with a sweeping bow.

Soon they were bowling through the countryside. She stopped off at the rectory and they took refreshment with Richard White.

Afterwards, she visited her son's grave. It was covered in golden daffodils and looked like a little golden chariot pulled by its angel. Odd that he was lying just a little way beneath her, and she couldn't take him in her arms. She would have loved the chance to cuddle him against her one more time. But she knew that once wouldn't be enough.

'I love you,' she whispered, before turning away, and tried not to cry because spring meant new beginnings and brought new life.

At least she knew where her son rested, she thought as she turned away. But not Francis. Where was her husband? Was he beneath the cold, restless sea, trapped inside the hull of a wreck with other drowned souls – a resting place that would provide no rest at all? She shook her head, dispelling the disturbing image.

It was a fine day. She wanted to walk for miles, but the shorter walk to Cheverton Manor would have to suffice. Pulling her mother's shawl around her shoulders she sent Sam Saynuthin and the carriage on ahead to the manor. 'Tell the servants I'll meet you there in a couple of hours or so,' she said, making sure he understood.

Breathing deeply, she strode away from him up into the hills. Beneath her the earth was stirring. Plants pushed against the surface, their roots nourished by the soil, their resilient tips spearing through to seek light and air. The grasses sent out tender green shoots, hares chased in crazy circles, disappearing down holes, to spring up again from others.

The air was colder here, but not chill. At the top of the highest hill she stopped to catch her breath. In the distance she could see the Isle of Portland. The sea was a good few miles off, the horizon pale grey, the sea and sky merging into a smudge of misty darkness.

Enjoying her walk, Siana felt her restlessness abate. She was eager to arrive at the manor now, where Maisie Roberts would make her some tea, and they'd sit and talk together for a while. She was also looking forward to seeing the progress of the refurbishment Marcus had ordered. It would be nearly finished by now. Not that he'd be in residence yet.

An hour later she entered the path through the copse, surprising a couple of squirrels who spiralled up a tree, scolding her. When the chattering died away she began to feel uneasy, for there was a rustle of feet through leaves, keeping pace with her. She stopped to listen. Nothing! How dark and dank it was in here, how dense the shadows. Too dense. Was that a man standing there in the thicket? Her skin prickled as she sensed danger.

A twig suddenly snapped underfoot. Nervously she shied, her heart beginning to race. 'Who is it?' she said.

The silence was unnerving. *Daniel,* she thought. 'A rabbit,' she said out loud, but not really believing it. She started forward again, her breath held back.

When somebody gave a low chuckle, the hairs on the nape of her neck, prickled. 'Is that you, Daniel? Show yourself.'

Still nothing, just a rustle of undergrowth. Panicking, Siana picked up her skirts and began to run. There was a scurry of sound now, the whip and snap of branches as somebody crashed through them at speed.

He stepped out from behind a tree, wild-eyed and

unkempt, his face a mess of weeping sores. She caught a glimpse of a raised arm, and gave a high-pitched scream when his clenched fist descended. There was an explosion of pain and everything went dark.

Francis Matheson stepped off the small coastal carrier at Poole with much relief.

He'd left Augustus in London. He had to present his report to the admiralty, and would then make all haste to inform the earl of their brother's survival.

Francis had enjoyed his brother's hospitality. The pomp and circumstance of life aboard the Royal Navy vessel had amused him, but he'd come to understand the need for discipline to be rigidly maintained on board a ship. Life at sea would not suit his independent nature, long-term, as Captain McPhee had ably demonstrated to him, for he'd not subjugate himself to any man.

It had been a short voyage from London round the coast, but Francis had enjoyed it not at all.

Used for coastal trade and conveyance of the occasional passenger, the little ship seemed flimsy after the solidly built *Turlington*. They'd sailed out from the mouth of the River Thames into the teeth of a stiff wind, their deck loaded with cargo. Immediately, they'd been tossed about in the choppy water like a cork in a flood.

Francis had taken heart that her captain, whose head had almost been swamped in an oilcloth hat as he stood at the tiller, had shown no concern. As soon as the second sail was rigged he'd sighed with relief, for the uncomfortable motion had ceased and the little ship had begun to fly over the water – taking him home to those he loved.

The captain had handed the ship over to a seaman and came to where he stood. 'I have a passenger cabin below if you'd like to crack a bottle and share a pipe with me, sir,' he'd said.

But the small space, although warm and cosy, reeked of the spirit lamp hanging from the ceiling. Soon, the cabin had been filled with a cloud of foul-smelling smoke, and the brandy they drank would have scoured varnish from the hull.

The atmosphere and movement of the boat had produced a soporific effect on Francis and his eyes had begun to droop.

The captain had handed him a coat. 'You can rest your head on this. It belonged to a gentleman I took to Poole a few days ago. A strange one, he was, talkin' to hisself and growling. He had sores on his face and kept banging his hands against his head and moaning, as if it were hurtin' him, poor soul. I was glad to be rid of him, though, lest he prove to be a Jonah.'

Francis had decided the coat might be a hazard to his health. He'd ignored the offer and drifted off to sleep on the wooden bench, his head cradled on one arm, his back hard against the hull.

He'd woken with a start, rested, but stiff, and just in time to watch a yellow and pink dawn arrive. There was a chunk of bread, a slab of cheese and a thick piece of ham laid out for breakfast. It was washed down by a mug of brandy and water.

Followed by raucous seagulls, they made fast time,

sailing past Brownsea Island and running into the crowded harbour. They'd tied up against other small craft of the same design, early in the afternoon and he'd stepped across to the quay, glad to be home at last.

His heart suddenly swelled with the need to see his family again. He turned towards the livery stable.

He collided hard with someone. They both apologized at the same time, then Josh gave a whoop and punched him on the shoulder. 'Doc? Dammit, man, we was told you'd drowned.'

Francis could hardly believe his eyes. It was Josh, tall, well built and prosperous-looking, complete with side whiskers and a moustache. 'Good God! You've become a man.'

Josh grinned. 'Shame on you, doc, did you expect me to grow into a skirt, then?'

'And your clothes? Tailored?'

'A proper gent I'm getting to be,' Josh said with abashed pride. 'I have my own office, and all. Though I haven't got much to do in it 'cept sit on my arse and bite my nails. Giles Dennings said I've got to get used to dressing like a gent if I want respect.'

'I was just going to hire some transport to take me to the manor.'

Josh's smile faded. 'Our Siana's living in the Poole house now, but she ain't there at the moment. Sam Saynuthin took her out to visit the Reverend White, and she'll probably visit Ashley's grave. Though she doesn't say it, she misses him something dreadful.'

'Ashley died?' Francis closed his eyes for a moment, recalling the handsome boy from his wife's first marriage. Sadness filled him as he imagined what Siana had been through in his absence.

Josh nodded. 'A lot has been going on you wouldn't know about. Daniel Ayres went looney from some disease in his brain. He murdered the Ponsonby girl, then nearly killed his wife. There was quite a hue and cry, but he escaped before they could arrest him. I've been keeping a good eye on our Siana, but there's been neither sight nor sound of him in the district, in all this time.'

'He threatened her?'

'More'n once.'

Francis dredged up a memory of Daniel presenting himself at the surgery with genital chancre a few years earlier. The chancre had cleared up, but he'd left for Italy shortly afterwards. It was entirely possible the disease had since progressed to his brain.

'Last week, they picked up the girl he fled to London with. But Daniel flew the coop. Siana sold the manor recently. She said she had no reason to keep it. Daniel had run the place into the ground. After Ashley died, he told her he was entitled to the estate and was going to take her to court over it. The bastard didn't have a ha'porth of sense, for farming or anything else. He just wanted to be lord of the bleddy manor.'

Things had been worse than Francis had imagined. A niggle of worry lodged in his brain. 'Will she be long, do you think?'

Josh shrugged. 'Hard to tell. It's spring, and you know what Siana's like. She's been restless for some time. Today, she got the itch to go up into the hills. She said that if she didn't have a good long walk she'd go insane. Can't see Sam going far, though. His body ain't constructed for much walking.'

Suddenly, Francis remembered the captain telling him of the man on the boat. Dread filled him. 'I have reason to believe Daniel might be back in the district. Would he go to the manor, d'you think?'

'Sure he would, for he thought he owned the place.'

'And Siana was Edward's wife,' Francis said heavily.

Josh's eyes suddenly filled with alarm. 'We'd best go and find her, then, for my sister is the only reason Daniel would risk coming back now. I've been very much afraid for her since he escaped from justice.'

He'd got a good crack in. Sebastian Groves bent over the dark-haired woman for a moment or two, watching the rise and fall of her chest. She'd been unconscious for at least five minutes.

There was a lump on her head. Blood oozed from her hair and a thin trickle ran from the corner of her mouth. She must have bitten her tongue as she collapsed. There was a delicate beauty about her which robbed him of breath.

Gently, he prised open her eyelid. He encountered a dark-flecked green eye staring straight back at him. She wasn't unconscious, she was feigning it! And she was as furious as all hell! Her other eye opened, the dark feathery eyelashes sweeping up with a suddenness that made him jump.

'Coward,' she taunted, but before Sebastian could put his case, her fist shot out and caught him a blow beneath his eye. As he reeled backwards with the unexpectedness of it, she scrambled to her feet and began to run.

Before she got very far she tripped on a root and fell flat on her face. He was there in a minute, his eye watering from the blow she'd landed on it. He stood back a little, soothing her. 'Don't be afraid, lady. It wasn't me who attacked you.'

She scuttled backwards on all fours like a crab. Coming up against the trunk of a tree she pushed herself upright, clutching a stout stick she'd laid her hand on. She held it before her, menacing him with it. 'Come one step nearer and I'll fell you.'

Sebastian grinned, he couldn't help himself. He was young and fit, and, despite her courage, the woman would be no match for him. He touched his bruised eye. 'You pack a mean punch.'

'If you didn't attack me, what are you doing here?'

'I was on my way to the manor. I heard you scream and came to investigate. I'm looking for a woman called Siana Matheson.'

She stared at him for long moments, the fright fading from her eyes when he didn't move towards her. He watched her glance go to his hair, then to his eyes. She drew in a deep, quivering breath, and said warily, 'I'm Siana Matheson. Who are you? State your business.'

'My name is Sebastian Groves, Mrs Matheson. I'm looking for my sister, who would be about seven years old now. Her name is Marina Groves.'

'*Marina Groves . . . Mariglowed . . . Marigold,*' she muttered to herself. 'Tell me the circumstances, Mr Groves.'

'Shouldn't we get you back to the house, first?' he suggested.

She seemed to be in no mood to listen. 'I'm not as delicate as I look. Now, please.'

'Marina and I lived in Somerset when she was small. Our father died, leaving the family destitute. I was sixteen, and my uncle in London, a printer, offered to take me in. He had no room for my mother and sister.

'My mother told me she'd secured a position as a housekeeper on a farm, where she could take Marina. The plan was that when I'd learned my trade she'd join me and we'd set up house together. We had no choice but to part company. I know now that she'd lied to me, for when I went to the farm for her, they'd never heard of her. I have made enquiries at every workhouse between here and London, with no result.'

Siana Matheson made a small sound of distress.

'Then I heard some gossip. There was a lady who'd found a dead woman, who had a young girl with her – a girl with hair the same colour as mine. That lady, from the goodness of her heart, had taken the child in to bring up as her own. My enquiries led me to you, Mrs Matheson and this is my third attempt to find you. I must know if the girl you found is my sister, for if she is, she's the only kin I have left.'

Her face was stricken now, drained of colour. She made a small noise in her throat as the stick fell from her fingers. Sebastian caught her before she fell and hefted her into his arms. He should have waited until she'd recovered from the blow to her head before telling her his purpose for being here, he thought.

But she'd known as soon as she saw him. He'd seen it written in her face.

The wind had begun to blow hard from the sea and rain spattered against his head. Sebastian decided he'd better head for the manor, before the madman he'd scared off came back to finish her off.

Siana woke to find a blurred Francis looking down at her. She closed her eyes, then opened them again. He was still there. Her heart set up a tumultuous clamour. She must be dead, but it didn't feel like it, because she had a headache. Confused, she stared at him. 'Was it Daniel? Did he kill me, then?'

The slow, beautiful smile he gave her was real enough. She'd forgotten the way that his smile made his whole face light up. His hair was greyer around the temples, she noted.

'He had a damned good try. You're concussed. The men are out scouring the countryside for him.'

Anxiously, she clutched at his sleeve. 'They won't hurt him, will they, Francis? He's ill, like a mad dog.'

'They might. He's dangerous, and would have killed you if he hadn't been interrupted.' Tears filled his eyes, her dear Francis was crying over her. She reached up and scooped a tear from his lashes with her fingertip. 'You're real, aren't you? You've come back to us.'

'Aye, I'm real.' He pulled on his gruff doctor's voice. 'Keep still whilst I examine this lump, woman. You're shaking, as if you've got a fever.'

She winced as his fingers probed at it, placed her hand

over his and drew it away. 'It's just a bruise. Why didn't you come home sooner?'

'It's too long a story to tell you now.'

She ran her fingertips over the bones of his face and the curve of his mouth, smiling when he stilled her hand to cup it against his face. He gazed down at her through eyes suddenly warm. 'If I thought I'd never see you again, that would have taken away my reason for living.'

'Oh, Francis, my dearest love. Even though they said you were drowned, I could feel you close to my heart. I never doubted you'd come home to us eventually.'

She slid her arms around his waist and he gently pulled her into a sitting position, hugging her close against his chest. 'There is so much to tell you. That man who saved me from Daniel—'

'Shush, my love. Sebastian's told me his story and I believe it. He has no intention of taking Goldie away from you. But he does want her to grow up knowing she has a brother.'

A gust of wind shook the house and a door slammed shut above them. The attic, she thought, and remembered the bolts as she heard the door begin to rattle. But one of the workmen might have opened it. She heard one of the stairs creak. Then another.

'He's upstairs,' she said, trying to keep the fear from her voice.

'Nonsense, my dear. It's one of the maids.'

But the footsteps coming down the stairs were too heavy for a woman. 'Didn't you say all the men had gone looking for Daniel?'

As Francis laid her gently back on the sofa and got to

his feet, the door crashed open. Daniel looked like a wild man with his unkempt beard. His face was puffy and red with weeping sores, his tawny eyes were bloodshot. He smiled when he saw her, keeping his hands hidden behind his back. 'Why is the doctor here, my love? And there's blood on your head. Have you fallen and hurt yourself?'

Francis stepped casually in front of her. 'She has, Daniel. Siana fell in the woods, don't you remember?'

He shook his head as if to clear it. 'I'm not Daniel, I'm the squire, Edward Forbes. This is my home and Siana is my wife. Come here to your husband, Siana.'

'She cannot move yet, Edward,' Francis said calmly. 'It would be dangerous for her, and she needs to rest.'

Daniel's eyes took on a wolfish cunning. 'You're trying to trick me, Dr Matheson. You want her for yourself, don't you? I've seen the way she looks at you. Well, you can't have her. She's mine.' Producing a pistol from behind his back, he took aim.

Dear God! Her heart in her mouth, Siana swept the nearest object from the table and flung it with all her might. It was a marble ornament. It hit Daniel in the chest and bounced across the floor before exploding into pieces. As Daniel staggered backwards Francis snatched the pistol from his hand. It discharged. Powder smoke filled the air, bits of the chandelier shattered and fell about the room.

Daniel stared at them for a moment, horror mirrored in his eyes, as if his mind had cleared and he'd just realized what he'd done. He turned and ran – straight into Marcus, who was coming in the opposite direction.

An arm snaked around Daniel's neck, a foot was placed behind his calf and a quick twist applied. Nudging a knee into Daniel's back, Marcus looked up at her, smiling. 'Mrs Matheson, how lovely of you to visit me. I hope you're not going to tell me this wretch is your husband, come home, at last.'

'Actually, *this* wretch is her husband,' Francis growled. 'May I ask who the hell you are?'

'Oh Francis, stop looking so fierce.' Siana couldn't help but giggle with relief as she stepped forward to place a kiss against the side of his mouth. 'This is Marcus Ibsen, the new owner of Cheverton Manor. Mr Ibsen, I have the honour to present my husband, Dr Francis Matheson, who has just shot your new chandelier into pieces.'

'Well done, man, I never really liked it,' Marcus drawled. 'I'd shake hands, but mine seem to be fully occupied.' He jerked Daniel upright.

Daniel gazed at her through reproachful eyes and said, 'I still love you, Siana.'

She moved to Francis's side.

'Do you have any laudanum?' Francis asked Maisie Roberts, who stuck her head nervously around the door.

Alerted by the shot, everyone came running in from all directions. Daniel was sedated, taken to the barred room and locked inside. There he would stay until the constables arrived with the wagon, and Noah Baines was called in to determine whether he was sane enough to stand trial, or not. Immediately, Daniel started banging his head with his hands and groaning.

'Give my regards to Miss Matheson and Miss Pansy

when next you see them,' Marcus called out when they finally left.

Francis took the reins from Sam and drove the rig himself, with Sam and Josh following behind on the two horses they'd hired from the livery stable.

'How are my girls? I'm longing to see them.'

'Growing up fast. They're in London with their aunt.' She gave Francis a loving smile. 'No doubt they'll come running home as soon as they hear the good news, for they're both opposed to the plan Prudence has to marry them off.'

He flicked her a grin. 'The right person will change their minds, just as she did mine.' And the conservative Francis Matheson did something she'd never imagined he'd do. He pulled the vehicle to a halt and kissed her on the mouth, right in the middle of a crowded street.

When her blush subsided, she asked him, 'Did you get the letter I sent out with Jed?'

'I did, and read it until it became so tattered it fell to pieces. It gave me something to cling to on the long journey home. I've been so looking forward to meeting my son.'

Siana was silent for a moment, hating to deceive him. But she must, for she couldn't break the fragile trust Maryse had placed in her, and the girl must never know of Bryn's true parentage. So she laid her face against his shoulder and whispered, 'Bryn has the Matheson eyes. He'll probably grow up to look just like you.'

And later, when the rapturous welcome from the children was over and they were tucked safely in bed,

Francis gazed proudly down at the small, sturdy boy, who had captured his heart in so short a time.

'He has nothing of his mother in him that I can see. He looks just like Maryse did at that age.'

'Perhaps the next one will look like me.' Siana's eyes could hardly meet his for the shame of her deceit.

He mistook her coy demeanour for shyness, and chuckled. 'Perhaps we should start on that next one right away. I love you, Mrs Matheson.'

'And I love you, Francis. I always have and I always will.'

As their eyes met she knew she must learn to live with the small lie she'd created, for to reveal it would damage too many lives.

There had been a reckoning.

She had paid for Bryn with the life of her daughter, buried in a lonely grave on a windswept Welsh hill. Sleep peacefully, Elen, my little Welsh maid, she thought, may our ancestors take you into their care.

Her lie had been paid for by the life of Ashley, riding in his little golden chariot. Sweet angel child. She must leave him behind, but he'd always have part of his mother's heart for company.

Hard lessons had been learned, but like the seasons, her life would gradually change.

Siana gave herself to Francis that night, daring to hope their loving act would result in another child to nourish against her breast.

For it was spring, and spring was the time of renewal.

The story of Siana Matheson will be
continued in
A HANDFUL OF ASHES

Don't miss the enthralling sequel to
Beyond the Plough

To be published in Pocket paperback in
September, 2004.

**POCKET
BOOKS**

Also by Janet Woods
A Dorset Girl

When her mother and stepfather perish in a fire,
Siana Lewis finds herself destitute, with a younger
brother and sister to support. Although her prospects
seem bleak, Siana's beauty and intelligence will
attract the attention of three men.

Daniel, her first love – the man who will betray her.

Francis Matheson, the village doctor, who admires
Siana's determination and thirst for knowledge.

And Edward Forbes, the local squire. A sensual and
devious man, Edward is used to getting what he
wants. He desires the beautiful peasant girl from the
moment he sets eyes on her – and he's determined
to have her. Whatever it takes.

'A thoroughly enjoyable saga with a delightful
heroine and vivid characters' Anna Jacobs

ISBN 0 7434 6799 X

PRICE £6.99

POCKET
BOOKS

A Sovereign For a Song

Annie Wilkinson

WINNER OF THE ROMANTIC NOVELISTS'
ASSOCIATION'S NEW WRITER AWARD

An impoverished miner's daughter growing up in
the small village of Annsdale, near Durham, young
Ginny Wilde yearns for adventure. But she gets more
than she bargained for when her dark good looks,
fiery spirit and beautiful singing voice capture the
attention of Charlie Parkinson, her employer's
unscrupulous brother.

Fleeing the wrath of her irate father, Ginny heads for
London where she embarks on a successful career as
a music hall artiste. But, unable to escape Charlie's
influence, Ginny finds herself increasingly unhappy
as she is sucked into his louche, womanizing
lifestyle. Can she ever find the courage to leave
Charlie and return to her beloved north-east? And
will she ever be able to recapture the heart of her one
true love, miner Martin Jude?

ISBN 0 7434 6882 1

PRICE £6.99

POCKET
BOOKS

This book and other **Simon & Schuster/Pocket** titles are available from your book shop or can be ordered direct from the publisher.

☐ 0 7434 6799 X   **A Dorset Girl**   **Janet Woods**   £6.99

☐ 0 7434 6882 1   **A Sovereign for a Song**   **Annie Wilkinson**   £6.99

Please send cheque or postal order for the value of the book, free postage and packing within the UK; OVERSEAS including Republic of Ireland £2 per book.

OR: Please debit this amount from my:

VISA/ACCESS/MASTERCARD ....

CARD NO ....

EXPIRY DATE ....

AMOUNT £ ....

NAME ....

ADDRESS ....

....

SIGNATURE ....

www.simonsays.co.uk

Send orders to: SIMON & SCHUSTER CASH SALES
PO Box 29, Douglas, Isle of Man, IM99 1BQ
Tel: 01624 677237, Fax 01624 670923
bookshop@enterprise,net
Please allow 14 days for delivery.
Prices and availability subject to change without notice.